"Who are you?"

Vince backed up a step from the door.

"I'm, uh, Vincent Cutler. You left a message on my—"

"Well, it's about time!" she exclaimed, and bent to grab a shopping bag by the door. "I've got a whole bag full of your mail here."

He looked past her. She'd done wonders with his old place. The apartment had a homey, put-together feel about it that he quite liked.

"Sorry about this. I don't mind coming after it again, if you'll just call. Here's my card."

"I'll send it. So long, Vince Cutler."

"Wait a sec. I'd like to know your name, at least."

She considered a moment. "Jolie Kay Wheeler."

His smile stretched into a grin. "Good night, Jolie Kay Wheeler. Maybe I'll see you around."

He didn't know why, but even as that door closed to him, he knew somehow that he hadn't seen the last of spunky, pretty Jolie Wheeler. Strangely enough, that thought was quite all right by him.

Arlene James has been publishing steadily for nearly four decades and is a charter member of RWA. She is married to an acclaimed artist, and together they have traveled extensively. After growing up in Oklahoma, Arlene lived thirty-four years in Texas and now abides in beautiful northwest Arkansas, near two of the world's three loveliest, smartest, most talented granddaughters. She is heavily involved in her family, church and community.

Indiana native **Dana Corbit** started her career in journalism. As an award-winning newspaper reporter and features editor, she had the opportunity to share wonderful true-life stories with her readers. She left the workforce to be a homemaker, but the stories came with her as she discovered the joy of writing fiction. A HOLT Medallion award winner and Booksellers' Best Award finalist, Dana feels blessed to share the stories of her heart with readers.

Deck the Halls

Arlene James

&

His Christmas Bride

Dana Corbit

LOVE INSPIRED
INSPIRATIONAL ROMANCE

LOVE INSPIRED®

INSPIRATIONAL ROMANCE

Recycling programs
for this product may
not exist in your area.

ISBN-13: 978-1-335-42503-4

Deck the Halls and His Christmas Bride

Copyright © 2021 by Harlequin Books S.A.

Deck the Halls
First published in 2005. This edition published in 2021.
Copyright © 2005 by Deborah Rather

His Christmas Bride
First published in 2009. This edition published in 2021.
Copyright © 2009 by Dana Corbit Nussio

This edition published by arrangement with Harlequin Books S.A.

For questions and comments about the quality of this book, please contact us
at CustomerService@Harlequin.com.

Love Inspired
22 Adelaide St. West, 40th Floor
Toronto, Ontario M5H 4E3, Canada
www.LoveInspired.com

Printed in U.S.A.

CONTENTS

DECK THE HALLS

Arlene James

For my husband, who has taught me how real and rewarding love can be.

Show me Your ways, O Lord;
Teach me Your paths.
—*Psalms* 25:4

Chapter One

The voice on the answering machine, while obviously feminine, sounded curt and cheeky.

"Come to your old apartment and get your mail before I trash it. Never heard of mail forwarding?"

Vince smacked the heel of one hand against his forehead. Where was his brain? He hadn't given a single thought to having his personal mail forwarded. In the past few weeks he'd been too busy settling into the new house, replacing his business accountant and hiring enough mechanics to fulfill a city maintenance contract to think about his personal mail.

Just about everything important came to the offices of Cutler Automotive, but that was no excuse. He should've realized that the new tenant of his old apartment would have to deal with his share of circulars and the other junk that routinely clogged every mailbox in the Dallas/Fort Worth Metroplex. Besides, something important did occasionally find its way into his residential mailbox. In fact, the materials he'd been expecting about the spring singles' retreat at his church would undoubtedly be among the papers waiting for him at the old apartment.

He hit a button and listened to the message again. Her irritation couldn't have been more obvious, but he found himself smiling at the huskiness of her voice melded with the tartness of her tone. He heard both strength and vulnerability there, an odd combination of toughness and femininity. Since he was still wearing his jacket over his work clothes, he decided that he might as well go at once, make his apologies and relieve her of the unwanted burden of his mail.

Picking up his keys from the counter, he jauntily tossed them into the air, snatched them back again and retraced his steps through the new, sparsely furnished house to the garage and the shiny, white, three-quarter-ton pickup truck waiting there. Glancing at the sign proudly painted on the door, he climbed inside and started it up. The powerful engine rumbled throatily for a moment before he backed the truck out onto the drive and in to the street.

As he shifted the transmission into a forward gear he tossed a wave at his next-door neighbor Steve, who was taking advantage of the clear, early-November weather in the last hour of daylight to walk his dog. The Boltons were nice people. Wendy, the missus, had been one of the first people to welcome Vince to the neighborhood. They were about his age and the proud parents of a sixteen-month-old curly-top named Mandy, who took most of their time and attention, but Wendy seemed determined to "fix him up" with one of her single friends. Steve had confided that his wife found Vince too "tall, dark and delish" to be still sin-

gle at twenty-nine, but that she'd have felt the same
way if he'd been a "bald warthog."

Vince didn't know about being "tall, dark and delish," but he didn't think he was a "bald warthog," either. He'd happily give up the single state the moment
that God brought the right woman into his life. So far
he hadn't stumbled across her—not that he'd exactly
been out beating the bushes for the future Mrs. Cutler.

He was a busy man with a booming business, three
garages and a large extended family, including his parents, four sisters and half a dozen nieces and nephews,
with one more on the way, not to mention the brothers-in-law and innumerable aunts, uncles and cousins.
That, church and a few close friends was about all he
could manage, frankly.

As he drove toward his old apartment building, a
feeling of déjà vu overcame him. He remembered well
the day, almost a decade ago, when he'd first moved
into the small, bland efficiency apartment. A heady
feeling of liberation had suffused him then. He'd felt
so proud to have left the home of his parents and struck
out on his own, leaving behind two pesky younger sisters and two nosy older ones.

Of course, with more freedom had come greater responsibility. Then had come the hard-won understanding that responsibility itself could be counted even
more of a joy than any foolish, youthful notions of
"freedom" that he'd once entertained. A fellow could
take pride in meeting his responsibilities and meeting
them well, whereas freedom—as he had learned—
could become an empty exercise in keeping loneli-
ness at bay.

Other lessons had followed. He'd found his best

friends in moments of difficulty rather than fun, though that was important, too. Most significant, Vince had learned that those who truly loved him—his family, particularly his parents—were bulwarks of support rather than burdens of bondage. The mature Vince possessed a keen awareness that not everyone was as richly blessed in that area.

For the life he had built and the man he had become, he had his parents, with their thoughtful guidance, patience, loving support and Christian examples, to thank. For his parents, he could only thank God, which was not to say that from time to time they did not make him wish that he lived on a different continent, particularly when it came to his single status.

By the time he pulled into the rutted parking lot of the small, dated, two-story apartment building, Vince was feeling pretty mellow with memories. He was by nature a fairly easygoing type, but he possessed a certain intensity, too, an innate drive that had served him well in building his business. Looking around the old place as he left the vehicle and moved onto the walkway, he saw that nothing whatsoever had changed, only his circumstances.

Onward and upward, he mused, setting foot on the bottom step of an all-too-familiar flight of stairs. His heavy, steel-toed boots rang hollowly against the open metal treads as he climbed. After passing three doors on the open landing, he stopped at the fourth and automatically reached for the doorknob. Only at the last moment did he derail his hand, lifting it and coiling it into a fist. Before his knuckles could make contact with the beige-painted wood, however, the door abruptly opened and a feminine face appeared. Obviously she had heard him coming.

"Who are you?"

Vince looked down into clear green eyes like pale jade marbles fringed with sandy-brown lashes. Large and almond-shaped, they literally challenged him. He backed up a step, lowering his hand and took in the whole of her oval face.

It was a bit too long to be labeled classically pretty, just as her nose seemed a bit too prominent to be called pert. But those eyes and the lush contours of a generous mouth, along with high, prominent cheekbones and the sultry sweep of eyebrows a shade darker than her golden-brown hair made a very striking, very feminine picture, indeed. The hair was the finishing touch, her "crowning glory," as the Scriptures said. Thick and straight with a healthy, satiny shine, it hung well past her shoulders, almost to her elbows.

Vince suddenly had the awful feeling that his mouth might be agape. He cleared his throat, making sure that it wasn't, and finally registered her question.

"I'm, uh, Vincent Cutler. You left a message on my—"

"Well, it's about time!" she exclaimed, sweeping her wispy bangs off her forehead with one hand and then instantly brushing them down again. "I've got a whole bag full of your mail here. You must be on every mailing list in the country."

He nodded in thoughtless agreement, but she whirled away too abruptly to notice. He watched the agitated sway of her hips as her long legs carried her across the floor. She moved toward the narrow counter that separated the tiny corner kitchen from the rest of the single room and he instinctively followed.

"I tried dropping it off at the post office," she complained, "but they just kept sending it right back to me. Doesn't matter that it hasn't got my name on it. It's got my address. That's all they care about apparently."

"Guess so," Vince mumbled, shrugging.

A raised ten-by-ten-foot platform set off by banisters denoted the sleeping area, and the remaining floor space served as dining and living rooms. A small bathroom containing a decent-sized closet opened off the latter. He knew all this without bothering to look, the apartment being as familiar to him as his own face in a mirror. Besides, his attention was fully taken by the tall, slender, feminine form in worn jeans and a simple, faded T-shirt, mostly obscured by the fall of her hair.

When she bent to open a cabinet door and reach inside, gentlemanly impulse sent his gaze skittering reluctantly around the room. Color jolted him as his eyes took in a bright-yellow wall and a neat, simple plaid of yellow, red and green against a stark white background. Potted plants were scattered about, and he registered a smattering of tiny checks and a few ruffles, but the room was not overly feminine, as his mother's and sisters' houses were inclined to be. The furnishings were sparse and dated, obviously used, but the overall effect was surprisingly pleasing, much better than the drab, often cluttered place that he had inhabited.

"Wow," he said, and the next thing he knew, she was flying at him, both hands raised.

"What are you doing? Get out! Get out!"

She hit him full force, palms flat against his chest,

propelling him backward. Vince threw his arms out in an attempt to regain his balance and then felt them knocked down again as he stumbled backward through the door, which summarily slammed in his face, just inches from his nose. Automatically reaching up, he checked to be certain that it hadn't taken a blow and felt the small familiar hump of a previous break. That was when he heard the bolt click and the safety chain slide into place.

For another moment, he was too stunned even to think, but then he began to replay the last few minutes in his mind, and gradually realization came to him. He slapped both hands to his cheeks. Good grief! She hadn't invited him in; he'd just followed her like some lost puppy, right into her home! *Her* home, *not* his, not any longer. No wonder she'd freaked! He dropped his hands.

"Oh, hey," he said to the door, feeling more and more like an idiot. "I—I didn't mean to alarm you. I would never...that is, I—I used to live here," he finished lamely.

She, of course, said nothing.

He closed his eyes, muttering, "Way to go, Cutler. Way to go. Probably scared the daylights out of her."

Shifting closer, he tried to pitch his voice through the door without really raising it; he knew too well how thin the walls were around here. "I'm sorry if I frightened you."

He waited several seconds, but there might have been a brick wall behind that door rather than a living, breathing woman. Actually, he had no idea if she was even still in the vicinity. She might have been cowering in the farthest corner of the room, though he couldn't quite picture her doing so.

No, a woman like that wouldn't be cowering. More likely she was standing there with a baseball bat ready to bash in his head if he so much as turned the door-knob. Clearly, a prudent man would retreat.

Despite recent evidence, Vince Cutler was a prudent man.

He turned and walked swiftly along the landing, then quickly took the stairs and swung around the end of the railing toward his truck. A certain amount of embarrassment mixed with chagrin dogged him as he once more climbed behind the wheel, his errand an obvious bust. Yet, a smile kept tweaking the corners of his mouth as he thought about the woman upstairs.

She was all dark gold, that woman, dark gold and vinegar. Spunky, that's what she was. He recalled that the top of her head had come right to the tip of his nose. Considering that he stood an even six feet in his socks, she had to be five-seven or eight, which would explain those long legs. It occurred to him suddenly that he didn't even know her name; that, more than anything else, just seemed all wrong.

As he turned the big truck back onto the street, he also turned his mind to mending fences. She still had his mail, after all, and he couldn't let things lie as they were. Good manners, if nothing else, decreed it. The question was how to approach her again. Frowning, he immediately sought solutions in the only manner he knew.

"Lord, I don't know what happened to my good sense. I scared that girl. Please don't let her sit there afraid that I'd hurt her. The whole thing was my fault, and if You'll just show me how, I'll try to make up for it."

Just then he drove by a minivan with the tailgate raised. It was parked in an empty lot and surrounded by hand-lettered signs touting Tyler roses, buckets of which were sitting on its back deck. A strange, unexpected thought popped into his head, one so foreign and seemingly out of nowhere that it startled him, and then he began to laugh.

That's what happened when you relied on God to lead you. As his daddy would say, when you ask God for guidance, you'd better get out of the way quick. Now all he had to do was pick his time and his words very carefully. That was to say, very prayerfully.

Vince polished the toe of one boot on the back of the opposite pants leg, not a work boot this time but full-quill ostrich, one half of his best pair of cowboy boots. Armed to the teeth with two dozen bright red rosebuds, he took a deep breath, squared his shoulders and rapped sharply on the door. He counted to six before the door opened this time.

Green eyes flew wide, but he thrust flowers and words at her before he could find himself facing that door again.

"I'm so sorry. I didn't meant to frighten you or seem disrespectful." When she didn't immediately slam the door in his face, he hurried on. "I guess I just lived here so long that it seemed perfectly natural to walk inside. I didn't think how inappropriate it was or how it would seem to you." She frowned and folded her arms, giving her head a leonine toss. He found himself smiling. "Honest. I feel like a dunce."

"You're grinning like one," she retorted, and then she sniffed.

His smile died, not because she'd insulted him—he didn't take that seriously—but because she'd obviously been crying.

"Oh, hey," he said, feeling like a real heel. "You okay?"

She swiped jerkily at her eyes and lifted her chin. "Yeah, sure I'm okay. You going to beat me with those flowers or what?"

"Huh?" He dropped his arm then quickly lifted it again, saying, "These are for you."

One corner of her mouth quirked, and humor suddenly glinted in those clear green eyes. "Yeah, I figured."

"For, uh, your trouble." He shifted uncertainly. "The mail and all."

"And all?" she echoed, arching one brow.

He gave her his most charming smile and waggled the roses in their clear plastic cone. "I said I was sorry."

She reached out and languidly swept the flowers from his grasp, drawling, "Right. Thanks. I suppose you want your mail now."

He nodded and fished a folded card out of his pocket, offering it to her. "I've already turned in one, but I thought you might want to drop that in the box yourself, so you'll know for sure that it's done."

She glanced at the change-of-address card, and that brow went up again. "That's you? Cutler Automotive?"

Nodding, he dipped into the hip pocket of his dark jeans and came up with a couple of coupons. "That reminds me. Maybe you can use these sometime."

She tucked the change-of-address card into the roses and took these new papers into one hand, cocking her head to get a good look at them.

"Hmm," she said, reading the top one aloud, "Fifty percent off service and repairs." She looked him right in the eye. "This on the up-and-up?"

"Absolutely."

"No catch? I don't have to spend a certain amount or agree to some extra service?"

"Nope. You just present the signed coupon, we knock fifty percent off your bill."

"No strings attached?"

"We don't accept photocopies," he pointed out, calling her attention to the smaller print at the bottom of the paper. "But that's it."

She nodded, apparently satisfied. "Okay. Great. If you wait right here, I'll get your mail."

"These feet are not moving," he promised, but the instant she turned her back, he craned his neck to get another look around.

She'd done wonders with the old place. Despite the dated furniture and faded fabrics, the apartment had a homey, put-together feel about it that he quite liked, and he told her so.

"Never looked this good when I lived here."

She laid the flowers on the counter and turned to face him. "No?"

He shook his head and shrugged. "Guess I just don't have the knack."

"What guy does?"

"None I know of, not many women, either, from what I can tell."

"You pay attention to that sort of thing, do you?"

she asked, seeming surprised. It had sounded a little odd, now that he thought about it.

"Lately, I do. Since the move."

"Ah."

She bent and extracted a small shopping bag from the cabinet.

"This is it," she said, carrying the bag toward him. "Two more pieces came just today."

He reached through the open doorway to accept the bag. It was stuffed with papers.

"I'm sorry about this. I usually take better care of business."

"I just hope there aren't any overdue bills in there," she said dryly.

"Naw, I try not to have any of those."

"We all try," she quipped wryly, but he detected a troubled note.

"Not all," he said, wanting to reassure her somehow. "You'd be surprised how many people make no attempt to pay their bills."

"Maybe they can't."

"Maybe," he admitted, "but if they try, we work with them."

She tilted her head and her brows bounced up and down at that. "Cutler Automotive, you mean."

"Yes, ma'am."

"Huh."

After a second or two it became apparent that she wasn't going to say anything else, and he couldn't for the life of him think of any way to rectify that. He shuffled his feet in place.

"Well, you have a nice evening."

She reached for the door. "Yeah, you, too, if you can

with all that to go through." She nodded at the sack in his arms. "If any more comes, I'll send it on your way now that I have a good address."

"I don't mind coming after it again," he assured her quickly, "if you'll just call."

"I'll send it," she stated decisively.

Defeated, he nodded. "Okay. However you want to handle it."

"That's how I want to handle it," she said flatly, backing up to push the door closed. "So long, Vincent Cutler."

He put up a hand. "Wait a sec. I'd like to know your name, at least. I mean, if you don't mind." He shrugged. "Seems strange bringing flowers to a woman whose name I don't even know."

She considered a moment longer then said, "Jolie."

"Jo Lee," he repeated carefully.

"No." She rolled her eyes. "Jolie. J-o-l-i-e."

"Ah. That's pretty. Jolie what?"

She flattened her mouth, but then she answered. "Jolie Wheeler. Jolie Kay Wheeler."

He smiled again for some reason. It just sounded... right. "Jolie Kay. I'll remember that."

"If you say so."

His smile stretched into a grin. "Good night, Jolie Kay Wheeler. Maybe I'll see you around."

"I doubt it."

He didn't. He didn't know why, but even as that door closed to him once again, he knew somehow that he hadn't seen the last of spunky, pretty Jolie Wheeler. Strangely enough, that thought was quite all right by him.

* * *

Jolie reached into the cabinet overhead and brought down a big pickle jar to serve as a vase. After filling it with tap water, she turned to the counter where the tightly budded roses waited. No one had ever brought her flowers before. Figured it would be some goofball like Cutler. First he doesn't bother to have his mail forwarded, and then he strolls right in as if he owns the place, as if an open door is an automatic invitation to invade the premises.

The good-looking ones were always like that, thought they had a right to the whole world just because they were easy on the eyes. He was easier than most, with that pitch-black hair, lazy, blue-gray eyes, square jaw and dimples. More polite than most, too.

He had immediately apologized yesterday for invading her space, but her heart had been slamming against her rib cage so violently that she hadn't found enough air to reply. Then embarrassment had taken over, and she'd mulishly let him stand there and wheedle until he'd given up and gone away.

Actually, he seemed harmless enough. Now.

The day before when she'd looked up and found him standing there in the middle of her apartment as if sizing up the joint, he'd appeared eight feet tall and hulking. Today, of course, he'd been his usual six-foot—or thereabout—self. She hadn't imagined those broad shoulders and bulging biceps, though, or the slim hips and long legs. The truth was, she had panicked, which wasn't like her, but then she didn't know what she was like anymore. Nothing was as it had been. Without Russell.

She pushed away thoughts of her nephew, rapidly blinking against a fresh onslaught of tears.

This was getting to be a habit. She'd be okay for a while, and then something would remind her of that sweet baby face, that milky, gap-toothed smile and little hands that grasped so trustingly, coiling themselves in her hair and shirt. The loss still devastated her. More, it made her angry, at herself as much as at her sister and brother.

She should never have let herself love little Russ so completely. She should have treated him as nothing more than a foster child, his presence in her life temporary at best. After all, she knew only too well how the game was played. Ten years of experience on one side of that equation should have prepared her better for the other.

Oh, she had been placed with foster families who had truly tried to make her feel a part of the group, but she had always known that it would end. Something would happen, and she would be on her way again, shuffling from one home to another with heart-numbing regularity.

Somehow, though, she hadn't let herself think that it could happen with Russell. When Connie had first gone to prison, pregnant and unwed, she had talked about giving up her child for adoption. Then, after his birth, when she'd asked Jolie to take him and give him a good home, saying that he ought to be with family, Jolie had seen her opportunity to really have someone of her own.

She and Connie had never discussed what would happen after Connie got out. For one thing, Jolie had never dreamed that a judge would actually hand over the child whom she had raised as her own to her misguided younger sister, no matter that said sister had given birth to him. It wasn't fair, and to have their adored big brother Marcus side with Connie had been the unkindest cut of all.

Jolie was still grieving, but she supposed that was to be expected. It had only been days since she'd last seen him, eleven days, two hours, in fact. She could know how many minutes if she was foolish enough to check her watch, which she wasn't. Of course she was still grieving. She'd grieved her mother's absence for years, until she'd found out that Velma Wheeler was dead. Strangely enough, knowing that her mother had died was easier than believing that her mother had simply abandoned her children to the uncertain kindness of strangers.

Jolie shook her head and willed away the tears that had spilled from her eyes, telling herself that she would get on top of this latest loss. She'd had lots of practice.

Reaching for the roses, she slid them from their plastic cone and began arranging them in their makeshift vase. She did not realize, as the pleasing design began to take shape, that she made it happen with an innate, God-given ability which those lacking it would surely treasure.

Never once in her entire life had she ever imagined that anyone could admire or envy anything about her.

Chapter Two

Jolie picked up the two small rectangles of heavy paper from the counter top and studied them again, each in turn. One was the fifty-percent-off coupon that Vince Cutler had explained to her. The other promised a free tow. She wondered again what the catch might be, but she wasn't likely to find out until she had need of the services offered. And the need was very likely to arise.

Her old jalopy was a garage bill waiting to happen. The thing had been coughing and gasping like an emphysema patient lately. She'd literally held her breath all the way to work this morning.

If the dry cleaners where she was employed had been situated just a little closer to the new apartment, she'd have walked it every day just to save wear and tear on the old donkey cart, but five miles coming and going on a daily basis was a bit more than she could manage, especially with the evening temperatures hovering in the thirties. Just to be on the safe side, Jolie tucked the coupons into her wallet—never know when they might come in handy—before going back to the ironing with which she augmented her meager income.

Since the death of his wife, Mr. Geopp, owner and operator of the small, independent dry cleaners where she'd worked for the past six years, had chosen to out-source the delicate work rather than invest in the new machines that could handle it properly, and he'd stopped taking in alterations and regular laundry altogether.

One day, Jolie mused, Geopp would retire, and then what would she do? Her heart wasn't exactly in dry cleaning, but she didn't seem to possess a single exploitable talent. It was a familiar worry that she routinely shoved aside.

With the tip of one finger, she checked the temperature of the pressing plate, judged it sufficiently cooled not to damage the delicate silk blouse positioned on the padded board and carefully began removing the wrinkles from the fabric. Her mind wandered back to the coupons.

If she took in her car for an estimate, would she see Vince Cutler again?

She glanced ruefully at the flowers he had given her. They were a pretty pathetic sight now. The buds had opened and half the petals had fallen, but she couldn't bring herself to toss them just yet. Not that she was harboring any secret romantic fantasies about Vincent Cutler. She wasn't in the market, no matter how goodlooking he was, and he was plenty goodlooking. Why, the only thing that saved the man from being downright beautiful was the little hump on the bridge of his nose.

She couldn't help wondering how his nose had been

broken, then she scolded herself for even thinking about him. Vince Cutler was nothing to her, and she intended to keep it that way. Secondhand experience had taught Jolie that romantic entanglements were more trouble than they were worth.

Her mom had been big on romance, and all that had gotten her was three kids by three different men, none of whom they could even remember. Still, every time some yahoo had crooked his finger at Velma Wheeler she'd followed him off on whatever wild escapade he'd proposed, often leaving her children to fend for themselves until she returned.

Sometimes they were out of food and living in the dark with the utilities shut off when she'd finally remember that she had a family. One day she simply hadn't returned at all, and eventually Child Welfare had stepped in to cart Jolie and her siblings off to foster care.

For years Jolie had harbored the secret fantasy that her mother would come back a changed woman, determined to reunite their scattered family, all the while knowing that Velma would have had to learn to care for them a great deal more in her absence than she ever had while present. Then one day Jolie had been told that her mother had died in a drunk-driving accident and been buried in a pauper's grave somewhere in Nevada. A simple typographical error had resulted in the misspelling of her name and an incorrect filing of records. Her mother had been gone four years by that time.

With Velma as their lesson, Jolie and her sister Connie had sworn that they would not go from man to man. Then Connie had somehow settled on that jerk

Kennard and doggedly refused to give up on him. Jolie understood that Connie had feared being a serial loser just like their mom, but only after Kennard had gone to prison for the rest of his life, taking a pregnant Connie along with him, did she turn away from him. Of course, Connie had claimed that she hadn't even known that an armed robbery was being committed that day, let alone a murder, despite the fact that she had been sitting in front of the bank in a running car.

Jolie had been inclined to believe Connie at the time. Now she just didn't know.

Maybe if Connie had made a better choice than Kennard…but then, Jolie reminded herself, she wouldn't have had Russell. It was worth any hardship to have a little boy like that. Wasn't it?

Jolie shook her head. Thinking that way could get a girl in trouble. Better just to go it alone.

Jolie had learned that lesson the hard way after the authorities had split up her and her siblings when sending them into foster care. At first she and Connie had been placed together, but that hadn't lasted for very long.

Oh, they'd maintained contact. The department was good about that sort of thing. But the years had taken their toll. Jolie had been nine, Marcus only a year older and Connie just seven when their mom had disappeared.

Two decades later, Jolie was again alone.

With Russell to fill her days and nights and heart, it had seemed that she had family again, but only for a little while. Now all she had was a pile of other people's clothing to iron and a single room with a private bath to call her own—so long as she could pay the rent.

That thought sent her back to the job at hand, and for a time she lost herself in the careful placement and smoothing of one garment after another. Funny how you could take pride in something so small and insignificant as smoothing wrinkled cloth, but a girl had to get her satisfaction where she could.

"Come on, baby, just a little farther."

Jolie patted the cracked black dash encouragingly, but the little car sputtered and wheezed with alarming defiance. Then it gave a final paroxysm of shudders and simply stopped, right in the middle of rush-hour traffic.

"Blast!"

Someone behind her did just that with a car horn.

"All right, already!" she yelled, strong-arming the steering wheel as far to the right as she could. The car came to a rolling halt against the curb.

Tires screeched behind her. Another horn honked, and then an engine gunned. A pickup truck flew by with just inches to spare. Jolie flinched, put the transmission in Neutral and cranked the starter, begging for a break. The engine turned over, coughed and died again. The second time, the engine barely rumbled, and on the third it didn't do that much. By the fifth or sixth try, the starter clicked to let her know that it was getting the message but that the engine was ignoring its entreaties entirely. Jolie gave up, knowing that the next step was to get out and raise the hood.

She didn't dare try to exit the car on the driver's side. Instead, she turned on her hazard lights, put the standard transmission in first gear, set the parking brake and released her safety belt to climb across the narrow center console and the passenger seat to the other door. Stepping out on the grassy verge between the curb and the sidewalk, she tossed her ponytail off one shoulder and kicked the front wheel of the car in a fit of pique. Pain exploded in her big toe.

Biting her tongue, she limped around to the front end of the car to lift the hood and make her situation even more visible to the traffic passing on the busy street. After that, all she could do was plop down on the stiff brown grass to wait for someone to come along and offer to help as there was no place around from which to make a telephone call. Looked like she might be trying out those coupons from Cutler Automotive sooner rather than later. Provided someone with a telephone stopped.

More than half an hour had passed and her toe had stopped aching before a Fort Worth traffic cop pulled up behind her aged coupe, lights flashing. Traffic moved into the inside lane to accommodate him as he opened his door and got out. He strolled over to Jolie, a beefy African-American with one hand on his holster and the other on his night stick.

"Ma'am," he said pleasantly, "you can't leave your car here like this."

"Sir," Jolie replied with saccharine sweetness, "I can't get the thing to move."

He rubbed his chin and asked, "Anyone you can call?"

"Could if I had a phone."

He removed a cell phone from his belt and showed it to her. Heaving herself to her feet, she walked over to the car to take her wallet from the center console. Pulling out the coupon from Cutler Automotive, she handed it to him. Nodding, he punched in the number and passed her the phone.

The number rang just twice before a voice answered.

"Cutler Automotive. This is Vince. How can I help you?"

Vince. She swallowed and shifted her weight. "This is Jolie Wheeler."

"Well, hello, Jolie Wheeler. Have you got mail for me?"

"Nope. I've got a coupon for a free tow."

"A free tow?"

"That's what it says. Any problem with that?"

"No, ma'am. Where are you?"

She told him, and he said he'd be right there before hanging up. She handed the phone back to the officer and thanked him. He nodded and turned to watch the passing traffic, trying to make small talk. They'd covered how the car had been acting and where she was going and where she'd been and the state of disrepair of the Fort Worth streets by the time the white wrecker, lights flashing, swung to the curb in front of her crippled car.

Vince bailed out with hardly a pause, and Jolie's heart did a strange little kick inside her chest. Then he walked straight to the grinning cop, ignoring her completely.

"Jacob," he said, shaking the other man's hand.

The policeman smiled broadly and clapped Vince on the shoulder. "How you doing, my man?"

"Staying busy. How're you?"

"Likewise, only with very little sleep."

"New baby keeping you up nights?" Vince asked, flashing his dimples.

It was at this point that Jolie folded her arms, feeling very much on the outside looking in.

"Oh, man, is he ever!" came the ardent reply. "Rascal's got a set of lungs on him, too, let me tell you."

"Well, he sure didn't get those from his soft-spoken mama," Vince said with a grin.

"Soft-spoken?" Jacob the cop echoed disbelievingly. "Soft-spoken? My Callie? Man, you know better than that. You've sat in front of her at a football game."

Vince just grinned wider. "I'm going to tell her you said that."

"Not unless you want to attend my funeral." Both men laughed and back-slapped each other before Jacob moved off toward his patrol car. "You're in good hands now, ma'am," he called jovially to Jolie as he sauntered back to his vehicle.

Vince shook his head, still chuckling, and parked his hands at his waist, striking a nonchalant pose before finally turning to Jolie.

"Well, I'm glad you got a nice visit out of this," she said sarcastically.

Vince Cutler arched his brows, but his smile stayed firmly in place. "Jacob and I attend the same church, but because of his schedule we don't often get to the same service, so I'm glad to have seen him. Now, what's the problem with your car?"

She threw up her hands, disliking the fact that he'd made her feel glad, jealous and petty all in the space of a few minutes.

"How would I know? The hateful thing quit, that's all."

"Uh-huh." He stepped up to the bumper and looked over the engine. Gingerly, he wiped a forefinger across one surface and rubbed it against his thumb. "No oily emission."

"Is that good?" she asked anxiously, her concern about her transportation momentarily overcoming all else.

"It's not bad."

Whatever that meant.

She flattened her lips and tried to see what he saw as he leaned forward and fingered first one part and then another, poking and prodding at hoses and wires and other unnameable organs. Finally he turned to lean a hip against the fender.

"So what happened, exactly, before it quit running?"

She pushed a hand through her bangs, tugged at her ponytail and sucked in a deep breath, trying to remember *exactly.* Finally she began to talk about how the car had been coughing and sputtering by fits and starts lately and how the dash lights had blinked off from time to time.

He listened with obvious attention, then asked, "Any backfiring?"

She considered. "No, I don't think so."

"Okay." Pushing away from the car, he moved toward the driver's door. "Keys in the ignition?"

"Yes."

He opened the door and folded himself into the seat behind the wheel. The starter clicked for several seconds then stopped.

Vince spent a few moments looking at the gauges on the dashboard, then he got out and walked back to the wrecker, returning quickly with a small tool box and a thick, quilted cloth, which he spread on the fender before placing the tool box atop it. He opened the box and extracted a strange gizmo that resembled a calculator with wires attached, which he carried back into the car with him.

Jolie walked around to the passenger window and looked in while he wedged himself under the dash and began pulling down wires. He separated several little plastic clips and attached leads from the gizmo to them, then he studied the tiny screen before turning the ignition key on and off several times in rapid succession.

"What is that thing?" Jolie asked, curiosity getting the better of her.

"I call it my truth-teller."

"Oh, they sell truth at mechanic's school, do they?"

"They sure do," he drawled, ignoring her sarcastic tone.

"That's not what I heard."

"You heard wrong, then."

He removed the leads, reconnected the clips and tucked everything back up under the dash. Then he rose and carried his equipment around to the front of the car again. Jolie joined him there, more curious than ever. He didn't keep her waiting.

"You've got a sensor going out, and I'd guess that the alternator needs to be rebuilt, too."

Dismay slammed through her. She covered it by rolling her eyes. "And what's that going to cost?"

He shrugged. "Can't say without checking a parts list."

"More than a hundred?"

"Oh, yeah. Plus, you've got half a dozen hoses ready to spring leaks and at least one cracked battery mount that I can see. That'll have to be replaced before your next inspection. And if I were you, I'd have the timing chain checked."

She caught her breath, stomach roiling. How would she ever pay for all that? she wondered sickly.

"I've reset the sensor," he went on, "so it should behave for a little while, and I'll give you a jump to get you started, but you really ought to bring the car in soon as you can because this *will* happen again. Just a matter of time."

Jolie bit her lip. Maybe he was just shilling for the garage. Maybe this would be all it took. Whatever, she had zero intention of taking the car in for repairs until she had no other option. She folded her arms again as he went back to the wrecker and returned with what looked like a battery on wheels.

"How much is today going to cost?" she wanted to know, not that she had much choice at the moment.

"This? *Nada.*"

Jolie blinked. "Nothing?"

"I can charge you if you want," he said, mouth quirking at the corners.

She wrinkled her nose. "Thanks, but no thanks."

He smiled knowingly, dimples wrinkling his lean cheeks. "Okay, then."

With that he got busy hooking up everything. Finally he got in and started her car. The engine fired right off and settled into its usual, uneven rumble. Jolie almost dropped with relief.

"Thank goodness."

He started disconnecting and packing away gear.

As he dropped the hood, she lost a short battle with herself and asked, "You won't get in trouble with your boss, will you? For not charging me, I mean."

Vince wiped his hands purposefully on a red cloth that he'd pulled from his hip pocket, holding her gaze.

"No problems there."

"You're sure?"

"Jolie, I *am* the boss."

She felt a tiny shock, but she'd practiced nonchalance so long that it came easily to her.

"Well, if you say so."

He folded the cloth and stuffed it back into his pocket with short, swift movements, saying, "Fact is, I own and operate three garages."

She blinked, impressed, but of course that would never do.

"All by yourself?" she quipped blandly.

He chuckled. "Not exactly. I have twenty-two employees, not counting the outsourcing, of course."

"Outsourcing," she echoed dully.

"Um-hm, bookkeeping, billing, that sort of thing."

"Ah."

And here she'd figured him for a regular joe. Just goes to show you, she thought, eying his dusky-blue uniform with reluctant new interest.

"If you call the shop tomorrow," he told her casually, "I can work you in." She lifted her eyebrows skeptically, and he went on, prodding ever so gently. "You really ought to have that work done."

Now she *knew* it was a scam. Soften up the mark with a little freebie, make her think you're as honest as the day is long, then get her in the shop and soak her good. Resetting that sensor was probably all the car had ever needed.

"We'll see."

"Okay," he said lightly. "Well, I'll be seeing you."

"Oh, really?" She tilted her head, studying him for signs of dishonesty. Had he somehow sabotaged her car so that she'd have to bring it to his shop?

He glanced away pointedly, his sculpted mouth thinning. "You know, not everyone in the automotive-repair business is a crook. In fact, despite our reputation for rip-offs, most mechanics are honest and highly trained."

To her absolute disgust, color stained her cheeks. "I didn't say you were a crook."

He just looked at her, his smoky-blue eyes flat as stone. "No, but you were thinking it."

Her chin rose defensively. "You have no idea what I was thinking."

"Don't I?"

He just stood there, staring at her, until she suddenly realized what he was waiting for. Her hauteur wilted in a pool of mortification. Still, she wasn't about to apologize.

"Okay, maybe I was thinking it, but you don't know how often someone like me gets ripped off."

"Someone like you?" he echoed uncertainly. "And what makes you so different from the rest of us?"

"I'm a single woman, for one thing."

His expression grew suspiciously bland. "I had noticed that."

"And I don't have a lot of money for another," she snapped, trying to offset the little thrill that his droll comment had produced.

"I would think that would make you less of a target for the unscrupulous, frankly," he said calmly.

Bitterly, she shook her head. "You would think wrong."

"I'm sorry to hear that."

She gulped at the sincere tone of his voice. "The thing is, I don't know enough about cars to guard against getting ripped off."

"You could learn," he suggested lightly. It sounded almost like an invitation.

She looked down at her toes. "I doubt that. I'm not the mechanical type."

"Just the suspicious type," he countered dryly.

Rolling her eyes up, she met his gaze. "I have reason to be."

"I wouldn't know about that," he said, his voice softening, "but I know this. You have nothing to fear from me, Jolie Kay Wheeler. On any score. Ever."

Now what could she say to that? Apparently he didn't expect a reply, for he started toward the wrecker.

"Well, you try to have a good evening."

"Yeah, you, too," she grumbled, disliking the mishmash of feelings that swamped her.

He flipped her a wave, climbed into the truck and drove off, leaving her standing there in the gathering twilight like some oversized, ponytailed traffic cone. Glancing around self-consciously, she made her way to the driver's seat of her little car and dropped down into it.

A sedan flew by with the blare of a horn. Traffic had moved back into the outside lane the instant Vince and his flashing lights had pulled away, but she had barely noted that fact. Shaking slightly, she switched on her headlamps, jammed the transmission into gear, put on her blinker, turned off her hazard lights and prepared to merge.

It hit her then. Like a ballpeen hammer to the back of the head.

She had never thanked him. A handsome, apparently successful man had gotten her car running for free, and she hadn't even had the grace to thank him properly. She tried to remember all the reasons why she had been right to suspect his motives, but somehow they didn't quite ring true.

Jolie brushed her bangs up, then down, blowing out a stiff breath and closing her eyes until the world righted itself and equilibrium returned and she could look at the situation dispassionately.

On second thought, it just didn't figure. He had to have some ulterior motive, something so slick and cagey that she couldn't even think of it. And maybe— good gracious—maybe he was just a nice man who liked to help people. Stranger things had happened.

Somewhere.

Sometime.

Telling herself that it didn't matter, she took a last measuring look at traffic, then pulled away from the curb.

The problem was, somehow it did matter. A lot. Enough to make her feel small and petty and unreasonable.

She was halfway home before it occurred to her that she still had both of those coupons.

Vince shifted in his seat, the safety belt biting into his shoulder. He craned his neck, trying to work out a kink there. It was ridiculous, getting this worked up over a little thing like having his motives questioned. Everyone was suspicious of everybody, at least until they got to know one another. He'd been accused of having ulterior motives before, though not in quite some time. It wasn't pleasant, but it wasn't fatal.

So she didn't trust him. So what? The world was full of people who expected automotive repairmen to rip them off. It was foolish to think she would be any different. And what difference did it make, anyway? God had obviously brought her into his life so that he could get her old car running for her again, and that was just what he'd done. End of story.

The thing wasn't going to run for long, though. With just a cursory inspection he'd found enough wrong under that hood to keep him busy for days, but he'd only mentioned the worst of it because it was obvious that she didn't have much money. It was just as glaringly obvious that she wouldn't be easy to help, either.

Maybe that was the point.

If so, he'd definitely be seeing her again. He believed that God had a purpose in all that He allowed into the lives of His children. So if he never saw her again, so be it. It wasn't his business, after all, to second-guess God, and he was just fine with that.

So why was he fighting the urge to turn around and give her a lecture on the stupidity of looking a gift horse in the mouth?

Ridiculous. Just ridiculous.

He didn't know her well enough to be this disappointed in her attitude. And he probably never would.

A hole seemed to open in his chest, burning hot around the edges.

Vince sighed and tried to concentrate on his driving. He passed an intersection on a green light and immediately heard the screech of tires followed at once by the crunching of metal. Automatically, Vince flipped on his warning lights and pulled out of traffic.

Looking around, he saw that two cars had collided in a grocery-store parking lot across the street. It didn't seem serious, and it wasn't impeding traffic, plus, he was off-duty. The fact was, he didn't make wrecker runs anymore. At least he hadn't until Jolie Wheeler had called. Well, that would teach him.

Shaking his head, he began making his way across the busy street to the parking lot. What was he going to do? Leave without making certain that no one needed his assistance? Not his style. Then again, neither was embarrassing himself, but he'd managed to do that twice now with Jolie Kay Wheeler. Twice was quite enough. Why couldn't he just leave well enough alone?

He reached the scene of the mishap, killed his engine and slid out onto the tarmac. Two women were glaring at each other over the hoods of their tangled cars. Vince put on a smile and waded into the fray.

"Can I help, ladies?"

Almost an hour later he'd managed to uncouple their bumpers and pull out a fender so both could be on their way, still angry but maintaining their civility even as they each contemplated a hike in insurance rates. Twenty bucks richer—the one with the crumpled fender had insisted on compensating him—Vince swung the wrecker through a fast-food lane to pick up a burger to eat at home. Alone.

He could've dropped in on his mom or one of the girls. They were always willing to set an extra plate at the table for him, but they were always wanting to know where he'd been and who he'd seen lately, too, and he just wasn't in the mood to answer questions about his nonexistent love life or hear how he worked too much. He wasn't in the mood to eat alone, either, but those were the options. With a sigh, he resigned himself to the latter.

It was only later as he bit into his burger at the kitchen counter that he wondered if Jolie would call on Cutler Automotive when her old jalopy finally conked on her again, because conk it would—and she still hadn't redeemed those coupons.

Feeling a little better, he enjoyed the rest of his burger.

Chapter Three

"**A**aargh!"

Jolie smacked the steering wheel with a closed fist. Not again! This time the engine wouldn't even turn over. No cough, no sputter, nothing.

She'd have cried if it would've done any good, but tears wouldn't pay for automotive repairs. Air wouldn't either, and that's what was in her checking account at the moment, with payday still two days away and rent due next week.

To make matters worse, she was going to miss at least a few hours of work this morning. The week was not starting out well. Sick at heart, she wrenched her keys from the ignition and crawled out of her old four-banger—*no*-banger at the moment—to head back upstairs.

Her first telephone call was to Mr. Geopp, who told her only to get into work when she could. He was a pleasant enough employer but somewhat distant personally. His late wife had been easier to talk and relate to. She'd cut Jolie every possible break, especially after Russell had arrived.

Jolie would stay with Geopp for no other reason than loyalty to the memory of his wife. She just wished that he would display a little more emotion, if only to let her know for sure where she stood with him in moments like this. It was one more worry on a long list of worries.

Jolie sat down to think through her options with the car. It had started before with a simple jump from a battery charger. Maybe that would work once more. She judged her chances of getting it done for free a second time at slim to none, however, especially if she called Cutler's again. After questioning Vince's integrity, she doubted that he'd cut her a break. Then again, neither would any other emergency service in town.

She thought of the coupons and shook her head in resignation. Cutler Automotive probably jacked up the price twice as high as normal before giving their fifty percent discount, but at least the towing would be free. They couldn't jack up free.

Sighing, she reached for the telephone once more. This time a perky-sounding female answered the call.

The wrecker arrived twenty-four minutes later.

Jolie was sitting on the bumper tapping one toe against the pavement when the familiar white truck swung into the lot. Her stomach lurched in anticipation, but then a stranger opened the driver's door and got out.

"You Ms. Wheeler?"

Nodding, Jolie tamped down her disappointment and straightened away from the car to look over this newcomer.

He seemed roughly the same age as Vince and had a shock of very dark hair falling forward over his brow, but that was where the similarities ended. This fellow was shorter and wider than Vince with a noticeable bulge around the middle and a slight under-bite that made his lower jaw seem overlong. His brown eyes twinkled merrily as he thrust out his right hand.

"I'm Boyd. What can I do for you?"

"You can make my car go."

"Well, let's have a look," he said noncommitally, taking a toolbox from the truck, "and while I'm looking, why don't you tell me what's been going on with it?"

Jolie started with that morning's fiasco and worked her way backward over the past couple weeks, leaving out only Vince's diagnosis. By the time she was through with her tale, he was nodding his head knowingly.

"Sounds like the alternator and probably a bad sensor. I'll try resetting the sensor and jump-starting it."

Jolie breathed a sigh of relief, but it was for naught. The sensor would not register, according to Boyd, and the jump did no good.

"Well, I'll tow her in and see what a full diagnostic turns up," he said blandly.

"What's that going to cost?" Jolie asked, fishing the coupons from the hip pocket of her jeans. "I have these."

Boyd took the coupons, kept the one for the free tow and handed back the other, saying, "These'll help."

"So how much?"

He shrugged. "Provided it's what I think it is and we don't find any other problems, I'd say about three hundred, but a lot depends on the parts. This is a domestic car, but a lot of the parts are foreign-made, so…" He shrugged again.

Jolie felt physically ill.

"Is that three hundred before or after the discount?"

He looked at her sympathetically. "After."

She momentarily closed her eyes.

"I can't afford that!"

"Aw, don't worry," he told her. "The boss will cut you a deal."

That would be the boss whom she'd practically called a crook.

"I wouldn't count on it," she muttered.

Boyd chuckled. "No, really. Vince is a good guy. He helps people out all the time. Between you and me, he'd probably give the business away bit by bit if I didn't keep reminding him that he was supposed to be making a profit. But then, the way I figure it, God takes care of His own."

Jolie didn't know about that. She just knew that life had suddenly gotten immeasurably more difficult for her personally, and it hadn't exactly been a walk in the park to begin with.

"I don't know how I'm going to manage this."

"Listen, just call the shop later and speak to Vince," Boyd urged. "Use the second number on the coupon. Okay?"

"Sure."

The two of them were probably working the scam together, she thought sullenly, and the nice-guy acts were just a carefully coordinated part of it.

Then again, the car wasn't faking it. The thing had been bugging out on her since well before Vincent Cutler had showed up on the scene.

Boyd had her put the car in Neutral so he could push it out of its parking space and "get a good hook on it." A few minutes were all that were required to secure the towing device. Then he just started up the automatic winch, and they stood there watching the front end of her car slowly rise off the ground.

"I have to find a ride to work," Jolie muttered to herself.

"Yeah? Where do you work?"

She told him, and he jerked his head toward the cab of the truck. "Get in. I'll drop you."

She brightened. That was the first bit of good news she'd had today.

"Really?"

"It's on the way."

"Great."

She climbed into the cab of the truck while he finished securing the tow. It was spotlessly clean, despite a gash in the vinyl of the bench seat, and sported a two-way radio, GPS system and some sort of miniature keyboard attached to the dash with an electronics cord.

As soon as Boyd slid beneath the steering wheel, he picked up the keyboard and typed in some letters and numbers, then he triggered the radio and informed whoever was on the other end that he was headed back to the garage with a car in tow, rattling off both make and model.

Soon Jolie was standing in front of the dry cleaners watching her car move away behind the wrecker, its front end pointing skyward. Mindlessly, she swept her bangs back and then smoothed them down again before turning to enter the shop. Bumping into one of their regular customers, she pasted on a smile. A glance showed her that the shop was full and the counter vacant while Geopp evidently searched for garments to be picked up. She went to work.

"How are you, Mrs. Wakeman?"

"Arthritis just gets worse and worse" came the usual doleful reply.

"That's too bad. How many pieces today?"

"Three, and be careful of the gold buttons on the blazer. They tarnished last time."

"Yes, ma'am."

The rest of the morning proved as busy as those first few minutes, but Jolie's mind was never far from her troubles.

Immediately after lunch, she called the garage, using the number on the card that Boyd had given her. Vince answered this time.

"Cutler Automotive. This is Vince speaking. How can I help you?"

She gulped inaudibly. "This is Jolie Wheeler again."

"Oh, hi. We've got the car on diagnostics now."

He sounded perfectly normal, as if she hadn't insulted him, as if they were friends or something equally ridiculous. For some reason that rankled, adding a dry edge to her voice.

"So you still don't know what's really wrong with it?"

"We don't have confirmation, no."

"And when will you have confirmation?"

"Shortly."

"Call me as soon as you know what it's going to cost," she demanded.

"All right."

"*Before* you do any work."

Several seconds of silence followed that, and when next he spoke, his voice was tinged with annoyance.

"No one's going to take advantage of you, Jolie."

She went on as if she hadn't heard him.

"Because I really can't afford a big repair bill." Or any repair bill for that matter.

He sighed gustily.

"I realize that. Look, why don't you just come by the shop after work? I'll show you exactly what's wrong with your car and what it's going to cost to fix it, and we'll figure out how to take care of it. Okay?"

He couldn't have sounded more reasonable, so why did she feel like needling him?

"And just how would you suggest I get over there without transportation? Take the bus?"

It was an entirely plausible possibility, which made what happened next all the more inexplicable.

"I'll pick you up," he said lightly. "What time to do you get off work?"

She didn't even balk, which in itself was appalling.

"Six o'clock."

"Okay. See you then."

They quickly got off the phone after that. Jolie stood staring at the thing for a long moment, wondering what on earth had possessed her to agree that he should pick her up, but then she shook her head.

Why shouldn't he? He had her car, after all. She hoped she could wangle a ride home out of it, too. Beyond that, she just refused to think, period.

Vince pulled up to the curb in front of the dry cleaners at precisely three minutes past six. The shop had

obviously seen better days. Its storefront looked out-
dated and rather dingy, but the area was clean and safe.
Because he was in a ten-minute loading zone, he kept
the engine running and settled back to wait.

He didn't have to wait long. The door opened just
moments later, and Jolie burst out onto the sidewalk.
He grinned at her dropped jaw. Her ragged little car
was purring like a contented kitten.

"It's fixed!"

He laughed at her delight, but then her face turned
thunderous. Her hands went to her hips, and he *knew*
what she was going to say. Even as she spoke, he released his safety belt, opened the door and stood, one
foot still inside the car, one hand on the steering wheel.

"I did *not* authorize any work."

"No, you didn't," he interrupted, "but it had to be
done."

"You said we'd talk about it first!"

"Jolie, how would you get back and forth to work
without your car?"

She put a hand to her head, ruffling her bangs and
then smoothing them again. Vince tried not to smile
at what seemed to be a characteristic gesture, something she did without conscious thought.

"I can't pay for it!" she suddenly wailed, as if he
didn't know that.

The sidewalk was not the place to talk about it,
however.

"Get in," he told her, indicating the passenger seat.
For a moment she just stared at him. "Get in," he repeated. "My truck's back at the shop. We can talk on
the way."

She trudged around and got into the car with all the

enthusiasm of a prisoner on the way to her execution. He chuckled despite his better judgment.

"It's not funny," she grumbled as he dropped down into the seat and clipped his belt once more.

"It's not tragic, either."

"Shows what you know," she snapped. "When was the last time you had to choose between paying the rent and other obligations?"

"It's been some while," he admitted, "but I have been there."

"Then you understand that there's just no way..." She gulped. "A—a few bucks a month, maybe, if I—"

"Will you just listen for a minute?" he urged, laying his arm along the back of her seat in entreaty.

She frowned at him, worry clouding those jade-green eyes.

"I have an idea about how we can square this."

Her mouth compressed suspiciously. It was a very pretty mouth, wide and mobile and full-lipped, but he couldn't help wondering what or who had fostered that mistrustful expression.

"How?" she asked.

He glanced at the front of the dry cleaners.

"Well, if it's not a conflict of interest for you, I need someone to do my laundry."

She blinked.

"Laundry?"

"Yeah, you know, dirty clothes and shop rags, some linens, that sort of thing."

The clouds were beginning to lift from her eyes, but her tone was tart as she retorted, "I know what laundry is, but why should I do yours?"

She buckled her safety belt, and Vince put the transmission in gear, turning away so that she wouldn't notice that he struggled with a sudden grin.

"Garages are dirty places," he began, nosing the car into traffic, "and I own all the uniforms that the guys wear. I thought I could do the washing myself, even bought a top-of-the-line, extra-capacity washer-and-dryer set, but it just doesn't get done in a timely manner."

"And you want to pay me to do it."

"Something like that."

She flipped the end of her ponytail off her shoulder, obviously thinking.

"I get it. You're talking about a barter arrangement, basically."

He nodded and signaled with the blinker that he was moving the car over into the next lane.

"Unless, like I said before, it's a conflict of interest for you, given that your regular job is with a dry cleaner."

"Not a problem. Mr. Geopp stopped taking in laundry a few months ago after his wife died."

"That's too bad, about his wife, I mean."

"Yeah, she was a good lady," Jolie said lightly, but something about her tone let him know that she honestly grieved the woman's passing.

"Were you friends?"

"Not really," Jolie replied, looking away. "About the laundry…"

He took the hint and dropped the subject.

"I have to warn you, there's lots of it."

"Good. That means I'll get the debt worked off sooner rather than later."

He nodded, signifying that they had come to an agreement in principle at least.

"Okay, so all we have to do is negotiate the particulars. I understand that laundry costs are figured by the pound or by the piece."

"That's right."

"I don't have any way to weigh it, so I say we go by the piece, then, if that's agreeable to you."

She named a price that was very much in line with what he'd expected, given that he would be providing the equipment and the necessary supplies. He proposed drawing up a debit sheet so she could mark off her work and subtract the cost of it from the repair bill, which would reflect the fifty-percent reduction that she'd been promised and that would include some extra repairs to her car that he felt were necessary but which he had not yet done.

"I only have two days a week to devote to this," she warned him.

"And what two days would those be?"

"Sunday and Monday. Those are my days off from the dry cleaners."

He shook his head.

"Sundays are for church. I'll be content with Mondays."

"No matter how long it takes for me to work off the debt?" she pressed.

"No matter how long it takes," he assured her.

She stared out the window for a long time, her expression hidden from him. He waited, confident of her decision. Finally she looked straight ahead.

"Okay, it's a deal."

He let her see his smile.

"Let me show you where you'll be working, then."

"Might as well." She sat up a little straighter.

"Obviously this street is Hulen," he pointed out, slowing to make a right turn. "We're going to take the Interstate up here and head west for about a mile."

She nodded, obviously making mental notes as he drove and talked her through the route.

When he turned the car down his street, she drew her brows together and said, "This can't be right."

"What do you mean? It's right up here."

"Here?" she echoed uncertainly, indicating the neighborhood around them with a wave of her hand.

The development was brand-new, not even half occupied yet, but that didn't explain her confusion to him. He let it go long enough to pass by the two empty lots between the corner house and his own at the top of the rise.

"This is it."

He couldn't help the note of pride in his voice.

By some standards, it was a modest home, but it was everything he had ever wanted, bright, roomy, well-appointed and undeniably attractive with its gabled metal roof and exterior of natural stone and rich red brick. He'd labored over every detail, probably to the point of driving the architect and builder nuts, but this was the place where he intended to live out the bulk of his life and, he hoped, one day raise a family.

Most folks didn't look at a first house as a long-term home, but Cutlers weren't the sort who "traded up." They were the kind of people who put down roots, sank them deep and let the years roll by in relative contentment. They believed in God, family, personal integrity, hard work and generosity, all notions that he'd once found boring and mundane. He'd gotten over all that, and he hadn't questioned his values again—until he saw the look on Jolie Wheeler's face as he turned her old car into his curving driveway.

She hated the place; he could see it on her face, and his gut wrenched. Disappointment honed a fine, defensive edge onto his voice.

"What's wrong with it?"

"What's wrong?" she echoed shrilly. "It's your house!"

"You expected me to take you to someone else's house?"

"I expected you to take me to your *business,* one of your garages!"

He stared at her, realization dawning.

"You thought I'd put a washer and dryer in one of my shops?"

"Of course I did!"

He stroked his chin, thinking. Guess he hadn't ever said that the appliances were at his house, and he *had* mentioned uniforms and shop rags and dirty garages.

"Never thought about putting a laundry room into the shop," he mumbled. "Might not be a bad idea. I'll have to look into that."

She threw up her hands, clearly exasperated.

"And in the meantime?"

He shrugged. "In the meantime we've got what we've got, don't we?"

She dropped her jaw, trying to see, apparently, just how far it could go without dislocating. He clamped his back teeth together and mentally counted to ten before drawing a calming breath and reaching way down deep for a reasonable tone.

"Look, I didn't mean to mislead you. The thought of putting a laundry room in the shop itself never even occurred to me."

"And you assumed that I understood you were taking me to your house?"

"Yeah, actually, I did."

She rolled her eyes at that.

"If you prefer," he offered grimly, "you can take the stuff to a commercial laundry somewhere."

"And who's going to pay for that?" she demanded.

"I will," he gritted out, hanging onto the wispy tail end of his patience, "but first you really ought to take a look at what my laundry room has to offer and what you'll have to haul around town if you decide that you just can't stand working here."

She turned her head to stare out the passenger window, drumming her fingers on the armrest attached to the door. He didn't know what else to say, what she expected him to say now, so he just waited her out. After some time she abruptly yanked the handle and popped up out of the car. Vince breathed a sigh of relief. He didn't know if his relief stemmed from her cooperation or the possibility that her disapproval was not directed at his home after all.

He killed the engine as she moved around the car toward the walkway. He got out, tossed her car keys to her and followed her along the curving walk to the front door. He didn't usually go in this way, preferring to park in the garage at the side of the house and enter through the back hall and kitchen, but he'd always admired the professional landscaping. In the summertime the flower beds beneath the front windows would blaze with purple lantana. Now he looked at it all with an especially critical eye, wondering what she thought of it, though why he should care was beyond him.

To put it bluntly, the girl was a charity case, and as prickly as a cactus. What difference did it make whether or not she approved of his house? Or him, for that matter? And yet it did. He couldn't help wondering why, but when it came right down to it, he was almost afraid to know.

Chapter Four

Jolie tried not to be impressed by the sprawling structure sitting proudly atop the gentle hill, but that wasn't
easy. It rose up gleaming and perfect, like something
out of a storybook, with its rock and brick exterior
and shining metal roof. The walkway underfoot was
constructed of the same red brick and brown stone
as the house and was flanked by billowing hillocks
of greenery and clumps of a spiky plant that looked
like a big, spiny artichoke to her. She didn't know one
plant from another, but she knew money on the ground
when she saw it.

She couldn't wait to see the inside of the place, even
if the hair had stood up on the back of her neck when
she'd first realized where he'd brought her.

His house, for pity's sake!

What'd he think, that she would be so impressed
she'd just fall all over him?

Not likely. No way. Uh-uh. She had better sense
than that, thank you very much.

But, oh man, what a place.

Vince slipped past her on the brick porch, which

was deeply inset beneath a tall arch, and jammed a key into the lock, giving it a quick twist. The tall, honey-colored wood plank door, inlaid with artistically rusted nailheads and iron bands, swung open soundlessly, revealing stone floors and smooth walls plastered in pinkish-tan adobe. The tall narrow windows flanking the door were made of stained glass depicting two spiny cacti in a delicate green with blossoms of rose red.

He stepped back to let her pass, and she'd have wiped her feet before entering if there had been a mat of any sort. As it was, she wiped her hands surreptitiously on the seat of her worn jeans, just in case they were dirty, then tugged on the hem of her T-shirt to cover the self-conscious action. She tilted her head back in the foyer, looking up at least twenty feet to the ceiling, past an elegantly rustic wrought-iron chandelier with cut-glass shades.

To her left was a hallway. To her right stretched a huge room set off by tall arches. It was completely empty except for a pair of light fixtures, larger versions of the one hanging over her head, and a leafy fern that sat on the floor in front of a window covered by a faded bed sheet. Straight ahead Jolie spied the back of a nondescript sofa and the overhang of a bar topped in polished granite.

"This way," he said, leading her through the foyer and into what was obviously a den.

The sofa sat in front of a massive stone fireplace. Flanking the fireplace was an equally massive built-in unit which could easily contain a television set as large as a dining table. Upon it were a small framed photo of several kids with mischievous grins and a pile of paperback books. The only other furnishings in the room were a low, battered table and a utilitarian floor lamp. At least here the windows were covered with expensive pleated shades in a dark red.

The bar, she saw, opened onto a large kitchen, as did the arched doorways on each end. Louvered, bat-wing doors stood open to reveal an island containing a deep stone sink. Behind it rose enough cabinets to stash away all the cookware usually offered for sale in a small department store.

The brushed-steel fronts of the appliances announced that no expense had been spared in outfitting the space, but the countertops were bare except for a small toaster and a coffeemaker. At the end of the kitchen, surrounded by oriel windows and two doors, one that opened to a hallway and another leading outside, was a dining area large enough to dwarf the small round table and two chairs situated beneath another unique light fixture.

"Who lives here?" she wanted to know.

"I do."

She rolled her eyes at him. "Besides you."

"No one."

Bringing her hands to her hips, she stared at him in disbelief.

"You've got how many bedrooms in this place, two, three?"

"Four, actually."

"And you live here all by yourself?"

"That's right."

She looked around her, dumbfounded.

"It's a little bare," he said sheepishly, and that was putting it mildly. "I really need to get somebody in here to help me do it up right. Just can't figure out who."

Good golly, Miss Molly, what she could do with a place like this!

She couldn't imagine living here, but it was practically empty, almost a blank slate, and she could see just what ought to go where, starting with a pair of big, leather-upholstered, wrought-iron bar stools so company could sit there at the counter enjoying a cold drink while the host prepared dinner. And that island just begged for a big old pot rack, something sturdy and solid, not that the place lacked storage.

"Hire a decorator," she told him. Obviously he could afford professional help.

He wrinkled his nose at that. "I don't know. I'm not much for trends and themes. It's not a showroom, after all, it's a home."

"But the right decorator could do wonders in here," she insisted.

"Yeah, but who is the right decorator?" he asked rhetorically. He then effectively closed the subject by lifting a hand and saying, "Laundry room's this way."

He led her through the kitchen and into the hallway. After pointing out that the garage lay to the left, he turned right. The second door opened into a laundry room large enough to sport not only a top-of-the-line, front-loading washer-and-dryer set but also a pair of roll-away racks for hanging clothes, a work table for folding and an ironing board, plus a sink and various cabinets.

Dead center on the tiled floor lay a heap of clothing big enough to easily hide a full-grown man. Sitting up. Jolie's jaw dropped.

"How long have you been accumulating that?" she asked, pointing at the pile.

"Week, week and a half," he said mournfully. "By Friday there'll be about half that much again."

"Good grief!" she exclaimed, mentally rolling up her sleeves. "Looks like I've got my work cut out for me."

He lifted his hands. "So do I load it up or not?"

"In what?" she asked dryly. "You got a dump truck around here?"

He chuckled. "Not that I've noticed."

"Well, then," she said with a sigh, "I guess we'll do it your way."

He just grinned, blast his good-looking hide, and well he might. In his place she'd be grinning, too. She was smiling on the inside as it was. Working in a place like this was going to be an out-and-out pleasure, even if it was only temporary. If he tried anything funny with her, she'd just walk out and leave him and his laundry high and dry without the least qualm.

Looking at it that way, she couldn't lose, because whatever happened, her car would be fixed. She almost hoped he *did* try to take advantage of the situation, but not until her debt was paid off because she didn't like owing anybody anything.

Yes, sir, smiling on the inside.

For once, things were going to go her way.

"This one?" Jolie slowed the car as they drew near the corner. Vince shook his head.

"No, the next."

She sped up again, laughing when the little car responded with more pep than usual. "I can't get over how much better it runs."

"It'll drive even smoother with the tires rotated and balanced," he told her. "You might notice a little improvement when we get all the hoses replaced, too, but probably not. You won't have to worry about another breakdown anytime soon, though."

"Music to my ears," she said, and he couldn't help smiling.

She drove as she seemed to do everything else, he noted, with an innate wariness. It certainly kept her on her toes and gave him some confidence in her safety on the road, but it also made him a little sad because she seemed to be constantly expecting trouble and catastrophe.

Over all, Jolie Wheeler struck him as a woman who'd had a lot of hard knocks in life, which was, he supposed, nothing new. The odd thing was that he didn't much like thinking of it.

The way she'd taken in his place had told him that she was unfamiliar with some of the more recent building trends. Later, she'd seemed to be mentally furnishing and decorating the space, and yet she'd remained oddly detached, admiring but certainly not gushing with compliments. He had sensed a kind of assumption on her part that she was out of her element in his house, and that had irritated him a little. Okay, a lot.

He was proud of his home. It was no mansion, but it was comfortable and spacious and extremely well-built. For the life of him, he didn't see why she shouldn't feel perfectly at ease in such surroundings, especially as he'd been particularly struck by how *right* the place felt for her. Maybe that accounted for the new idea noodling around in the back of his mind.

What he'd told her about needing help with furnishing and decorating the place was true. In fact it had begun to take on a certain urgency as his mother and sisters had started pressing him to let them have a go at it. He shuddered mentally, imagining what that might mean. If he wasn't very careful he'd walk into his own house one day soon and find it outfitted in chintz and lace and filled up with kitschy knickknacks.

He liked what Jolie had done with the apartment much more than what his mother and sisters had done with their respective homes. Could she be talked into giving him a hand with his place? He was trying to think how to broach the subject when his stomach gurgled and growled—more like roared, actually. It was so loud that Jolie burst out laughing.

Mildly embarrassed, he clapped a hand over his belly.

"Feeding time at the zoo, I take it," she teased.

"Hey, I'm a hardworking man, and it's dinnertime, okay?"

"Okay by me," she grinned.

Suddenly his heart was beating a little too pronouncedly as he made a spur-of-the-moment decision. He shifted in his seat, wondering if it was wise but knowing that he was going to do it. Fearing she could get the wrong idea, though, he made the suggestion as casually as he could manage.

"Listen, there's a pretty good restaurant up here on the right. Why don't we stop off and grab a bite?"

For a second, he got no reaction. Then she made a face, and he was sure that she was going to tell him to go soak his head. To his surprise, though, her answer was fairly ambiguous.

"I'm not really fit for going out after a day at the cleaners. It's dirty, smelly work, and—"

"You look good to me," he blurted and then could've bitten his tongue off—until she slipped him an almost hopeful glance out of the corner of her eye. "It's a casual sort of place," he added quickly. "I'm, uh, not exactly dressed for anything fancy, either." He indicated his uniform with a wave of one hand.

They came to a red light, and she gave him another one of those sideways looks.

"Just dinner," she said.

It could have been a question or a warning, but he decided to take it as the former, quipping, "Sure. You didn't think I was going to insist on going roller-skating afterward, did you?"

Her mouth quirked up in a smile.

"Do people still roller-skate? Isn't it all roller-blading now?"

He relaxed.

"Doggoned if I know. If you don't do it in a garage or on a field, I haven't had much experience with it."

They both chuckled and drove on in silence for a couple more blocks.

"That's it right up there," he said, and she turned off the street into the parking lot. "Best chicken-fried steaks in town," he told her as she parked.

After killing the engine she said dryly, "Let's hope there's something a little healthier on the menu."

"Well, sure," he teased, "they've got fried chicken, too."

She rolled her eyes as she climbed out of the car. Chuckling, he let himself out on the other side.

"The menu lists a bunch of salads," he assured her as they walked toward the restaurant. "I've even been known to eat one a time or two."

"I'll bet it had fried chicken on top of it," she retorted as he pulled open the door and held it for her.

So it had, but he let his grin be his admission, to her obvious amusement.

The hostess hurried toward them. A teenager in baggy cargo pants a size too large and a T-shirt a size too small, she wasn't dressed any better than they were. She greeted them with a smile and led them to a booth with bench seats and a plank table.

Vince ordered iced tea, chips and salsa as an appetizer and the chicken-fried steak for a main course. Jolie went for an Oriental salad with grilled chicken and mandarin oranges. They both asked for extra lemon with their tea.

Business seemed unusually slow, so the service was especially prompt, leaving them little time for talking. Even at that, he did most of it.

"So, Jolie Wheeler, tell me something about yourself."

She shrugged and said, "Not much to tell."

"What about your family?"

She looked down at the thick paper napkin in her lap.

"Don't have much. What about you?"

"Too much." He chuckled and took it back. "Naw, not really. Thing is, I've got four sisters, and I'm smack dab in the middle."

"That must be trying at times."

"At times," he admitted. "The older two want to baby me all the time, and the younger two think their big brother is supposed to baby them. At least I got four brothers-in-law out of the deal."

"So they're all married then?"

"That's right, and they hate that I'm not. It's like their mission in life is to see that I am, theirs and Mom's."

"And why aren't you?" Jolie asked lightly.

He shrugged. "Haven't found the right lady yet."

"Oh, like you've been out searching high and low for her," she said, sounding very skeptical about that.

He rubbed his palms against his thighs and admitted, "Not lately. I'm open to it, though."

She seemed surprised by that.

The chips and salsa arrived then, and he was hungry enough to dive in, but from long habit, he bowed his head first and silently said grace over his food. When he looked up again, reaching for a crisp triangle of fried-corn tortilla, she was sitting with both shoulders pressed to the back of her seat, her mouth compressed in a straight line.

"What's wrong?"

"I…were you *praying* just then?"

"Yeah. What of it?"

"Nothing." She shook her head and glanced around. "So you're, like, a God freak or something?"

"You could say that. What about you? Aren't you a believer?"

His stomach muscles clenched as he waited for her answer.

"Yeah, I am." She did that thing with her bangs, and

then she positively astounded him, muttering, "Actually, my brother's a minister."

"No kidding!"

She nodded, then looked away and back again.

"I never asked you, how do you like your shirts done?"

The abrupt change in subject startled him.

"Oh. Uh."

"Starch?"

"Well…"

"They stay cleaner longer, but it takes extra time," she told him matter-of-factly. "Spray starch gives it a nice finish, but a lot of men like the extra weight and feel of the real thing."

"Spray starch is fine," he said, realizing that she was trying to avoid talking about her brother. Or God. Vince wasn't sure what to think about that. Either way, it troubled him, but since she was obviously unwilling to get into it, he had no choice but to let it go.

His stomach growled again, and he loaded up one of the chips, inviting her to help herself. They'd emptied the basket by the time the main course arrived, and he'd told her his sisters' names and those of his nieces and nephews, except the one on the way, but she hadn't said another word about her own family or much of anything else.

"So how'd you get into the car-repair business?" she asked as he cut up his plate-sized steak.

"Went to school, went to work, saved up some cash, made an investment. I reinvested that and started looking for a property. It grew from there."

She stabbed a piece of lettuce with her fork.

"You make it sound easy."

He shook his head, chewing the tender steak, and swallowed.

"Lots of hard work and pinching pennies."

She waved a fork around and asked, "You do this sort of thing all the time?"

"What sort of thing?"

"Bartering with people who can't afford to pay cash for their car repairs."

He shrugged. "It seems a good way to take care of the problem."

"Seems chancy to me. How do you know you're coming out even?"

He laid down his knife and fork and rested his forearms on the table. "Listen, I'm not ashamed to say that I've worked hard because I have, but the truth is that I've been very richly blessed in life, too. It would be pretty selfish and self-centered of me not to try to work with folks who haven't had my breaks. Don't you think?"

"Yeah," she admitted bluntly, "I do."

He chuckled at her refreshing honesty and got down to some serious eating.

At least they agreed on *something*. So what if she was wary and kept her distance? Maybe she wasn't a "God freak," as she'd put it. She obviously had some standards, and that was okay by him.

If his stomach muscles sometimes clenched around her, well, he'd figure out what that meant later. Meanwhile, they were both getting their needs met. She needed her car in good running order; he needed his laundry done. And maybe they could help each other in additional ways, too. Time would tell.

* * *

"About Monday," he said, preparing to step out of her car in front of his office, "I'll be there to let you in, and if I'm not there when you need to leave, you can just lock up on your way out."

"All right."

"Meanwhile, I'll expect you to drop the car by on Saturday morning to get those hoses changed."

She nodded. "I'll do that." He had his head out the door when she impulsively stopped him. "By the way..." He relaxed back into his seat and turned to face her.

"Yeah?"

She felt awkward saying it, but she knew it was the right thing to do.

"I wanted to thank you. For everything. I—Including dinner. I really didn't expect you to buy."

He smiled. "No biggie. Consider it my way of apologizing for failing to tell you up front that you'd be working at my house."

"All right."

"That mean I'm forgiven?"

"Let's just say I'm willing to overlook your lapse in judgment. Again."

"Ouch."

She laughed, so he wouldn't figure it was too big a lapse in her estimation.

"Take care now," he said, getting out of the car. He flipped her a jaunty wave and walked toward a big white pickup truck with the shop's name and information painted on the sides. Thoroughly bemused, Jolie put the car in gear and headed home.

She had to say this for Vincent Cutler. He was one

of a kind. First he'd frightened her, then he'd charmed her, then angered her and then charmed her again. That ought to be a recipe for distrust and disaster, but somehow she felt that he was basically harmless. In fact, he seemed like a real nice guy.

More puzzling still, he seemed actually to like her, and she hadn't really given him anything much to like. That made her wonder if he didn't have a hidden agenda, but if he did, she couldn't figure out what it was. He didn't seem to be the self-righteous, pie-in-the-sky type that she'd too often found religious people—including her brother Marcus—to be. Then again, he didn't appear to be out for whatever he could get, either. He just seemed to be…well, so far as she could tell, he was just a really nice man, which, in more ways than one, was surprising.

For one thing, Vincent Cutler was a handsome man, and he had the easygoing self-confidence that all handsome men seemed to possess. In addition, he was ambitious, but in a hardworking, down-to-earth way, not at all as if he figured the world owed him success for being what he was.

It didn't quite seem fair that on top of all that he should also be nice. Could be for show, of course. He might be the most clever of con men, but somehow she didn't think so.

She owed him money, and he was willing to barter for services rendered, but what assurance did he have that she'd even bother to show up for work? The majority of the repairs that her car needed were already done, and since she hadn't actually authorized any of them, she could pretty much tell him to take a leap if she was of a mind to, which she was not.

So, okay, she had to figure that he was a good judge of people, too, but that didn't explain why he'd done what he had. He'd fixed her car, knowing that she very probably would not be able to pay him and had not authorized the work but would likely try to do the right thing. That made him kind, willing to take a chance and a good judge of character.

His list of attributes was getting longer all the time, not that it mattered one tiny whit. She honestly didn't expect to see him much after tonight. They'd made their bargain, and she would fulfill her end as he'd already done his, and that would be that. Wouldn't it?

Somehow she sensed a flaw in her reasoning.

All right, so she'd be working in his house. That didn't mean he'd have the time or the inclination to babysit her. The man had a business to run, and obviously he wasn't worried about her stealing from him. Why should he? She was no thief.

Of course, he couldn't know that at this point. But she couldn't very well steal a house, and she hadn't seen much inside worth the taking, which made it all the more remarkable, even suspect, that he was willing to go out on a limb for somebody like her.

What did he hope to get out of it? Except a fair exchange of services, that is.

Truth to tell, she just didn't know what to make of Vince Cutler, and maybe she never would. What did it matter anyway, so long as her car was running well and she wasn't choosing between eating and paying a mechanic's bill?

It should not have mattered at all.

But somehow it did.

She told herself that she didn't like surprises, that

the world was easier to navigate if people just stayed in their assigned boxes and did what was expected of them. The truth was, though, that Vincent Cutler was turning out to be something of a godsend, and she really didn't want to think about that.

After all, if God was looking out for her, how did she explain losing Russell?

Chapter Five

When he opened his door to her on Monday morning Vince couldn't help smiling. She just looked so good standing there in her simple jeans and a faded red tank top under a soft yellow, short-sleeved shirt hanging open down the front. Her biscuit-gold hair, loose except for the narrow band that held it neatly behind her ears, flowed down her back. Without so much as a dab of makeup or a single piece of jewelry, and dressed for a day of real work, she still managed to look every inch a woman, a woman who was not best pleased, if her frown was any indication.

He supposed it had to do with the dirty, dark-blue shadow on his chin and jaws. His mother and sisters certainly scowled if he went around unshaven, but sometimes a fellow just couldn't face a razor in the morning, and Monday was the one day of the week when he didn't have to, provided, of course, that he didn't have errands to run or a meeting of some sort.

Today was such a day, which meant that he'd seen no reason to shave. Now, rubbing his prickly jaw with one hand, he wished he'd lathered up anyway.

Putting on the best face that he could under the circumstances, he broadened his smile and bade her a cheery, "Good morning."

"Morning," she muttered, glancing down at his bare feet before sliding past him into the foyer. "Am I too early?"

He closed the door. "Not at all. I like an early start on the day myself."

"Hmm, well, I'll just head to work and let you finish getting ready to leave."

His smile wilted.

"Uh, I'm not going anywhere."

Her chin jerked up, eyes wide as saucers.

"Not going anywhere?"

She couldn't have looked more appalled. Vince shifted his feet.

"Monday's my day off, too. Didn't I make that clear before?"

She folded her arms.

"Obviously not."

He brought his hands to his hips, fighting down a surge of irritation, though whether he was more irritated with himself or her he didn't know. How many times and in how many ways could he mess up with this woman?

"I guess I assumed, since we're both in service industries, that you'd naturally figure…" He broke off, reaching deep for patience. Grasping it, he said, "If it'll make you more comfortable, I'll find somewhere to go."

"Why don't you just do that, then," she retorted, lifting her chin so high that he found himself practically staring down her nostrils.

"Fine," he snapped. "If that's what it takes to make you happy."

Grinding his back teeth together, he stomped off toward the back of the house, across the den and through the shallow alcove that opened onto the master bedroom.

Of all the testy, high-handed, downright unfriendly women in the world, he told himself, Jolie Wheeler purely took the cake.

Ripping a shirt from a hanger in the large walk-in closet, Vince yanked it on over his white T-shirt then went to the dresser to locate a pair of clean white socks. Plopping down on the side of the bed, he jerked on one of the socks. He was about to poke his toes into the other when he heard the front doorbell chime again. Rising, he managed to get the second sock on and take a step toward the door in the same movement.

He hadn't even made the den when one of his sisters—Olivia, he thought, or maybe Sharon, he couldn't always tell the voices of the older two apart—called out, "Hey, Vince! You decent?"

Wincing, he answered. "Yeah."

Great, that was all he needed, his nosy sisters barging in right in the middle of another misunderstanding with Jolie.

He hurried into the den, relieved to see that Jolie was absent. Maybe she hadn't heard the commotion.

Helen, the sister just younger than him, walked into the den. Olivia, the sister just older than him, was on her heels.

"Where are your boots?" Olivia asked, as if he was a two-year-old who'd forgotten where he'd escaped from his shoes.

"Waiting for my feet," he told her dryly. "Actually I was just getting ready to leave."

Maybe that would get them on their way.

Fat chance.

They looked at each other and said in unison, "Hope it's not important."

Obviously no one was going anywhere anytime soon.

Vince stifled a sigh. His sisters were often exasperating, but they were all so crazy about him that he couldn't be unhappy to see any of them. Opening his arms, he wrapped each of them in a one-armed hug and quickly bussed their cheeks, hoping to get them on their way none the wiser.

Heaven knew what they'd think if they were to clap eyes on Jolie.

"Okay, what's up? You two are out and about awful early."

"Earlier than you," Helen teased, rubbing the spot where his unshaven chin had grazed her.

"Like I've never seen either of you running around at mid-morning in fuzzy slippers with curlers in your hair."

Helen chortled and Olivia sniffed, tossing her dark curls.

"That's different," Olivia argued. "I've got three boys to corral."

"And who's corralling those hooligans today?" he asked, grinning at the thought of his nephews.

"Mom."

"But she's got Bets to help her," Helen added with a grin. Vince laughed.

Four-year-old Elizabeth Ann, known affectionately

by the family as Bets, effectively commanded the co-
terie of Cutler grandchildren, numbering six in all.
An only child, to the growing dismay of her parents,
she'd never had any trouble holding her own against
her five older cousins, four of whom were boys.

Now that Donna, Vince's youngest sister, was expecting, however, Bets was showing signs of insecu-
rity at losing her position as the baby of the family. As
a result, she'd become a bossy little termagant whose
orders the older five obeyed slavishly in an unspoken
conspiracy to reassure her.

The whole thing was rather sweet to behold and
would resolve itself, everyone was certain, in time.

"So what's got you two over here hassling me at
this early hour of the morning?" Vince tried again.

Olivia slipped out of his embrace and moved to
the center of the sparsely furnished room, holding
out her arms.

"Do you even have to ask? My goodness, Vince,
you might as well still be living in that little cracker
box of an apartment."

"This house needs proper furnishings," soft-spoken, light-haired Helen added, leaning into him.

"And since you show no signs whatsoever of finding a wife to take care of the matter for you," Olivia
began sternly, "we'll just have to do it."

Vince felt a spurt of panic. The very last thing he
wanted was his sisters outfitting his house for him.
Just the possibility made him shudder.

"Now, look here, sis—"

"Don't you look-here-sis me. I've wiped your snotty
nose, not to mention your—"

"Olivia!"

Undaunted, she wagged a finger at him.

"You still haven't bought so much as a throw rug! If we leave it to you, you'll be sitting here alone ten years from now on this same old ratty couch eating your supper out of a can. Now, the alone part you'll have to fix yourself—with God's help, of course—but the other we're willing and able to take care of. So, you can either come shopping with us, or we'll do it without you, whichever you prefer."

He rolled his eyes, preferring a hard jab with a hot poker to either alternative, and caught sight of Jolie's head easing around the casement of the kitchen door. An audacious idea burst into his mind, one he'd been mulling around in some fashion since he'd gotten a look at what she'd done with his old apartment. He knew that the idea was born of desperation and would likely blow up in his face, but he let it out anyway.

"As a matter of fact, that won't be necessary," he said calmly. "It's already in hand."

He beckoned Jolie, weighting the gesture with a hopeful look that he prayed his sisters would miss. She frowned at him but edged into the room, her cheeks a becoming shade of pink.

"I, uh, didn't find any color-safe bleach in the sack of supplies you left in the laundry room."

"No? Could've sworn I picked some up. I'm sure it was on your list."

Actually, he was positive that it was on her list of needed supplies and that he'd bought a big plastic tub of the stuff on his way home Saturday evening. It appeared that her curiosity had gotten the better of her and that she was too embarrassed to admit that fact, which suited him just fine in the present circumstances.

He waved her further into the room, saying to his sisters, "Girls, I'd like you to meet Jolie Kay Wheeler. She's helping me out around here."

Two heads pivoted and tilted. Jolie might have been a bug under a microscope, the way they were studying her. Vince cleared his throat.

"Jolie, these are two of my sisters. Olivia." He nudged the elder, and she jumped as if he'd stuck her with a hat pin. "And Helen."

His sisters looked at him, then each other and finally at Jolie again. Both melted into smiles.

Helen leaned forward slightly and asked in her sweetest voice, "Would that be *Miss* Wheeler?"

"Uh. Um-hm."

Suddenly those smiles were beaming around the room with the force of a lighthouse on a dark and moonless night at sea, and the next thing Vince knew, they'd swarmed her like a pack of locusts, both chirping at once.

"Oh, it's so nice to meet you!"

"He hasn't said a word, the brat. We spoiled him rotten, you know, only boy and all that."

"But he's really very sweet, not half as stubborn as he seems. A little impulsive, maybe, but manageable."

Vince rolled his eyes at that, but no one paid him the least mind.

"Are you a professional decorator?" Helen asked.

"Have you known each other long?" Olivia wanted to know.

"All right, all right."

Vince waded into the fray and rescued Jolie with

a hand firmly cupping her elbow to draw her to his side. She glared daggers up at him, and he could see the demand in her eyes. What was going on?

He tried to think of a way to explain it and came up only with the truth. "I, uh, I've been meaning to ask you if you'd help me outfit this place. I mean, yours looks so great." He shot a desperate volley at his sisters, saying, "I really love what she's done with her apartment. It's just my kind of thing, you know? Very tasteful, very…chic."

He wouldn't know chic if it bit him, but he didn't think it involved being upholstered in chintz or layered with doilies.

Jolie stared at him for a full five seconds before she slowly asked, "You want *me* to help you furnish and decorate this place?"

"Yeah. Sure. Absolutely."

She put a finger to her chest. *"Me?"*

"I know it's a lot to ask," he told her, instinctively pulling her closer, both elbows cupped in his hands now. "But I really like the look of your apartment. I like it better than anything else I've seen. And I *really* need the help." He slid a glance over her head toward his sisters before bringing it back to plumb those soft jade eyes. "Please."

Jolie dropped her gaze, lifted a shoulder in a casual shrug, and lightly conceded, "Okay."

He could have kissed her. He might have kissed her, if his sisters hadn't been standing there grinning like idiots and soaking up the whole thing. As it was, his right hand just sort of slipped around to the center of her back, finding its way beneath the heavy, silken fall of her hair.

He beamed at his sisters.

"See. Good as done."

They ignored him, as usual.

"Now, sugar," Olivia said to Jolie, stepping closer, "if you need anything at all, you just give a yell. All four of us would be delighted to pitch in and help out."

Jolie inched closer to Vince, apparently intimidated by the gleam in his sister's eyes. What could he do but slide his arm around her? He couldn't help noticing that she was a perfect fit.

"In fact," Helen was saying, "why don't you come to dinner on Sunday so we can talk about it all together? Mama would be thrilled, wouldn't she, Vince?"

"Oh, uh, sure."

It was the bald truth, never mind that what his sisters were assuming was not.

"I—I couldn't intrude," Jolie said, obviously unprepared for this full-frontal assault.

"No intrusion!" Olivia exclaimed, seizing and squeezing both of Jolie's hands. "Really, the whole family would be thrilled." She abruptly switched tactics. "Make her come, Vince."

"Oh, please come," Helen added to Jolie.

"All right. Okay. Enough," Vince interrupted firmly, literally putting himself between Jolie and his sisters. "I'll take it from here." He reached out and started sweeping them toward the door with one arm. "Thanks, girls. I appreciate your stopping by, but frankly you're holding up the show now, so if you don't mind…"

"Yeah, yeah, we're going," Olivia conceded drolly. She pecked him on the cheek and strode for the entry, beckoning Helen to follow. Helen paused long enough to go up on tiptoe and throw her arms around Vince's neck. He bent forward to accept her kiss and hear her whisper in his ear.

"I'm so glad. She's very pretty."

"Um," he answered noncommittally, feeling terrible about misleading them and ironically pleased at how it had gone so far.

"It was very nice to meet you, Jolie," Helen said with a last smile in Jolie's direction.

With her light-brown hair and dark-blue eyes, Helen was the sweetest and most soft-hearted of his sisters and at times his favorite, though he could say the latter of all of them at various moments.

"Nice to meet you, too," Jolie murmured, nodding.

It struck Vince that she actually meant it, and an unexpected feeling of warmth swirled through him. He sent her a grateful look and hurried after his sisters to see them safely out.

He knew that the whole family would soon be thinking, as Olivia and Helen must, that Jolie was his girlfriend, which meant they'd naturally assume that they would see her on Sunday at dinner, and he wouldn't disabuse them of that notion. Yet.

He didn't mean to lie to them. He'd just make the truth clear to them a little later, like after he'd gotten Jolie to agree to help him out. He really did want, need, her help decorating and furnishing his house, and who knew? She might even be willing to come over to his mom's for Sunday dinner. Wouldn't hurt to ask. He hoped.

Jolie stood right where he'd left her until he returned from seeing his sisters out. She'd gotten over her embarrassment at being caught eavesdropping—mostly, anyway. When she'd heard the doorbell and then female voices, curiosity had simply gotten the better of her.

For a moment she'd thought that some girlfriend, or two, had come to call, but she'd quickly realized that they were his sisters. It had become obvious that he didn't want them decorating his house, and she hadn't minded helping him out with that, but of course, he wasn't serious about her doing it. Was he?

She couldn't imagine what had made him desperate enough even to suggest such a thing.

"So what's the deal with your sisters outfitting this place?" she demanded the moment that he reentered the room.

"None at all," he said quite happily, "that's the point."

She glanced at the battered, mismatched furnishings in the room.

"No offense, but you could use some help, not to mention some decent furniture."

"Don't I know it, but not from my family. And with you to help me, they won't have to."

"But you don't really want me to help you furnish and decorate this place," she said confidently, only to watch his face rearrange itself into a blank mask.

"That mean you're backing out on me?"

She gaped in astonishment. He really meant it!

"I'm not a professional decorator," she pointed out.

"So what? Neither are any of them."

"That's not the issue!"

"What is the issue?" he asked sharply. Then, before she could even answer, he turned out both palms beseechingly. "Look, I'll pay you for your help. All right? How would that be?"

"But I'm not a professional decorator!" she repeated, more forcefully this time in case he'd missed it the first.

"I know that!" he retorted. "I don't want a professional decorator. I want a helping hand from someone whose taste I appreciate."

What was he talking about? She didn't have any taste; she couldn't afford *taste*.

Didn't he understand that she'd never had two whole nickels to rub together? Whatever "decorating" she'd done at her place she'd managed with old sheets and stuff. It was all done of necessity. She'd never had the luxury of actually picking out things.

Her world was one of make-do. His was… She looked around her and gulped. This house was a palace, an empty palace.

"You can't mean it."

He thumped the side of his head with the heel of one hand and muttered at the far wall, "I know I'm speaking English, so it couldn't have gotten lost in translation."

She parked her hands at her hips, too astonished to take issue with his jibes.

"You actually *do* mean it."

"Hello! Houston, we have contact."

She flattened her lips and narrowed her eyes at him to let him know that he wasn't funny, at least not to her, but her heart was suddenly racing.

"I don't get it. You've got family ready, willing and able to help you. Why ask *me*?"

"Because I've got family ready, willing and insisting on helping me."

She noted that he had not said able.

He sighed gustily.

"Have you ever seen those old fifties movies where the walls are all papered in big bouquets of flowers and even the lampshades have ruffles on them?"

Jolie made a face, disliking the picture he'd created in her mind.

"I love my mom dearly," he went on, "but she has never met a doily or a chintz pattern that she didn't like. As for my sisters, it's the same song just different verses. They've all got their themes, you know? With Sharon, it's chickens."

"Chickens?" Jolie echoed, eyebrows rising.

"Chickens everywhere," he told her. "The throw pillows in the living room have chickens on them. Chicken-patterned chintz."

He shuddered, and Jolie's mouth twitched.

"With Olivia, it's cows," he went on blandly, "black-and-white cows. Black-and-white cows with red in the kitchen, black-and-white cows with blue in the living room, black-and-white cows with green in the bedroom. Black-and-white cows with yellow in the bath. My brother-in-law swears that late at night he can hear mooing."

Jolie snickered and clapped a hand over her mouth, but despite his woebegone expression, he seemed to be enjoying himself.

"Helen, now, Helen's more sedate," he said. "Helen's whole house is tan. Even the flowers on her chintz sofa are tan. The flowers on the wallpaper are tan. The flowers on the throw rugs are tan."

"Oh, no." Jolie bit down on a sputter of laughter.

"But Donna," he managed to say, despite his own grin, "she's the avant-garde one. Her chintz is polka-dotted. Navy blue on white. Or white on navy blue for contrast."

Jolie guffawed, imagining his house done up in flowered chickens and polka-dotted cows in every color of the rainbow. With doilies.

"S-so you can s-see my problem," he chortled. Swallowing, he managed a serious tone. "Hey, I'm just trying to avoid hurt feelings. And chintz of any sort."

He shuddered spastically, and Jolie nearly fell over, laughing so hard that her sides hurt. He threw an arm around her for support, burbling and bumping hips with her.

"I—I'm a desperate man," he managed, sucking air.

After a moment they both calmed somewhat.

He caught a breath and wiped an eye, saying, "I really don't want to have to hire a professional. I don't want a showplace. I want something homey and comfortable but *me,* and I know I'm more apt to get that with you than with any of them. For one thing, I can be honest with you."

She nodded and dabbed at her eyes with the back of one wrist.

"Okay, I get it now."

He clapped his hands together and turned his face up to the ceiling.

"Thank You, God."

She shoved an elbow into his ribs.

"Get serious."

"Sweetheart, I *am* serious," he told her, sounding it. She ignored the *sweetheart* part—just a figure of speech, after all—and the little thrill that came with it, concentrating instead on studying her surroundings. She discovered, to her surprise, that she really wanted to do this thing.

Suddenly, her mind was hopping with ideas.

"I just don't know how much good I can do for you," she admitted forthrightly. "I don't have much experience."

"You've got style, though, and it more or less mirrors mine, or what I'd like mine to be, anyway. And I meant what I said about paying you."

She shook her head. "I can't take money for something I'm not trained or qualified to do."

He held out both hands again, this time in a stalling motion. Then he snapped his fingers.

"Tell you what, let's stick with the barter plan. I'll give you a year, make that two years, of free automobile upkeep for your help."

Her eyes widened, but before she could reply to that generous offer, he held up an index finger.

"This time, though, there are strings attached."

She grinned.

"Let me guess. No chintz."

"That's one, but there is another."

She folded her arms in mock resignation.

"Let's hear it."

He dipped at the knees, scrunching up his face in a wheedling gesture.

"You have to come to dinner on Sunday."

Was that all? She opened her mouth to ask, but he hurried on.

"My family will be disappointed if you don't. The girls are used to getting their way, frankly, but they always mean well, and after refusing their help with the house, I just don't want to have to explain why I couldn't convince you to accept their invitation to Sunday dinner."

She was ready to capitulate after the first sentence, but she didn't let him know that. Vince Cutler groveling was a very pleasant experience.

"Well," she mused, stroking her chin, "I guess I could."

"Great!" He clapped his hands together. "How's this? I'll pick you up for church and afterward we'll go straight to Mom's."

Jolie frowned, suspicion instantly rearing its ugly head again.

"Church? Who said anything about church? I thought we were talking about dinner."

"Dinner's always first thing after church," he told her, matter-of-factly. "Mom usually puts something in the oven or slow-cooker before she leaves the house for services, and it's ready when she gets back."

Jolie bit her lip. What was it with this guy? Every time she thought she had him figured out, he threw her some sort of curve. Was this about his sisters' expectations, his empty house or getting her to church?

What was it with church people, anyway? They came on as caring, then turned on you. Marcus had.

"I don't know," she muttered, more to herself than to him.

"Fine," he said lightly. "I'll pick you up immediately after the service. Just be ready and waiting. Mom hates it when we're late to the table. It's her all-time pet peeve. But it's not too far from your place. If we hurry we'll be there in time."

Jolie figured she'd be nuts to refuse. Two years of no worries about her old car! Plus, she'd have the pleasure of outfitting this grand house.

She nodded decisively.

"Just tell me what time."

"Twelve o'clock noon," he told her, sounding relieved. He smacked his hands together again, rubbing them as he glanced around. "Oh, man, I can't wait to get started. When can we, do you think?"

She shrugged, considering.

"Well, I suppose we could do some preliminary window-shopping as soon as I get the laundry done."

"In that case," he exclaimed, turning toward the kitchen, "I'll help you."

"That's not necessary," she told him, laughing and hurrying to catch up as he strode off on stocking feet.

"I can at least help you sort," he insisted, forging ahead.

Jolie paused to roll her eyes. What kind of guy got this excited about decorating his house? In some ways, she was afraid to find out.

She swept into the laundry room to discover him knee-deep in the pile. He'd started tossing clothes every which way. She stood shaking her head, her hands on her hips, until he plopped a pale-blue dress shirt that would look stunning with his eyes into a pile of jeans. She plucked it out again, then started making a few more corrections, and somehow they fell into a pattern.

Before she knew it, they were standing side by side at the work table treating stains at her direction with one of a trio of products.

When the first load was ready, Vince picked it up

and stuffed it into the washer while she measured the correct amount of liquid detergent. She poured it into the dispenser and turned some knobs to adjust the water temperature; then he pushed a button, and water started to fill the tub.

An odd sense of satisfaction settled over her, but she didn't have long to enjoy it. He grabbed her hand and tugged her toward the door.

"Come on," he said, "I want to show you the rest of the house."

She put on a smile, nodded and prepared to be delighted, but that had nothing whatsoever to do with Vince. It was strictly about his house and the unexpected pleasure of getting her hands on it. At least that's what she told herself.

Chapter Six

"Might as well start at the beginning," Vince said, dropping her hand.

He felt all too aware of her for some reason, but he simply wouldn't think about it: better to concentrate on the house.

"You've probably guessed that this big empty space at the front is supposed to be formal living and dining," he quipped, then went on to explain, "I wanted everything open for entertaining, you know? This way, even the entry, which is often just wasted space, becomes a part of the whole, flowing right into the den with the beverage bar and, of course, the kitchen. At Mom and Dad's we're always hanging out in the kitchen."

He glanced over his shoulder as they passed beneath one of a pair of tall, wide arches that opened off the foyer. Leading her to the center of the long space, he let her take the room's measure.

"You could hold a ball in here!" she finally exclaimed.

"I don't think it's that big," he muttered sheepishly.

Smiling, he pointed out what seemed to him to be the salient architectural touches.

"The set-backs are perfect for displaying things, figurines maybe or... I don't know."

"Plants," she mused, looking over the nooks and crannies that stair-stepped up the front wall, creating a deep inset for the tall, multipaned window, "and maybe some pottery."

"I like the look of leaded glass," he went on, drawing her attention to the window itself, "but I didn't want anything too formal, so we went with this oxidized surface on the metal parts." He chuckled. "Mom says rust is not a decorative finish, but I think it looks cool."

"Like it's been around a long time and will be forever," Jolie commented, lightly brushing her fingertips over the window casing.

He couldn't have been more pleased.

"That's it. That's it exactly. Besides it just seems more..." He curved his hands, trying to grasp the right word.

"Masculine," Jolie supplied.

He felt a tiny shock at that. He hadn't realized that was the effect that he'd been going for until now.

"Yeah. Yeah, it is at that."

"Which means we can throw in a little elegance without making the room too feminine."

He liked that thought. Elegant but not frilly.

"That sounds right. Now, back here..."

He hurried her across the foyer and into the hall branching off it.

"This first door, that's the powder room."

She craned her neck around a bit before he herded her away.

"These three rooms on the front are bedrooms. The first two share a bath."

Walking her through quickly, he threw open empty closets and pointed out the window seats before moving back into the hall.

"The last one here at the end I think of as the guest room because it has its own bath."

He let her look around for a moment, though the room was basically an empty box with a nice window. The small bath contained a tub with a shower in it, unlike the other two full baths in the house, which boasted both tubs and shower stalls.

They started back down the hall on the other side, toward the powder room.

"This," he said, pushing wide double doors, "is what I call the study."

It was a long room with a single window in the end, lots of bare bookcases and two built-in desks. A computer sat rather forlornly atop one, but he hadn't gotten around to hooking it up yet. Didn't see the point until he at least got a desk chair. Jolie wandered into the room, her jaw dropping.

"You have your own library!"

"I would if I had any books," he said. "I thought this would be a good place for the kids to do their homework and maybe play some video games, that sort of thing."

"Kids!" she exclaimed, whirling on him. "You have *kids*?"

For a moment he wasn't sure what she was asking. Maybe she wondered if he *wanted* kids. Or was she saying that she didn't want them? Then again, it was a pretty straightforward question, even if it didn't make any sense.

"Of course not. How can I have kids when I'm not even married?"

She literally snorted.

"In case you haven't noticed, you don't have to be married to have children."

"*I* do," he stated flatly, frowning.

She stared at him for several seconds, as if verifying the truth of what he'd just said.

Apparently satisfied, she nodded briskly and swept past him, muttering, "Good for you."

His jaw descended. Had he seen the sheen of tears in her eyes? Before he could think better of it, he went after her, catching her by the elbow just as she reached the foyer.

"Jolie, are you okay?"

She nodded, but she didn't look at him.

"I guess it's your religion that makes you think like that. Lots of men don't."

"It's my faith, yes," he said, "but it's common sense, too. Plenty of men feel the same way. They know that children should have two parents."

"But lots of them don't."

"And most of them turn out fine," he conceded, "but it means twice the effort for a single parent."

"True." It came out barely more than a whisper.

He caught her chin with the crook of his fingers and angled her face so he could gauge her expression. For a moment she stood with her eyes downcast before suddenly lifting her eyelids. The jade of her irises sparkled with tears.

"Jolie?"

He was almost afraid to ask why she cried, but she pulled away from him and gave him an answer anyway.

"My sister has a little boy." Her voice cracked at the end. "His father's in prison for killing an off-duty policeman during a robbery."

Vince pushed a hand over his face, horribly relieved even as he drawled, "Aw, Jolie, I'm sorry to hear that."

"Russell's better off never knowing him," she asserted defiantly.

"I'm even more sorry about that," Vince said quietly.

She turned away then, and he watched that steel rod slide into her spine.

"We don't all get the ideal parents," she told him almost grudgingly.

He wondered about her parents, but he didn't think asking would get him anywhere just then, not with her defenses back in place.

"I'm sure there are times," he said carefully, "when one parent is better than two. I was speaking in generalizations before."

"I know." She glanced at him and moved away, mumbling, "I should check the laundry."

"Sure. We can finish the tour later. There's just the master suite."

He stood there until she disappeared into the kitchen, then he sighed and jammed his hands into his pockets.

What would he have done, what would he have said, if it had been her and not her sister? It wasn't his place to judge, of course, but he did believe that his values were right, and it made his belly burn to think that she might have been used by some man and then abandoned by him.

He went into the living room and sat down to think, but Jolie Wheeler couldn't be puzzled out with what little information he had. He bowed his head and let the Spirit guide his prayer.

He asked God why Jolie Wheeler was suddenly a part of his life. She'd said that her brother was a preacher, but she spoke about faith and God as if she didn't quite understand them, almost as if she carried certain resentments. Was he supposed to help her deal with that somehow? Or did God have something else entirely in mind?

There had been moments when he was showing her through the house just now, when being with her had felt exactly right. Then there were those moments of confusion, like now.

He shook his head, asking God not to let him do anything foolish until he had this thing figured out. Oh, and he could use some help keeping his temper, too, because she had a way of setting him on edge, which just went to show how confused he really was.

Vince rarely lost his temper, rarely even felt the emotion of anger, but he seemed prone to step wrong where she was concerned, and then the yelling started. He hadn't raised his voice to a woman other than his sisters in his whole life, and he hadn't done it with one of them since he was maybe fourteen.

What was it about Jolie Wheeler that got under his skin?

Jolie slipped into the kitchen some time later, not quite sure what she expected. It wasn't to find him making lunch.

"What are you doing?"

He turned a glance over one shoulder, smiled and waved a knife smeared with mustard.

"What does it look like I'm doing?"

She folded her arms, relieved at his bantering tone.

"It looks like you're building a wall with bread and meat."

"There's lettuce and tomato in there, too," he told her with mock defensiveness, nodding at the gargantuan sandwich, "and pickles and cheese and bell peppers, even some sliced mushrooms." He slid one half of the monstrosity to the side. "Hope you like mustard."

She blinked, oddly touched, and barely bit back the words, *For me?* They sounded mewling and pathetic even inside her head.

"You want to get that cantaloupe out of the fridge and carve it up?" he directed, pointing with his chin. "I'm in a cantaloupe mood. How about you?"

She walked over to the refrigerator and opened the door.

"I like cantaloupe."

"You can use that paring knife there on the counter," he said. "I rinsed it after I sliced the peppers. Oh, and grab that pitcher of iced tea. There's a bowl of sliced lemon in there, too. Got a white lid on it."

"I see it."

She placed everything on the counter, then carried the melon to the sink, where she split, cleaned, peeled and sliced it, dropping the crescent-moon-shaped slivers into a plastic bowl which Vince had set out for her. While she worked, he got down mismatched plastic tumblers and filled them with ice, tea and lemon, then put the sandwiches on plates and carried everything to the island in the center of the room.

Producing a bag of chips, he leaned a hip against the counter, munching, until she rinsed and dried her hands. With a swipe of one foot, he pulled out a short, rather wobbly stool for her. Then he hopped up onto the counter and lifted his plate onto his lap.

"I could eat a horse," he said, spearing a piece of melon with a fork.

"Is that in here, too?" she teased, eyeing the sandwich mountain on her plate.

He didn't answer, and when she looked up, it was to find his head bowed. She quickly looked down again.

"We thank You, Lord," he said easily, "for Your many blessings. I especially thank You for saving me from the chintz squad and, most importantly, giving me a way to keep from hurting their feelings. You know I love them, Lord, and I know they mean well, so thank You for bringing Jolie along to help me out. Amen."

She didn't know what to think about him mentioning her in his prayer, but what she said was, "Do you always do that?"

"Pray before I eat?" he asked, and quickly devoured the melon slice in two bites. "Yep. Don't you?"

She answered him honestly, but for some reason it made her uncomfortable.

"No."

"How come?" He wrapped his hands around the enormous sandwich. "Wasn't it the done thing at your house?"

"I never had a house," she blurted.

He lowered the sandwich.

"Around your home then."

"Can't say as I really ever had one of those, either."

"You had to grow up somewhere."

She picked up her own sandwich and took a bite just so she couldn't answer him. He did not, however, let the subject drop, just changed his tack.

"Guess your folks weren't the praying kind."

"Wouldn't know. Probably not."

"How is it you don't know something like that?" he asked softly, shifting his plate to the countertop.

She felt her shoulders lift in a shrug, and that was when she knew she was going to answer.

"Never even met my father," she said with a swallow, "and Mom was gone at least half the time."

"Where was she gone to?"

She studied her sandwich, but in truth, her appetite had disappeared.

"The better question is *who* was she gone *with*."

"Who?"

His voice could be so gentle, so warm, sometimes. It made her own sound harsh and sharp.

"Some man or other."

He said nothing for a moment. Then he moved his plate to his lap again and picked up his sandwich.

"Who raised you then?"

She picked a pickle slice out of the sandwich and popped it into her mouth.

"The system."

"The system?" he echoed.

"The state. Child Welfare."

"Ah. I have a real good buddy who was raised in foster homes. You met him, I think. Boyd."

She looked up in surprise, and he bit off a huge chunk of sandwich.

"Wasn't he the guy who towed my car?"

Vince nodded.

"Doesn't he work for you?"

"Um-hm."

"And you still call him a real good buddy?"

He worked the food in his mouth and swallowed.

"What's so odd about that? We were friends before he came to work for me."

They were both aware that she was steering the conversation away from her and back to him, but Vince didn't seem to mind. She let herself relax somewhat.

"Isn't it hard to keep the business part separated from the friendship part?"

"Don't know," he said succinctly, readying his sandwich for another assault. "Never tried."

She rolled her eyes, suddenly enjoying herself again.

"Now that's some attitude for a business owner."

"What's wrong with it?"

"What's wrong with it? Somebody has to be the boss, that's what's wrong with it."

"You sound just like Boyd. Sissy and I are always telling him that he's more concerned about my business than I am." He chuckled.

"Who's Sissy?"

"Boyd's wife. We grew up together, Sissy and me. She ran tame with my sisters, Helen and Donna. You probably wouldn't like her. She's sweet as sugar and soft-spoken as a running brook."

Jolie huffed, knowing full well that she was being baited but enjoying herself too much to care.

"I have been insulted. You have just insulted me, Vince Cutler."

He laughed and leaned forward, confessing, "Actually, she spits and hisses just about as much as you. The two of you would either get on like a house afire or you'd rip each other to shreds, and I'm not taking bets on which." He winked then and added, "But she's not as cute as you are."

With that he hopped down from the counter and carried his plate across the room, where he ripped a paper towel from the roll and proceeded to wrap his sandwich for easier handling.

Jolie inwardly sputtered for a moment, but then she blinked and let an unfamiliar feeling wash over her.

Cute. He'd as much as said she was cute.

She began pulling the filling from between the slices of bread, poking it into her mouth bit by bit, and found that it was difficult to chew and smile at the same time.

"I've been thinking about it," Vince said, checking his rearview mirror, "and we don't really have to do those two bedrooms up front. Let's concentrate on the living and dining room for now, and then the den and kitchen."

"That's fine," Jolie said, feeling as though she was sitting on top of the world there in the cab of that big, brutish pickup truck.

She didn't like leaving the laundry unfinished to go shopping, but Vince Cutler could be *very* persuasive. She didn't even like to think how persuasive he could be, so she put her mind on the business at hand.

"However," she said, "the first thing you should do is get some drapes up, especially in those two front bedrooms. Until you get those windows covered, the house is going to look empty from the street."

"I hadn't considered that." He rubbed his cleanly shaven chin, glancing at her. "Where do we find them?"

Jolie considered a moment.

"I've heard there's a store down on Camp Bowie that specializes in window treatments."

"Camp Bowie it is."

"I don't suppose you know the measurements of the windows?" she asked hopefully.

He shook his head. "Not off hand, no, but I think I'm still carrying around a set of house plans tucked behind the back seat."

"Then I'd say we're in business," she told him confidently.

Famous last words.

It turned out that the windows in Vincent's custom-built house were not standard sizes. A persistent questioning of store personnel elicited the name of a custom draper, who was only too happy to show them styles and fabrics and quote prices, astonishingly high prices to Jolie's mind. In just over two hours at the draper's shop, however, they gained a good idea of what it was going to take to get the windows covered, but they were no closer to actually having done so.

"I think I'm going to have to put together a budget," Vince said thoughtfully, letting the shop door close behind him.

"A budget's good," Jolie agreed, moving across the sidewalk to the truck, which was parked directly in front of the building. The prices of custom-made draperies had shocked her, and her mind was reeling in search of alternatives. "You know, I've got an old sewing machine that I picked up at a garage sale. It's not fancy, but it does a good job, and I've been sewing up curtains and such for years now. Maybe I should—"

Vince cut her off in midthought. "Nope."

He stepped up to her side, and she frowned at him. "No? Why not? You saw the price of those things."

"Yes, I did, and they're high, but there are other drapery shops." He lifted one booted foot to the front bumper of the truck and balanced his forearms atop his knee. "Besides—and I don't mean any offense—I want this done right *and* quick. Now, I know you'd do good work, but you don't have time for sewing. You're already working three jobs, remember?"

Four counting the extra ironing, she thought, and one of them she'd left unfinished. Piles of laundry waited for the washer back at his house. Still...

"It's going to cost an awful lot of money."

"I'm aware of that. I figure at this point maybe five thousand for window treatments and three, maybe four, times that much for furnishings."

Several seconds passed before Jolie realized her mouth was hanging open. Even then some effort was required to snap it shut again, and she had to swallow before she could speak.

"That's your idea of a budget?"

He dropped his foot to the ground.

"I told you, I want it done right. I'm looking for quality, classic furnishings that won't need upgrading every couple years."

"And you're just going to toss me that much money and expect me to produce what you're looking for?"

"No," he said reasonably, "I intend to oversee every purchase. I want you to tell me what works best where."

She let out a long, slow breath.

"Man, oh, man. Did you ever pick the wrong girl for this job. That's more money than I've made in the past year."

"Jolie," he told her, "I've been planning and saving a long time for this, and I want to get it right. Your job is to tell me what you think will look good. I know what I like, but I'm not sure which of the things I like will go together."

She shook her head, insisting, "You ought to hire a professional."

"We've been through this. I don't want a professional." He strode for the driver's door, fishing in his jeans pocket for his keys. "Now are you getting in or are we camping on the sidewalk?"

She got in.

"Want to take a look at some furniture?"

"Guess it won't hurt to look," she muttered.

Wrong again.

They hit four different stores before a helpful salesman finally directed them to a place that actually carried the rustic Western style that they both seemed to be envisioning. Vince declared the store perfect for their purposes the instant that they walked into the showroom, but Jolie took one look at the price of a leather sectional and insisted that they could do better elsewhere.

"I've seen handmade, one-of-a-kind pieces in this very style at the outdoor market for half the price," she hissed.

"What outdoor market?" he asked in hushed tones.

"Over in Dallas, downtown in the warehouse district. They open these big sheds on the weekends, and the artisans and craftsmen haul in their goods." Vince looked down at his toes. "I can get a Friday off if I ask in advance," she whispered, all but pleading. "We can at least look."

He tucked his fingertips into his waistband, rocking back on his heels.

"This Friday?"

"I'll see," she promised. "Maybe. I haven't had to ask off lately." She held back a wince at that. She hadn't had to take time off from work since she'd lost Russ. Pushing aside thoughts of her nephew, she fixed her mind on the issue at hand. "I'm sure I can get at least half a day."

Vince caught her arm and steered her toward the door, calling out to the anxious salesman, "Gotta run. We'll catch you later. Thanks for your help."

"I don't know why I didn't think of it sooner," she said once they reached the sidewalk. "I guess I didn't know exactly what you were looking for until you honed in on that last piece."

"Now that," he said, hooking a thumb over his shoulder, "is my idea of a comfy couch. It seats six and has recliners in each end."

"Two pieces would be easier to shift around," she pointed out cautiously. "Besides, that's better suited to the den than a so-called formal living room."

"Hmm, maybe you're right about that. See there." He beamed at her. "You do know what you're doing."

She turned away, rolling her eyes.

"Can I get back to some real work now?"

He chuckled, following her across the parking lot. "You act like that laundry is going somewhere."

"Not unless I get it done, it isn't."

He unlocked the door and handed her up into the tall cab before making his way around to the driver's seat.

"You'd think we were spending *your* hard-earned cash," he teased.

"Yours is not as hard-earned as mine is or you'd feel the same way," she grumbled.

He shook his head and drove her back to his house, where he busied himself elsewhere while she worked at the laundry and envisioned, room by room, what she really wanted to do with the place. It didn't take long for her to realize that what she needed was a comprehensive list of what it would take to achieve the look she was after. Just knowing how much money she had to play with set her imagination whirling.

She hadn't realized what fun simple dreaming could be.

Chapter Seven

Jolie was at the ironing board, down to the last dozen shirts in need of pressing, with a load of laundry in the washer, another in the dryer and two more still heaped on the floor, when Vince strolled into the room.

"Enough," he ordered. "The rest can wait."

She straightened to work a kink out of her back.

"At the very least, the pants have to be hung or they'll wrinkle and need pressing, too. And the towels have to go into the dryer before I can leave."

"Okay, I'll help you finish up. Then I want you to get out of here," he ordered, "or else I'm going to make you dinner."

"Ooh," she quipped, shuddering theatrically, "how diabolical."

"I should inform you that the sandwich constitutes the sum of my kitchen skills."

"Yuh," she said, perfectly serious, "how diabolical."

"It wasn't that bad!"

She giggled. "It wasn't bad at all, especially if you happen to be a giant—or eat like one. But I couldn't let you feed me twice in one day."

"I don't see why not."

"Meals are not part of our deal, that's why not."

"Speaking of that," he began, "I think we ought to approach this new project from a different angle. What do you think about making a list of everything we know we're going to need and—" He broke off when she burst out laughing.

"That's just what I've been doing." She tapped her temple with the tip of one forefinger. "Just haven't got it down on paper yet."

"There you go," he said, grinning. "Great minds thinking alike."

"I don't know about that," she retorted playfully, "but I have a suggestion. Why don't you make your list, and I'll make mine, and on Friday we'll compare them, provided I can get time off from the cleaners."

"Sounds good to me. Then on Sunday we'll have something to show the girls. You do remember that Sunday comes with a meal, don't you?"

"Of course I remember."

"I see, so it's okay for my mom to feed you but not me. I think that's some sort of double standard."

She rolled her eyes. "It's not about the meal. It's about showing your family that you're making headway on furnishing this house."

"Don't be surprised if you have to make a progress report."

"That I'll leave to you."

The buzzer on the dryer went off, indicating that the load was finished, and she hurried to pull out the uniform pants before they could wrinkle.

He went for the rolling rack of hangers, saying, "So

I'll pick you up at the cleaners about noon on Friday unless you call to cancel. Right?"

"Right. I'll have my list on paper by then."

"Me, too."

They worked for several minutes, folding, creasing and hanging the pants. The washer stopped before they were finished, and Jolie shifted that load into the dryer. All in all, it had been some day.

"Take off now," he ordered, "and I'll see you Friday."

"Yes, sir, boss, sir."

He brought his hands to his hips in a sarcastic pose.

"Right. You and Boyd, great respecters of my authority."

She just grinned, unplugged the iron and gathered up her handbag and keys.

"See ya." She turned for the door.

"Hey, Jolie."

She whirled in midstride.

"Yeah?"

He rocked back on his heels, gaze targeted on his toes. Then he looked up at her from beneath the smooth jut of his brow.

"Just wanted to say that I'm glad you moved into my old apartment. And got overloaded with my mail. And needed work on your car and…you know, all the rest."

Warmth spiraled through her, followed quickly by a spike of pure fear. She was getting caught up in something that she didn't quite understand here, and she wasn't sure how to feel about it, so she just nodded and went on her way.

It would have been a lot easier to deal with if she

could have convinced herself that she wasn't glad about how things had turned out, too.

They spent an hour at a table in a favorite chain restaurant of his, comparing their lists and debating the contents until they came up with a master list. The girl was nothing if not stubborn—and close with a buck.

Since it was his buck that she was wringing, Vince couldn't be too put out about her thrifty ways, especially since it was a habit which she obviously had developed from pure necessity. Strangely enough, that only made him want to spend more, either to irritate her or to delight her, he wasn't entirely sure which.

The tentative excitement lighting her eyes when she talked about actually picking out articles for purchase seemed reason enough to splurge all by itself, but he couldn't deny that arguing with her had become something of a favorite pastime, especially once he'd figured out that her tough exterior was just that, a front that she used to protect herself.

The question became by what, or whom, did she feel threatened?

Vince had no answers for that, but he exercised his better judgment and curbed the impulse to dump wads of cash on her, sensing that she wouldn't find the actual spending of it as enjoyable as he would find watching her spend it. That didn't mean that he wasn't tickled by her building enthusiasm for the project, however, and try as she might, she couldn't hide the evidence of it. At times, she practically bubbled, and it was in those moments that Vince found himself almost aching for the woman he glimpsed behind those jade eyes.

They spent the balance of the afternoon in Dallas wandering around old warehouses and new sheet metal barns. The mid-November weather was glorious, with bright sunshine overhead and air crisp enough to feel like autumn while requiring nothing more onerous than a sweater or light jacket. It was Vincent's favorite time of the year in Texas.

The suffocating heat of summer had waned with September and the weather had run mild for weeks, gradually cooling. The trees were ablaze still, though some of the leaves had started to fall, but the weather would hold, maybe even right up into December, when the temperatures would take a plunge. Winter would bring one or two ice storms, but they would be brief and would lack the danger of the spring tornado season.

Yes, autumn was the heavenly season in Texas, at least as far as Vince was concerned. Jolie called it "perfect shopping weather."

He liked what he saw at the market. Much of it was imported from Mexico and, to a lesser extent, other countries, but most of it came straight out of workshops in Texas or one of the surrounding states. He absolutely went nuts over an easy chair covered in deerhide, manufactured by a retired aerospace engineer in Fort Davis, west of the Pecos River. The vendor stuck a hold sign on it for them, and they tore through the rest of the market putting together a complete roomful of furnishings built around that one chair.

Problem was, he wanted that chair in the den where he could relax in the evening and watch a little TV or read. Jolie carped about deviating from their plan, but he could be stubborn, too, and in the end he got his way without too much tussle. Then she found the perfect dining-room suite, which sent them off on another search for coordinating pieces.

Vince wasn't completely sold on the living-room stuff that she picked out, but the vendor assured them that anything they didn't love once it was installed in the house could be returned. They arranged for delivery on Monday, and before he knew what had hit him, Vince found himself the proud owner of half a houseful of brand-new, handcrafted furniture, for much less than he'd have paid in a regular retail store.

All in all, it had been a very productive day.

"Wait until the girls hear how much we've gotten accomplished," he said as he drove Jolie back toward her car at the cleaners.

Jolie chewed her lip for a moment before saying, "I hope they won't think I've been extravagant."

"If they think anybody's been extravagant, it'll be me," he pointed out. "It's my house and my money, after all."

"Yes, but it's my plan."

"What difference does that make? I have final say. Besides, it isn't any of their business."

"If you really believed that you wouldn't have insisted that I go to dinner on Sunday with your family."

"I didn't insist! I asked politely, and you kindly agreed." He narrowed his eyes at her. "You're not backing out on me, are you? Because I've already told Mom that you'll be there."

"Who said anything about backing out?" she demanded indignantly.

Vince laughed. He couldn't help it. Even their arguments—and they were constant but completely without rancor—engaged him in a way that no interaction with any other woman ever had. He fought the impulse to reach across the cab of the pickup and chuck her under the chin, but he couldn't deny himself the occasional glance.

She was growing on him, this Jolie Kay Wheeler, prickles and all. He found himself wondering if she might be the one, but then he reminded himself that he still knew little about her. God had not yet revealed His plan. Still, Vince couldn't deny a growing undercurrent of awareness between them. At least he suspected that it was mutual.

Then again, it wasn't wise to take anything for granted where Jolie was concerned.

Vince dropped Jolie off at her car behind the cleaners. It was later than they'd anticipated returning, so the rush hour was well past. He offered dinner, but Jolie said she had much to do. He didn't question her, but he did insist on following her home just to make certain that she got there safely.

She told him that he was a sexist, high-handed Neanderthal, and that she'd been taking care of herself for a quarter of a century at least, which prompted him to drawl, "I didn't think you were that old."

"I'm twenty-seven, thank you very much, and don't change the subject."

"And what is the subject? Oh, yeah, my gentlemanly impulse to see you safely to your own front door."

"Whatever," she replied with a huff, slamming the door to the cab.

He grinned, enjoying himself, and followed at a discreet distance until she turned her little jalopy into the apartment parking lot.

Twenty-seven, he mused. That seemed to him just about the right age for a woman. Funny, but in some ways she seemed younger. And in some ways she seemed older. It was as if she maintained some measure of innocence while carrying the weight of the world on her slender shoulders.

"Lord," he prayed, "show me how to lighten her load."

She was trembling. He felt it in the hand that he placed at the small of her back as he began the first of many introductions to be made.

"Mom, Dad, this is Jolie Wheeler. Jolie, these are my parents, Ovida and Larry."

Jolie timidly offered her hand to his mother, who clasped it and held on for dear life as if afraid that her one chance for a daughter-in-law would escape before they could get her well and truly tied down.

"Sugar, you are as welcome as rain in the summer! My, isn't she a pretty thing, but of course Vince could always have his pick."

Vince groaned inwardly when Jolie shot him a startled glance. Why hadn't he set them all straight? He'd meant to, but somehow it hadn't seemed important. He should have realized that his mother would make her assumptions obvious. His dad had always said that Ovida was about as subtle as her flaming-red hair.

The hair that curled softly around her squarish face had faded over the years, but Ovida remained as bluntly spoken as ever. Vince cleared his throat, hoping she'd get the hint, and all but wrenched Jolie from her grasp, moving on to his eldest sister and her husband.

"This is Sharon and Wally and their two kids, Jack and Brenda. You've met Olivia, and this is her husband Drew and their three boys, Mark, Matthew and Michael. Helen you also know. That wild man she's married to is John."

"Don't you believe a word of it," John put in, winking at Jolie and giving one corner of his beloved mustache a tweak.

Vince playfully tugged the other corner of his old running buddy's facial hair and kept going.

"The little redhead is Bets, and finally here's my baby sister Donna and her crackbrained other half Martin, whom we lovingly refer to as Chrome Dome."

Unperturbed at the teasing insult, Marty rubbed his perfectly bald head, wrapped his arms around his wife and patted her distended tummy, saying, "And this is either Anthony or Ann."

"We wanted to know which, but the baby didn't cooperate," Donna divulged, having inherited both her mother's red hair and frank manner. "Must take after Marty."

"Man, let's hope not," Vince retorted, straight-faced.

"Now, y'all get to the table," Ovida ordered. "The gravy's jelling."

The family turned en masse and swiftly moved into the dining room, leaving Vince and Jolie to bring up the rear. He dropped a reassuring smile on her, figured that he knew what her beetled brow was about and felt a hole open in the pit of his belly.

What on earth, he suddenly wondered, had possessed him to throw her into the arena with his family like this? He knew perfectly well that they all thought she was his girlfriend. It wasn't like him to exacerbate unfounded assumptions. Trouble was, he'd started thinking that maybe it shouldn't be unfounded.

The family scrambled for seats, leaving two places at the top of the *T* for him and Jolie. Vince had hoped that his mother would put the kids in the kitchen as usual, but instead she'd opted for the "holiday seating," which meant that the kitchen table had been carried into the dining room and fitted to the longer table there so that the two formed the shape of a *T*. The whole had been laid with her very best china. He wished that for once the good dishes had stayed in the hutch.

The Cutlers were solidly middle-class folk who lacked for nothing and wanted for little, but their lives seemed embarrassingly rich to Vince just then with all seventeen of them—Jolie made it eighteen—crowded around a table practically bowing beneath the weight of food. Obviously his sisters had pitched in even more than usual, and Jolie was looking a bit overwhelmed by it all. As if worried that she wasn't dressed well enough, she kept tugging on the hem of her simple white blouse, which she wore with black slacks and black loafers.

He pulled out a chair for Jolie and patted her arm in a gesture of encouragement. She didn't so much as glance at him but kept her gaze targeted on her lap. Bets howled about something, was gently scolded by both her parents and shushed by all her cousins, but then everyone settled into place.

His mother disappeared into the kitchen and quickly returned carrying two huge steaming bowls of hot biscuits draped with matching white dish towels. She placed one on each table and took her seat at the end of the top of the *T* opposite his father.

"Daddy, give us the blessing please."

Larry cleared his throat and bowed his salt-and-pepper head and delivered the requested prayer of thanksgiving. The rest of the family echoed his "Amen," and Vince squeezed Jolie's hands, realizing only then that he'd reached over to cover them where they were clamped together in her lap. He quickly withdrew his hand, hoping that no one else had noticed, only to catch several knowing smiles.

For some time, conversation was curtailed by getting everyone served. Eventually, however, the "interview" began. It would be, of course, Olivia who fired the opening volley.

"So, Jolie, where do you work?"

Vincent watched as casually as he could the very careful manner in which Jolie swallowed and laid aside her fork.

"Actually, she's doing some work for me," he blurted. "Laundry, decorating the house. I think I mentioned that when you came by the other day."

Jolie pressed her heavy linen napkin to her mouth and spoke.

"Mainly, I work for Geopp's Dry Cleaners."

"Oh, I know that place," Ovida said brightly. "I used to take our things there all the time, but I thought it closed down after sweet little Mrs. Geopp passed."

"Just for a couple of weeks," Jolie said softly.

"I'll have to start using them again, then."

"I'm sure Mr. Geopp would appreciate that."

It was Sharon's turn.

"Do you have family?"

Jolie toyed with her fork.

"An older brother and a younger sister. And a nephew."

"That's nice," Ovida gushed. "Do they live around here?"

"Yes, ma'am, but, um, we're not really very close."

"Oh, that's a shame."

Jolie hunched a shoulder in ambiguous reply.

"What do you do for the holidays?" Donna wanted to know, and again Jolie merely shrugged.

"Well, you'll just have to spend Thanksgiving with us," Ovida announced brightly.

Vince nearly choked on a hunk of steamed carrot.

"Oh, no," Jolie replied quickly. "I couldn't impose."

"As if one more will make a difference around here," Ovida said dismissively. "Now, I won't take no for an answer, seeing as how you have no other plans. Vincent, take a drink."

Vince croaked out a "Yes, ma'am," and gulped down half a glass of tea.

At least no one had asked about her parents. That was information which he preferred to impart privately. In fact, he should have done so before today. He wondered why he hadn't. Then he realized that he had wanted them to get to know her first, to *like* her first, not that they would hold her raising against her. He just wanted them to see her in the very best possible light.

This was getting a little scary. He couldn't remember another time when he'd felt this way about a woman.

The impulse to try to control the situation was very

strong, so strong that he heard himself asking, "Have I told you how Jolie and I met?"

Of course, he hadn't, so he did so now.

"She leased my old apartment, and like a clunkhead I forgot to have my mail forwarded."

"I didn't know you got any mail there," Sharon said.

"Not much," he admitted.

"Not much!" Jolie yelped. "I'd accumulated a whole shopping bag full of his stuff before he finally came and got it. The post office and I played ring-around-the-rosy with it until I went to the library and looked up his phone number on the Internet."

Laughing stiltedly, Vince said, "Guess idiocy pays off sometimes." He caught Jolie's questioning glance and added, "You should see what she's done with the old place. That's what inspired me to have her help me out with my place. Why, if the apartment had looked that good when I lived there I might have stayed."

This brought groans and comments from all around the table.

"Took us ten years to get him out of there."

"And it still looked like a room in a frat house."

"At least he took down the pizza boxes."

"Yeah, how's that for decor? Pin empty, flattened pizza boxes all over the wall."

"I'm not sure he even scraped the cheese off first."

"Okay, all right," Vince objected, holding up both hands as if to fend off further comment. "The pizza boxes went the first year, and you know it."

"Then it was pages out of sports magazines."

"I wasn't even old enough to vote!"

"Hey, he could've gone to hamburger wrappers," Jolie quipped, and everyone laughed.

"So he's 'cooked' for you, has he?" Donna teased, crooking her fingers to indicate quotation marks.

Vince no longer tried to restrain his rolling eyes as everyone laughed at his expense.

"Y'all leave him alone," his mother scolded without the least heat before abruptly changing the subject. "So, Jolie, where do you go to church, hon?"

Jolie coughed behind her hand, smoothed that hand over the napkin in her lap and mumbled, "I, um, haven't been in awhile."

Vince felt a welling of unreasonable panic and didn't even realize that he was going to speak until he opened his mouth. "Her brother's a preacher, though."

Jolie shot him a look that lanced straight into his heart.

"Is that so?" his mother gushed avidly.

With a strained smile, Jolie said softly, "He has a small church in Pantego."

Ovida Cutler literally beamed. "How interesting. What kind of church is it?"

"What difference does it make?" Vince asked quickly, picking up his fork. Almost at the same time, Jolie answered, so that they talked over one another.

"You're right," Ovida said with a smile. "What difference does it make?"

Vince knew from the gleam in her eye that she was pleased. Jolie, on the other hand, was not, and he couldn't blame her. He wondered all over again what he was doing—and how likely he was to get in trouble by doing it.

All in all, dinner was a trial, but somehow they made it through. Jolie insisted on helping clean up afterward, which caused Vince some uncomfortable moments. He resisted the urge to follow her into the kitchen and run interference for her with the Cutler women, but just barely.

It seemed he need not have worried, however, for when they all trooped back into the den, where the guys were watching television, they were chatting like old friends. Then Jolie retrieved the folder of papers that she'd left with her purse and invited his sisters and mother to take a look at what she'd accomplished so far with his house.

They all exclaimed over the prices she'd given for the furniture.

"That's amazing!"

Jolie beamed, assuring them, "It isn't junk, either."

"Well, of course not," Ovida said. "Vincent wouldn't settle for junk."

"Oh, right, like that ratty piece of horsehair he's been sitting on all these years isn't junk," Olivia said.

"That was Grandma Sledge's sofa," Vince pointed out.

"Sentimental junk then," Sharon retorted.

"Oh, dear," Jolie worried aloud, "does that mean we shouldn't get rid of it?"

"No!" his sisters all exclaimed in unison.

"It really should be retired," Ovida agreed, and they all laughed. Vince took himself off to the safe company of the menfolk.

Some time later he realized that Jolie and his sister Donna had put their heads together for a fairly lengthy discussion, and once more his protective instincts stirred, but when he wandered over to ask what was up, Donna smiled secretively and answered only, "Girl talk, big brother, girl talk."

He knew too well what that meant, as did every other male in the room, but just in case he'd missed it, John translated for him.

"In other words, it's none of your business."

Vince did not agree, but he figured it was best not to probe too deeply at that moment. He'd survived this harebrained scheme so far by the skin of his teeth, but he was well aware that it could blow up in his face at any moment, which was nothing less than he deserved, frankly. Once he figured out what the dickens he was doing, he'd have some confessions to make, not to mention some apologies. Until then, he might just do best to keep his mouth shut, and thereby keep his head attached firmly to his shoulders.

He hoped.

Chapter Eight

Later, driving Jolie home at twilight, Vince figured that it was safe to ask what she'd thought of his family.

"Oh, they're great," she replied easily, "and your sisters and mom actually seemed to like what we're doing with the house."

He nodded, surprised but pleased about that himself.

"So what were you and Donna talking about for so long?"

Jolie smiled enigmatically, and he resigned himself to disappointment on that score, but then she said, "Decorating, of course. What else?"

He snorted at that. "I can think of a few dozen subjects I'd just as soon she didn't bring up, frankly."

Jolie laughed. "She just wanted to know what sort of furniture she could find at the market where you and I shopped."

"And?"

"And I expect that she and Martin will be spending some time in downtown Dallas next weekend."

It was his turn to laugh.

"Remind me to rub it in when Marty's griping about her buying new furniture."

She tilted her head to one side.

"Don't you like your brother-in-law?"

"Love him like a brother. I actually introduced him to my sister."

"Really? Just so you can irritate each other?"

He grinned. "It's a guy thing."

She arched an eyebrow but said nothing else, which was just as well, because he felt keenly the need to broach another subject. Shifting in his seat, he decided how to phrase it.

"I know it's none of my business, but I can't help wondering what's going on with you and your family."

Her eyes frosted, and she lifted her chin. "You're right. It is none of your business."

Like that was going to stop him, he thought, amazed at himself.

"I was just wondering if there was anything I could do to help. Family is important, and you seem so sad when you talk about yours."

Her gaze dropped to her lap, and she muttered, "There isn't anything you can do, believe me."

He was prepared to let it drop after that. What he wasn't prepared for, even after she turned her gaze out her side window and fussed with her bangs, was the tears that streamed down her face when she finally looked back to him. Instinctively he whipped the truck off the street and into the empty lot of a defunct car wash.

"Jolie?"

She shook her head, biting her lip. He slammed the

transmission into Park, words tumbling out of his own mouth heedlessly.

"Honey, what's wrong?"

She gulped, and he leaned across the center console to wrap his arm around her shoulders.

"It's all right. Please don't cry."

"I c-can't help it," she finally whispered.

He brushed aside a strand of hair caught in the moisture on her cheek.

"I'm sorry. I didn't mean to make you cry."

"It's not you. It's…my life."

"Won't you tell me about it? You can talk to me, you know. I mean, we're friends now, aren't we?"

"I suppose we are."

She blinked and dabbed at her eyes with the edge of her sleeve. He scrambled in the console for a tissue and came up with a creased paper napkin.

"Thank you." She sniffed and pressed the napkin to her cheeks. After a moment she sighed and let her hands fall to her lap. "I told you that my nephew's father is in prison," she began softly. "What I didn't tell you is that my sister went to prison, too."

Vince rocked, knocked back by this revelation.

"Oh, man."

"They got her for abetting a crime," Jolie went on, "but Connie's always sworn that she didn't know what her boyfriend was doing when he went in to rob that bank branch, and she did turn him in when she heard on the news that he'd shot a guard."

"Well, that's good," Vince murmured, wanting desperately to say something positive, though he felt completely out of his depth here. Prison, for pity's sake.

"The guard was an off-duty police officer," Jolie

went on, "and he died, so they sentenced her to five to eight years, but she actually served less than two."

"Sounds like she behaved herself."

"Model prisoner, they said." Her voice dwindled away with the next words. "That's why they gave Russell back to her."

Jolie choked and began to sob.

Russell? Vince's mind was whirling. Obviously he didn't have the full story yet, but all he could think to do at the moment was to wrap his arms around her and croon sympathetically.

"I'm so sorry. I really hate to hear this. I—I mean, I'm glad that she did well, but...you've obviously been though a great deal."

About the time he ran out of comforting words, Jolie calmed, turning her face into the hollow of his shoulder.

"I knew you'd understand."

Understanding had not yet been achieved, actually, but he didn't say so. Instead, he opted to ask the question uppermost in his mind, "Who, um, is Russell?"

That set her off again, and he could've kicked himself—except he still didn't know what it was all about. He figured all he could do was wait out the tears, and eventually she gulped, wiped and pulled in a shuddering breath.

"Russell is my n-nephew."

Her nephew. So that's why they'd given Russell to her sister; the sister was his mother. Vince sighed, pretty sure that he knew now where this was going, and already his heart was breaking for her.

"You took him, didn't you? While she was in prison."

Jolie nodded, blinking rapidly.

"C-Connie found out she was pregnant not long after she went in, and e-everyone thought it would be best if the baby was with f-family." She pulled in a deep breath and went on more calmly. "So I got certified as a foster parent and found us a little house. The state gives you a monthly stipend, you know. It was enough for two bedrooms and a little yard." She closed her eyes as if remembering. "He was perfect, just perfect. We were so happy, the two of us." Her hands plucked at the damp napkin. "Then just before Connie got out, my brother came to see me." She shrugged. "I didn't think anything of it. We saw him often."

"What happened?" Vince asked.

She closed her eyes and pinched the bridge of her nose. "He wanted to talk about Connie and Russell, about reuniting them. I couldn't believe it!"

Vince tightened the loop of his arms about her, feeling torn. On one hand, he couldn't argue against reuniting a parent and child, provided there was no history of abuse. On the other hand, Jolie had evidently cared for that boy for over a year, presumably from his birth. Did no one consider her feelings or what was best for her? Had no one prepared her for the day that the child's mother would reclaim him? However it had happened, it was plain that Jolie had been terribly hurt.

"So your brother helped your sister take back the boy," Vince surmised, and she nodded miserably.

"I guess I should have expected it, but the caseworker was always talking about *if* Connie could reclaim the child, and it just didn't make sense to me that she could go to prison and come out somehow a better parent than *me*!"

Vincent laid his head against hers, feeling her pain and the neediness that she tried so hard to keep hidden behind that tough-cookie mask of hers. Maybe she'd set herself up for disappointment, but that didn't make her grief any less real or poignant. Plus, she'd done a very good thing, caring for her nephew for at least the first year of his life. It must seem grossly unfair to be paid back with such a loss.

"I'm so sorry," he said against her temple. "And I'm sure you *are* a wonderful parent."

"You've no idea how much I miss him," she whispered, leaning into Vince. "I just couldn't believe they'd take him away."

"I guess there was a hearing?"

She nodded, becoming animated. "And Marcus testified on Connie's behalf," she said bitterly. "He talked about her 'spiritual maturity' and how she took parenting classes and college courses. He even let her and Russell move in with him! What hurt most of all was when he said that he feared it would be 'unhealthy' for Russell to be left in my care."

That, Vince could not imagine, and he was almost shocked by how easy it was to feel outraged on her behalf.

"Pure nonsense. Surely he didn't mean it the way it sounds."

"Maybe not," Jolie conceded, "but that doesn't change the fact that Russell is with them now, and I'm alone again."

Again. What a wealth of information and meaning that one little word contained.

"You are not alone," he protested automatically,

tilting her face toward his with a finger curled beneath her chin.

"I've always been alone," she whispered, and he saw by the tortured look in her eyes that she really believed that.

"God never allows His children to walk through this world alone," Vince assured her, believing it wholeheartedly.

He'd once heard Hell described as complete and utter separation from God, and he shuddered to think of an eternity spent bereft of the slightest nuance of love. Somehow he understood that Jolie had felt too little love in her lifetime and too much separation.

Could he convince her that he wasn't going anywhere? Should he even try? Any words he might have given her to that effect seemed abrupt and premature, so he did the only thing he could think of to show her that he wanted to be a part of her life. He lifted one hand and cradled her cheek.

The impulse to kiss her shook him right to the marrow of his bones, but he subdued it.

Even as she drew away, color staining her cheeks, he understood that he was taking a big risk by opening himself up to the possibility that they could be more than friends. They were from very different backgrounds, and she did not seem able to trust. Yet.

She had issues to be resolved and wounds to heal, and he suspected that it would take a lot of patience and some very deft handling on his part to get them both to the place where they would have to be for anything more than simple friendship. But he couldn't ignore what he was feeling.

"I can't believe I told you all that," Jolie said with a grimace. "I hate it when people feel sorry for me."

"I don't feel sorry for you," he corrected firmly. "I feel sorry for what you've been though."

She smiled softly. "How is it that you always say the right thing?"

"We both know better than that," he said, "but if I got it right this time, I'm glad. In fact, I thank God."

She blinked and looked down shyly. He watched her pull together her usual bravado, enjoying every instant of the transformation. She was plucky, this woman. *His* woman?

Maybe. In time.

She fluffed her bangs and nervously smoothed them again, saying, "I'd better get home."

He took the hint and leisurely settled back behind the wheel.

He'd see her tomorrow, after all, and as often thereafter as he could manage until they both understood, individually and together, everything that God had in store for them.

Jolie had finally gotten a handle on the ever-plentiful laundry, so they were able to spend Monday afternoon shifting around the newly delivered furniture until everything was placed just right.

Vince was delighted to see that Jolie had been absolutely correct about the living-room stuff, and he told her so, which made her loft her eyebrows practically into her hairline.

"Frankly, I'm not sure which one of us is more surprised," she admitted, and suddenly he found himself slinging an arm around her shoulders as they both laughed.

Then she looked up at him, and he caught his breath as awareness sizzled in the air. Before he could figure out what he should do about it, she had whirled away, ducking down slightly to extricate herself from the loop of his arm.

"About Thanksgiving," she said, glancing away.

He reached for a nonchalance that he couldn't quite find and asked, "What about it?"

"I don't think I should come."

He caught his frown before it fully developed. "Why not?"

She shrugged. "Your family could get the wrong idea about us."

"My family's had the wrong idea since my sisters first walked in and found you here."

"Have you tried to tell them different?" she asked pointedly.

He wouldn't lie to her. "No."

"How come?"

"I don't know." He laid a hand against the nape of his neck. "You've met them. Do you figure it would do any good?"

She looked him square in the eye. "Probably not."

"Well, then, what's the point?"

She bit her lip. "I don't want to mislead anyone."

"Neither do I."

"So I'd better not come," she said decisively. Yet, he heard the faintest note of question in her tone.

He looked down at the toes of his boots and said baldly, "I want you to come."

"Oh?" She sounded a teensy bit hopeful.

He stuffed his hands into his back pockets and nodded. "I couldn't enjoy myself knowing you were sitting home alone at holiday time."

"No?"

"Not a bit."

She seemed to consider. Then, she shook her head. "It's not your problem."

"What's that got to do with it?" he wanted to know. "You'll still be alone, and I'll still be thinking about that instead of enjoying myself."

She rolled her eyes, and he scuffed a toe on the carpet.

"Unless there's a chance you might join your own family, after all."

"No chance of that," she stated flatly, folding her arms, "and I told Marcus so."

Vince felt a jolt of shock. "You mean he invited you to join them?"

She lifted her chin. "Surely, you don't think I could!"

He didn't know what he thought at the moment, but if she was determined not to join her own family, she'd just have to make do with his because he really couldn't enjoy Thanksgiving knowing that she was sitting out the holiday alone. He pulled out the big guns.

"Mom will be awfully disappointed if you don't come, you know, and how am I supposed to explain your absence? Saying that you can't abide being mistaken for my girlfriend would go over big."

She threw up her hands, as if it was all a great inconvenience, and exclaimed, "Well, I guess I'd better come then!"

He bit back a smile, sensing that her capitulation was less onerous than she pretended. "I guess so."

"I certainly wouldn't want to offend your mama after she's been so kind to me."

"Thanks," he drawled wryly. She didn't seem to have any qualms about offending him, but he'd take what he could get at this point. "Well, that's settled then. I'll pick you up about ten o'clock Thursday morning, if that's okay. Mom says we'll eat as close to noon as possible, but she likes everyone to be there early."

Jolie muttered something about sleeping in, but she nodded her agreement and left soon after, almost running to her car.

He chuckled about it, but later he sat in his special deerhide chair and thought about her or, more to the point, his feelings for her and whether or not he was supposed even to have them.

Looking around at the changes she had already wrought in his home, he tried to decide whether or not God meant her for him, or if he was supposed to somehow help her settle her differences with her family. Apparently they were willing, or at least the brother was.

Maybe that was all there was to it.

Or maybe this was about mutual need. Maybe she was just someone who could literally help him get his house in order, and maybe he was just someone who could fix her old car.

And maybe he would never know why God had brought her into his life.

All he could do was pray for guidance and trust that understanding would come when it was meant to—

and that he wouldn't do something stupid like getting his heart broken in the meantime.

Jolie set down the iron and sighed, wiping her brow. She was beginning to hate ironing with a passion. Iron, iron, iron, that was all she seemed to do. That and laundry and planning designs in her head and shopping and arranging and…daydreaming about Vince Cutler.

In the beginning she hadn't wanted anything more than simple friendship from him, if that. Truth be told, she'd have settled quite happily for a cordial working relationship, but somehow one thing had led to another and before she'd known it, they were friends. From there, one short step had brought her to the possibility that they might be more to each other, which was ludicrous.

For one thing, she didn't want anyone in her life. Caring for people just got you hurt. She'd learned that all too well. For another, she was not the sort for Vincent Cutler. Vince came from a nice, normal family. He would definitely want a nice, normal girl, and that sure wasn't her, not with her background and her baggage.

Disgusted with herself for even briefly entertaining the idea that she might be more to Vince than a charity case, she turned her back on the ironing board and went to the sink for a cool drink of water. The outside temperatures were in the low forties, but in this tiny apartment standing over a hot iron, the air felt downright sultry.

So why did she feel cold inside?

She didn't have to look far for a convenient answer.

It was all Marcus's and Connie's fault. They'd used her and then betrayed her. They'd let her take care of Russell and then taken him away from her.

How could Vince even think that she'd accept an invitation to spend the holiday with them?

Wandering over to the counter, she picked up an envelope. Twice now she'd started to peel back the flap, and twice she'd stopped, telling herself that she didn't care what was inside. She'd recognized the handwriting on the front immediately. God knew that she and Connie had corresponded often enough in the past two years for her to know her sister's handwriting at a glance. She should have dropped the envelope in the trash the moment she'd realized who had sent it. Instead, she ripped the back flap off completely.

The card inside slipped out easily into her hand. The front was embellished with a cross and a white dove bearing an olive branch, symbols of peace and forgiveness. As if she had anything to be forgiven for, she thought resentfully, flipping the card open.

The verse printed inside was a quotation from Genesis 31:49. "May the Lord watch between you and me when we are absent one from another."

Jolie thought of her little sister's big green eyes and elfin face, and a lump rose in her throat. Willfully, she pictured Russell's bright coppery head and beaming smile, and the lump turned bitter. Quickly, dismissively, she scanned the short message that her sister had written.

It was all about how Connie missed her and wished they could have a "real family Thanksgiving." She asked Jolie to call her and wrote how sorry she was for "the misunderstanding between us." Some misunderstanding, Jolie thought disdainfully. She had been used, plain and simple, by her own sister. And brother. She wouldn't forget his part in it. They had used her and then cast her aside.

Even knowing that, however, she'd gladly do it all over again, just for Russell's sake. Even knowing that she would eventually have to give him up, she could never have walked away from the fat, cherubic little bundle who had been placed in her arms that day. Only hours old, he'd squinted and blinked at the bright world, pushing his tiny pink tongue against his lips hopefully, and she had instantly wanted for him all that she had missed: a stable and loving home, healthy meals, safety, laughter, a true sense of belonging.

She had tried so hard to give him those things, and he had been happy, so happy. Did he miss her? she wondered wistfully. She loved him enough to hope that he didn't, and yet her heart cracked open a little wider at the thought that he might not.

Closing the card, she stuffed it back into the envelope and dropped it into a drawer. Out of sight, out of mind.

Please, God, she prayed silently. *I just can't bear to think about it.*

Then she remembered that God did not answer her prayers. If He did, she'd still be chasing Russell around on the floor, removing dangerous objects from his reach, rocking him to sleep, playing giggling games of peek-a-boo.

Emptiness overwhelmed her.

In the silence she heard the faint click of the thermostat kicking off or on inside the iron as it attempted to regulate the temperature of the pressing plate. Jolie gulped and swiftly moved back to the ironing board and the work at hand, desperate for anything that would take her mind off Russell.

She concentrated on placing and ironing the next garment, on getting the lay of a lace applique just right. Her hands moved by rote, and her mind wandered to something more challenging. The kitchen in Vince's house was bare and bland. He needed some attractive but useful items to scatter about the place. She tried to remember what he had, what he could use. She remembered the sandwich he'd made for her, the easy way in which he'd leapt up onto the counter to eat his share, the way his gaze moved over her face from time to time.

The slight dilation of his irises as he'd leaned close, his hand warm against her cheek, his arm about her shoulders.

With a jerk she realized that she was fantasizing again about that moment in his truck on Sunday evening when it had seemed that he might kiss her. Just as it had then, her heart beat a rapid staccato inside her chest and heat rose up all the way to her cheeks.

What was she doing?

She already knew that she was not the sort for Vincent Cutler. No man was the sort for her. Any man whom she might want would never really want her, and she would not be like her mother, constantly used and tossed aside. She'd had enough of that already. She wouldn't be foolish enough to open herself up to more. Never would she wind up like her mom or even Connie.

Never would she have a child of her own.

Russell had been her one chance at real family, at

motherhood. Without him she had nothing, not even the brother and sister to whom she had clung for so many years, despite the separation of different foster homes.

She was alone in the world, but at least she was safe from the pain of loving and losing.

Still, if she didn't have the Cutlers to spend Thanksgiving with this year, she wasn't sure how she would make it through the holiday.

The Lord never allows His children to walk through this world alone.
The Lord watch between you and me while we are absent one from another.

"Please, God," she whispered, "just this once. I can't go on thinking about them anymore. Isn't it enough that I've lost my family? Can't I please just have some peace now?"

God, it seemed, was just not on her side.

Chapter Nine

"Evening."

"I see you're ready to shop," she said wryly, looking pointedly at his uniform as she slipped through the door of his house.

It was easier than looking at his face. Staring at that handsome face was much too dangerous. Besides, for some reason he looked especially inviting with a five o'clock shadow, very virile. Steady, she told herself. Vincent Cutler was just another guy, nicer than most, maybe, but in the end as much trouble as all the rest of them.

He shifted his feet self-consciously. "Look, I got held up at work. The drapery shop closes at seven, and I've got prayer meeting tomorrow evening, and with Thanksgiving being the next day, it's either tonight or wait until next week to check out this place, so I didn't take time to change. Do you mind?"

She rolled her eyes. The uniform was rumpled but clean and neater than her work clothes, which consisted of an old T-shirt and jeans worn to a pale gray-blue.

"I'm just teasing, okay?"

He lifted his brows at her tart tone but made no rejoinder.

"We'd better get a move on," he said, shepherding her through the house toward the garage. "It's not far, which is why I asked you to meet me here."

"And how did you hear about this place, again?"

"The fellow who built this house for me brought his car in for repairs today, and it occurred to me that he might have a lead on a good drapery place, so I asked him for a recommendation."

She nodded as he handed her up into the truck.

Not forty minutes later, she was climbing back into it, thoroughly disgusted. "And we thought the first place was high!"

"They *were* on the expensive side," he agreed, sliding behind the steering wheel. "Oh, well, nothing ventured, nothing gained."

"Nothing gained is right," she grumbled, buckling her safety belt. How dare that builder waste their time like this? she fumed silently. He probably knew what Vince was worth and figured he could afford such ridiculous prices. "Probably getting a kickback or something," she muttered, folding her arms.

Vince slid her a glance but said nothing. They drove back to his place in silence. Thankfully, it was a short trip. Jolie hopped down out of the truck and let herself into the house before he had the brake set. He caught up with her in the foyer, halting her progress toward the front door with a hand clasped around hers.

"Whoa," he said, drawing her around to face him. "Now why don't you tell me what's really bothering you?"

In the space of four weeks—and it was four weeks to the day, she realized with a jolt—he had somehow learned to read her like a book. Moreover, she seemed powerless to stop him.

"You're in a snit, and it's got nothing to do with overpriced drapery."

"I am not in a snit!" she defended hotly, but then she caught the concern in his gaze and gave up. "Oh, all right. I'm in a lousy mood, and I admit it. Happy?"

"Not until you tell me why."

She sighed gustily, but she told him. "I got a card in the mail from my sister Connie yesterday."

"I see." He led her into the living room, not releasing her hand until they were seated side by side on the couch. "What did she say?"

Jolie dropped her gaze, her fingers smoothing over the supple leather at her side.

"Not much. She's sorry for our 'misunderstanding,' like she didn't know taking Russell away from me would break my heart."

He didn't exactly rush to condemn her sister's actions. "Is that it?"

Jolie swallowed, feeling petty and frankly irritated about it. What had happened to her was *not* petty, but he was right to think there was more. "She wants me to call her."

"Are you going to?"

"No! Of course not!"

"How do you know it's not about Russell?" he asked softly.

Folding her arms, Jolie reluctantly told him, "She says that she wants a 'real family Thanksgiving.' As if we've ever had such a thing."

"Maybe it's time to start."

Her gaze zipped to his face. "How can we possibly? Connie and Marcus took Russell away from me!"

"And this might be a way for you to have him back in your life," Vince argued gently.

She couldn't believe what she was hearing.

"For moments here and there? I don't think so. It would be like losing him all over again every time we parted!"

Vince placed a comforting hand on her shoulder. "Don't you want to know if he's well and happy? Wouldn't it *help* to know that he's well and happy?"

She hungered for even the tiniest detail about Russell, but every thought of him still brought pain. Far worse, however, was the worry.

"And what if he isn't well and happy?" she whispered.

"Then you go to bat for him again," Vince said placidly. "You contact his caseworker, report what you've seen…"

She'd started shaking her head as soon as he mentioned the caseworker.

"They won't do anything! It would mean admitting that they were wrong."

"You don't know that."

"I can't do it!" Jolie leapt to her feet and began to pace. "I can't put myself through that again. You don't know what it's like to love a child and lose him, to finally be part of a family and have it ripped away! I'm better off alone."

He came to his feet beside her and stopped her in her tracks, his hands clamping her upper arms.

"You are not alone. You have never been alone. You never will be alone."

She cut him a scathingly skeptical look. "You're a great guy, Vince. You're kind and generous and caring, but I haven't lived the kind of life that you have. I didn't have model parents and a stable home. I didn't have a home, period!"

Dropping his hands from her shoulders, he said, "Maybe not, but that doesn't mean you were alone. You had your brother and sister, didn't you?"

"So what? I don't have them now, and don't try to tell me that it could be any other way, not after what they did to me!"

"What about God, Jolie?" he asked. "God is our constant companion. He's always there, always here. You just have to reach out to Him."

She could tell that, like Marcus, Vince was utterly sincere, and she wanted to be contemptuous about his beliefs, but she couldn't. Instead, she found herself being honest.

"Don't you think I've reached out? If God is here for me, Vince, then why did He let me lose Russell?"

"I don't know, honey," Vince admitted, "but I have to believe that He has a reason, a plan, and I know that God cares for you. I can prove it."

She was shocked by how much she wanted him to do just that, so much that when he led her back to the couch and gently seated her, she did not resist. Sitting down next to her, he wrapped an arm around her shoulders and bowed his head. Without even thinking, she bowed her own.

"Gracious Lord God, please help Jolie feel Your presence. I know how much You love her, but she's in so much pain that she can't feel it. She needs the peace and healing that come from truly knowing how much You love her. It's so easy to lose sight of that fact when we're hurting, but no one can understand her pain better than You can, and no one but You can heal her heart. Please help her to see, to feel, that she's not alone. Help her to accept that she is loved, truly, deeply, constantly loved. Amen."

As he prayed, Jolie felt a warmth flow through her, and for a moment, just a moment, she did believe. Then doubt reared its ugly head.

She told herself that the warmth she felt was nothing more than Vincent's arm and her own wishful thinking. Trusting in God's presence and care would just leave her open to more disappointment because she wasn't the sort whom God could love, not *personally.*

She wasn't even the sort a mother could love—or a man like Vince.

She didn't say so. Instead she smiled limply, thanked him and said that she had to be going. Vince didn't argue, but she saw the disappointment in his eyes.

"I'll pick you up tomorrow morning at ten," he reminded her solemnly.

She smiled and flicked her hair off her shoulders with a toss of her head. "Sure."

How long would it be, she wondered as she left him, before Vince cut her loose just like everyone else in her life had done?

"Hold on there, scamp!" Vince snagged his nephew Matthew by the collar of his shirt and hauled him to a stop. "I'm pretty sure I heard your mom tell you to stop running in the house."

Matthew turned up his freckled snub of a nose and regarded his uncle with impish defiance. "Nuh-uh."

"Oh, right," Vince said, bending to bring himself muzzle-to-muzzle with the little miscreant. "That was *me*."

Matthew giggled uncertainly, his mind processing the backhanded order. When he had reached the obvious and only safe conclusion, he sobered conspicuously.

"Okay, Uncle Vince."

Vince smiled and straightened, patting the boy on the head.

"Good choice. Spread the word. The next one I catch running in here is going to be the *last* one to the table."

Matthew's face registered horror, and he went off at a fast walk to deliver the edict. Vince glimpsed Jolie hovering uncertainly just inside the kitchen door, where his mother and sisters churned around like marbles in a blender.

Jolie had been all smiles that morning, as if she couldn't be bothered to spare a thought for her estranged sister and brother or her absent nephew, but Vince knew that wasn't the case. He'd prayed long and hard about the situation the evening before, and he'd come to the conclusion that until Jolie made peace with her family, she wouldn't be able to trust anyone else. And he wanted her trust, wanted it very much.

Matthew's mother exited the maelstrom with a plate of deviled eggs. On the way to the dining room she patted Vince's cheek and teased, "Practicing to be a parent, are we?"

"Chapter and verse, son," his dad called over his shoulder from the easy chair in the den, his gaze never leaving the fuzzy picture on the old television set. "You've got to read 'em chapter and verse."

"For all the good it'll do," Matthew's father, Drew, said dryly. The other brothers-in-law had gone out front to look over a neighbor's new boat.

Vince changed the subject. "Hey, did I tell y'all that I've decided to get me one of those new big-screen TVs?"

"Excellent," his father said, glancing in his direction. "Super Bowl party's at your house this year. But aren't those sets pretty expensive?"

Vince shrugged. "Jolie's saved me a bunch of money on the house decorating, but I'm still shopping around. I figured I'd better do it while I'm in a spending frame of mind."

Abruptly Drew bolted upright on the couch and hooted, pumping his fist in the air while Larry flopped back in his chair and groaned. Vince switched his attention to the television, becoming aware at the same instant of a presence at his side.

"What happened?" Jolie asked, looking to the set.

Controlling his surprise, Vince answered calmly, "Drew's team scored." Jolie wrinkled her nose, and he laughed. "What? You don't like them?"

"They've got the lamest uniforms in the NFL," she complained. "Just look at that logo. I know what it's supposed to be, and I still can't identify it."

"That's no reason to dislike a team," Drew protested.

"Yeah, well, their quarterback's got a shallow draft," Jolie went on knowledgeably. "He falls back only two steps, and then he does this double-pump thing that totally alerts the defense to his target." She shook her head and added, "He'll run out of stunt plays soon, and then the other team will clean his clock for him, I don't care how good his line is." With that she turned back into the kitchen.

Vince blinked, aware that his brother-in-law and his father were staring at him with mouths slightly ajar. It had taken concerted effort and drastic measures to get his sisters even minimally interested in live football, and they still wouldn't watch more than five minutes of a televised game. His mother had no interest, either, and in her case nothing seemed to make a difference, not tickets to a pro game, not autographed photos, not detailed explanations. Jolie, on the other hand, came already programmed. Vince grinned and shrugged at his father and brother-in-law, letting them know that he was as surprised as they were.

Drew shook his head as if to say that it wasn't fair. Then a roar from the television yanked them all back into the game. It was Larry's turn to hoot.

"Hey, Jolie!" he crowed. "The game's tied! Ran it all the way back from the kick-off!"

She popped her head out of the kitchen in time to catch the replay. Afterward she dismissed the play with a dry comment.

"Lucky break. Special teams have been sputtering all season."

Vince and Drew laughed at the look of consternation on Larry's face.

As soon as she disappeared again, Larry looked at Vince and admitted softly, "Too bad she's right."

"I heard that," Jolie informed them loudly.

Larry ducked his head, grinning as everyone else laughed.

Vince privately marveled. Who'd have guessed that she could fit in like this? He leaned back against the wall and perked up his ears, wondering how it was going in the kitchen with the female half of the clan.

As usual, they all seemed to be talking at once, but he heard Donna say, "Mmm, Jolie, these potatoes are good. What'd you put in them?"

"A little broth. Cuts back on the fat."

"Don't let Dad hear you say that," Olivia counseled wryly.

"It's Thanksgiving," Sharon said, mimicking their father's voice. "It's a feast. We're *supposed* to eat fat."

"And do we ever!" Helen chortled.

"They're yellow enough. He'll never know the difference," their mother said. "Somebody turn up the oven. These rolls are almost ready to go in."

"I'll do it," Donna volunteered. Vince heard the screech of chair legs against the floor and pictured his heavily pregnant sister hauling herself up out of the seat into which she had dropped earlier, complaining of a backache.

Just then a blood-curdling scream erupted from the closed-in back porch where the kids were playing. Olivia somehow recognized the voice of her youngest and yelled, "Michael?"

Drew popped up onto his feet, announcing loudly, "I'll go." He headed toward the back of the house. "Michael? Matthew? Mark? What's going on out there?"

Content that Jolie was holding her own for now, Vince wandered over and dropped down onto the end of the sofa that Drew had just vacated. His dad leaned forward, propped his elbows on his knees and jerked a head toward the kitchen.

"So what's her story then?"

Vince didn't pretend to misunderstand him. He'd been prepared for this question. He gave out the capsulized version.

"So she's not close to her brother and sister," Larry surmised correctly. They were much alike, father and son, not only in build and coloring, but in attitude, too.

"Actually, they're estranged," Vince admitted, still very troubled by that. "Long story short, for various reasons Jolie wound up taking care of her nephew for the first year or so of his life. Then a few months ago, her sister took the boy back and their brother helped her do it."

"That's tough." Larry shook his head sorrowfully.

"The thing is, she can't seem to come to terms with it."

Larry clucked his tongue. "Well, give her some time, son. I know women as well as any man can, and I figure she's dealing with a real sense of loss and betrayal right now. Those are especially big issues for women, and given what you've told me, it must be even more difficult for her than most."

"Yeah, I suspect you're right there."

He worried that if she didn't soon find peace with her situation and form some reconciliation with her family she would grow even more angry and resentful than she already was. She'd close herself off entirely then, and he didn't want that. He just didn't know what to do about it. God could and would help her accept, forgive and conquer her pain, if only she was willing to let Him. Getting her back in church seemed to be a logical first step in the right direction, but she'd already refused one invitation to attend with him.

Lord, how do I reach her? he prayed silently.

Before he could follow that thought, his mother rushed into the room, a dripping ladle in one hand, a wild look in her eyes.

"Larry, get the car!"

"What?" His father twisted around in his chair.

Ovida didn't answer him. Instead she abruptly addressed Vince. "Get Marty in here. Now!"

Vince stood, still not sure what was going on, and caught the murmur of concerned voices in the other room. He glanced through the doorway, straight into Jolie's pale face, and suddenly he knew.

Bolting for the front door, he heard his mother's exclamation. "Her water broke!"

Forget the turkey, they were having a baby!

Jolie stood with her mouth open like some spectator at a train wreck.

It was pandemonium, with the women cramming food into the refrigerator and shouting out instructions to one another, the men zipping around in the background, and the kids crowding around the kitchen door to stare at the laboring mother as if expecting the baby to burst from her belly like some alien in a horror movie.

The only calm one of them, Donna herself, was

right at the center of the storm. Despite her white lips, guttural moans and roiling belly, she managed to sit patiently, smile and work her way down a mental checklist while her family careened around like Keystone Kops in a panicked attempt to shut down dinner preparations and get her to the hospital.

"My suitcase is all packed and sitting inside the closet door," she said to no one in particular. "The doctor's telephone number is programmed into Marty's cell phone. All I've had to eat is a hard-boiled egg and crackers. There's a list of people to call on my bedside table."

She looked right at Jolie, who couldn't seem to do more than gape, as she said that last. Then she reached out, sucking in a sharp breath at the same time. Instinctively, Jolie wrapped her fingers around Donna's and squeezed.

Sinkingly aware of the others rushing from the room, she asked, "Are you all right?"

Panting, Donna nodded, gulped and gripped Jolie's hand even tighter. "St-strike the family names from the list," she instructed. "That'll leave the church and two others. Vince can make those calls after we get to the hospital. Okay?"

"Uh-huh."

Marty skidded through the doorway into the dated but homey kitchen, Vince on his heels. He went down onto his knees at Donna's side, demanding, "What's wrong?"

"Nothing."

"B-but Vince said—"

"I'm having a baby," Donna snapped. "It's perfectly normal."

"But it's not due yet!"

"Tell that to the baby!" She grimaced at his look of worry and added softly, "A month early is nothing to worry about. Everything will be fine."

He placed his hand on her belly and fervently said, "From your lips to God's ears."

Stepping up behind Jolie, Vince cleared his throat and said, "John's sedan is waiting out front." His hands settled gently upon Jolie's shoulders, and she fought the most astonishing urge to lean back against him.

"Who's behind the wheel?" Marty asked anxiously.

"Dad."

Martin shook his head. "No, no, he's too slow. You're the wheel man. I want you."

Donna rolled her eyes as Vince flexed his hands on Jolie's shoulders. "No problem," he said mildly. "Let's go."

Donna tugged on Jolie's hand as she began pushing her way up out of the chair. Bracing herself, Jolie helped haul her up, Marty hovering solicitously at his wife's side.

"Mom sent Sharon for a clean robe for me to wear, and Helen's gone for towels," Donna said, plucking at her wet clothes. Jolie blinked. She'd missed those details entirely.

"Let's head for the door," Vince said, stepping back to make way. "Mom and Olivia are herding the kids into Wally's van."

"Oh, I can stay here with the kids," Jolie offered, glad to have something to contribute.

Donna just laughed. Vince squeezed her shoulders again.

"Thanks, hon, but it would take a battalion of armed

soldiers to make that work. The Cutler clan descends en masse for every family event."

"Just hang on," Donna instructed. "They'll need every hand at the hospital."

"Oh, no," Martin moaned. "I think I'm going to be sick."

"For Pete's sake, Marty," Donna chided, her free hand on her belly as he hurried away. "Make it quick, will you?" She lifted her arm. "Vince, lend a hand."

He slid to her side, wrapped an arm around her back, murmuring, "I've got you, sis."

"Nothing new there," she muttered and kissed his cheek.

The trio sidled through the door, Jolie taking up a position on Donna's other side. Helen rushed past with the towels, shouting, "John, put Bets in the car with us. Vince and Jolie are going with Donna."

"Tell Dad I'm driving," Vince called out as she disappeared through the front door.

"Good grief, Marty," they heard her say. "Could you do that in the grass?"

Donna moaned, then she laughed. "Poor Martin. You be nice to him, Vincent Cutler, or I'll pull your ears off your head."

"Me?"

"Don't pretend you won't tease him," Donna scolded.

"Never occurred to me." Vince winked at Jolie over the top of his sister's head, and a smile quirked her lips. The next instant she was blinking back tears.

Jolie couldn't help thinking about Connie going into labor all alone and in a hostile place instead of surrounded by loving, teasing family. They were like nothing she'd ever known, these Cutlers. Donna was so fortunate, and Jolie sensed that she knew it and also that even now, in the midst of happy crisis, she was doing her best to make Jolie feel included.

Sharon met them at the front door with a black bathrobe.

"Here you go, sugar. This won't show stains."

"Isn't this Dad's?" Donna asked, pausing to shove her arms into the wide sleeves.

"He never wears it," Sharon told her dismissively, "so don't you worry about it. Where's Marty?"

"Throwing up on the lawn," Vince answered smugly.

Sharon laughed, and to Jolie's surprise, Donna sniffed and a tear rolled down her nose.

"He loves us so much," she said in a happy, shaky voice, rubbing her belly.

"Of course he does," Vince said solicitously, shoving open the screen door. "Here we go."

What would it be like, Jolie wondered enviously, to feel such love?

She stuck to Donna's side as they again negotiated a doorway.

It was chilly in the shade of the porch, but the sun shone brightly overhead despite the clouds scudding along pushed by a brisk wind. An ashen Marty wore a jacket draped about his shoulders, and Sharon's husband Wally was busily dispensing coats to everyone else.

"Over here," Vince called, holding out one hand. "The corduroy and the denim."

"And the fur," Sharon added, striding forward to receive all three coats. She draped the bronze-colored faux fur around Donna, did the same for Jolie with the ivory corduroy walking coat and tossed Vince his denim jacket as they drew up at the car. Larry was waiting with the rear door open and the motor running.

"Marty, you go around," Donna said, presenting her cheek for her father's kiss. "Vince is going to drive, Daddy."

"Whatever you want, doll." He went around her and got in on the passenger side.

Donna ducked down and carefully edged into the car, the seat of which was lined with towels.

"We're right behind you," Sharon promised, moving toward another vehicle.

Jolie hung back hesitantly, until Vince placed a hand at the nape of her neck. She looked up at him, and he dropped a smile on her, saying, "Let's go, sweetheart. Hurry."

Sweetheart. Once or twice he'd called her honey or hon, but sweetheart seemed so...so...*romantic*.

Gulping, Jolie slid in next to Donna, who immediately gripped her hand again, despite the supporting arm that Marty had wrapped around her shoulders. Vince quickly swung down behind the steering wheel, reaching for his safety belt.

"Okay, let's get this show on the road."

"Owww," Donna moaned as the car backed out of the drive.

"Isn't this happening too fast?" Marty asked Jolie worriedly. Before she could formulate an answer for that, Larry reached into the back seat and covered Donna's and Jolie's linked hands and began praying aloud for a safe delivery and a healthy mother and child.

The other family members echoed his "Amen." Then Donna gasped and dropped her head onto her husband's shoulder.

"Let's move it!" Martin ordered, suddenly taking charge. Vince flicked on the hazard lights, pressed down on the horn and gunned the engine through a yellow light at the corner.

Donna was going through her mental checklist again by the time they pulled up under the canopy at the hospital. It seemed to help her keep the pain at bay.

"Suitcase in the closet. List on the bedside table. Oh, and the vent in the baby's room should be opened. We want the nursery nice and warm when we get home."

"I'll take care of it," Marty promised, bailing out, but as he disappeared into the hospital, Donna turned to Jolie.

"Tell Sharon. She'll see it gets done."

"Sharon," Jolie promised. "A-and Vince is to call."

Marty reappeared with a nurse pushing a wheelchair. Larry got out and hurried around to the door that Marty had left open. Donna scooted forward, pausing long enough to pat her brother on the shoulder.

"Getting off easy, buddy, with all the family in one place."

"Yeah, considerate of you," Vince cracked, glancing into the rearview mirror. "Take care of yourself, sugar," he added as Donna slid awkwardly out of the car. "See you soon."

"Fifth floor," Marty informed them, closing the door as his wife settled into the wheelchair. Vince sighed and readjusted his mirror to meet Jolie's gaze.

"Never a dull moment," he quipped, and started the car forward again.

That, thought Jolie, was as gross an understatement as she'd ever heard. How very blessed the Cutlers were!

Chapter Ten

Vince found an empty spot and parked. His family members were already piling out of vehicles in other places as he opened the back door of the sedan for Jolie. She took his hand as she rose to her feet.

"Are you sure I should be here?" she asked uncertainly, eyeing the horde of Cutlers swarming toward the hospital.

He looked down at her, brushed a strand of hair from her cheek and clasped her hand tightly in his.

"Yeah," he said. "Yeah, you should."

Suddenly, Jolie knew that there was no other place in the world where she would rather be. Perhaps it was odd, but she felt welcome. The Cutlers had a way of doing that. They were probably like that with everyone, though, not just her. Still, she felt special, included.

"Why would you think you shouldn't be here with the rest of us?" Vince asked.

Jolie shrugged. "It just seems odd." A heartbeat later she softly and unexpectedly added, "I wasn't there when Russell was born."

Out of the blue, longing stabbed her, so sharp that it felt like a knife between her ribs. One moment she was fine, and the next she'd have given her last breath to see Russ. And Connie, Marcus, all of them. How she missed them!

Despite all that had happened, she missed her brother and sister. How weird was that?

Vince slipped his arm around her and turned her to follow the others at a rather sedate pace, telling her, "You were there when it counted most."

"I guess so," she murmured uncertainly.

"You did a good thing with your nephew, Jolie," he told her firmly, "and I'm sorry you got hurt because of it, but it grieves me that you aren't at peace with your family. Won't you consider seeing them, trying again?"

Her heart swelled painfully at his gentle words, but then it contracted with fear.

"I'd just be letting myself in for more heartache," she said tremulously.

Vince dropped his arm and strolled at her side, silent for the moment.

"It's a risk, I admit, but isn't the possibility of mending the rift worth it?"

He couldn't understand how it would be, how it had always been for her and her brother and sister.

"Vince, you have a big, wonderful family. You can't know how much I envy you. But the Wheelers aren't like the Cutlers. Our parents were never there for us, and we kids haven't really been close since Child Welfare split us up."

"What about before that?"

"Before that," she echoed, remembering with sudden clarity.

She didn't even realize that she'd come to a halt as the images and sensations flowed over her.

Connie had been little more than a baby with her pale, wispy locks and frequently trembling chin. Jolie remembered the urgent strength in her thin, ropy arms as they'd banded about her, seeking solace and reassurance. Only two years older, in many ways Jolie had felt responsible for her sister. Unfortunately as Connie had grown and matured into a very beautiful girl, she had continually reminded Jolie that she was not *that* much older, the implication being that she was not that much wiser and shouldn't give advice.

Marcus had been an avenging angel during their childhood. How fierce he had been! When the other kids had made fun of their mismatched clothing and perpetually runny noses, he had lifted his chin and pressed back his shoulders and stared them down with fists clenched. Every time their mother disappeared he'd solemnly taken over the task of caring for his sisters, and Jolie had believed that he could do no wrong.

With adulthood, his thick hair had warmed to a light, toasty brown which just missed blond. His solemn green eyes no longer seemed overly large for his face, a face that had been too thin and rawboned for a boy. He had changed in other ways, too. He was calmer, more confident. How calmly he had stated his case against her and devastated her world!

In retrospect, she realized that it wasn't the first time. Their world had come apart the day that Marcus had gone next door to beg food from the neighbors. With the gas cut off and no groceries, they'd had to

force down macaroni without cooking it. The bread
had been growing blue stuff, but they'd eaten it anyway. Finally, all they'd had left was a mushy piece of
tomato. Marcus had said what they'd all known, that
their mother was not coming back, but Jolie couldn't
believe it when he'd said that he couldn't take care of
them anymore.

Rage swamped her all over again at the memory
of it.

Strong, hard hands closed around her upper arms.
"You're trembling."

Jolie shook off the difficult memories, saying automatically, "It seems to have gotten cooler."

"Let's get inside." He linked his fingers with hers
and tugged her toward the brown brick building.

"Are you sure I won't be in the way?" she asked
again, dragging her feet.

Surely she didn't belong with these nice, normal
people.

"Hey, what's one more when it comes to the Cutlers?" Vince replied teasingly.

"Remind me to ask the nurses that," Jolie retorted,
giving back as good as she got and falling into step
beside him.

Vincent grinned. "They're probably shuddering
to see us coming. It's not the first time this has happened, you understand."

"Obviously."

"And it won't be the last," he added, squeezing her
hand.

Jolie's heart fluttered, and she dared not even wonder why. All she knew was that she'd somehow gotten
swept up in the Cutler universe and, oddly enough,

that she liked it. She didn't know how that had happened, but she did know that it couldn't last.

Nothing good ever did, not for her. But at least she was a small part of something normal and happy now. She supposed that was as good as it was going to get.

"Oh, man, look at that, will you?"

Vince pressed his palms against the glass partition between the waiting area and the nursery. His newest nephew lay screaming, tiny limbs flailing beneath the taut blue blanket, his face a jowly mask of pasty red flesh below a tiny, white knit cap.

Beside him, Jolie stood very still, her hands splayed against the glass partition. Vince could feel the ache in her. He knew that she was remembering her nephew as a newborn, and his heart went out to her.

She cleared her throat and commented in a voice that was almost normal, "Your dad says they're going to name him Anthony."

"Anthony Martin," Marty confirmed proudly, coming through the door that he'd been popping in and out of for almost five hours now. He hadn't stopped beaming since he'd first given them the news.

"How's the new mama doing?" Larry wanted to know.

"Mad as hops," Marty announced happily. "Doc's told her that she has to stay flat on her back for several hours when she wants to be up rocking the little squaller in there. Ovida's making sure she stays put for now."

"She'll be praying for somebody to keep her down this time next week," Olivia observed dryly.

"Hopefully it won't be too bad," Marty said, "My

folks are on their way from Tulsa, and Mom's planning to stay a couple of weeks. You know how first-time grandparents are."

"God bless them," Sharon said with a nod, and that started a mild squabble about how she, as the oldest daughter, had gotten the lion's share of attention and assistance after giving birth to the firstborn grandchild on *both* sides of her family. In the midst of it, a nurse pecked on the nursery window.

"They're going to let me take him in to her again now that they've got him all cleaned up and charted," Marty said, disappearing once more through the door.

"That'll make mama happy," someone said.

A general silence descended. Then Drew suddenly asked, "Has anybody thought about the game?"

That brought several exclamations from around the room. Vince's was among them.

"Hey, that's right. It's just ten days away. Will Donna be able to go, do you think?"

"I wouldn't count on it," Helen answered.

"Doubtful, very doubtful," Olivia confirmed.

"Even if baby Tony had come on time, she was cutting it close," Sharon pointed out. "She told me that if she couldn't go they were planning to give her ticket away."

"Maybe Marty will take his dad in her place," someone said.

"He's declined in the past," Drew noted. "I think the only sport he cares for is golf."

"Well, Larry, looks like you'll get to be one of the sibs this year," Wally said, but the family patriarch shook his head.

"Naw, naw, that's a deal for the younger generation. I'll stay home with Mom as usual. Y'all take Jolie there. She's a football afficionado."

All eyes, save those of the children who were standing with their noses pressed to the nursery glass, turned to Vince and Jolie. It hadn't occurred to Vince even to mention this Cutler family tradition to Jolie, but the opportunity to include her suddenly seemed golden, for more reasons than one.

"What do you say, Jolie? Want to see a pro football game?"

"You're kidding."

He shook his head. "Not at all. We've been attending the first local game after Thanksgiving for years. Used to be just us guys, but gradually the girls got in on it, too."

She looked thunderstruck. "You're serious? A live pro game?"

"We buy the tickets at the beginning of every season," he confirmed. He was sure that Marty would be glad to let him take this year's extra off his hands.

"You're going to love it," Drew assured her, leaning back as best he could in his stiff, shallow chair.

Vince could tell from the look in Jolie's eye that she was afraid to get her hopes up.

"Don't worry," he said. "It's a week from this coming Sunday."

Her eyes brightened. A weeknight would have been problematic, but she didn't work on Mondays, at least not at her regular job. He could guarantee that her other "boss" would understand and be extremely flexible about starting times.

"Thing is," he went on mildly, "there are strings attached. The deal includes church."

"Church," she echoed uncertainly.

"Yeah, see, the timing's a little sticky so we'll all be attending early service together and leaving straight from there."

She nodded, biting her lip. "Uh-huh. Are you sure they haven't made other plans for the ticket?"

"No, I don't think so," Sharon said.

"I think Donna was holding out in hopes of making it herself," Helen said with a glance at her sister.

Sharon shrugged. "Maybe so."

"What do you say?" Vince asked Jolie. "Want to go?"

She took a deep breath—and smiled. "Sure! I'd love to go."

"Excellent."

Vince clapped his hands together and breathed a silent sigh of relief. He'd tried to get her to go to church before, but she'd resisted for one reason or another. He had sensed her ambivalence, even anger, though he doubted she would admit to it, and he could understand to a certain extent, since her brother was a minister. She had reason to be hurt, and he knew that the anger she was feeling directly resulted from her pain and loss. Unfortunately, he suspected that until she released the anger, the pain of her loss would not release her, and it seemed to him that the way to do that was to get her back into church. At least he hoped so.

Lord, let this be a first step in that direction, he silently prayed, even as the conversation continued.

"Wear flat shoes," Sharon warned her.

"And bring some warm pants," Helen added. "I always wear two pieces, like a sweater and a skirt. Then

I just slip my pants on in the ladies' room after church, tuck the skirt into a bag, and I'm good."

"And don't forget your coat and scarf," Olivia warned. "The seats are about halfway up in the stadium, and it can get real chilly."

"Especially if the weather turns," Wally said, prompting a discussion about the year an errant wind had driven sleet through the hole in the roof of the stadium right into their faces.

The air was thick with jolly reminiscence by the time his mom stuck her head through that door and waved at his dad.

"Grandpa, get in here."

"About time," he exclaimed, getting to his feet.

"Wally and Sharon, you're next."

"I want to go!" Bets pleaded as Larry moved swiftly past her. "I want to hold the baby."

"Not today," Helen said flatly.

"Please, please, *pleeease*."

"She can go in my place," John said, and that set up a wail from the other kids.

"Brenda can go in for me," Wally announced.

"Just let the girls go," Drew proposed.

"No way," Vince said. "I'm going in."

"What about you, Jolie?" Sharon asked. "You ought to get to go in."

Feeling her immediate withdrawal, Vince piped up again. "She'll stick with me."

"Oh, no, that's all right," she began, but he sensed that this was something she needed to do, whether she realized it or not.

Seizing her hand, he bent his head close to hers.

"Donna will expect it. You don't mind, do you?"

She gulped, and he prodded a little harder, keeping his voice low.

"I know it's difficult, but it would be a shame not to see this thing through to the end. Come on. He's just a little baby."

Finally she drew a deep breath and nodded uncertainly.

"That's my girl," he crooned, sliding an arm around her.

He realized as he said it that it was true, at least he'd like to make it true. Against all odds, Jolie Wheeler had somehow carved out a niche for herself in his life. She'd lodged herself in his heart, and he instinctively wanted to keep her there. Whether he could or not remained to be seen. Vince knew himself to be an all-or-nothing kind of guy, and he understood that the make-it-or-break-it point of any new relationship could be just around the bend, but there was no turning back now, not for him.

He draped his arm casually around her neck and drew her closer. It was something he might have done with his sisters, and she seemed to take it that way, but he let himself imagine what it could be like if she was his girl. Full of hope, he listened to his family's banter and held Jolie at his side where, God willing, he meant to keep her.

It was, no doubt, a mistake to hold little Anthony Martin, but when Ovida matter-of-factly dumped the impatiently fussing little guy into her arms, the weight of him felt so right cradled against her chest that Jolie hadn't possessed the strength to immediately pass him on. She thought of Russell and his sweet, placid nature. How frightened she had been when he'd first been placed in her arms. Then she had looked into his blinking, unfocused eyes and fallen head over heels in love. She would never feel that again, never hold a child of her own. How could she when she was obviously meant to live her life alone?

They were a touchy-feely lot, the Cutlers, always hugging and kissing each other's cheeks, patting and holding hands, so she wasn't particularly surprised when Vince stepped up behind her and casually surrounded both her and the baby in a loose embrace. Looking over her shoulder, he cooed to the baby, who blinked his big, navy-blue eyes and stopped mewling long enough to listen to a voice other than his own.

Suddenly what she would be missing hit Jolie with the impact of a bullet fired at close range. She felt as if she was bleeding from the heart. It wasn't just Russell whom she was missing. It was all those children she would never have.

Unless…

She turned away from the temptation of that thought and gave up the baby to one of his aunts. When Vince patted her shoulder, she knew that he understood at least some of what she was feeling.

Somehow that made it even worse.

Friendship was one thing; a future was something else again. She must not let herself believe that she could have the kind of future for which Vincent Cutler was obviously destined. She was not meant for that kind of life; nothing in her experience had prepared her for it.

Sidestepping, she put her back to the wall as if making room in the crowded hospital suite. Vince folded his arms.

When Donna declared that she was too exhausted for company and that they all needed to get out so she and little Tony could rest, Jolie was secretly relieved. If she could have found a polite, subtle way of doing it, she'd have gone home, but when she hinted to Vince that she, too, was tired, he insisted that she couldn't skip the Thanksgiving meal even if it had been delayed.

They convoyed to the Cutler home, and everybody pitched in to reheat the food and get it on the table. The family seemed determined to make a great celebration, even without Donna, but Jolie's heart was no longer in it.

Marty stayed only long enough to gulp down a plate of food, and Jolie toyed with the idea of asking him to drop her off on his way back to the hospital, but his eagerness to return to his wife's side would not allow her to impose. Besides, she felt duty-bound to help with the clean-up.

Finally, Vince drove her home. When he casually inquired if she had plans for the weekend, she felt a spurt of annoyance. All she wanted at the moment was to be alone with her misery.

"What weekend?" she retorted, implying that she'd be working Friday and Saturday as usual. "If you mean Sunday, I intend to do nothing at all."

The truth was that Geopp had elected to shut down the business for a couple of days so he could visit with relatives in Louisiana. Ever since she'd learned of this unexpected holiday, she'd been wondering what she was going to do with herself. Now she only wanted to lock herself away until her defenses were shored up again.

One corner of Vince's mouth crooked upward in what could have been a grimace or a grin, but he said nothing more on the subject.

Relieved, Jolie told herself that she needed the time to rest. She felt emotionally and mentally drained. Indeed, by the time she climbed the stairs to the landing, she was practically asleep on her feet. She fell into bed and dreamed of infants wailing forlornly as she tore through hospital corridors searching for something she could never find.

She woke in the morning to despair. Her thoughts turned immediately to Russell and to Donna and baby Anthony. And to Connie and Marcus. And to Vince. And to everything else she had spent her life wanting and could never have.

Chapter Eleven

When the telephone rang on Saturday afternoon, Jolie's first thought was that it was Vince, but the caller ID revealed that the call originated from her brother Marcus's number. After a surprising moment of agonizing indecision, she let the machine get it and then erased the message without listening to it and turned off the telephone.

Why not? She had no more business talking to Vince than to her brother or sister. There was not a single person in the world that she must talk to, and it was better that way. A solitary life was safest, simplest, easiest. She didn't have to get her heart broken repeatedly to learn that lesson.

By Monday morning, she'd convinced herself that she wanted no deeper involvement with Vince Cutler than a casual friendship, which was as it should be. They had made a business deal that was mutually beneficial, and as honest people of good will, they had formed a friendly working relationship, nothing more. The dinner invitations with his family and the upcoming football game were incidental offshoots of their business relationship, and it would be beyond foolish to seek anything more. She resolved to keep her distance.

It should have been easy.

When she arrived at his house for work, he was dressed and ready to go out. That was fine by her. In fact, it was preferable to having him underfoot all day.

"I see you're ready to leave," she said airily, moving toward the kitchen and the laundry room beyond.

"Not me," he said, snagging her hand and drawing her to a halt. "We. Or have you forgotten about the drapes?"

She had. She'd forgotten everything after the events of Thanksgiving, everything but the laundry waiting for her. "I have work to do now."

"You sure do," he agreed, towing her toward the garage.

She dug in her heels. "First things first. Let me get the laundry done, then if there's time—"

"We'll make time," he insisted, bringing his hands to his hips. "The laundry can wait a little while. I'll help you with it later."

"It's *my* job," she reminded him sharply. "I'll do it."

He tilted his head, studying her. "Fine. Then you'll do it *later.*"

Jolie set her back teeth, gritting out, "You're the boss," as she swept past him. What he said under his breath she didn't catch, mostly because she didn't want to.

"You going to glower at me all day?" he asked, following her into the house after another unsuccessful shopping trip.

"I'm not glowering at you," she snapped. "I'm frustrated. Doesn't this town have a reasonable drapery supplier hidden away somewhere?"

"I don't think it's the store owners who are being unreasonable," he muttered.

She rounded on him. "That's a hateful thing to say! I'm only looking out for your best interests! You may like being cheated and ripped off. I don't!"

Irritation flared. "Face it, Jolie," he told her flatly. "The drapes are going to cost what they're going to cost. We've been to every shop in town. Pick one, and let's get this thing underway."

"You pick one!" she shot back. "It's your house." With that she whirled and flounced down the hallway to the laundry room.

He let her go, not trusting his own temper at the moment, and trudged into the kitchen. His intuition told him that something more than the obvious was going on here. She'd been stiff-arming him all day. Why didn't she just set up barricades and tattoo Do Not Touch on her forehead? So much for taking the next step toward a real relationship.

Rubbing his own forehead with the heel of his hand, he leaned against the counter and told himself that he shouldn't have backed off after Thanksgiving. At the time he'd thought he was giving her room to decompress after all the excitement of the baby coming early and the family reaction to it. On a normal day the Cutler crew could overwhelm a person, even him! A self-contained soul like Jolie didn't stand a chance. Obviously she'd used the weekend to reinforce that protective shell she'd built around herself. Now he'd have to chip another hole in it.

He bowed his head and asked God to show him what to say and how to say it. The answer was quick in coming. With a sigh, he turned and ambled into the laundry room. She was stuffing a load into the washer as if it was trying to escape.

"I'm sorry," he said to her back.

She froze for a moment, poked a few stray ends and bits into the tub and slowly shifted around to face him.

"I know you're doing your best for me," he went on, "and I know that it goes against your grain to pay more for something than you feel you should. I'm sorry I let my impatience get the better of me."

She gulped and turned her back on him again, busily dumping detergent into the washer and twisting dials.

"It's not your fault," she finally said without turning around. "I'm in a lousy mood. But you're right, I don't like paying more than I think I should. I don't like for *you* to pay more than I think you should, either. And don't bother saying that you can afford it. That's beside the point."

"Is that really what this is about?" he asked cautiously.

She turned, shrugged and leaned back against the washer, arms akimbo as she braced her hands on her hips. "What else?"

He let the possibilities percolate for a minute. "You get another letter from your sister?"

She immediately got busy cleaning out the lint trap in the dryer. "Nope."

He wasn't fooled. "Your brother?"

"No." But she hesitated first.

"One of them call or come by?"

She balled the lint into her fist, closed the dryer door and walked over to the trash can. "He might have called."

"Might have?" Vince echoed.

She dropped the ball of lint into the trash and then watched it lie there. "I saw his number on the caller ID."

"But you didn't talk to him."

He hadn't meant it to sound accusatory, but she evidently took it that way. After slitting a quick glance at him from the corner of her eye, she pinched the bridge of her nose.

"Look," he said, "I'm not spoiling for a fight. I understand the situation with your brother and sister. I'm just wondering what this mood of yours is really about."

"What mood? I don't know what you're talking about."

"I think you do. I think you know I like you. A lot."

She shot him a quick, sharp look, too quick for him to tell if it was astonishment or dismay.

"Well, I—I should hope so."

"And I think you like me, too," he forged on.

"Of course." She said it lightly.

He wasn't fooled. "I think you like me a lot," he went on doggedly, "a lot more than you want to."

She turned to face him again. "That's ridiculous."

He had her now. "Oh, good." He rocked back on his heels. "Then there's no reason you won't go to dinner with me Thursday night."

She blinked. "Uh."

"You're not busy Thursday night, are you?"

"Uh."

"Friends do that, you know, have dinner together."

Her lips flattened. "Friends. Right."

"Excellent! I'll pick you up about six-thirty, give you time to change after work."

"We can talk about the drapes," she said emphatically, obviously trying to set boundaries.

"Right," he said, grinning. With that, he walked away and left her to her work.

They could talk about anything they wanted to talk about, anything at all, the weather, the economy, philosophy. They'd talk about whatever pleased her, but they would be talking as more than mere friends this time. Of that he had no doubt.

Jolie feared that he'd drag her off to a showy, upscale restaurant and spent hours trying to figure out what to wear. In the end she chose a pair of black jeans faded to charcoal gray and a simple burnt-orange turtleneck. It wasn't fancy, but it was the best she could do.

Vince showed up in jeans, complimented her looks with a casual comment and took her to a popular chain restaurant serving Mexican food.

After ordering, they talked about what sort of drapes she had in mind for the house and what they were obviously going to cost. Jolie had accepted the fact that the draperies were going to cost more than she'd like. After that, it had been a relatively simple matter to decide which of the custom drapers should get the work. Vince approved her choice and suggested that they make an appointment to revisit the shop on Monday. Jolie agreed, and he said he'd take care of it.

When the food came, he prayed over it as usual, but

this time he took her hand before he did so. Jolie felt compelled to bow her head alongside him. She really had nothing against speaking a blessing over her meal, and she could admit privately now that a part of her previous reaction to his habit had been aimed, not at him or the act of praying, but at her brother.

Sometimes it seemed that she could not escape Marcus or reminders of him no matter what she did. She'd see a pair who looked similar in appearance and wonder if they were brother and sister. Even children, who were easier to identify as siblings, caused her a pang because she couldn't help remembering how close she and Marcus and Connie had once been.

It was no different that night. As soon as she lifted her head after the prayer, Jolie came eyeball-to-eyeball with a little girl sitting next to her older brother in a booth across the way. The child smiled, rattling her appetizer plate against the ta-bletop, and the boy calmly dropped more tortilla chips on it without interrupting the parents' conversation. Jolie had to look away.

Only when she pulled her attention back to her own table did she realize that Vince still held her hand in his. He gave her a sympathetic look and squeezed her fingers. Quickly she smoothed her napkin in her lap, requiring both hands to do so. It disturbed her that he seemed able to read her thoughts so easily, but she couldn't deny, even to herself, that his concern left her with a warm feeling.

Despite her best intentions, she found herself relaxing, and that made conversation flow more easily. Soon they were bantering and teasing like…well, like the friends they were. The food disappeared, and the check was settled, and yet they lingered at the table, talking and laughing—until the little girl and her family across the way rose and began to leave the restaurant.

Jolie couldn't help glancing at them one more time, and that prompted Vince to say, "You must miss them. I know I'd sure miss my sisters if something happened to drive a wedge between us."

She didn't pretend to misunderstand.

"I do miss my brother and sister, but this is not some silly childhood argument. Frankly, I've never been so hurt or disappointed in anyone."

He nodded and changed the subject, sort of.

"One day when you have your own children, you can use this to help them value their relationship and get along."

Jolie opened her mouth to say that she would never have children of her own. She'd have to fall in love and get married before that could happen, and she had no intention of letting herself get that close to anyone. Still, she couldn't seem to force out the words. She told herself that it was because he would almost assuredly try to talk her out of her decision to remain alone, but the truth was that saying it aloud felt too much like making it real.

She settled for an inarticulate, "Mmmm," smiled and said, "We probably ought to go and free up the table."

He nodded, rose and held her chair while she slipped out of it. Then he helped her with her coat and escorted her from the building. She tried to re-capture the mood, but she kept thinking of what he'd said about using her experiences as a parenting tool. That made a certain sense—for a person planning to make a family, a person whose experience had taught her that family was not for her.

Before he dropped her off at her apartment building, he reminded her that the football game was coming up on Sunday and that she would need to be ready by eight o'clock in the morning. She assured him that she wouldn't forget, and assured herself that Sunday would be about fun and friendship only.

She awakened early after yet another restless night. Marcus had called the afternoon before and left another message. She'd stood there and listened as he'd spoken to her answering machine, but she hadn't picked up the telephone, telling herself that there was no point in doing so. If she hadn't slept well, she chalked it up to the excitement of attending a pro game.

Never in her wildest dreams had she ever imagined that she would do such a thing, but then much about her life seemed beyond her imagination. That thought preoccupied her throughout the morning, so that when Vince knocked on her door, she was in an agony of indecision, despite having thought she'd resolved the issue of what to wear.

"Does this sweater go with this skirt?" she demanded of him anxiously.

He answered automatically. "Sure."

Irritated and impatient, she stomped a foot, brought her hands to her waist and demanded, "Look at me! I'm trying to figure out what to wear."

He let his gaze wander from her feet upward. By the time it got to her face, he was smiling. "No, I guess the sweater does not go with the skirt, after all."

She threw up her hands and whirled away, snapping, "Why didn't you say so?"

He just chuckled as she hurried into the bathroom to change the sweater for a simple, tailored blouse which would work well with the double-breasted navy wool coat that she'd picked up at the military surplus store.

It was hard to justify spending good money on a fashionable winter coat in Texas, but she did her best to dress up the outfit with a wooly scarf. After stuffing knit gloves into her pockets, she took one last look in the mirror, adjusted the dark-blue knitted headband that she wore to keep her hair out of her face, fluffed her bangs and went out. Vince was standing exactly where she'd left him, his hands in the pockets of his brown corduroy jacket.

"I'm ready."

"You look terrific," he told her. "Stop worrying."

She rolled her eyes. "I'm not worrying, but thank you."

"You're welcome. Shall we?"

He offered her his arm. She linked hers with it and went out to embrace what she hoped would be a red-letter day.

She didn't expect church to be the highlight of the outing. Feeling betrayed, Jolie had stopped going to church when Marcus had first broached the subject of returning Russell to his mother. She'd told herself that if God didn't care enough about her to keep Russell with her where he belonged, then God didn't care whether she was in church or not. Ever since she'd accepted Vince's invitation, however, she'd secretly felt a certain relief.

As it turned out, Vince's church provided an eye-opening experience. For one thing, Vincent Cutler, good as he looked, good as he was, couldn't carry a tune in a bucket. She, however, could.

Jolie had always enjoyed singing along with the radio, and Russell had seemed to like her voice well enough, but she'd learned to love singing hymns at Marcus's small church. Vince's church was quite large, large enough to boast a hundred-voice choir and a state-of-the-art sound system, with a large video screen that showed the words to each song. Given the season, the place was packed, even for the early service, and all those voices lifting heavenward in praise made her feel as if she might float right up to the ceiling.

"We usually sit down there on the right near the front," Helen had whispered before the service had begun. She'd pointed over the balcony rail. "The pastor likes to leave the back seats for visitors. You know, so they don't have to go searching for an empty spot in a strange place. That's him there."

When the hymn-singing portion of the service had concluded, the pastor stepped up to the pulpit, bade the congregation rise for prayer and read off a list of names of those in need. Next he read a list of those with praises. When he mentioned that Donna, Marty and the new baby were home and well, he waved up to the balcony, and quite a number of heads turned to smile and offer silent congratulations to the family. Most of those seemed to take note of Jolie standing beside Vince.

As if in answer to a collective question, Vince took her hand in his, so that they stood side by side, hand in hand, with heads bowed throughout a long but eloquent and obviously heartfelt prayer.

Once they sat down again, a quartet provided special music. Jolie couldn't imagine hearing better vocals. At the end of the selection, the pastor returned to the pulpit and placed his burgundy Bible atop it. After instructing them to turn to the twenty-fifth psalm, he began to read in a strong, dramatic voice.

Jolie hadn't remembered to bring the Bible that Marcus had given her for Christmas some years earlier, but Vince leaned forward slightly and laid his own Bible in her lap, open to the correct passage. He lifted one arm about her shoulders and with the other hand pointed out where they were. She took the Bible into her hands, and her eye picked up on the fourth verse.

"Make me know Thy ways, O Lord. Teach me Thy paths. Lead me in Thy truth and teach me, for Thou art the God of my salvation. For Thee I wait all the day. Remember, O Lord, Thy compassion and Thy loving kindnesses, for they have been from of old. Do not remember the sins of my youth or my transgressions. According to Thy loving kindness remember Thou me, for Thy goodness' sake, O Lord."

The preacher looked up and asked a simple question. "Have you asked God to teach you His ways?"

Jolie felt a thunk, as if something had dropped from her chest into the pit of her belly. She forgot about Vince's arm draped casually about her shoulders and let the preacher's words fill her.

"If not, why not?" he went on. "Our God is the God

of salvation, the God of compassion, a loving, kind God who forgets, just wipes out, our sins and transgression, all for the asking. 'Well, pastor,' you say, 'if I ask to know God, He's going to expect something of me.' I don't deny it. On the other hand, friend, if you ask to know God, He's going to *make* something of you."

Jolie listened, fascinated, and what the pastor had to say made a lot of sense. This was very different from what she had experienced from time to time as a child, when church had seemed a confusing, often boring, kind of punishment, and from what she'd known at Marcus's church. As his sister, she'd often been more concerned with how others saw and heard him than with the contents of his sermons or how they might apply to her.

She wondered with a pang if she had been unfair to Marcus. He had often urged her to consider the words that he delivered from the pulpit, but she'd had a difficult time doing so. He was her brother, not some oracle from God. She'd been proud of him, but she hadn't wanted to take his sermons seriously. Why not?

The answer came in a blinding flash of insight, and suddenly she found herself caught up in a maelstrom of emotion. Tears welled into her eyes, and even as she listened to the pastor with suddenly sharp ears, she came to a clear and abrupt understanding of herself. She hadn't listened to Marcus because she'd already been angry with him.

"Some of you don't want to know God," the preacher was saying, "because you don't want to know yourselves. You want to maintain your illusions. You think you've got the world and yourselves figured out.

Knowing the Maker of both would just confuse things, throw your little make-believe world into a tailspin. Well, make-believe is a prison, ladies and gentlemen. Always remember that the truth is what sets us free."

The truth was that even before Marcus had sided with their sister and taken Russell from her, Jolie had been angry with him. Deep down, she'd been angry with him for years. Ever since the day Child Welfare had arrived to cart them off to foster care, she and Connie to one home, Marcus to another, Jolie had been bitterly angry with her brother.

He had gone to the neighbors. He had abdicated his place as their protector and caretaker. Her heroic, solemn, big brother had turned out to be only a boy, after all. The protracted absence of their mother had given him no choice, really, but at the time it had seemed to Jolie to be the ultimate betrayal. She'd known it was unreasonable even then, and perhaps that was why she was only just now facing that anger.

"You push God away," the preacher was saying. "He's reaching out to you, but you keep pushing Him away with your indifference and your defensiveness and your cynicism and your wrath. This world isn't perfect, so you label God a tyrant, unfair, uncaring. 'What's He ever done for me?' you say. It's a very long list, but I'm going to give you a one-word answer that says it all. Jesus."

Jolie shuddered with something she couldn't describe, not an emotion really but a knowing, an opening. It left her feeling shaken and vulnerable, and suddenly she yearned with a startling ferociousness for her brother. She heard his voice inside her head just as she'd heard it on the answering machine the previous day.

"Hello, Jo," he had said, sounding sad and wistful. "Hope you're well. We're all fine. Russ is growing like a weed, really running around the place now. You did good by him, Jo, he's a happy, loving little boy. We were wondering, Connie and I, what your plans are for Christmas. We missed you Thanksgiving, but we prayed that you didn't spend it alone. Every day I pray that you'll pick up the phone and call. Please, Jolie, let's be a family again. Please think about it."

She did think about it. For a moment, she could see and feel it so clearly, how it had been to be a real family. Then she realized that everyone was getting to their feet. They sang another hymn, and she managed to go through the motions, but she was too distracted by thoughts of her brother, sister and nephew to make sense of the words. She felt as if she were reeling, and she reached mechanically for the old pain and resentment, anything to steady herself.

Surely, she told herself petulantly, Russell missed her as much as she missed him. How could Marcus say that he was fine? How could any of them be fine after all that had happened?

And how could they ever be a family again? Too many years and too much hurt had gone by since they had been a real family. Maybe if they hadn't grown up in different foster homes, maybe if Connie hadn't gone to prison, if they hadn't teamed up to take Russell away from her after she'd stepped in to care for him, if her mother had just once thought of her children instead of the latest man to whisper promises in her ear...

"You okay, hon?"

The sound of Vince's voice jolted her. "Huh?" She looked around to find that the building was quickly emptying.

"The girls are going to change for the game. Did you want to go with them?"

"Yes!"

She grabbed her bag and turned to follow Helen along the curving row of seats and out into the crowded aisle, aware of Vince watching her, his hands at his waist. She dared not look back. Everything seemed to have bobbed to the surface, all the hurt and anger and longing that she'd suppressed all these years, and if he saw her face, he would undoubtedly know.

Following along in Helen's wake, Jolie carefully tucked away all her mental and emotional corks, but something told her that it would only be a temporary fix at best.

Chapter Twelve

Inside a stall in a surprisingly opulent ladies' room, Jolie changed into her jeans. The sisters did the same, chattering about Donna's Thanksgiving baby and how little sleep the new mother had gotten since they'd come home from the hospital. Several others had crowded into the small space, and Sharon made a few introductions, but Jolie knew that she'd never remember who was who despite the friendly smiles and speculative looks.

Finally the foursome hurried out to greet the men, throwing on their coats. Sharon and Olivia seemed especially enthusiastic about the game. Helen, who was the quietest of all the sisters, seemed to be missing Donna. She and her husband John automatically fell into step beside Vince and Jolie, who suddenly realized that Marty was missing, too.

"Is Marty meeting us there?" she asked as they pushed out onto the sidewalk.

John shook his head, and Vince said, "Guess he didn't want to leave Donna and the baby. He called this morning and told us to give his ticket away."

"Give it away!"

"Sure, why not?" Vince asked, taking her hand as they crossed the traffic lane and moved toward the parking lot. "If he's not going to use it, somebody else might as well."

"He's not going to try to sell it or anything?"

"Scalping is illegal," John said matter-of-factly.

"Technically," Wally added over his shoulder. "There are ways around that."

"Yeah, and one of them is to give the ticket away," Vince said. "Marty says he has too much to be thankful for to worry about missing a game and losing a few bucks."

"I think it's a nice thing to do," Helen put in. "Why don't we all pitch in and pay him for it, then we'll each have a part of giving it away?"

"That's a good idea," Olivia agreed, turning around to walk backward as they made for her minivan. "If each couple gave just twenty-five dollars, that would leave Marty and Donna with an equal stake. Then we'd all be giving away the ticket."

Everyone agreed to that, everyone but Jolie who stopped dead in her tracks, gaping at the thought of a ticket that cost a hundred and twenty-five bucks! It took everyone a moment to realize that she wasn't with them, then they all stopped and Vince walked back to ask, "What's the matter?"

"Who paid for my ticket?" she wanted to know.

She hadn't really thought about it before. Somehow, though, she'd assumed that the family had bought the tickets together and that they'd cost maybe thirty or forty dollars each, which seemed like a lot to her. Three or four times more seemed outrageous, and she couldn't let Donna and Marty give that kind of money to her!

Vince reached out and fingered the lapels of her coat, stepping close.

"Better face the facts, Wheeler," he told her softly. "I paid for your ticket because you're my date." He stepped closer still, bringing his forehead near hers and staring down into her eyes. "It's better than letting Marty take the hit for two tickets he couldn't use, isn't it?"

His date. A couple. How on earth, she wondered wildly, had this happened? She shook her head, thoroughly confused, but then his face clouded and she found herself nodding. Vigorously. He grinned and grabbed her hand, turning back to the others and dragging her along with him.

"What are you waiting for?" he asked loudly. "We've got a game to go to!"

That seemed to light a fire. Wally pumped his fist, and the whole group piled enthusiastically into the van. Jolie and Vince crammed into the back seat with Helen and John, leaving Sharon and Wally to the shorter middle one and Olivia and Drew to the front buckets. Vince sat on the outside edge, crossing his legs and extending his feet out into the space between the shorter middle seat and the van's sliding side door.

On their way to the stadium and while inching forward into the parking lot, they talked enthusiastically, the men dissecting the opposition, the women anticipating the food and the people. Sharon and Helen entertained Jolie with stories about fan hijinks, and it became clear to her that they watched the crowd more than the players. They all talked over one another, joking and laughing and generally just having a good time.

That laid the pattern for the remainder of the day. After hiking in from the "back forty" as Drew called the parking area to which their seats entitled them, they gave Marty's ticket to a grateful young couple who traded the seat in for a cheaper one and used the difference to pay for a second. After making their way to the seats, the women shed their coats and handbags and announced that they were going for food. Vince crammed bills into Jolie's hand and asked for nachos, sausages (plural), a burrito, a large soda and a dill pickle, adding that she should get herself anything she wanted.

She looked at the money in her hand and wondered if he expected her to order filet mignons, then she got a look at the actual prices and wondered who in his right mind would spend that kind of money for junk food! The Cutlers apparently, because the sisters loaded up, teasing one another about wearing the goodies on their hips as they made their way back to their seats.

"Good thing we only do this once a year," Helen remarked.

"Speak for yourself," Sharon quipped drolly. "You can look at my fat behind and know this isn't a rarity for me."

Sharon was pleasantly rounded, like her mother, but Jolie didn't think of her as "fat." The other girls, who took after their father, as did Vince, immediately protested the self-description, and by the time they rejoined the men, Sharon was prancing around like a beauty-pageant contestant, dipping and swirling comically.

As soon as the bounty was passed out, the group huddled together for a quick prayer, then settled into their seats just as the opposing team emerged from the locker room. Jolie had never felt quite so avid. Vince glanced at Jolie's single sausage on a bun and asked if that was all she was going to eat.

"It's not even lunchtime yet," she said.

"But it's game time!" Drew crowed, stuffing a dripping nacho into his mouth.

"Yeah, if you're going to hang out with this crew," Olivia said, leaning forward to peer around Vince, "you're going to have to learn to pig out."

"How else can you date our pig of a brother?" Sharon piped up. Jolie looked down. Was she dating Vince or was it all for show on his part? Just then Vince reached around Jolie to lightly smack his oldest sister in the back of the head just as she was about to bite into her hot dog. The result was chili on her chin and nose and a lot of laughter.

The home team burst onto the field just then, and the crowd rose to its feet, including the Cutler contingent. Vince took a napkin and cleaned Sharon's face for her. She stuck out her tongue at him, then darted around Jolie to kiss him on the cheek. Jolie couldn't help feeling a little envious of the easy, teasing camaraderie that the siblings and their spouses enjoyed.

She would never again have the same with her own brother and sister. *Unless I can somehow forgive,* she caught herself thinking. Immediately, she tried to push that thought away. How did she put away her hurt and anger?

The question stubbornly clung to the back of her mind throughout that long and amazing afternoon.

* * *

Vince slung an arm across Jolie's shoulders companionably as they strode toward his truck in the church parking lot. Behind them, Drew tooted the horn of the minivan as it turned onto the street. Lifting his free arm high in farewell, Vince gave in to the impulse to pull Jolie a little closer.

"So what do you think?"

"About the game?" she asked, smiling.

"The game, the crazy Cutlers…the service this morning."

"It was great, all of it," she replied sincerely.

Vince smiled. "So, what was your favorite part?"

She shook her head. "This whole day has been… words fail me."

She'd laughed with the rest of them all afternoon, and she'd really gotten into the game, making some astute judgment calls about various plays and rulings. She'd even loosened up enough to splurge on fajitas. Still, throughout the day he'd sensed that she was experiencing some sort of emotional turmoil. It could have been his imagination, of course, but he decided to go with his gut feeling.

"Want to talk about it?" he asked gently as they drew near his vehicle.

She stiffened, but her reply was flippant. "Sure. Let's see." She struck a pose, one arm folded across her body, one finger tapping her chin, as he fished out his keys and unlocked the passenger door. "We should not have lost that game," she concluded, climbing up into the seat.

Vince chuckled. He'd given her the perfect out. Next time he'd choose his words a little more carefully. After walking around the truck, he inserted himself behind the steering wheel, unsurprised when she took up right where she'd left off, rattling on and on about the game.

"The team's just too young, you know. Can't take the pressure."

Vince nodded agreement. Really, he couldn't quibble with her assessment, but that wasn't why he let her get away with dissecting the game play by pivotal play as he drove her home.

At one point he interrupted long enough to ask, "How'd you get so into football, anyway?"

"What else is there to do during football season? I mean, that's all that's on television Sunday afternoons and Monday nights."

"Which just happen to be your two days off from your regular job." And of course, she would not have cable, he added mentally, making her pretty much a captive audience of whatever stations she could pick up with a pair of rabbit ears.

"There you go," she confirmed matter-of-factly.

He smiled, thinking that he had unintentionally benefited from her straitened circumstances, while she launched into a story about Sharon's hips or some such thing. He wasn't really paying attention any longer. Instead, he was weighing the advisability of pressing her to reveal what was actually going on inside that pretty head of hers.

By the time they reached the apartment building, he'd concluded that no good cause would be served by letting the matter go. Sooner or later, she would have to deal with some of her issues—or he was going to have to reconcile himself to simple friendship with her, something he didn't want to contemplate. He sent up a silent prayer and shut off the engine.

"Can I come up? We need to talk."

She blinked at him, frowning slightly. "Sure."

Smiling to let her know that this didn't have to be a frightening conversation, he let himself out of the truck. She was already doing the same, so he waited for her to join him. Side by side, they headed for the stairs.

As they entered the apartment, she flipped on the lights and asked if he wanted something to drink, but he groaned at the very thought.

"I am stuffed. I won't have to eat or drink for at least two days."

She arched a censorial eyebrow, announcing airily, "I am not surprised."

Laughing, he said, "Come on, let's sit down."

He lifted a hand, but instead of putting hers in it, she turned toward the sofa and dropped down onto one end of it.

"What's wrong?"

He sat down next to her and calmly replied, "That's what I want to know."

She shook her head, gaze skittering away. "Not following."

Carefully considering his words, he folded his hands.

"There were moments today when you were somewhere else entirely, and I don't think it was a happy place."

She sighed and rubbed her hand through her bangs, muttering, "Nothing gets by you, does it?"

"Couldn't say. All I know is that I like to keep it

real, especially between us, and when something's
bothering you, well, seems that it bothers me, too."
Surprisingly, tears sprang into her eyes, and without
even thinking, he slid close and drew her into the circle of his arms. "Hey, now, it wasn't my intention to
upset you."

She gave him a watery snort, insisting, "I'm not
upset, I'm…confused."

"What about?"

She bowed her head, and for a moment they simply
sat together. Finally, she spoke.

"It's almost too much, you and your family, me and
my family, what the preacher said today."

He lifted his arms from about her and locked his
hands, meshing his fingers.

"Let's start at the end and work backward. What
exactly did the pastor say that's got you thinking?"

She spoke hesitantly at first and then with growing
agitation. Who could really know God? Why would He
forget the bad things we do? Vince answered her patiently and in some detail. Knowing God, he told her,
was a lifelong process. One had to believe, of course,
and then ask and keep on asking to know God's will.
Most importantly, one had to pay careful attention to
God's replies.

"As for forgetting our transgressions," he explained,
"it pleases God to forget how those whom He loves
hurt Him. Again, all that is ever necessary is that we
ask for His forgiveness, and afterward He wipes out
our sins as if they never existed."

Jolie admitted that she just didn't understand how
that could be.

"Don't make the mistake of saddling God with our

human weaknesses," he told her. "And understand now that His strength is also ours for the asking."

"But why?" she demanded.

He considered for a moment.

"Let me ask you a question. Don't you want to forget the pain?" Her eyes widened. "Our sin pains God, but He loves us, so why would He want to remember our sin?" Vince went on. "God *chooses* to forget, but before forgetting must come forgiveness. If you want to forget your pain, Jolie," Vince said, "first you have to forgive."

Her brow wrinkled, and she whispered, "I'm not sure I can. If it was rational, maybe, but…"

"If what was rational?" he asked. When she hesitated, he urged, "Tell me."

To his gratification, she trusted him with the story of her childhood, with the anger she had discovered only that day. Coupled with what she felt was her brother's betrayal in the matter of her nephew, the realization obviously rattled her. He listened until she had talked herself out, sometimes weeping, sometimes bitter, more often just plain hurt and confused. Afterward, they sat quietly, taking comfort in each other's company until the emotional storm had truly calmed and Vince felt that he could broach the last difficult issue.

"You know, this whole tangle might unsnarl itself if you'd just see your brother and sister."

"How can I do that?" she demanded, sitting up straighter. "How can I risk that kind of heartbreak again?"

Vince leaned forward, bracing his elbows on his knees.

"Doesn't it make a difference that you wouldn't be coping with it alone this time?" She blinked at him, and he saw immediately that she was as afraid to trust in that as in anything else. "No, of course, it doesn't," he answered himself.

He sat up again and turned slightly to face her, praying that what he was going to say was the right thing.

"Has it occurred to you that this isn't about you? You're hurt. All right, I understand why that is so, but what if this really is best for your nephew? What if knowing his mother loves him is more important than knowing that you love him? And why shouldn't he have both?"

For a long moment, she stared at him as if he'd sprouted horns. Then she shifted around until their knees touched. "Do you really believe that?"

"I don't know," Vince told her softly, "but I believe that God always has a reason for allowing what goes on in our lives, and it makes sense to me that Russell could only be better off for having a loving relationship with both his mother and his aunt."

"I want to forgive," she said after a moment, "but I don't know how."

Vince smiled and took her hands in his. "It starts with a prayer," he began.

They slipped to their knees, and Jolie poured out her heart, all her hurts and fears and failings. She begged God to help her forgive.

After a long while, they rose

"Thank you," she whispered to Vince, dabbing at her eyes with a tissue pulled from her pocket.

"My pleasure. I hope this means that you're willing to talk to your brother and sister now."

"Forgiving and opening yourself up to more hurt are two different things, Vince," she hedged uncertainly.

"Just think about it," he urged, "and while you're considering it, I'll be praying for you."

She nodded, half smiling. He saw a glimmer of trepidation in her eyes and knew that she had not yet conquered her fears. He understood instinctively that she must, but it was only as he drove himself home a little later that he realized why.

Not only did her happiness depend on it, but theirs together did as well.

And they *could* be happy together.

In fact, Vince was beginning to believe that they *should* be happy together. It seemed to him that God was blatantly leading them in that direction.

At least his heart seemed to think so.

Vince ran a fingertip around the rim of his cup and glanced up just as his father came through the door of the coffee shop. Waving, Vince snagged Larry's attention and sat back into the corner of the booth, one elbow propped atop the edge of the seat back. As he slid onto the bench opposite Vince, Larry turned up his coffee cup and signaled the waitress with a look.

"Cold out there," he commented, rubbing his hands together.

Vince noted that his father's fingers had grown knobby and stiff.

"Arthritis acting up?"

Larry nodded. "Yeah, that twenty-two-degree temperature drop last night kicked it up a notch."

"Well, that's Texas for you."

"You're telling me? I've seen it drop forty degrees in two hours and without a cloud in the sky."

"Blue norther," Vince recollected, but then he changed the subject. "I need your advice."

"Figured something like that," Larry said, pressing back in his seat as the waitress arrived with the coffeepot. She poured the steaming black liquid, ascertained that they didn't want anything else and departed again. "What is it then?" Larry asked, leaning forward to hunker around his cup. "Jolie?"

Vince smiled wryly. "How'd you know?"

"Well, it wouldn't be business. Nothing I can tell you there. And if it was about the family, you'd be talking to your mother. So I figure it's got to be Jolie. You in love with her?"

Vince nodded matter-of-factly. "Yeah. Yeah, I am."

"How come?"

The blunt question momentarily shook Vince, and to his surprise he found himself growing angry.

"How come? What do you mean, how come? What's wrong with her?"

"I didn't say there was anything wrong with her."

"She's a little rough around the edges, okay?" Vince retorted defensively. "Who wouldn't be, given all she's been through. In fact, it's a wonder she's not selling herself on some street corner, but instead she's managed to maintain her dignity. She lives her life with a certain sense of honor, and if that makes her a little standoffish, then who are we to judge?" He pecked himself on the chest. "I've lived a life of pure bliss compared to her, and I know that if our roles were reversed I'd be the worst sort of thug. If you really want to know the truth, she's too good for me!"

Larry sat back with an air of satisfaction.

"Well, that answers that question. Now how about her? Is she in love with you, too?"

Rubbing the back of his neck, Vince ducked his head and admitted, "I don't know. I think she could be if she'd let herself."

"Trust issues," Larry commented mildly, lifting his cup. "Not surprising."

"Big trust issues," Vince confirmed morosely, "and it's all centered on her family. I know in my gut that if she can't patch it up with them, we can't go forward."

"What are you going to do?"

Vince toyed with the spoon on his saucer. "What would you think about me arranging a surprise meeting with Jolie and her brother and sister?"

Larry kept his eyes averted while he considered, but then he shook his head. "An emotional ambush isn't the answer, even if your motives are good. That would just make her mad at you."

Vince scowled and shoved a hand through his hair. "I wouldn't mind her being mad at me for a while if it patched up her family."

"Except it might not work that way," Larry pointed out, "and forever afterward she'd know that she could count on you to try to handle *her* business *your* way."

Vince grimaced. "I see your point, Dad, but—"

Larry lifted a hand, palm out. "No buts, son. This is where you give your own faith a real workout. God's in charge here. Let's keep it that way. I have an inkling that she'll come around when it's the right time for her to do so. If your patience gets a little test in the meanwhile, well, you must need it."

Vince's mouth crooked into a lopsided smile at the twinkle in his father's eye. "You're right. You're absolutely right. It's just that I feel so strongly that if she can't open herself up to her family again, she'll never be able to open herself completely to me."

Larry nodded sagely, saying, "Then we'll pray that way and trust God to work it out."

"And until He does, I guess I'm cooling my jets," Vince muttered with a resigned sigh.

"I don't see that you have much choice in the matter, son. She's got to resolve these issues before she can be the wife you want and need. That is what we're talking about, isn't it?"

"Yes, and I know you're right, but I'll admit that I was hoping for something else."

"I'll make a covenant with you," Larry said, placing both of his gnarled hands flat on the tabletop. "I'll pray for both of you every day until God works this thing out. In fact, let's start right now. Okay?"

Vince copied his father's posture and bowed his head. While Larry softly prayed aloud, Vince thanked God for the man sitting across from him, for the life he had led, for the wisdom to which he was privy and for not having had the sense to forward his mail.

Chapter Thirteen

Christmas rushed toward them. It spilled out of the shops and onto the sidewalks in sometimes garish displays of tattered decorations and sometimes poignant and surprising beauty. Neither moved Jolie, who had never enjoyed Christmas.

The so-called joy of the season had always eluded her. Oh, once or twice her mother had found a way to provide a modest celebration for her three children, but even the best of those memories were pretty dismal.

Jolie recalled cupcakes with sprinkles, a bitter red punch and a doll with matted hair and gaps in her eyelashes.

Once Marcus had gotten roller skates so old that the leather had been cracked, but he'd skated around their barren little apartment, careening into walls and wobbly furniture, until he'd outgrown the things. He hadn't dared skate outside for fear of the junkies and thugs who would as soon have robbed a child of his battered old skates as shoplift a candy bar.

As for Connie, she had wagged around a huge plastic piggy bank for a couple of years, and for a time

they'd all scavenged coins conscientiously. Unfortunately, their cache had been raided so often that they'd
never been able to fill more than the piggy's plastic
feet.

Usually, their holiday gifts had been nothing more
than cardboard puzzles, cheap boxes of crayons, new
socks or cans of soda, if that. Sometimes the holiday
had passed without anything at all to mark it. Then
at the end, their mother had not even bothered to be
at home.

Christmas with the various foster families had
been more rewarding gift-wise, but Jolie had always
felt like an outsider and a fraud at those celebrations.
The gifts had never felt personal or appropriate, and
she had gone out of her way to destroy more than a
few of them, which she now realized had only served
to make her seem ungrateful and incorrigible, as she
had, in fact, been.

Since she'd reached adulthood, Marcus had routinely invited her to spend the holiday with him and
his foster family, with whom he maintained a close
relationship. Jolie had tagged along with him the year
that she was eighteen, but not since. It hurt too much
to see the easy, affectionate manner with which he and
his foster family dealt with each other.

Marcus had actually found himself in a family
who had truly wanted him, but they obviously hadn't
wanted two mulish little girls to go along with their
five boys, natural, adopted and foster. As Marcus had
explained many times, she and their sister wouldn't
have "fit in." She understood *now* that the house had
been small, and that the boys had slept dormitory-style
in one large bedroom, but she still couldn't escape the

idea that Marcus's foster parents hadn't wanted her. So far as she could tell, *no one* had wanted her or Connie.

Maybe that was why Connie had latched on to Russell's low-life father, and why she, Jolie, couldn't seem to latch on to anyone at all. Until now.

She still couldn't quite fathom how it had happened, but somehow Vincent Cutler had become such a large part of her life that when Marcus called on the Tuesday following the big game to say that he and Connie and Russell would be celebrating the coming holiday at home and would like her to join them, Jolie had used Vince as an excuse.

If she hadn't been expecting Vince to call and if she hadn't had her hands full of ironing, she wouldn't even have answered the phone without checking the caller ID first. As it was, she found herself actually talking to her brother for the first time in months.

"Um, Vince probably has other plans," she said into the phone in instant reply to Marcus's rushed invitation to join him and Connie for the holiday.

It wasn't a lie; she hadn't said that Vince had plans which included *her*, but she realized now that she was hoping he did.

"Vince?" Marcus echoed. "Is that your boyfriend?"

Boyfriend. The word had a dangerous, incredulous ring to it. She took a deep breath.

"Uh, more just friend, really, and sort of my boss. Sort of. Temporarily."

Marcus seemed to brush that off. Even more surprisingly, he seemed genuinely pleased that she might have someone in her life.

"That's great, Jo! Tell me about him."

For one long, troubling moment, Jolie fought the

urge to do just that, but then she reminded herself that she and Marcus weren't really on speaking terms. He had no right to know about her life.

She said flatly, "I don't think so."

"He must be good to you," Marcus surmised correctly, gently probing. "Otherwise, you wouldn't put up with him." His voice softened, lowered, then. "I've always admired that about you, Jo. You know your own worth."

"And what am I worth, Marcus?" she retorted bitterly. "Whatever it is, it doesn't make me good enough to raise a child, does it?"

"Jo, you know that's not true," he said, sounding pained. "Neither Connie or I would ever have placed Russell with you if we weren't absolutely convinced that you would be a great parent."

"Then why take him away?" she wailed.

She could feel her brother's exasperation, but his voice was mild, gentle when he said simply, "She's his mother, Jo."

"I've been more his mother than she's been!"

His voice dropped a chord, as if he didn't want to be overhead on his end.

"He's her only chance, Jo. Can't you see that?"

"He was *my* only chance!" she cried just before she hung up, but even as she said it, some part of her knew that it wasn't necessarily so. At least she was starting to believe that it might not be.

You wouldn't be coping with it alone this time.

The implications of that were breathtaking. She wanted to believe that Vince had been talking about more than friendship, but he hadn't said that. Somehow she'd gotten the feeling that his reticence had to do with her situation with her family, and that felt patently unfair to her.

Couldn't he see how she had been treated? In a very real sense, she had been used by her own brother and sister, used and then discarded.

Well, all right, not quite *discarded*, but the same as. Almost. Except she had been the one to turn her back on them, a little voice reminded her. And why shouldn't she? she countered angrily. After what they'd done, who could blame her? Why should she feel guilty about it?

She did, though. Worse, she couldn't quite deny the subtle yearning that had begun in her when she'd first heard Marcus's voice on the telephone. Yet how could she ever trust her brother and sister again? How could she bear seeing Russell and then letting him go home with them?

Suddenly she wanted two things very, very badly. She wanted to fold little Russ close, even knowing that they would take him away again afterward, and she wanted Vince to do the same with her.

When Vince showed up at the cleaners on Friday, Jolie abandoned the presser to greet him.

"Hey!" She couldn't help smiling because he was smiling, his mouth bracketed with the grooves cut by his dimples.

"Hey yourself." He leaned on the counter to talk to her. "You busy?"

She leaned backward to catch a glimpse of Mr. Geopp, who at the moment was pretending to be deaf, dumb and blind.

"I can take a minute. What's up?"

"Two things. Everybody's going bowling tonight. Want to come?"

She wondered just who "everybody" was, but the words that fell out of her mouth were, "Of course."

Dimples again.

"Excellent."

"But, um, I'm not very good," she put in quickly. "I've only tried a couple times."

"No problem."

"Oh, well, if you're sure."

He reached out and tapped the end of her nose, saying, "Absolutely positive. Now then, question number two." He briefly held up two fingers before tucking his hands into his coat pockets. "Mom wants to know if we can count on you for Christmas."

A tiny thrill mingled with relief shot through Jolie. To cover it, she glanced at the frosted window and the paper snowflakes that Mr. Geopp had taped to it.

She'd once expected to spend the holiday with Russell. Without him the whole Christmas season had seemed like a huge insult, something to be endured. She'd been dreading it more than she could even let herself admit, but since Thanksgiving she supposed that she'd been waiting for Vince to invite her to spend the holiday with him and his family.

He was like a glimmer of light at the end of what felt like a long, dark tunnel. She blinked and let her smile brighten.

"Thanks. I'm not big on Christmas really, but I'll try not to put a damper on the fun."

He chuckled. "Don't count on as much excitement as Thanksgiving. We're not expecting any new little bundles of joy. That I know of."

She laughed. "Just a humdrum Cutler holiday, hmm?"

He scratched an ear, admitting wryly, "I wouldn't count on humdrum, either."

She laughed again. "No? Really?"

He nodded in acknowledgment of the absurdity of a humdrum Cutler gathering of any type.

"The schedule usually goes something like this. Christmas eve supper around six at Mom and Dad's, followed by the reading and then the gift exchange and church at ten."

"The reading?"

"You know, the Christmas story."

"Oh, of course."

"We do it in parts so everyone gets at least one line."

"Ah."

"Anyway," he went on, "Christmas eve is the big do at our house. Mom puts on a lavish buffet for Christmas Day, and people pop in and out all day long, but Christmas eve is reserved for family. The sisters sometimes drop by on Christmas Day and sometimes don't, depending on the families of the son-in-laws. Or is it sons-in-law? I always forget."

"Sons-in-law," Jolie murmured automatically, still wondering about the reading, but it was the gift exchange thing that truly gave her pause. "Listen, Vince, I—I can't really afford…that is, there are so many of you to buy for."

He lifted a placating hand.

"Don't worry. You'd only have to buy one gift, and nobody goes overboard. We draw names because no one can buy for everybody. Mom and Dad always get together a little something for each of the grandkids, but no one else does. We do a little name-drawing ceremony that we jokingly call the family lotto. That'll be this Sunday after church. Or if you want, this year we could keep the gift thing just between the two of us."

This year. Jolie's heart kicked. This year. As if they'd be doing this again next year. As if they might actually have some sort of future together.

"I—I don't mind drawing names," she replied a little breathlessly.

"Does that mean I can count on you for church Sunday?"

She felt an unexpected spurt of eagerness. "Sure. Why not?"

He grinned. "Better and better. I'll tell Mom to expect you for dinner. We'll draw names right after."

"If you're sure it's no trouble."

"You know better than that," he told her cheerfully.

The lovely part was that she really did believe she'd be welcome.

"But, ah, there's just one thing. I-if I get you or one of the other guy's names, you'll have to give me some idea what to buy. I've never…"

"Never bought a guy gift before?"

"Only for my b-brother."

She held her breath, wondering if Vince would bring up the situation with Marcus and Connie again, but he just smiled and rocked back on his heels.

"Good. That's good."

"Is it?"

"Oh, yeah."

She couldn't account for the shyness that slipped over her then. Suddenly she couldn't quite look him in the eye any longer—not with Mr. Geopp just there on the other side of the gliding rack hung with recently cleaned garments arranged in alphabetical order according to the last name of the customer.

"Tell you what," he said, "I'll give it some thought and be prepared to dish out advice after the name-drawing. How's that?"

"That's fine." It came out almost as a croak. She cleared her throat before asking, "What time should I be ready for bowling tonight?"

"Six-thirty too early?"

She shook her head. "Gives me just enough time to get home and change."

"Then I'll pick you up at the apartment at half past six."

"Okay."

"See you then." He gave her a wave and turned to go. She wasn't really ready to let him.

"Vince?"

He swung around, as eager as a puppy.

"Yeah?"

Her heart beat so pronouncedly that it almost strangled her.

"Thank you. For Christmas, I mean."

"You bet."

"And thank your Mom for me, too."

He chuckled. "Okay. See you later."

She nodded, smiling, and he turned with a wink to pull open the door and move swiftly through it.

Jolie watched him stride down the sidewalk and out of sight, his image blurred by the frosting that had been sprayed on the window. Lifting a hand to her chest, she marveled at the way her heart had sped up at the first sight of him.

It was ridiculous, really. Just because he was handsome and kind and caring, that was no reason to overreact. Why, it was almost as if... Surely she wasn't... hadn't...

She sat down hard on the tall, three-legged stool that Mr. Geopp kept behind the counter for when his legs were aching. Her face felt flushed, and her pulse rapped a quick staccato as the truth hit her.

So this was what it felt like to fall in love.

Oh, no. This was awful!

Or so she told herself.

It didn't feel awful, actually.

It felt hopeful, so very hopeful that it was terrifying.

She closed her eyes and thought, *Dear God, oh, please don't let me be like my mother. Please don't let me be like that.*

She could almost understand now why Velma had chased after every man who had come along. She'd been chasing this feeling, this sense of hope in an otherwise hopeless life. But Vince was different from all those losers her mom had hooked up with.

Vince was good, genuinely good.

So what's he doing hanging around with you? asked that pesky little voice she'd been hearing so much from lately.

Panic swept through her. He wouldn't hang around for long. Of course he wouldn't. No one ever did, not her father, not her mother, not Russell, not one of the foster families with whom she'd lived. Why should Vince be any different? Unless...

"Oh, God," she whispered, without even knowing

what she was pleading for, "Oh, God, please." And it came to her then that Vince was in her life because he wanted to be.

She hadn't pursued him, just the opposite. In fact, she'd been downright disagreeable in the beginning. Yet gradually, patiently, he'd made himself a place in her life and in so doing had worked his way into her heart.

Now she could only pray that he didn't break it.

Jolie released the ball and watched it fly down the very center of the lane, gradually straightening as it whirled nearer its target. She was a better bowler than she'd known. Then again, she hadn't had an expert like Vince to show her what she was doing wrong until now.

She backed up a step, afraid to breathe lest it affect the trajectory of the spinning ball. It plowed into the head pin, just slightly to the right of center, and sent every pin but two flying in different directions.

"You can do it," Vince called encouragingly. "It's the same spare as before. Half step to the right. You can do it."

Jolie lifted her ball from the return, scooted right and hefted the ball into place just below chest height. Taking a deep breath, she stepped off, swung her arm back, bent and released.

Once more the ball whirled straight down the alley, this time knocking out the remaining two pins. Jolie leapt straight up into the air, coming down again into Vince's arms as he had rushed forward to congratulate her. They almost toppled onto the floor, but he planted his feet and anchored them both, laughing, before releasing her.

"That's my girl!"

Jolie tried not to read too much into that while the others either applauded or groaned dramatically, depending upon which team they were on. The group consisted of Helen and John, Drew and Olivia, Donna and Martin and Vince's friend and employee Boyd and his wife, Sissy.

Neither Donna nor Helen were bowling, Donna because it was still too soon after the baby and Helen because she seemed to want to keep her sister company.

Sissy had immediately latched on to Jolie, and Jolie found that she quite liked the extremely tall, rather plain woman. Sissy was slender to the point of emaciation, though she ate like a stevedore, and had lank, dark-blond hair that hung to the bottoms of her ears on the sides and was spiked rather unflatteringly on top.

"Thyroid condition," she'd announced cheerfully as she'd consumed her second order of onion rings, having already downed a double-meat burger and a large soda.

Sissy sauntered up to bump hips and elbows with Jolie in a goofy kind of congratulatory dance, seeing as they were on the same team with Vince and Boyd. Her hip bones were like blades.

"Trust Vince to come up with the only true sportswoman in the bunch," Marty groused good-naturedly.

Sissy took issue, planting her bony hands on her bony hips. "Hey! I'll have you know that I played varsity volleyball all through high school and college."

"Now if only she could bowl," Boyd cracked with a straight-faced sigh.

"Her score's better than mine," Jolie pointed out as Sissy glowered.

Suddenly Boyd grinned and pulled his wife down onto his lap.

"I know. I just like to see her bristle."

Her long, skinny arm wound around his neck as she giggled and kicked her feet. The two were obviously mad about each other. It gave Jolie a warm, cozy feeling, especially when she felt Vince's hand slide possessively into the dip of her waist.

"Want a cola?" he asked softly.

She shook her head and leaned into him a little. Just having him close was reward enough for that spare or any other achievement she could dream up, for that matter.

He gave her a smile and asked loudly, "Whose turn is it?"

"Does it matter?" John replied drolly, getting to his feet.

"Only to the winners," Vince retorted goodnaturedly.

Actually they were behind by three pins, but nobody seemed to be paying much attention to the score. It wasn't about competition. It was about fun and fellowship.

The "midnight" leagues actually started at ten o'clock, so they were out of there by nine-forty-five. Their team had lost by six pins, but the others magnanimously refrained from rubbing it in.

Marty and Donna hurried away, saying that it was time to feed the baby. Donna gave Jolie an absent-minded peck on the cheek before making for the parking lot. Helen did the same, then hurried back to ask

Jolie if she wanted to join the sisters for a Christmas shopping junket the next day.

"Oh, I have to work on Saturday."

"Rats," Helen said. "Well, maybe another day."

"Monday afternoons are about the only time I have," Jolie began.

"Excellent!" Helen said, "the stores won't be so crowded and we'll know whose names we've drawn by then."

"Oh, I didn't mean…that is, I'll be working at Vince's on Monday afternoon," Jolie went on apologetically. "We haven't quite finished the house."

Helen frowned. "Ah, that's okay. I just remembered that Mom can't babysit on Monday, and Donna won't leave little Tony with just anyone."

"I'll keep the baby," Vince offered.

"Really?" Helen brightened.

"But what about the house?" Jolie asked uncertainly. "We still have the library and your room to do."

"We'll do them later."

"Are you sure?"

"Absolutely. I'll even go over to Donna's place to keep the little guy there."

"It pains me to say it," Helen told him, kissing his cheek, "but you are the best big brother."

"You used to say that when I'd loan you my sweaters to wear, too," he reminded her, "then you'd return them with stains and smelling like cheap perfume."

Helen ignored that, saying to Jolie as she hurried away, "I'll talk to the others and call you."

"Does she even have my number?" Jolie wondered, waving.

"I'll give it to her," Vince said as they walked toward his truck. Obviously, he approved of her spending time with his sisters. Jolie tried not to think what that might mean. Given the gregariousness and generosity of the Cutlers, probably nothing out of the ordinary.

Olivia and Drew were the last to exit the building. They called and waved. Jolie and Vince waved back. A sleek, black, two-door coupe rumbled up beside them with Boyd hanging out the passenger-side window.

"Hey, you guys want to come over for a while? It's early still."

"Naw, us guys have to work tomorrow," Vince reminded him, "and that includes you."

"Oh, yeah, so it does," Boyd mused, playing dumb. "Oh, well, my boss is a sweetheart. He won't mind if I'm a little late."

"You just try it, mister, and I'll forget to sign your paycheck."

"In that case, I'll be there bright and early."

"Never doubted it."

Laughing, Boyd rolled up the window, his wife calling out, "See you soon, Jolie!"

"I look forward to it," she shouted at the heavily tinted window.

She and Vince stood where they were until the car pulled away.

"You wouldn't believe it to look at her, but that Sissy's an excellent cook," Vince said conversationally. "On the other hand, you might believe it looking at Boyd."

Jolie chuckled. "They're great."

"Yeah, they are. Did you know that they were high-school sweethearts?"

"So they've been together a long time then."

"Married the day after we graduated."

"But they still don't have kids?"

Vince grimaced. "It's that thyroid thing. They've always said that they would adopt when the time was right. They're looking into it now."

"I see."

"I think they'll take an older child because Boyd remembers too well what it was like to want and need a family and be passed over time and again by couples desperate for babies."

"I understand that," Jolie stated matter-of-factly, remembering all too well herself. "Marcus could have been adopted," she went on. "At least he said he could have, but it never happened."

"Wonder why?" Vince mused.

"I always figured that there was something wrong with the family he was with. They'd already adopted two other boys and had two of their own. Marcus never wanted to talk about it."

"Hmm."

They'd reached the truck, and he handed her up into it, then walked around to slide behind the wheel.

"So what are you going to shop for on Monday?" he asked, fitting the key into the ignition.

"That depends on whose name I draw and what that person wants."

He let his hand fall away from the ignition switch and half-turned to face her, one forearm draped across the top of the steering wheel. "I could tell you what I want if you're interested, but you aren't going to find it in a store."

Whatever that meant, she couldn't believe that Vincent Cutler would make an unsuitable suggestion, and she liked the idea that they might trade gifts apart from the family.

"I don't see why we couldn't exchange gifts privately," she said.

For a moment he simply stared through the windshield into the distance. Then he faced her once more.

"Jolie, I've thought about this for a long time. I've prayed about it endlessly."

"That sounds so serious," she said, trying for a light tone even though her heart had begun beating like a jackhammer.

"There's just one thing I want for Christmas," he was saying.

Could he possibly be asking for a serious relationship? she wondered wildly. Were they about to become a formal couple? Surely they were too old to go steady! But not to get engaged. The very thought left her breathless. She was ready for anything—except what he actually said.

"I want you to try to work things out with your brother and sister."

Chapter Fourteen

Jolie rocked back in her seat, feeling as if he'd sucker-punched her. *"What?"*

He repeated himself, word for word, slowly, in case she hadn't heard him the first time. "I want you to try to work things out with your brother and sister."

Anger and disappointment roared through her. How dare he? Who did he think he was to ask such a thing of her? She'd thought he cared about her!

"You don't know what you're asking!" she exclaimed.

"I know it's difficult," he said. "It may be the most difficult thing you ever do, but I believe it's so important for you that I'm willing to take this risk."

"What risk?" she snapped. "It's no risk for *you*."

"Isn't it?" he asked softly, his smoky-blue eyes plumbing hers. Then he sighed and seemed to mentally shake himself. "You can do this, Jolie. I know you can. You're a strong, loving, intelligent woman."

She stared at him with incredulous eyes. "Why are you doing this?"

"Because I truly believe that if you don't make

peace with your family, it will color the rest of your life, and I just care too much, Jolie, to let you do that to yourself. Don't you see that you have to at least try to put this pain behind you?"

She pressed her fingertips to her temples. "It seems to me that it's just adding another level of anguish to what I live with every day."

"I don't want you to live this way," he said urgently, "tied up in angry knots for the rest of your life. I certainly can't live like that."

"No one's asking you to!"

"Maybe not, but would you want it for me if it was the other way around?" he asked softly.

He knew. He knew how she felt about him! He wasn't saying it outright—obviously he didn't want to embarrass her—but he knew, And he was trying to show her that he cared for her in his own way, too, in a deeply spiritual way that he had already demonstrated over and over again. Maybe he didn't care for her the way that she wished he did, but the big, sweet lunk really did think that it would be best for her to make peace with her brother and sister.

Maybe it would. She just didn't know anymore. She closed her eyes and such a longing came over her that it was literally physical. It was a longing for the family she had lost, for the nice, normal family that she'd never quite had, and also for the family and life that only Vince himself could offer her.

"Just think about it," he urged softly. "Please, Jolie."

She *was* thinking about it; she couldn't stop thinking about it now. It was as if a hungry little something had lodged itself in the center of her chest, begging and pleading. She put a hand over her mouth. How had she gotten so needy, so weak? This was what wanting Vince in her life had done to her.

She'd been so careful not to want anyone or anything. Her whole life she'd known that to want too much was to face the bitterness of disappointment again and again, and losing Russell had just proven that. Then how could she now want Vincent Cutler? How could she not?

More importantly, what if he was right and by not doing this she would forever curtail her life in some way?

Yet, how could she work out an acceptable understanding with Marcus and Connie? There was Russell, after all. She just didn't know if she could bear to see him with anything approaching regularity and live with the knowledge that he wasn't hers, would never be hers.

Still, if trying was all that Vince asked of her, if he really thought it was best...

Doesn't it make a difference that you wouldn't be coping with it alone this time?

What if this really is best for your nephew? What if knowing his mother loves him is more important than knowing that you love him? And why shouldn't he have both?

"I'll think about it," she finally said, brushing away the tears that she only just realized were on her cheeks. "I can't promise more than that."

"I can't ask more than that," he answered, his voice thick and quivery.

She turned her face away, one hand lifting automatically to ruffle her bangs and smooth them again.

"Let's get you home," he said briskly, starting the engine. "Tomorrow's a work day."

She nodded dumbly, wondering if she was going to get much, if any, sleep that night. Dark fear and bright hope blended together within her, swirling into an ever-changing mosaic of emotions sharp enough to cut her heart to ribbons.

How ironic that in this season of peace she should feel such overwhelming inner turmoil.

Those next days were the longest of Vince's life. He couldn't sleep, couldn't concentrate.

What if he was wrong?

He didn't know Marcus or Connie Wheeler from Adam. They could be the worst sort of hateful, manipulative people. Just because Marcus was a minister didn't mean that he was trustworthy. They could break Jolie's heart all over again, just as she feared they would.

But at least she would have tried, he argued with himself. She would have done all in her power to mend the rift.

Would she, though, come out of it trusting him?

If she allowed him to push her into reconnecting with her brother and sister and then it went badly, she'd have every right to question his judgment. Worse, she might never feel for him what he felt for her.

Pushing her to make peace with her family suddenly seemed a terribly presumptuous, meddlesome, even arrogant, thing to do. He'd told himself that he was acting in her best interest, but had he acted out of selfishness instead? Oh, why hadn't he kept still and bided his time as his father had counseled him?

No longer sure of his own position, all he could do now was pray that God would guide her, give her wisdom and strength in this situation—and the ability to forgive if he was wrong about everything.

She attended church with him and his family on Sunday as planned. Afterward she joined the family for dinner. She smiled and teased and pitched in to help just like everyone else, but it all felt a little forced. She seemed brittle, shadowed, her smile honed to a fine edge. Her gaze felt guarded and diffident, as if she couldn't bear to look at anyone or anything too long, especially him.

When it came time for the family lotto, as it was jokingly called, they all gathered around the table in the kitchen.

Every year his mother baked an elaborate gingerbread display just after Thanksgiving to kick off the season, and the family had long ago incorporated the name-drawing with the gingerbread. This year as a centerpiece for the dining table, Ovida had fashioned a country church, complete with bell tower, steeple and stained-glass windows made of crushed hard candies melted into shapes and designs. For the name-drawing she had made twelve large gingerbread men and seven smaller ones, each with a name written on the back in icing that had hardened before the cookie was turned over to hide them. The children would draw for children's names from the smaller cookies, and the adults from the larger ones.

Before the actual choosing of cookies—and names—began, they all drew slips of paper with numbers printed on them to establish order. Ovida drew the number one, Vince a six, and Jolie a nine. Ovida began the game by choosing the cookie with her son-in-law John's name on it.

"Whoo-hoo! Just pack me a big box of that home-made Christmas fudge of yours," he crowed, patting his middle.

Helen goosed him playfully in the ribs. "And you told me you wanted a new nine iron."

"New iron," Ovida muttered, pretending to write that on an imaginary list. "I didn't even know you were concerned about pressing your clothes, John," she remarked innocently, knowing perfectly well that Helen had referred to a golf club and not a steam iron.

When the laughter died down, the drawing continued. Vince's turn eventually came, and he drew Sharon.

"Okay, I know just what I want," Sharon announced gleefully. She held up one hand as if admiring a ring or bracelet. "I'm thinking three karats at least."

"Three carrots," Vince drawled, borrowing his mother's joke and pretending to take notes in the air. "Would you like peas with that? Green beans maybe? A side of ham?"

"You are the ham," Sharon shot back.

More laughter followed, then Donna drew her own husband's name.

"Rats," he said good-naturedly, "and no, that's not a request, but it might as well be because I'm losing a gift in this deal."

"I'll still get you a sweetheart gift," Donna assured him, leaning into his side as she gently burped the baby on her shoulder.

Marty smiled at their child. "You already have."

"And an expensive gift it is, too," Drew quipped. "You'll be paying on it for a lifetime."

Olivia elbowed him in the ribs.

The laughter and the drawing continued.

When Jolie's turn came, she turned over a cookie bearing Vince's name.

He caught her sudden intake of breath, dimly heard the hum of speculation around them, and wondered again if he had ruined everything for them by urging her so strongly to make peace with her family. He felt the sudden need to blurt that he wanted…something, anything, a new shirt, a garden hose, a picture frame, anything at all except what he'd already said. A glance at his father had him biting back the words, but he made up his mind to take Jolie aside and tell her privately that he was wrong to stick his nose into a situation that clearly was none of his business and that she should follow her own instincts and wishes in the matter.

He never got the chance.

The right moment just never came. They were not even to have a private moment as he drove her home because as they were walking out the door, his mother asked him to drop off a casserole for an elderly friend who had difficulty cooking for herself and Olivia abruptly decided to ride along and say hello.

"You don't mind dropping me at my house after you drop off Jolie, do you, sweetie?" Olivia said, throwing on her coat.

What could he do but smile, shake his head, and tell himself that he would call Jolie later?

Later, however, she seemed to have taken the phone off the hook, because the number rang busy for over an hour before he gave up. It was getting too late to call anyway, and besides, what was the rush?

She'd be over in the morning as usual to do the laundry and work on the house before her shopping trip with his sisters. They would sit down and talk then. He would apologize for butting in, affirm her concerns and they'd be right back where they'd started.

"Oh, Father," he prayed aloud, dropping his head into his hands, "what have I done? What should I do?"

He prayed late into the night, and woke heart-heavy, no closer to certainty than before. Dragging himself out of bed and into his clothes, he went about his morning routine, making coffee and breakfast. He carried a second cup of coffee with him, sipping from it while scraping off his morning beard and combing his hair. He drained the cup before brushing his teeth, and was standing with the brush protruding from a mouth full of foam when the telephone rang.

Quickly, he rinsed and moved into the bedroom to pick up the receiver of the cordless phone beside the bed.

"Hello."

"Vince?"

He knew the instant he heard the quaver in her voice that something had happened.

"Jolie, what's wrong? You okay?"

"I—I'm not sure frankly. Can you come over?"

"Now?"

"Half an hour or so. I-it should be about that."

That didn't make a lot of sense, and when she gulped audibly, it scared the daylights out of him. He started yanking on his boots, the telephone receiver cradled between his head and shoulder.

Everything else was forgotten, especially when she added softly, "Just come over."

"I'm on my way."

He broke the connection and tossed the cordless phone onto the bed, reaching for his jacket.

All the way on the drive over, he prayed that she was all right, that he would have the wisdom and intelligence to deal with whatever had happened. He felt in his bones that it had to do with her brother and sister, and he knew that if he had caused new heartache for her they could both carry the scars of it for the rest of their lives.

Jolie opened the door and almost wilted with relief. "Thank heaven it's you."

Vince strode inside, sweeping the door closed behind him, and pulled her into his arms, holding her against his chest, her head tucked beneath his chin.

"Are you all right?"

She sighed, relishing the comfort and closeness for several seconds before gulping down the lump in her throat.

"So far. I didn't sleep much, though."

"Me, either," he rumbled. "But tell me what's happened? Why am I here?"

She took a deep breath and looked up at him.

"I spoke to my brother last night."

His reaction was not what she'd expected. Instead of breaking into a smile, Vince stepped back, his hands going to her shoulders, concern clouding his face.

"Jolie, honey, listen. I didn't mean to pressure you. It was wrong of me to meddle in something that clearly wasn't my business."

"You were just concerned for me."

"I know, but—"

Another knock at her door interrupted whatever he'd been about to say. Jolie stiffened, her heart leaping into her throat once more.

This was it then, the moment of truth. They were all about to find out just how strong and daring she was.

For Vince, she told herself, *and for Russell,* but then she was honest enough to add, *and for me.*

Drawing Vince's name had been like a message straight from heaven for her. Once she'd gotten home afterward, she'd plucked up her courage and called her brother. They'd talked for a long while, and she'd come to understand that he'd felt he'd had no choice except to do what he had—and very likely he'd been right. She couldn't blame Connie for wanting her son, and she couldn't blame Marcus for helping her gain custody of him.

In some part of her heart and mind, she'd always known that, but old emotions from the past had been reactivated by the prospect of losing physical custody of the child whom she'd come to love so much, and she'd allowed herself to lash out in pain and anger. Now with Vince on her side, she was ready to put it behind her. The only concern was Russell. She just didn't know how she would react when she saw him again.

Would the past rear its ugly head again? Or was she really ready to go forward? There was only one way to find out.

Squaring her shoulders, she put on a tremulous smile for Vince and whispered, "Merry Christmas," just before she reached for the doorknob.

He gasped and settled his hands upon her shoulders

as she opened the door. The weight of them soothed and steeled her, so that she was able to greet her brother and sister with a semblance of control.

"Hello."

"Hello, Jo."

Of average height, Marcus stood just a little over three inches taller than her. He had a lean but solid look about him, and his light golden-brown hair was still damp from its morning combing. In a short while, she knew, it would begin to fall over his forehead from its straight side part as it dried. The poignant smile upon his handsome, beloved face nearly smashed her control, so she quickly glanced away.

Beside him, Connie looked pretty and petite, her golden-blond hair, now cut to chin-length, feathering softly about her face and playing up her big, muted-jade eyes. She wore a vulnerable, uncertain air, as if questioning her welcome, but it was the child in her arms who wrenched the sob up from deep inside Jolie's chest.

She clapped both hands over her mouth in an effort to prevent its escape and felt Vince squeeze her shoulders as she failed. Then Connie abruptly stepped forward and literally shoved her son into Jolie's arms.

"There's your aunt JoJo," Connie said, her voice thick with emotion. "We're so happy to see her!"

Marcus laid one hand on Connie's shoulder and reached for Jolie with the other, clasping her forearm and biting his lips as tears filled his eyes. Russell, God love him, dropped his bright red head onto Jolie's shoulder and wrapped his little arms around her. She sobbed. She couldn't help it. She was so happy to see him, to hold him!

He had grown! He felt heavier, stronger and not at all troubled by the momentous event taking place around him. Aware, yes: troubled, no.

Jolie felt an immense sense of relief. He was well, happy. Whatever they had done to one another, Russell was going to be okay because, she realized suddenly, Russell was loved by those who should love him. What could be better for a little boy than that?

Somehow she felt…*freed* by the realization that she could truly trust this child's welfare to his mother. She hadn't expected that.

Vince lifted a hand to ruffle Russ's short, glowing, coppery locks, and Russell looked up, grinning at this friendly stranger. A watery laugh erupted from Jolie.

"Let's sit down," Vince suggested.

"Yes, let's," Connie replied brightly, blinking back tears.

Nodding, Jolie turned and led them toward the sofa with Russell in her arms.

"What a big boy you're getting to be," she murmured, surprised and delighted when he nodded his agreement. "I'm so happy to see you," she whispered.

He opened his arms wide and hugged her again.

She dropped down into one corner of the couch, Russell in her lap, as Vince introduced himself. She hadn't thought to do it herself.

"Vincent Cutler," he said simply, offering his hand to Marcus, who gave it a hearty shake.

"Jolie's mentioned you," Marcus replied. "And I'm Marcus, of course, and this is our sister Connie."

"Good to meet you," Vince said, nodding at Connie, who folded herself down onto the edge of the chair opposite the sofa.

Jolie was rubbing foreheads with Russell when Vince dropped down onto the arm of the sofa next to her.

"He looks wonderful!" she gushed to no one and everyone.

"He is wonderful," Connie said softly, "thanks to you."

Jolie swiped at her eyes, which kept leaking tears. Words just seemed to be falling out of her mouth. "I've missed him so much!"

"Oh, Jo!" Connie gasped, suddenly launching from her chair to a spot right next to Jolie. "He's missed you, too. We've all missed you. Please come back to us!"

Before Jolie could say anything to that, Connie threw her arms around her, sobbing brokenly, and then Marcus was crouching in front of them, one arm reaching out to each.

"None of us will ever be able to thank you enough for all you've done, Jo," he began, then he paused to stretch his lips tight over his teeth to control their trembling. "We never wanted to lose you, though. We just want the family back together finally. We've waited so long for that. Decades, Jo. We've waited decades to be together again. Please—" He bowed his head.

"I'm so sorry," Connie wept. "It's all my fault! If I'd been as good as you, as strong as you, none of this would have happened."

Good? Jolie thought. Strong? After wallowing in self-pity and anger all these weeks? Surely if they could overlook and forgive that, she could manage the rest. It might not be easy, but it didn't have to be as difficult as she'd been making it, either. With Russell in her lap, she gathered her brother and sister into her arms as best she could, too overcome at the moment to speak.

"JoJo," she heard Russell say, and then she felt Vince's strong, comforting hand on the crown of her head.

"Yeah, that's our JoJo," he told the boy softly, "and how blessed we all are to have her."

Jolie laughed even as she cried.

"Oh, no you don't!" Marcus exclaimed, launching off the couch to run down Russell, who'd decided that it might be fun to try to climb the curtains.

He brought the boy back dangling between his hands, which were clamped around Russell's little torso beneath his chubby arms. He plopped down on the sofa again, Russell in his lap.

"You are a little chunk."

"I can't believe how much he's grown," Jolie mused wistfully. "He was just an infant last Christmas."

"You don't even have a Christmas tree this year, Jo," Connie noted gently, folding the tissue with which she'd been dabbing her eyes.

They all seemed inclined to alternate between bouts of tears and laughter, but in Vince's estimation even the tears were happy now. *Thank You, God,* he said silently, a refrain that he had repeated over and over again as the morning had progressed.

Jolie shrugged and admitted, "I didn't see the point."

"Without Russell here," Connie surmised. "I understand."

"We had a tree last year," Jolie said quickly, and

Vince realized that Connie had missed that first Christmas with her son, "but he was too little even to notice."

"He's certainly intrigued this year," Marcus said, doing his best to contain the writhing bundle of toddler energy in his lap. "We bought a four-and-a-half-footer."

"Marcus even built a nice platform for it," Connie added.

Marcus grinned wryly. "Yeah, I had this bright idea that if I made it tall enough and wide enough, he wouldn't be able to reach the tree."

"Which is true," Connie pointed out with a chuckle, "so he just climbs up onto the platform instead."

"And helps himself to the ornaments," Marcus continued.

"The whole bottom half of the tree is bare now," Connie chortled.

"And only God knows how many pine needles he's managed to swallow," Marcus confessed with a wry twist of his mouth.

"Of course, he doesn't have any understanding of Christmas yet," Connie said, mirroring Jolie's smile, "but he loves that tree."

"Tee," Russell echoed happily, kicking out with both legs in an attempt to get to the floor.

Suddenly he stopped and yawned so widely that they all laughed. With a sigh he rolled onto his side and stuck two fingers into his mouth. Connie checked her watch.

"My goodness, it's past his nap time."

Taking him from Marcus, she gathered him against her chest, rocking gently back and forth. He bucked for a few seconds, then dropped his head onto her shoulder, his sleepy eyes smiling at Jolie. Vince curled his hand around hers. It was going to be all right. Everything was going to be all right. *Thank You, God.*

"Speaking of Christmas," Marcus said, leaning forward to capture Jolie's attention. "We were hoping that this year we could all be together."

Jolie sat up a little straighter, flicking a glance sideways at Vince. "Well, I… I've already made plans."

Marcus clamped his jaw and nodded, clearly disappointed.

"That's no problem," Vince piped up, sitting forward slightly. "The three of you will just join us at my parents' house."

Marcus and Connie traded a look. "We couldn't impose," Connie said gently.

"But you wouldn't be imposing," Vince assured her.

"That's kind of you to say," Connie told him, "but your family doesn't even know us."

"That doesn't matter," Vince said. "They'd be delighted to get to know Jolie's brother and sister."

Connie smiled, but she shook her head in refusal. Vince saw Jolie's disappointment; it was mirrored clearly in her brother's eyes.

"Marcus, won't you be spending at least part of the holiday with your foster family?" Jolie asked.

He shook his head, explaining, "Dennis has moved to Colorado with his wife and kids, and Maggie and Dad are going there this year."

"I—I thought Dennis was divorced. He's the oldest one, isn't he?"

Marcus nodded. "Yeah, they got back together. Trying to make a new start in Denver. The folks feel they really have to get behind it."

"Marcus and the other guys insisted," Connie put in.

"Well, that settles it then," Vince declared heartily, "and I won't take no for an answer. I've got to warn you, though. The place is a zoo at holiday time. You've got these two," he said to Marcus, wagging a finger between Jolie and Connie, "but I've got *four*." He held up the appropriate number of fingers in emphasis.

"*Four* sisters!" Marcus yelped.

"Hey." Connie folded her arms in mock outrage. Both men grinned.

"Two older and two younger," Vince confirmed, "which means I get it from both directions."

"Oh, they're wonderful, and you know it," Jolie scolded, slinging an elbow, which Vince easily caught. He grinned at Marcus. The two had just come to a new understanding of one another.

"Did I mention that they're all married?" Vince asked. "That's the good thing about sisters. They give you brother-in-laws."

"Brothers-in-law," Jolie and Connie both corrected.

Marcus and Vince looked at each other and burst out laughing.

"What?" Jolie asked. Connie shook her head, seeming just as mystified as Jolie. Marcus and Vince only laughed harder. "What?" Jolie demanded, finding a soft spot with her elbow this time.

Vince covered his midsection with a forearm, gasping, "It's a brother thing."

"Or rather, a sister thing," Marcus said, still grinning.

"I don't think I like that," Connie muttered, but she was grinning, too.

Marcus lifted a hand placatingly. "Now, now. What would I do without the two of you to correct my grammar?"

"And organize your life," Vince added.

"And redecorate my house," Marcus said.

"Tell me about it!" Vince hooted. "At least your sisters have good taste. Well, Jo does. I assume Connie's is similar."

"Not bad actually."

"Count yourself doubly blessed," Vince told him heartily. "My whole clan is hung up on chintz, which Jolie saved me from, by the way."

"It's not as bad as he's making it out to be," Jolie argued, seeing her brother's raised eyebrows.

"You'll see at Christmas," Vince countered, giving them a little verbal nudge. "Come on. Say you'll be there."

Marcus and Connie consulted each other with another look.

"You're sure your family won't mind?" Connie asked.

"I guarantee it," Vince stated firmly, "and if you refuse, I'll just have to have Mom and the girls badger you into it."

Marcus lifted both hands in a gesture of surrender. Jolie looked at Russell now sleeping heavily on his mother's shoulder.

"Vince has seven nieces and nephews, the youngest born on Thanksgiving Day," she told Connie. "You know Russell would love playing with all those kids."

Connie rubbed his little back. He sighed contentedly, and Connie nodded in acceptance. Vince launched into an explanation of the Cutler family's holiday schedule, and when he got to the Christmas eve church service, Marcus interrupted.

"I conduct a true midnight service, starting around eleven-thirty. Our congregation is small, but nearly everyone attends."

"Where is your church again?" Vince asked.

"Pantego."

"I don't see why we can't make both services. Ours is short. We'll go there first and join you at your church by eleven-fifteen or so."

"You could spend the night with us," Connie said eagerly to Jolie, "and be there for Russ to get his Santa gifts on Christmas morning."

"You can have my room," Marcus added encouragingly. "I'll sleep on the couch."

"Oh, no, I want her to share with me," Connie objected. She looked at Jolie again. "Remember, we always shared when we were little. I had the hardest time learning to sleep without you. It'll be like old times."

"Better," Jolie said, gripping her sister's hand. "Much better."

Vince put his head back, sighing inwardly. It wasn't the first time he'd caught himself teetering on the edge of tears that morning. Sometimes joy came with its own strings attached.

Thank You, God, he prayed again. *Thank You. Thank You.*

If he said it all day, it still wouldn't be enough.

They stood at the railing on the landing and waved one more time at Marcus, who dropped his own hand

and slid behind the wheel of his small sedan, his smile still gleaming white. Jolie felt as if her heart had grown too large for her chest. If she wasn't careful she might float right up into the sky.

Pulling her cardigan tighter against the cold, Jolie turned and ambled back into the apartment. Vince followed, closing the door and propping a shoulder against it, arms loosely folded. He looked very pleased with himself. She'd allow him that.

"Thank you for inviting my family to have Christmas with yours."

"I'm looking forward to it," he said heartily.

"You're sure it'll be all right with your mom?"

"What do you think?"

She thought the Cutlers were just about the warmest, most wonderful people in the world, one in particular.

"And thank you for everything else," she said simply.

Pushing away from the wall, he walked forward and wrapped his arms around her. She laid her cheek against his chest, sighing. She'd never dreamed how lovely just being held could be.

"I am so proud of you," he said. "And you don't know how frightened I was."

"You?" She lifted her head. "Why?"

"If it hadn't worked out…" He licked his lips. "I wouldn't have blamed you for hating me."

Her jaw dropped. "Don't be silly! I could never hate you, not after everything you've done, fixing my car, working out a deal to pay for it, the maintenance agreement—"

"Which you have also paid for," he reminded her, "big-time."

She went on as if he hadn't spoken. "Thanksgiving, the game. And now this." She shook her head. "I wasn't big enough to do this without you. I'd have gone right on being mad at the world and—"

"Hush," he said. Bending his head, he gently pressed his lips to hers as if to stop the flow of her words that way.

Jolie felt her heart take flight. After a moment she drew back, studying his gaze hopefully. Dare she believe that this was more than a friendly gesture?

"Jo," he said. Cupping her face in his hands, he pressed his thumbs beneath her chin and tilted her head back. "No one's ever given me a finer Christmas present." He grinned and added, "I wonder how you'll top it next year?"

Jolie caught her breath. There it was again. *Next year.* He really must mean that they had some sort of a future together. The look in his eyes certainly seemed to say so, but how could she be sure?

"Is that a hint that I should put my thinking cap on?" she asked lightly. "Am I setting a pattern for Christmases to come here?"

He answered her with another question, his voice a deep rumble. "Is that what you want, Jolie, more Christmases to come?"

She didn't know how to answer that, wasn't even quite sure what he was asking, so she backed up a step, flapped a hand through her bangs, chuckled awkwardly.

"Isn't that what everyone wants?"

"I thought you didn't particularly like Christmas."

She shrugged. "Maybe I'm learning to like it."

He laughed. "That's good to know."

She looked down. "That's not all I've learned."

"A wise person never stops learning," he told her. "Life has made you very wise, Jolie."

"I doubt it." She rolled her eyes and caught sight of the clock on the wall beside the door. "Oh, my! Your sisters are expecting to meet me at your house! We're supposed to do lunch before we hit the stores."

"Well, what are you waiting for?" he teased. "Get your coat."

She hurried to do that, thinking that the warmth she felt inside just might be all she'd ever need against a Texas December.

Chapter Fifteen

❧

Dressed in a bright holiday sweater and a long green skirt, Ovida sported a wreath of holly in her fading red hair. She seemed as gay and giddy as the children, who were obviously on a pure sugar high, sweets grasped in their hands. Jolie felt a bit underdressed in her simple brown knit slacks, matching turtleneck and off-white cardigan, but as always Ovida immediately put her at ease, greeting her with a hug. Certainly, she welcomed Jolie and her family with all the warmth that the holiday engendered.

"Thank you so much for coming! What a pleasure to meet you. Good grief, that one could be a Cutler!" she exclaimed, rubbing a hand over Russell's bright hair. "Girls, look at this doll."

Her daughters moved forward, and Connie and Russell quickly disappeared into a gushing gaggle of Cutler sisters. Olivia broke away briefly to look over Marcus and declare him entirely too handsome for a minister.

"And single, too!" she exclaimed after a word from Connie.

That elicited a blush from Marcus and speculative remarks from the sisters. "Carolina Fowler," someone suggested suddenly.

"Or Audrey Hart."

"Wynona Phillips."

This last suggestion met a chorus of agreement.

Horrified at the obvious matchmaking, Marcus glared at Vince, who covered his laughter with a hand. Jolie shot a conspiratorial glance at Connie and found her fighting her own amusement, a rapt Russell perched upon her hip. Ovida abruptly thrust cups of hot, buttered apple cider into their hands and sent Larry after a plate of elaborately decorated sugar cookies.

This was going to be a Christmas to remember. Tomorrow would bring the delight of watching Russell's face light up when he spied his Santa toys beneath the tree in Marcus's living room, but tonight belonged to the Cutlers.

As usual, it was chaos, exuberant, delightful chaos, and Jolie loved it. She loved everything at the moment. In fact, she'd never been happier.

The last eleven days had been among the brightest and busiest of her life. Between work, finishing Vince's house—she'd wanted it done in time to decorate for the holiday since it was his first in his new home—and getting reacquainted with her family, the days had flown by in a happy blur, much like the children who ran through the room to the flash of John's camera as he wandered around, capturing the celebration on film.

He snapped Larry shaking hands with Marcus, then

paused long enough to copy the greeting, while the other brothers-in-law lined up to follow suite.

Smiling, Jolie looked around her.

The Christmas tree, which had gone up in the living room on the day after Thanksgiving, was surrounded by a miniature mountain range of colorfully wrapped gifts. A cheery blaze flickered in the brick fireplace, and carols wafted softly from speakers placed around the lavishly decorated house. Stuffed angels, hand-sewn of patterned chintz (of course) and decorated with wisps of organza, velvet, lace and sequins, with yarn for hair, were tucked into every available corner and niche. Vince and Marcus had traded rueful glances over that small fact.

Within minutes of their arrival, the newcomers were all laughing and talking with clusters of the Cutler family as if they'd known one another for ages. Eventually, Bets took center stage, clapping her hands and stomping her feet until she got everyone's attention.

"It's time. It's time," she announced, sounding very adult. "And I want to be Mary!"

"I get to be Elizabeth!" her cousin Brenda announced.

"Tony's Baby Jesus!" one of the boys shouted.

"An honorary role only," his father admonished the infant teasingly.

"Time to read the Christmas story," Vince explained as he escorted Jolie to the hearth, where they perched side by side on plump chintz (what else?) pillows.

The other adults began sorting themselves into seats, couple by couple, more than half on the floor, as Ovida passed out folios bound in red and green construction paper and decorated with bits of rick rack and ribbon. She handed one to Marcus, who took up a spot on the floor next to Jolie, his back to the long, brick hearth.

"You'll read Zacharias for us, won't you, Pastor Wheeler?"

"My pleasure," Marcus said, "but please use my given name."

"Marcus, then." She smiled before turning to her husband. "Daddy, you'll be the narrator. Mark, you're Herod. Matthew, Michael, shepherds."

Connie wound up on a chair next to Donna and Marty, who held baby Tony against his shoulder. Ovida must have handed out a dozen of the bound scripts before passing around simple stapled copies to the others. Jolie and Vince got one to share. Jolie saw immediately that the story was taken from several books of the Bible since the passages were denoted in the margins.

When everyone had settled down, Larry cleared his throat, opened his copy and began to read what was obviously a familiar and beloved story. It began with an encounter between Zacharias and an angel who announced the coming birth of a son for the elderly priest and his previously barren wife, Elizabeth. That child would turn out to be John the Baptist, cousin and forerunner of Christ. Jolie listened and followed along, fascinated. Everyone, she mused, knew the story of the Baby Jesus, but she'd never before heard this part.

The reading, some of which was very dramatic and moving, took all of forty minutes, and when it was done, Jolie marveled at the extent of what she had not known, the fulfillment of prophecy, including the flight into Egypt and Herod's murder of the male children in an attempt to remove any king of the Jews who might one day challenge him for power. No one had ever mentioned to her, for instance, the encounters of Simon and the prophetess Anna with the Holy Infant in the temple.

There was so much more to the story than she had realized! She determined to give the Biblical accounts a careful reading at the first opportunity, including the Old Testament prophecies. It was one of these with which the reading ended, a quotation from the ninth chapter of Isaiah, verse six.

"And His name will be called Wonderful Counselor, Mighty God, Eternal Father, Prince of Peace."

With those final words, a moment of reflective silence descended. Marcus closed his script reverently.

"This is really marvelous," he said. "It's straight from Scripture, but I don't think I've ever seen it arranged so clearly. Could I possibly have a copy to share with my congregation?"

"Take mine," Vince said, handing over his white paper copy.

Bets leaned forward with a mischievous gleam in her eye. "Since we're giving away stuff, can *I* have my presents now?" she asked witheringly.

Laughter and a mild scolding followed, but Larry ultimately made the decision. "Everyone can have their gifts *after* we pray." The whole group quieted, and Larry looked to Marcus. "Would you like to lead us?"

"Oh, no," Marcus answered immediately. "Surely that honor must fall to you."

Larry didn't protest, merely bowed his head and

began to speak. He finished by saying, "Most of all, I thank You, Father, for the special ways You've moved in the lives of our family this holiday season. You've always blessed us with amazing and undeserved generosity. You cleanse our souls and mend our hearts, and for that most of all we praise You. Now make us agents of Your love in this season of love and always. These things we pray in the holy name of Your Son. Amen."

"Amen," Jolie whispered, turning her gaze on Vince. He smiled benignly and squeezed her hand before popping up to help the children distribute the gifts.

All of the adults had at least a single gift to open. Due to the so-called "sweetheart" gifts, most had two, as did each of the children, one as a result of the "family lotto" and the other from their grandparents. Ovida and Larry had been good enough even to provide a gift for Russell, as had Jolie. She'd wanted Vince to have something under the tree, too, so she'd bought him a hand-tooled leather cover for his Bible and sent it along with his sisters after their shopping trip. Jolie herself had several gifts waiting for her, one from Sharon, who had drawn her name, and one each from her brother, sister and nephew.

In addition to this bounty, the grown Cutler children had joined together to buy a gift for their parents. This seemed to be a yearly event, and this Christmas the gift was a large-screen television that the sons-in-law carried in from the garage where they'd hidden it earlier. Clearly, Larry was delighted.

"The Super Bowl Party is here this year!" Drew announced, but Vince immediately objected.

"No way. I got my big screen last week, so I've got first dibs. It's already agreed."

"You've agreed," Donna pointed out. "Jolie hasn't."

Jolie glanced around in surprise. "It's not up to *me*."

Obviously that was so, because the matter died instantly. Donna wasn't even looking at Jolie anymore. Instead, she was taking Tony from her husband, and saying something to Connie. Vince had gone back to directing the opening of the gifts.

All the gifts had two tags attached to them, one of which had been removed and deposited into a large glass bowl as the packages were passed out. It was Vince's job to draw the tags, one by one, and announce the name to the assembly. That person could then open the gift of his or her choice, saving the other for next draw. The fun part was the anticipation of hearing one's own name and the absolute delight that everyone seemed to take in watching one another open gifts.

Jolie's name was called early on, and she first chose a package from Marcus. It was a new Bible bound in supple tan leather with pages edged in gold. Inside, he had written an inscription. "To Jolie, one of the two dearest sisters in the world. May God bless you with every good thing, shelter you from harm and fill your life with love. Marcus."

She hugged him and treasured his whispered, "I love you, sis."

"I love you, too."

Next time around, she opened Connie's gift, a touching photo album filled with old pictures of them as children and recent ones of Russell, Connie and Marcus. They spent several minutes with their heads together, looking through the pages, remembering and laughing as they'd done as children.

"I can't believe you managed to save these," Jolie said, brushing her fingertips across a sheet of old photos.

"I can't believe I have my sister back," Connie said softly, blinking away tears.

Jolie trumped her handily. "I have my sister, my brother and my nephew."

"Wanna trade?" Olivia cracked, lightening the mood and making everyone laugh.

"No, thank you," Jolie replied smoothly, widening her eyes as if in horror.

Everyone laughed again. Vince put a stop to it by plunging his hand back into the bowl. Some time later he finally drew his own name.

Even though he'd said he only wanted to see her reunited with her family, Jolie hoped he'd like her other gift. He broke the ribbon, ripped away the wrapping paper and lifted off the top of the box, batting back the tissue inside. For a moment he simply stared at the leather Bible cover handstitched and dyed with a Western motif and embossed with his name. Then he smiled, reached out for her and, to her mingled embarrassment and delight, kissed her soundly on the mouth before showing off his gift to the company at large. Larry especially seemed to like it. He examined the cover in detail, murmuring that it was "Neat."

"Thanks, babe," Vince said. "I wasn't expecting that." He slid her an apologetic look and added, "Guess I should've put something under the tree for you, too."

"Oh, that's all right," she said.

She hadn't expected anything from him, certainly

not a "sweetheart" gift as it was termed. It would have been nice, true, but she looked at Russell, saw how engrossed he was with the stacking blocks she'd given him and recognized the understanding smiles on the faces of her brother and sister. It was enough. How could she ask for more?

With his free hand, Vince drew another name and another and another. Eventually Jolie opened her gift from Russell. It was a framed photo of him. He'd been allowed to scribble on the mat with a crayon, which set off the photo charmingly. And finally she unveiled the beautiful silk-blend sweater from Sharon.

"This is beautiful!"

"It's the very color of your eyes," Sharon told her proudly.

Jolie looked at the lovely green sweater and beamed.

When the last gift had been opened, pronounced delightful and appropriately envied, Vince turned over the bowl as a demonstration of its emptiness and placed it on the floor.

"Guess that's it, folks. Pretty good haul, eh?"

General statements of agreement followed. Bets noted that the children still had Santa gifts to look forward to, and her parents teased her about the possibility of her only receiving coal and switches. She didn't seem very worried.

Jolie rose to help Sharon begin gathering up the trash, but Vince stopped her with a hand on her wrist.

"Wait a minute," he said rather loudly, drawing a small gold-foil bag from his jacket pocket. "Looks like we have one more gift, after all."

Jolie laughed, sure that the pretty gold-foil bag was for her, and sank back down onto the hearth next to

Connie, who had squeezed in earlier while looking at the photo album. She couldn't help feeling a little thrill because Vince had bought something for her, after all, not a *sweetheart* gift, of course, but it was enough that it was personal.

Marcus left Russell playing happily on the floor and eased up onto the corner of the hearth next to Connie.

Vince placed the small bag in Jolie's hand, and she felt something hard and cubic inside. Pulling the bow from the fringed draw string, she emptied the sack of its contents. A small, white velvet box tumbled onto her lap, just the right size for a ring.

Jolie immediately dismissed the crazy possibility that popped into her mind. It couldn't be. She'd let her own wishful thinking completely run away with her. And yet… Her heart was beating pronouncedly as she looked to Vince for some clue as to what she would really find inside that tiny box. The glow in his eyes literally took her breath away.

"Oh, no!" she gasped.

Chapter Sixteen

Vince felt his heart plummet to the pit of his stomach. He'd been so sure. Christmas eve, surrounded by her family and his, had seemed the perfect moment. But now…well, there was no backing out now. His whole family knew what he was planning.

He blew out a deep breath, slipped off the hearth, crouching before her, and reached for the jeweler's box in her lap. She hadn't yet touched it. Her hands hovered about her shoulders, as if she feared the thing would bite her.

More likely it would bite him.

Mentally whispering a quick prayer, he closed his hand around it, dropped that hand to his side and murmured softly, "Am I refused before I've even asked, then?"

What was he going to say to his family? They all expected a happy announcement. Jolie clapped both hands over her mouth as if to say that wasn't going to happen.

"Guess I'm not as clever as I thought I was," Vince said with a self-deprecating grimace. He tried for a smile and failed miserably. "That's what I get, going for the grand romantic gesture."

He cleared his throat and would have risen if she hadn't reached out to capture his face in both her hands, forcing his gaze to hers. Tears shimmered in her eyes, eyes that brimmed to overflowing. With love.

And disbelief.

"This can't be happening," she said in a tiny, shaky voice. "Not to *me*."

Vince tilted his head and felt the tremble of her fingers against his skin. Hope blossomed, the hope that he had misunderstood her initial reaction.

"Why not to you?" he asked patiently, aware that everyone else in the room seemed to be holding their collective breath.

Jolie gave her head a truncated shake. "I'm not the sort of person who…we're not like you." She waved a hand broadly, looking up at the arrested assembly. "Cutlers are…you're *normal*."

Relief washed through Vince, relief mingled with a shade of irritation.

"Whatever that is," he snapped. Then he reached for his patience. "Normal is one of those things that can't be easily defined, but all right, so you're not like us. So what? I wouldn't want you if you were."

Only the instant the words left his mouth did he realize how true they were.

Okay, she'd had issues that had needed settling, relationships that had needed mending, but that didn't mean that he wanted her to change who she was. He loved her as she was. She was perfect for him as she was. Why hadn't he told her that earlier?

He sighed, realizing that he'd handled this whole

thing badly. Bowing his head, he quickly prayed for God to give him the right words.

"We're blessed, we Cutlers," he began, trusting God to put the words into his mouth. "We've had nice *normal* lives, wise, caring parents. God must have known that we couldn't handle anything else. Or maybe He was just preparing me for you, the way He was preparing you for me." He fitted his hand around the gentle curve of her jaw, feeling a certain peace, a rightness settle over him. "He gave you a special kind of strength, Jo. You've never had a stable home life, parents who protected and guided you, and yet you're one of the best people I know."

"I'm *not*," she insisted tearfully. "I've been so selfish, so angry."

"So human," he amended. "Honey, the shocker is not that you've had negative emotions as a result of negative experiences, it's that you continue to be so caring, so honorable, so forgiving, so solidly, stubbornly *you*."

"That sounds like the sort of man *you* are," she told him wonderingly, "not the sort of woman *I* am."

"Do you know what sort of woman *you* are, Jolie?" he asked, and then he answered his own question. "You are exactly the sort of woman I need, exactly the sort I could love for the rest of my life if you'll just— Whoa!"

She nearly bowled him over, flying off the hearth and throwing her arms around his neck.

He dropped the box to the floor and caught himself with one hand. Laughter rushed up out of his throat as he steadied them both. He heard gasping and sniffles in the background and the sweetest squeaking in his ear.

"I love you so much!"

Now they were getting somewhere. He hugged her tightly for a moment, torn between elation and relief.

"Let's try this again. Okay?"

"O-o-kay," she managed.

Easing her back onto the hearth, he groped for the box with one hand. At the same time, he was having some trouble getting her to let go of him, but he managed it with little squeezes and pats and tugs. She quaked all over, like the first leaf of spring meeting the last icy blast of winter. He felt a sharp tap on his shoulder. Looking up, he found his precocious niece at his side.

Bets grinned down at him and shoved her hand at his face. On her palm, just beneath his nose, rested the white velvet box that had started all of this. Trust Bets to get herself into the spotlight.

He picked up the tiny box between his thumb and forefinger, saying wryly, "Thanks."

She inclined her head, grinning, spun on her tiptoes and paraded back to her seat, her hands clasped behind her.

"I would make a very good flower girl, by the way," she announced cheekily.

Laughter sputtered, eddied, faded while Vince hung his head in mock chagrin.

Bets had temporarily upstaged him, but he knew who held the major roles. Now it was time for this little drama to reach its climax.

Taking a deep breath, he rocked forward onto one knee, reached out and clapped a hand around the nape of Jolie's neck, steadying both of them and feeling her lovely hair slide beneath his fingers. She had worn it down, a simple rhinestone clip at one temple.

Plain and simple, that was Jolie.

No, not plain.

She had to be one of the most beautiful women in the world, and—incredibly—she was meant for him. He knew it at the very core of his being, and that certainty gave him strength, peace, joy.

"Jolie Kay Wheeler," he said in a firm, even voice, "will you marry me?"

She made a strangled noise and burst into tears. His heart stopped again, then Marcus grabbed his hand and began pumping it while Connie hugged her sister comfortingly.

"Hang on. Hang on," Vince instructed, wanting this thing settled in no uncertain terms. She hadn't actually said yes yet.

He dropped the box into Jolie's hands. She stared at it for a moment and then began wrenching at it, sobbing or laughing, he couldn't tell which. Impatiently, he snatched the box back, snapped it open and plucked out the ring, holding it up so that the two narrow, red satin ribbons that he'd attached to the band hung down in front of her.

This time, he was sure that it was laughter which shook her. Smiling, he explained himself.

"It comes with strings attached."

"Yes," she said, scrubbing at the tears on her face.

Since he wasn't exactly sure what that meant, he proceeded, lifting one thin ribbon with an index finger.

"This one is love."

She giggled. Jolie, his Jolie, actually *giggled*.

"You have to say it so everyone else can hear it," he instructed around a smile.

"Yeah, otherwise nobody'll believe it," Marty cracked.

Everyone laughed, the sound rich and ebullient.

"I love you!" Jolie declared to mild applause.

Vince was having a really good time now. He hadn't done so badly, after all. He lifted the second ribbon.

"This one is marriage."

Another wave of applause washed through the room as Jolie reached for the ring, but Vince was determined to hear it plainly said, so he jerked the ring back. She caught the tail end of the ribbon, and for a moment they performed a little tug of war. Something told him that it wouldn't be the last.

He couldn't have been happier. God knew he'd be bored inside of a week with a meek, compliant little mouse of a woman. Besides which, the other Cutler women would eat her alive! A prickly, sassy, strong-willed but good-hearted female was exactly what he needed, and even she seemed finally to know it.

"You knucklehead," she said, sniffing, "of course I'll marry you."

The room erupted, as did Vincent's heart. Jolie yanked the ring out of his grasp and threw her arms around him again. He caught her against him, rocking her wildly as blows of congratulations rained down on his shoulders.

Connie sat on the hearth, openly weeping and laughing, her son standing at her knees, while Marcus was on his feet, shaking hands and accepting congratulations as if he was the bridegroom.

Suddenly Vince felt himself close to tears. Jolie seemed to know it instantly.

She pulled back far enough to place her forehead against his and whisper, "I do love you, Vince, with all my heart."

"I know that," he said, hugging her tight once more, "but it's no more than I love you. We're going to be so happy, Jo."

After a moment, they both sank back onto their heels. Vince took the ring, admiring the single, brilliant-cut diamond—not *too* large because Jolie wouldn't like anything ostentatious—and slipped it onto her finger, ribbons and all.

It was a tight fit with the ribbons still attached, but he wasn't ready to remove them just yet. He'd tie them around her wrist if he could. Or his own. He settled for cupping her face in his hands and kissing her firmly.

His sisters were planning the wedding aloud in the background.

"Valentine's Day," he heard Olivia say.

"It's perfect," Donna declared.

Vince climbed to his feet, taking Jolie with him, his anxious gaze on her face, but she put her head back and laughed, saying, "Don't look at me. I'm not about to get in the way of that."

Vince relaxed, Jolie's hand clutched tightly in his, and half teased, "I'm counting on you to keep them from decking me out in ruffles and a red tuxedo."

"On the budget you've given us?" Sharon scoffed. "We'll be lucky if we can get *her* properly outfitted."

"Oh, wait!" Helen exclaimed, rushing over to spin Jolie around and take her measure with a critical eye.

Abruptly she nodded. "Mother," she announced, "Jolie can wear your dress."

"That old thing?" Ovida gasped, but even Vince could hear the delight in her voice. "It's from the sixties, Empire waistline, little wedding ring collar, straight skirt."

"And sleeveless," Sharon pointed out. "In February."

"We'll get a little lace jacket," Donna suggested eagerly. "No, velvet, white velvet. Simple, sleek, elegant."

Jolie literally clapped her hands, eyes bright, the lines of her face softened with happiness and laughter.

Suddenly, Vince couldn't contain his joy a moment longer. He wrapped his hands around her waist, lifted her and literally spun her in a circle.

The Cutlers were big on celebration, big on family, big on faith and big on love. Their collective past was glorious with holiday memories and shared joys, but this was surely a year that would stand out among all the rest. A Thanksgiving baby, a Christmas engagement, hopes and dreams fulfilled. A perfect, God-given love.

* * * * *

HIS CHRISTMAS BRIDE

Dana Corbit

To the Baxter boys—Brock, Dylan and Logan—
who have inspired my fictional stories
in more ways than just by lending me your names.
You are all amazing young men, who I'm sure will
be real-life heroes in the future. Also, to Melissa,
my own Amy Warren. And, as always, to the
POTLs, the six amazing women who inspire
and push me to tell stories from my heart.

And Jesus looked at them and said,
"With men it is impossible, but not with God;
for all things are possible with God."
—*Mark* 10:27

Chapter One

The house looked like a fire-department statistic just waiting to happen. Either that or the trigger for a power outage the likes of which southern Indiana had never known. Jenna Scott couldn't decide which as she tromped up the walk toward the redbrick colonial, passing a riot of Christmas lights and a holiday amusement park along the way.

On one side of the walk, a half-scale crèche rested serenely on the lawn with animals, shepherds and wise men focused on the Christ child. On the other side, a trio of plastic carolers sang a scratchy version of "O Little Town of Bethlehem," and a herd of mechanical reindeer bent to munch on artificial snow.

Could someone say "over the top"?

Her mother hadn't been exaggerating when she'd mentioned that the Warrens' Christmas display was "a sight to behold." The celebration was also another excuse for best friends and matchmakers Trina Scott and Amy Warren to force their adult children together. They'd been campaigning for an event like this ever since the Scott-Warren matrimonial merger six months before. Jenna figured that whatever the evening held in store for her personally, it promised to be entertaining.

As she stepped to the door, decorated in green-foil gift wrap, a hum of voices spilled from inside, competing with Elvis bellowing "Blue Christmas."

"So much for a quiet Christmas at home," she told the life-size Santa doll that smiled at her from a wicker chair on the porch.

Suddenly that bah-humbug spirit filled her again, making the winter wonderland feel claustrophobic. It was only the second Christmas since her father died, and she doubted it would be any easier than last year. Visiting Markston wasn't like coming home for the holidays, anyway. Markston wasn't her home. Nowhere was, really.

Someone yanked open the door before she had the chance to knock, and Jenna found herself wrapped in a hug warm enough to cut through the December freeze.

"Jenna, dear, you finally made it," Mrs. Warren said.

She stepped out of the woman's embrace, glancing back at the outdoor decorations. "Wow. This is great."

"I'm glad you like it. Now come in out of the cold before you catch your death." Already Amy Warren was pulling Jenna into the entry where the rest of the Scotts and Warrens were gathered. Just being in the house again made butterflies flutter in her stomach.

Her mother gripped her in a tight hug. "We thought you'd never get here."

"I told you my flight would get in after dinner, and I came straight from the airport." Jenna gestured toward the deep-blue airline-attendant uniform she'd been wearing since she'd left her apartment that morning in Romulus, Michigan, and headed to Detroit Metro.

"It doesn't matter now because we're all here together again," Trina told her.

"All here?" Jenna asked.

She scanned the faces of the other guests waiting to greet her. Newlyweds Matthew Warren and her younger sister, Haley, smiled over at her, Matthew's four-year-old daughter, Lizzie, resting on his hip. Jenna's other sister, Caroline, stood next to them, and the youngest Warren brother, Logan, was there, as well, but appeared to be inching toward the door.

They were not *all* there—the one member of the Warren family she'd hoped most to see was missing: Dylan. He was the whole reason she'd agreed to participate in this joint holiday celebration in the first place. The whole reason she hadn't canceled the trip and stayed in Michigan.

"Am I missing something?"

Jenna startled at the sound coming from behind her, butterflies continuing their mad dance inside her belly. Taking a deep breath, she turned toward the gruff voice she would have recognized anywhere. Leaning over the staircase railing with his wavy brown hair falling forward on his forehead was the best friend she'd ever had. The one who'd left a hole in her life when he'd removed himself from it.

For the space of a few breaths, she could only look up at him, following the lines of his face and settling on his warm chocolate eyes. Those eyes were amazing. If he were anyone else besides Dylan Warren… Jenna blinked, surprised by the strange path her thoughts had taken. But this was Dylan, even if the passing years had put more granite in the chiseled cheekbones, which had always contradicted his teddy-bear personality. His smile probably would look as friendly and unassuming as it always had…if he was smiling. He wasn't.

"Hey, Dylan," she choked out over the knot that had formed in her throat. "Oh, I mean, Dr. Dylan." Now that he'd finished his doctor of optometry degree at Indiana University and had joined a local optometry practice, he'd earned that title, even if he didn't look much like a medical professional now in a tan flannel shirt and jeans.

"Hi." He cleared his throat. "Dylan's fine."

Only Dylan didn't appear to be fine. He didn't even make eye contact with her as he shuffled down the stairs and joined the others in living room. Her heart sank.

Jenna didn't know what she'd expected. That when he saw her, the four years of distance and the misunderstanding that caused them would fall away so they could resume their friendship as if it had only been a pause in their conversation? Hadn't the awkwardness between them last summer at Matthew and Haley's wedding clued her in that it wouldn't be so easy? But she'd wished, anyway.

She couldn't allow herself to be discouraged, though, not when she'd prayed for a chance to try to make it up to Dylan for the day she'd treated his feelings so cavalierly. This visit might be the chance she'd hoped for.

Four years ago, she'd excused her actions by telling herself she hadn't realized that their plans had been firm, let alone that he'd thought it was a real date, instead of just hanging out. Now she saw that situation—saw a lot of things—through new eyes.

Before she could say anything, Jenna was swallowed in one of those Warren-Scott hug fests where she couldn't distinguish one form from the next in the crush. She couldn't be sure, but she didn't believe Dylan was among those who hugged her.

"Now that we're all here," Amy Warren began after all the greetings ended, "we need to get started on the Christmas festivities."

"Yeah, we'd better hurry up and get started before Easter comes and we've missed it," Logan piped up, earning a frown from his mother and a few chuckles from the others.

Jenna realized she was looking again at Dylan and quickly began to scan the indoor holiday decorations. Too much of a good thing was the only way she could describe the pine garland that was draped over every stair railing, curtain rod and windowsill.

The coffee table had been transformed into a miniature Christmas village. Several manger scenes and a Madonna figurine covered other tables and shelves. The individual pieces were lovely, but when compiled this way, they created a frenzied feeling in the room, which did nothing to help Jenna calm her nerves.

"The only thing missing is a tree," Jenna breathed.

Logan tapped his head as if she'd just given him a great idea. "Good thing we're going to the Christmas-tree farm to cut one down."

Jenna turned to her mother and raised an eyebrow. Now the way Dylan and the others were dressed and the line of hiking boots by the door made sense.

"Didn't I mention we'd be tree hunting tonight?" Her mother wore a sheepish grin.

"No, you didn't. Anyway, didn't you look at the weather forecast?"

"The rain isn't expected until after midnight."

Caroline stepped closer to Jenna. "Mom didn't warn me, either. She only said we would be participating in the Warren family's Christmas traditions this year to celebrate the new connection between our families."

Jenna nodded, having heard the same story. She hadn't been thrilled with the idea of sharing in another family's holiday traditions. Her own family's celebrations had been portable at best because of her father's frequent corporate relocations. She'd needed no reminder of how their wreaths and ornaments had hung in different family rooms every year or so.

Jenna glanced over to where the middle Warren brother stood. Dylan would understand those bittersweet memories. He'd been her only constant after each of her family's moves—only a phone call or a text message away. But as she watched him now, his attention was focused on something in the family room, as if he hadn't heard the conversation. Or didn't care.

"Come in here," Amy Warren said as she ushered them into the room where Dylan had been looking. "Then I'll give you our agenda."

Jenna followed gamely as Amy led them toward the huge sectional sofa. She took her place on one end, noting that Dylan sat at the opposite end.

Amy stood in the center of the L-shaped couch as if leading a class. "Okay, we'll begin with tonight's tree cutting. Reverend Boggs and his wife, Lila, were supposed to join us, but he called to say something came up at church."

"Did he say if everything was okay?" Matthew asked. As an attorney who also worked as the weekend music minister at Community Church of Markston, he was usually in the loop regarding most church matters.

"He only said they would catch up with us here later." Mrs. Warren sent a glance Jenna's way, noting her outfit. "We have clothes for you upstairs."

"See how well they outfitted me?" Caroline modeled a red flannel shirt with sleeves that hung off her hands.

"Is that how Dylan's shirt fits you?" Trina asked her daughter, a secretive smile playing on her lips.

"Quit it, Mom," Caroline warned in a low voice.

"I'm not doing anything."

"Keep it that way."

No one could blame Caroline for being cautious after their mothers tried to arrange a match between Caroline and Matthew Warren last spring, only to have Matthew and Haley fall in love, instead. Caroline wouldn't appreciate any more shenanigans from their two moms with their ridiculous plan to arrange marriages among their children.

Their matchmaking attempt this time was particularly funny. Jenna's type-A, corporate-ladder-climbing-retail-executive sister matched with quirky, laid-back Dylan Warren? That was enough to pull the smirk right off her face: she didn't like the idea of Dylan being set up with Caroline.

It was a fleeting, silly thought, but as Jenna tucked it away, a more powerful musing settled into its place. Their meddling mothers had already enjoyed one success in their matchmaking scheme, which they'd always jokingly referred to as The Plan. Did their achievement mean they would up their games now? Would they be able to convince Dylan and Caroline that their mothers knew best, no matter what their initial objections? She tried to picture herself at Dylan and Caroline's wedding and almost had to leave the room. She didn't like this. She didn't like it one bit.

Tonight was even tougher than Dylan had expected it would be. The prospect of having Jenna Scott in town for an interminable two weeks had already scored high on his dread scale, but the combination of sitting in the same room as Jenna *and* listening to his mother tell them her plans for another dysfunctional Warren family Christmas had topped even that.

Both reminded him of things he could never have. Both evoked humiliating memories best left in the past.

"Remember, tree trimming is only the beginning," Amy told her captive audience, rubbing her hands together like a child waiting to open her Christmas presents. "Tomorrow we'll start the cooking and baking. First the treats and then the pierogi and cabbage rolls."

Dylan felt tired, and they weren't even elbow-deep in cookie dough yet. Christmas always had been a trying experience for Dylan and his brothers. Their mother had made each celebration bigger, better and brighter than the last as she tried to make up for her husband's absence in the boys' lives. Dylan knew from experience that nothing could make up for that.

Now his mother wanted to share the humiliating, sideshow event with the new in-laws. She acted as if the two families had been joined in marriage, instead of just his older brother and Jenna's baby sister. If only he could have found another optometry conference to attend, he could have avoided this year's festivities and the holiday guests with a legitimate-sounding excuse.

When his mother started describing the thirty or

so goodie platters they would make for church friends and neighbors, Dylan cleared his throat.

"You know, Mom, maybe we should consider cutting back on the baking this year. Maybe make fewer platters. Or just give gifts from your bakery."

"Give gifts from the shop?"

From her incredulous tone, he would have thought he'd just suggested giving day-old bread from the supermarket as gifts rather than the scrumptious, designer cakes his mother created at her bakery, Amy's Elite Treats.

"And why would we cut back, anyway?" She waved away his suggestion with a brush of her fingers through the air. "We have more hands in the kitchen this year."

That's the point, he wanted to say. Fewer recipients would mean less baking and less time spent with all those extra hands. "Just a thought."

His mother rolled her eyes, turning back to the group. "Then Monday night we have tickets to see the *The Nutcracker.* Third row." She shot her arm into the air as if she'd just won a medal. "And then we'll take a car tour to see the Festival of Lights."

Dylan's frustration built with each event his mother listed. Why couldn't she see that all this busyness had nothing to do with the true meaning of Christmas? And of all the women in this world, why had Matthew chosen to marry a Scott sister? Okay, he would concede that point. Haley and Matthew were too perfect together for God not to have planned that one.

But if Matthew had married someone else, they could have been enduring these excessive Christmas festivities with another family. Instead of this one. Now he would have to spend a miserable holiday trying to

avoid the one person who'd always been able to send
his stable life crumbling into invisible fault line: Jenna.
Always Jenna.

She represented his life's biggest disappointment—
the person he'd always loved who'd always been out of
reach. She'd made him question everything he knew
to be true: his values and even his faith. How could
he not when he'd always been so certain that God intended them to be together? Even now, after working
as hard to forget her as he had to finish his degree, he
could no more prevent his gaze from shifting her way
than he could have given time a lunch break.

At twenty-six, she looked impossibly young with all
that caramel-colored hair wrangled into a long ponytail. The only difference between the way she'd worn it
in junior high and the style now was the longer bangs
off to one side. Her face was thinner now, too, but that
only magnified the impact of the high cheekbones and
generous lips that were Scott family traits. She was
painfully, perfectly beautiful.

Stop. He looked from side to side to be certain he
hadn't said that aloud. After four years he should have
been unaffected by those eyes, the color of iced tea,
and that skin, like a porcelain doll.

He hated that she still had such an effect on him.
Why, around her, had he always been like a kid with a
milk allergy who couldn't resist a scoop of ice cream?
Would he ever be able to look at her and feel innocuous
familiarity and nothing more? Because the answer to
that question could incriminate him, Dylan was grateful to Jenna for the night she'd pressed his hand regarding their friendship.

It wasn't the first time Jenna had behaved selfishly—far from it—but it was different from the rest. After he'd spent months scraping up the courage to ask her on a date, he'd finally asked and she'd accepted. Then, as he was leaving for his five-hour trip to the Michigan State campus to meet her, she'd called to re-schedule their "buddies' weekend" because some rugby player had asked her to a movie.

In that moment, when the proverbial straw broke the camel's back, he'd told her he was finished with her. He wouldn't be her friend anymore. If not for that night, he might still be there, serving as her long-suffering best friend and always wishing for more.

"Dylan, are you listening?"

He shifted, glancing up to see his mother watching him, her arms crossed over her chest. "Sure, Mom." At least he was now.

"After church Sunday, we can get started on the Christmas-ornament project." Amy turned to explain to the Scotts. "We do one every year. We need to find a new service project, too."

She paused finally, tapping her head with her index finger as though wondering if she'd forgotten anything. "Oh. Right. Rehearsal for Christmas Eve services. It's our tradition to sing together in the choir, and I'm sure Matthew could use the extra voices."

Matthew appeared apologetic as he turned to his wife's sisters. "I can always use every available voice." He took his new bride's hand. "I've already recruited one Scott sister for the choir."

"As if I had a choice," Haley offered with a wink.

"Now for the events on Christmas Day," his mother began again.

Amy Warren must not have heard Logan's sigh because she prattled on, describing the elaborate Christmas dinner they would share. Dylan tuned out again, his attention pulled by something as strong as gravity toward the face he had no business looking at, the person who was toxic to his best interests.

Jenna caught his gaze this time, pink lips lifting in a tentative grin. Ignoring the jolt he would probably always feel when she smiled at him, he turned away from her and focused on his mother again. Jenna wanted things between them to be the same as they'd always been. She'd made that clear enough in a few letters and during a stilted conversation at the wedding. But their relationship could never be the same.

They were different people. At least he was. He was an adult now, a respected member of the Markston community, not the everyman she'd found so easy to overlook. And this new Dylan Warren refused to allow Jenna Scott to get under his skin again.

Dylan planned to keep his distance from her during this visit just as he had for the past four years, just as he had at the wedding. Although he still felt guilty for using his graduate studies as an excuse to avoid going to Michigan for her father's funeral nearly two years before, he couldn't think about that now, not when he needed to focus on giving her a wide berth during her visit. If he could avoid caving in to her attempts to get close to him for the next two weeks, maybe he could finally exorcise her from his heart for good and get on with his life.

His plan in place, Dylan sneaked another look at Jenna to test his resolve. Immediately he realized his mistake. As she listened to his mother's speech, Jenna had tilted her head to the side, revealing a long expanse of her elegant neck above the collar of her uniform. The impulse to brush her skin there was so strong that Dylan had to fist his hands and turn away to shake it. He was in trouble, and he knew it. If he wanted to have any hope of maintaining his distance from Jenna Warren this Christmas season, he needed to start praying for strength right now and keep right on doing it through the New Year.

Chapter Two

Dylan slipped out of his muddy hiking boots and gave his head a hard shake, sending droplets of water from his hair flying every which way. Dripping less than he had before, he stepped through his mother's front door.

"I'd like to see a Currier & Ives painting of that precious holiday scene," he groused.

"I heard that, Dylan Thomas." His mother came down the hallway and handed him a towel.

"Sorry, Mom." He toweled off his hair.

He didn't know how his mother could still call her twenty-six-year-old son by both his names when he annoyed her, any more than he could understand how she was still in a festive mood after such a disastrous tree-cutting outing. It had begun to sprinkle the moment they'd pulled up at the tree farm, and by the time they'd left with that gigantic, soggy Scotch pine, Dylan had been looking around for animals lined up two by two.

Matthew opened the storm door and stuck his head inside, raindrops running down the lenses of his glasses. "Hey, little brother, we could use a hand out here. We're setting up the tree in the garage so it can dry out."

Dropping the towel on the tile, Dylan retrieved his boots and followed his brother. So much for his much-needed break from being around Jenna.

"Any chance Mom's decided to cut festivities short tonight?" Matthew asked over his shoulder.

"Are you kidding? She and your mother-in-law already have the hot chocolate simmering on the stove, and I could hear their bad duet of 'We Wish You a Merry Christmas' as soon as I walked in the house."

"I figured we wouldn't get out of it," Matthew said. "Never let it be said that a little rain could keep our mom from her holiday celebration."

"At least you aren't the newest matchmaking target."

Matthew laughed the laugh of someone who'd been there. "Stay strong, brother."

As they stepped into the garage, Caroline and Jenna were holding the tree upright while Logan crouched below, twisting the braces of the tree stand into its trunk.

"Could you two hold that thing straight?" Logan called up from the bottom.

"Come on, Nature Boy, don't you know how to deal with trees once they're cut down?" Caroline chided.

"I can with some proper help. Who cut this trunk, anyway? It's crooked."

Jenna caught Dylan's eye and laughed, and even he couldn't resist smiling at that. Logan, the resident park ranger among them, had cut the tree himself. They rested it on its side so Logan could even up the trunk and remove the lowest branches. Then, with several hands and a lot of grumbling, they finally secured the tree in its stand with only a slight lean.

Their work finished, they filed into the house, leaving their boots and soaked coats near the door.

"Everyone in here," Trina told them, ushering them into the family room, where Amy sat on the edge of the brick hearth.

Although they'd had only minutes to put the party together, the mothers had risen to the occasion. Now orange and yellow flames danced in the gas fireplace, strains of recorded Christmas carols filtered from the stereo speakers, and a spread of finger sandwiches and snacks rested on the side table. And because no Warren-Scott gathering would be complete without them, two of his mother's famous cakes were arranged on cake stands.

They were preparing to say grace when the doorbell rang, and Matthew hurried to let Reverend Leyton Boggs and his wife inside. They conferred in hushed voices as they hung up their coats and then made their way into the family room, their faces stoic.

"Is everything all right, Reverend?" Amy Warren asked.

The minister smiled in that comforting way he'd used in every memorial service Dylan had ever attended. Something was wrong.

"Late this afternoon, there was a fire downtown that destroyed a young family's home," Reverend Boggs began. "Brad and Kelly Denton were already struggling since Brad was laid off from his job, and their car wasn't running, so this fire came at a particularly tough time. The home was rented, and they had no insurance."

"How awful for them," Jenna said. "Do they have children?"

Lila Boggs nodded. "Two boys. Seven-year-old twins named Connor and Ryan. But praise God, they all got out safely."

"Yes, praise Him for that." The minister told how the Dentons had been trying to provide at least a simple Christmas for their sons, only to have their few gifts go up in flames along with the rest of their possessions.

Empathetic murmurs filled the room as the minister told more of the specifics. But Dylan barely heard the details. The story made him so uncomfortable that he found it hard to sit still. A family already limping along through life now had the burden and indignity of being homeless at Christmas. He'd heard dozens of those tragic holiday stories before, but this one touched him in a special way.

It had to be the mention of those two little boys that spoke to him. His heart ached as he imagined the confusion they had to feel after today's events, after the security blankets of home and safety had been ripped from them. He'd known a day like that once himself: the day his father left. At twelve years old, he'd been older than these boys, but he remembered how powerless and small he'd felt. How frightened he'd been that his world would never be right again. Now he grieved for these children, who'd lost their childhood just as he had.

"I spoke with the Dentons by phone, and then Lila and I drove them to the Markston Inn for the night. I paid for their night's stay with church emergency-relief funds," Reverend Boggs was saying when Dylan tuned back in to the conversation.

"But they're going to need more than temporary help. We've offered on behalf of the church to adopt this family through the holidays, so I'll be seeking support from church members like yourselves..." He let his words trail away as he waited for someone to step up to the challenge.

"Of course, we'll help," Dylan's mother answered. "We've been looking for a Christian service project, so we'll make a donation."

"That's a great idea," Logan said, and the others chimed in their agreement.

"I knew I could count on the Warrens and, of course, the Scotts." The minister smiled. "I'm sure this young family will appreciate whatever you can give."

Neither the accolades nor his mom's best chocolate walnut torte sat well with Dylan tonight. He felt as if they were all taking the easy way out—himself included. What they were willing to offer just didn't feel like enough.

Reverend Boggs glanced at the wall clock. "Some Indianapolis news vans were at the scene of the fire, so the story should make the ten-o'clock news."

"Hey, somebody turn it on," Logan called out.

Dylan stretched toward the sofa table and retrieved the remote, flicking on the flat-screen television in the corner.

"The holidays will be a little less bright for a young Markston family who narrowly escaped tragedy today when a blaze broke out in their northside rental home," said a reporter whose bright red coat appeared too festive for the somber news.

As the reporter continued her story, the camera panned first to the smoldering structure and then to the couple and their sons, huddled together in the chilly rain with blankets draped over their shoulders.

No longer hungry, Dylan set his plate aside. The story had been stirring enough, but to put faces to the tragedy brought the sad situation right into the family room. He'd pictured those children in his mind, but on the screen they appeared smaller than he'd imagined. Defenseless. Their bright eyes peeked out from beneath their parents' arms as they watched the firefighters wage a losing battle with the blaze.

Stark reality was clear on Brad and Kelly Denton's faces. Dylan remembered that his mother wore an expression like that during the early days after his father left. Matthew had looked that same way after his first wife had deserted him and Lizzie. The Dentons might have escaped with their lives, but the young couple, like his mother and his brother, had been unable to protect their children from life's unfortunate truths.

In the next shot the reporter was standing with the family, all of them under the shelter of two large umbrellas. Brad Denton squeezed the boy next to him and said, "We feel blessed that we all got out safely. As long as we're together, we'll figure out the rest."

Dylan could only stare at the screen. He'd been feeling sorry for himself all night when people like the Dentons, who had real problems and every right to their own pity party, were counting their blessings. He'd forgotten to count his.

Around him the room had fallen silent as the news broadcast moved to commercial break.

"It's a sad story," Reverend Boggs began again as Dylan shut off the television. "Still, I feel God has a blessing planned here. I'm sorry to run, but I need to call some of the other church members."

"It won't be necessary to make any more calls, Reverend." Dylan waited as the others turned their surprised expressions his way. He couldn't blame them—he wasn't usually the idea man in this crowd, but he had to be this time. No one else was stepping forward, and he couldn't turn his back on those little boys.

"Look at all of us." He held his hands wide to indicate the size of the group. "Sure, we can write a check, but I think we can do a lot more." Out of the corner of his eye, Dylan could see Jenna watching him, a strange expression on her face. He pressed on. "Between our two families, we should volunteer to adopt the Dentons ourselves."

Everyone spoke up at once—that is, everyone except Jenna. She was too busy staring at Dylan, who didn't sound at all like the Dylan she'd once called her best friend. Who was this take-charge guy? *Her* Dylan would have been more than happy to let other people make plans and then join in for the ride.

That he'd spoken aloud the exact idea she'd been bouncing around in her head surprised her even more. How could they not do more for that poor family? Her worries about reconnecting with Dylan seemed small when compared to those of these young parents who had no place to live and no way to feed and clothe their children. It wasn't right for her to warm herself by the fire while this family had been huddled under blankets, trying to shield their children from the cold.

"He's right," Matthew said, his voice rising above

the rest. "We have so much. We don't need anything for Christmas. The Dentons will need everything."

"That's a great idea," Haley chimed in.

"We have to help them," Jenna told them. Her throat clogged with emotion as she tried to put herself in the shoes of those young parents. She could only imagine the hopelessness they felt.

Mrs. Warren stood up, shaking her head. "I don't know. That's a big project you're taking on, Dylan. We can help, but it might be better if we spread the load among various church members." She frowned as if realizing more pitfalls. "And we would have to cancel some of our holiday plans—"

"Not cancel, Mom," Dylan said, standing beside her and wrapping his arm around her shoulders. "Just tweak. Remember, you wanted us to spend quality time with the Scotts during the holidays, and what could be better than spending that time helping others?"

"We wanted to share our Christmas traditions, too." Mrs. Warren's face fell in disappointment.

"And we will," Dylan assured her. "Some of them."

"We already have," Logan said. "We found the tree."

Mrs. Warren shrugged as she sat on the hearth. "If you're sure we can handle that much work…"

"Of course we can." Dylan nodded as if to emphasize his words. His mother's reticence appeared to surprise him. Jenna, too, found the woman's reaction strange. Mrs. Warren was one of the most kind-hearted people she knew, so Jenna assumed something else was bothering her.

"What did you have in mind?" Matthew asked after a long pause.

"We could put some of the money and effort we

would have used for Mom's great list of activities toward making Christmas bright for someone else."

Although Dylan glanced his mother's way, the first response came from someone smaller.

"Do we have to give away our Christmas tree?" Lizzie asked, her eyes sad.

"Of course not, silly." Dylan crossed the room and scooped up his niece. "But don't you think that other family should have a nice Christmas, too?"

When she nodded, he tugged on one of her braids and lowered her to the floor. Jenna couldn't help smiling at the sweet gesture. Dylan really seemed to adore Lizzie. The two of them had been so inseparable at the wedding that Jenna had been ashamed to be jealous of a child.

He turned to the minister. "Now, Reverend, you and Mrs. Boggs have met the Dentons. Can you give us an idea of what their needs are?"

"You'll need to start with the basics. Food, clothing and shelter. Lila and I are planning to meet with the family for breakfast tomorrow morning to find out the specifics. We wanted them to rest tonight."

Dylan nodded. "Would you mind if a few of us joined you so you could introduce us?"

"That might be best," Lila answered for her husband.

"You should go, Dylan." Matthew gestured toward him from the sofa. "This was your idea."

Dylan appeared surprised by his older brother's suggestion, but he nodded. He was probably as used to Matthew assuming plans in his family as Jenna was with Caroline taking over organizational duties in theirs.

"I would like to go."

He smiled that boyish Dylan smile that Jenna had missed while he'd been dodging her efforts to talk to him all evening. He hadn't been mean exactly, unless treating her as if she was invisible counted as mean. She marveled at his compassion for the Dentons. She could only hope that one day he would send some of that kindness her way and finally forgive her.

Jenna realized that she'd never thought to appreciate Dylan for the gift he was. She wished he would give her the chance to tell him how sorry she was for that and to show him she wasn't the same selfish person he used to know. God had made sure of that change.

"Who else would like to join us for breakfast?" Reverend Boggs asked as he took a seat next to his wife.

Jenna's mother spoke up. "Caroline should go."

Caroline was already shaking her head when Matthew offered a suggestion.

"Jenna should go. She and Dylan are buddies, and they haven't seen each other in a while."

Matthew probably thought he was helping his brother out by offering him an escape from their mothers' matchmaking efforts, but Dylan looked like a man stuck between two unacceptable choices and hoping for a third.

Jenna jumped in before he found one. "That sounds great. I'd love to have the chance to meet the Dentons."

She knew better than to look at Dylan because his gaze wouldn't be tossing daisies at her. Dylan probably thought she'd only accepted Matthew's suggestion to get the chance to spend time with him, but it was more than that. The Denton family's story had touched her, too, and she wanted to reach out to them.

"That's fine," Dylan said finally, but he didn't look at her. Instead, he grabbed a legal pad out of the drawer in his mother's roll-top desk.

"We'll know more tomorrow, but we can divide up the general areas now. Housing, furniture, clothing and food." He wrote as he spoke. "If we split into teams, we'll be able to accomplish more."

"They should be teams of two, one from each family," Jenna said the moment the idea popped into her head. "I'll work with Dylan."

"Wait." Amy exchanged a glance with Trina before she turned back to Dylan. "I thought it might be nice if you worked with—"

Caroline stood to interrupt. "I'd like to get the chance to spend time with my new brother-in-law." She turned to Matthew. "Okay with you?"

"Fine with me."

"I'll work with Jenna, then."

Although Dylan's tone might have been more enthusiastic if he'd just volunteered to clean Porta-Johns, Jenna was pleased to have won the point. He would probably raise eyebrows if he refused to work with her.

Dylan teamed up the remaining family members, pairing his mother with Jenna's mother, and Logan with Haley. Because the youngest Warren brother and the youngest Scott sister had been like oil and water together ever since they were in diapers, he assigned Lizzie to work with them to keep the peace. That complete, he started dividing the work.

"I had planned to deal with food, but since I'm working with the premier shopper—" Dylan paused, glancing Jenna's way "—we'll take clothing, toiletries and Christmas gifts."

The minister stood and crossed the room to collect his coat. "Well, Dylan, it looks as if you have this under control. I'll have to remember your organizational skills the next time we need a new committee leader at church."

Jenna agreed with the minister's praise and would have said so, but the look Dylan sent her way made her keep her opinion to herself. Her plan of working on a team with him didn't seem like such a great idea, after all. Did she really think forcing him to be with her would help her to restore their friendship?

No, she'd gone about this the wrong way. Instead of approaching him slowly and letting him remember why they once were close, she'd forced her way into his space, reminding him of how selfish she'd always been. She'd wanted to prove to him she was different, and all she'd done was show him more of the same.

What was she supposed to do now? Once again, she'd messed things up with Dylan, but she would just have to work within the uncomfortable situation she'd created. She'd committed to helping the Dentons, and she intended to follow through with her commitment. Maybe if Dylan saw that, he would eventually be able to forgive her, after all.

Chapter Three

Brad Denton looked as uncomfortable as a cowboy in a tuxedo as he took a seat next to his wife at Home Cooking Café the next morning. Well, Dylan could relate to his discomfort. As if it wasn't awkward enough meeting the Dentons for the first time, Jenna was sitting next to him. He wished he could ignore her, but the coconut scent of her shampoo invaded his senses every time she turned her head, and the chime of her laughter filtered into his ears. If only his senses hadn't picked today to become sharp enough to detect a noise in the next room or hear a butterfly fluttering its wings.

He'd counted on her being a no-show this morning—like all the other times—but that hadn't worked out for him, either. Why she'd picked this morning to come through on one of her commitments, he wasn't sure. She wasn't doing anything halfway, either. They'd barely made it to their seats, and she was already playing hostess, chatting with Lila Boggs and Kelly Denton.

"Do you think we should send out a search party

for the boys?" Reverend Boggs asked as he opened his menu.

Brad glanced over his shoulder toward the restroom where Connor and Ryan had hurried before the hostess could seat them. He spoke conspiratorially to Dylan. "Two more minutes and we're going in."

The men's room door opened then, and the boys rushed out, saving the adults from that covert mission. The boys hurried across the room, looking like matching wind-up toys, not technically running—their mother had warned them not to—but close to it.

As the twins scrambled into the two remaining seats at the long table, mischievous grins on their faces, Dylan's thoughts cleared. He remembered why they were all working together in the first place: for the sake of these little boys. He'd only just met them, and already they inspired a fierce protectiveness in him.

Dylan couldn't get over the fact that Connor and Ryan were laughing and playing as if they'd already forgotten about yesterday's fire and were ready for their next adventure. Children were definitely resilient. He knew from experience. But he also knew that they scarred just as deeply as anyone else did.

Those boys and their parents deserved the best his family and the Scotts could offer, and nothing—not even Jenna—should distract him from giving it.

"I sure hope after all that time in there that you two washed your hands," Kelly said to her sons.

"We did, Mommy." Only one of them answered, but they both held up their hands.

The waitress took their order, and soon the twins were wolfing down their waffles as if they hadn't eaten in months. Not true, of course, since their parents had already mentioned the pizza they'd eaten in their hotel room late last night.

"Boys, you need to slow down. This isn't a race," Kelly admonished them as she set her fork aside.

Dylan shook his head. "Obviously you weren't a boy who grew up with brothers. In my house, everything was a race or a contest."

"I can vouch for that," Jenna told them. "The Warren brothers competed over who could spit the farthest or cross his eyes the longest, even who had the most ear wax."

Because Dylan couldn't help smiling at the shared memory, he was glad she wasn't looking his way. But she would know about those things. She'd been there for many of those contests and other incidents. He remembered clearly just how important it was to him to win when Jenna was around.

"You really do understand our boys, then," Brad said.

"It sounds as if you've known each other a long time." Kelly looked back and forth between them, searching for a connection.

"Since birth...or a little before," Jenna said, smiling. "Our mothers are best friends, so they stuck us kids together a lot."

He hadn't intended the comment to sound so harsh, but he failed, and an awkward silence settled over the table. He suddenly felt bad—he didn't want to hurt Jenna. He just didn't want to get pulled back into a friendship that had caused him so much pain. But being around her brought back so many memories, most filled with laughter rather than sadness. It confused and frustrated him that though he knew he should steer clear of her for his own good, part of him was willing to be drawn in again. It didn't do any good for him to wish he could have found an excuse not to work on a team with Jenna. He simply had to work with the situation as it was.

"Anyway... I think we've addressed all the details." Dylan glanced down at the list of tasks in front of him and then to the list of clothing and shoe sizes next to Jenna's coffee cup. "Can any of you think of anything we haven't covered?"

"Will Santa miss us this year because he doesn't know we're at a hotel, instead of our old, burned-up house?" Ryan asked, suddenly serious.

Dylan swallowed, his heart aching for the child's distress. The twins' concerns might not have been as obvious as those of their parents, but they were there.

The adults glanced at one another across the table. The boys wouldn't fully understand how much they'd lost in the fire for a while—the memories and surety that they would always be safe. The grown-ups already knew.

Connor tilted his head to the side. "Do you think Santa will get it if we leave a note for him at our old house to tell him where we are now?"

"As long as we put a cookie and some milk with it." Excitement replaced the worried look on Ryan's face.

"Hey, those are clever ideas, boys." Kelly managed a reassuring smile for her sons.

The waitress stopped by the table to leave the check, and Dylan nabbed it before anyone could look at it. He pulled his wallet from his back pocket and set his credit card with the bill.

Brad glanced at the credit card that represented a

free breakfast, and he gripped his hands together. "I don't know if all this is the best idea. Your church has already done so much with the hotel room and all."

Kelly leaned her cheek against her husband's shoulder. All through breakfast, the two of them had been holding hands. "You'll have to forgive my husband. It's hard for him to accept help. We've always made our own way before, and…" As her voice broke, she glanced away, dabbing her eyes with her napkin.

"Pride. It's a tough thing." Brad tried to laugh, but his voice was thick with emotion. "With me out of work and now…this, we're not in a position to be able to turn down help, for the boys at least. So thank you for everything."

"Okay, then," Dylan said. "First we'll—"

Brad rushed on as if Dylan hadn't spoken. "But as soon as we're able, we'll repay every cent."

Reverend Boggs held his hands wide. "Now, Brad, there's no need to worry about that right now. These two families are just trying to do as our Lord directed to feed and clothe those who need it. You would do the same if the situation were reversed. Remember in Matthew 25:40, Jesus said, 'Truly, I say to you, as you did it to one of the least of these my brethren, you did it to me.'"

"It's just hard." Brad shrugged, not quite on board.

In a surprising move, Jenna reached over and squeezed Brad's hand. "Think of it as only temporary." Her smile was warm enough to convince even the most determined person to change his mind. "When you're back on your feet, you can help out somebody else who's going through a tough time. That way the help keeps moving."

When Jenna released his hand, Brad sat straighter in his seat. "Okay. We'll do that."

It was all Dylan could do not to stare at her with his mouth gaping open. He'd never seen her like this before, so generous and selfless, so focused on someone else's need. She was…different.

Don't go there. You can't afford to. Not again.

"That's great." Jenna pushed back from the table and stood. "Now why don't you all get back to the hotel? You probably could use a relaxing day after yesterday. We'll take care of some of these details and have you resettled in no time."

Reacting to her cue, Dylan came to his feet. The others around him stood, as well.

"In no time," he repeated, stepping over to shake hands with Brad.

Jenna was less formal, hugging Kelly first and then bending to offer each of the boys a squeeze. They only grimaced a little.

As she moved on to hug Brad and the minister and his wife, Dylan slanted a perplexed look her way.

He couldn't help but think about how she'd tried to make it easier for the Denton family to accept assistance, seeming to care as much about their feelings as their physical needs. The Jenna he remembered wouldn't have thought to reach out to anyone else. She'd always been too preoccupied as the epicenter of her own universe. But was it possible that she *had* changed.

Again, he forced himself not to read too much into her efforts. She was probably just hurrying the process along so they could finish their charity project and get on with their Christmas activities.

Preoccupied, he didn't see it coming, but Kelly caught up with him, wrapping her arms around him in a fierce hug.

"God bless you for your kindness." Kelly squeezed again and then released him. "Let us know what we can do. We're not afraid of work."

"We definitely will…after you relax today."

Dylan had to admit that Jenna's suggestion was a good one. And he preferred not to have the family present for some of the delicate discussions that might have to take place with additional donors.

He stole another glance at Jenna, who was reassuring the boys about Santa, and his breath caught. Today would be tough. He grimaced. If he was having this much trouble ignoring her with a crowd around them, he couldn't imagine how hard it would be when the two of them were alone together. Maybe if they kept busy the whole time, it wouldn't be so bad. Maybe he could even send her off shopping for clothes while he took on another part of the project. Independent subcommittees, so to speak. Yes, staying busy and dividing duties, that would help. No time to look into her beautiful eyes. No time for her to bring up the day that forced him to put her out of his life. No time for him to change his mind.

Jenna didn't have to look Dylan's way to know he was watching her, instead of the Dentons, as they crossed the parking lot to return to their hotel. The way he'd been studying her the past twenty minutes, she wanted to tell him to turn up the microscope's magnification and take a good look.

She hated guessing that shock was the reason for

his sudden curiosity. Was he really so surprised that she'd been kind to the Dentons? Someone would have to be missing a heart not to want to reach out to that great couple and those sweet little boys. Did he believe she was that type of person? Sure, she'd been a little narcissistic in the past, but she couldn't have been that bad. At least she hoped not. And even if she had been, she was different now.

He might not realize it, but she wasn't the only one who'd changed, and from what she'd seen so far, some of his changes hadn't been for the better. He might be this new assertive-doctor type, but where were his sweetness and vulnerability? The qualities that made him Dylan? He was barely recognizable under all of that authoritarian veneer.

Frustration welled up inside her. Dylan would never give her a chance to restore their friendship. She didn't know why she'd ever thought he would. Four years had passed. If he'd wanted to reconnect with her, he would have done it by now, and if she'd expected to have the chance to make amends, she should have tried *before* now.

She didn't want to believe it was too late. Hadn't her mother always told her it was never too late to do the right thing? It had to be the right thing for her to at least apologize for hurting him, whether he forgave her or not. And even if he didn't believe she was the kind of person to think of others, she intended to help the Dentons have the merriest Christmas possible. She had too many blessings in her life not to share them with others.

She would work with Dylan, even if he wasn't happy about working with her. She would pray through the process that they would somehow reconnect. He wasn't the same boy she remembered any more than she was the same girl, but Jenna sensed that buried deep inside him—maybe intentionally hidden from her—was the person she'd once been closer to than anyone else. With God's help, she was determined to find him.

"This is one thing you could have done without me."

At this newest round of Dylan's grousing, Jenna looked over her shoulder at him and grinned. "And have you miss all this?"

She gestured toward the rows of sweaters in the discount store's women's department. He was bored, but if she had agreed to his suggestion that they divide the list of stores and meet up at the end of the day, she wouldn't have had the chance to see him all afternoon. So much for not forcing him to work with her. She sighed. This was getting more complicated by the minute.

"Have some mercy, will you?"

Dylan leaned his elbows on the hand grip of the shopping cart and rubbed his eyes, yawning. They'd already found several outfits and coats for Brad and the boys at the charity clothes closets and resale shops she'd marched him through for hours, but they were purchasing a few clothes for Kelly now. Jenna was in her element, and she wanted her purchases to be just right.

"Okay. I'll be finished here in a minute." She made her final selections and dropped them in the cart. "How does someone so impatient survive a job where you stare at people's eyeballs all day?" she teased.

She would have taken the strange sound he made as a laugh if he'd chuckled at any of her other jokes today.

"Believe me, even just asking, 'Better or worse?' and 'Which is clearer, A or B?' is more interesting than shopping for women's clothes."

He did chuckle that time—at least something had brightened his spirits. He checked his watch again.

"You see," he said, "I was right. At least in this one store we could have gotten more done, faster, if we'd separated and met up at the cash register later."

Jenna frowned as she gathered several items in her arms. "We also would have gotten half as many things for twice as much if we'd done that. Haven't you ever heard of comparison shopping? You can't just march up to the undershirt display and pick the brand with the best commercials. You have to look at price. We only have so much money, and we want to get as much as possible."

"But I could have handled toiletries."

"Probably."

"Probably? How do you think I earned my professional degree? Bid on it on an Internet auction site?"

When she whirled to look at him, Dylan had his arms crossed. Even with his chin tilted up that way, he looked…oddly appealing.

"No. Not the Internet. But can you tell me what kind of shampoo wouldn't sting a kid's eyes or would give long hair like Kelly's a nice shine?"

At first he frowned, but finally he raised his hands in defeat. "Fine. You win."

With this part of their shopping complete, Dylan wheeled the cart out of the women's department and hurried with apparent relief toward Health and Beauty. Jenna had to jog to keep up with his longer stride.

"It wasn't that much of a defeat, was it?" she asked

when he finally slowed down in the toothpaste aisle. "What would you know about kids' or women's shampoo? Besides, you always hated to shop. You hated malls, too. Your mom used to bring clothes home for you to try on. She had to return the ones that didn't fit."

"Guilty." He picked up the most expensive tube of cinnamon-flavored toothpaste, but when she lifted her brow, he set it back on the shelf and gestured for her to select one. "But in my defense, malls are just consumer prisons where they pipe in music with subliminal shopping messages and where the lights are so bright they convince you that whatever you're trying on looks good on you."

Jenna picked up a tube of toothpaste next to a sale sign and moved on to the toothbrush display. "Next you're going to tell me about conspiracy theories and grassy knolls."

"A little before my time, don't you think?"

He had smiled at her comment. Finally. A success. She thought back to all the times he'd regaled her with stories from documentaries about the assassination of President John F. Kennedy or the sinking of the *Titanic*, realizing now that she'd only half listened. A better friend would have listened more closely as he spoke about his interests. Note to self, she thought.

Jenna selected two adult toothbrushes on a two-for-one deal and picked two junior-size brushes for the boys. "I still don't understand why you assigned us to the clothes committee when you hate clothes shopping."

Dylan pulled one of the toothbrushes from her hand and tapped her on the head with it. "Are you kidding? How could I not pick the shopping committee when

I was working with the crowned queen of shopping? That would have been a waste of your talents."

Jenna laughed, and for a second, it seemed like old times between them as he grinned at her. She smiled in return, and they just stood there for a moment until Dylan seemed to catch himself. He quickly turned away.

Jenna grabbed a container of dental floss and crossed it off on the list before moving on to the razors and shaving cream.

"I bow to your expertise here." She waved toward the merchandise. "Just watch your prices."

"At least I'm good for something here." He pulled shaving cream, a reasonably priced razor and a pack of replacement blades off the shelf, even grabbing a set of disposable razors for Kelly.

"Do these meet your specifications?"

With all the items checked off on this first list, they went through the checkout line and headed to the car. If the others had accomplished as much as she and Dylan had, they were well on their way to a successful project.

"Whew," Dylan said as he pulled on his seat belt. "Now that was an ordeal."

Jenna didn't say anything for a moment. He might think it had been challenging shopping with her, but if he thought that tomorrow she would agree to working separately on different portions of the project, then he had another think coming. They were making progress. She could feel it. And she wasn't going to give up.

"You know we're not done, right?" she asked.

Dylan looked at her with what she hoped was mock dread.

"After we meet with the boys tomorrow to help them

write their Santa's lists, we're headed to the mall for Christmas shopping. You better rest up if you thought today was tough."

Dylan groaned and leaned his head on the steering wheel. She reached over, laughing, and gave him a quick pat on the shoulder. He didn't even stiffen at her touch.

Yes, they'd definitely made progress.

Chapter Four

Dylan followed the enthusiastic chatter into his mother's formal dining room. Already from the cars parked outside, he had no doubt they were the last to make it back to the house. And if all that laughter was any indication, they'd all had an enjoyable afternoon.

Had he? He wasn't prepared to answer that question.

Stowing their coats in the closet, Dylan led Jenna down the hall to join the others. Last night he'd wished for any excuse to avoid the family reunion, but now he was anxious to join the crowd. He needed a break from spending time alone with Jenna before he said something he'd regret, something that put him right back where he was before he'd cut her out of his life.

All day he'd tried to work with her and keep his distance at the same time, a tough enough challenge without her making it even harder by being sweet and funny. Combine all that with the fact that he hadn't been able to keep his eyes off her, and he had every reason for the exhaustion he felt now. He'd thought he could tuck away his personal battle and handle the work without breaking a sweat, but compartmentalization like that took practice.

"Aunt Jenna and Uncle Dylan are here," Lizzie announced as they stepped into the doorway. "We went shopping today."

"You did? Did you buy lots of food?" Dylan heard the false-sounding enthusiasm in his voice and grimaced. He would have to try harder if he planned to convince everyone that all was well in his corner of Markston.

"Even yucky stuff like peas."

The look of horror on the child's face had the whole table laughing.

"You're just in time," Amy said as she came through the swinging door from the kitchen, carrying two steaming bowls of Dylan's favorite beef stew.

"Here, Jenna, you sit next to Haley." Amy gestured toward a vacant space. "Dylan, you take your usual spot. We were just about to say grace."

Dylan felt a flash of annoyance when he discovered that he'd been seated next to Caroline and not Jenna. He chose not to dwell on that thought. Caroline acknowledged him with barely a nod. He wasn't the only one who'd realized they were matchmaking targets, and she was keeping her head low.

Matthew's enthusiastic prayer of thanksgiving made him curious, so as soon as he released Caroline's hand on one side and Mrs. Scott's on the other, Dylan leaned forward. "So it sounds like we've had some success today. Does anyone have a report?"

"Why don't you two go first?" Haley suggested. "What were the Dentons like?"

Jenna had just started to take a bite, but she lowered

her spoon. Her eyes sparkled as she spoke. "They were amazing. And those boys were so cute. I just wanted to hug them to pieces."

Logan didn't miss a beat. "Haven't they had a hard enough week already?"

The sound of Jenna's laughter made Dylan feel warm inside—too warm. If today was any indication, he'd be crazy by the time the holidays were over. "They even volunteered to help with whatever they can, but I don't know what that would be," he said.

"We know exactly how they can help," Caroline declared before suddenly looking Dylan's way. "I mean... if you think it's a good idea."

Dylan couldn't help but grin. Even the Scott family's resident control freak had given him a vote of confidence. "Okay, what's your plan?"

"Matthew convinced one of his friends to allow the Dentons to stay in one of his rental properties rent-free for one year," Caroline announced.

A chorus of cheers erupted around the table, with Logan throwing in a whoop for good measure.

"That's amazing, you guys." Dylan breathed a contented sigh. If all their plans fell together this easily, they would have the Dentons sipping cocoa by their own fireplace by the first of the week.

Matthew lifted his index finger. "There's one caveat. The house is one of Kevin's new purchases. It's going to require work before it's even inhabitable. Kevin's willing to split the cost on the materials, but we'll have to supply all the elbow grease."

Dylan thought for a minute. This project, which had started as an exercise in hunting and gathering, had just morphed into an undertaking of brawn and sweat.

His mother's warning didn't seem so out of place now. "I guess Brad and Kelly will appreciate having the chance to help."

"Many hands make light work." Mrs. Scott used the old adage she and his mother used to pull out when they were sending their six children off for kitchen duty.

His mother leaned forward in her chair. "So it's a good thing we have ten pairs of willing adult hands."

The others chimed in their agreement, but his mother's response had surprised Dylan the most. "You're right, Mom. With this many hands, we can do anything."

He smiled at her, glad to see she was becoming more interested in the charity project. She hadn't been wild about having her Christmas plans ditched, but he knew better than to think it was because she didn't want to help a family in need. It was just hard for her to give up the Christmas traditions that were so important to her.

"What needs to be done to the house?" Dylan braced himself as he waited for the answer. Although he and his brothers had learned how to repair things like leaky faucets and holes in walls, which were the results of an absentee dad and overenthusiastic wrestling respectively, he wasn't qualified to take on advanced plumbing and electrical work.

"Most of it's cosmetic," Caroline explained. "Just a deep cleaning and some fresh paint. The place was in pretty bad shape when Matthew's friend bought it."

Dylan took reports from the other committees and then asked the two mothers to add researching new and used kitchen appliances to their list, since the house would require them.

"I have a few leads for those things," Mrs. Scott said.

"Speaking of leads," Haley began as she hurried to the living room. She returned holding a few pieces of paper. "They gave us these at the food bank. They're long-term aid sources the Dentons might qualify for. But most won't be available until after the holidays."

"Need doesn't take a holiday," Dylan groused.

"I found the same thing when I checked with a few of my legal clients to see if they had leads on jobs for Brad and Kelly," Matthew said. "Basically nothing until after the New Year."

Dylan shook his head. "Who knew it was so tough to get help?"

"Only the people who really need it."

Until Jenna answered his rhetorical question, Dylan hadn't even realized he'd spoken it aloud. He swallowed as he looked across the table at her. The compassion that filled her eyes tugged at his heart with some unnamed emotion. The connection he'd always felt with her was right there again, but it had shifted somehow. This new, kinder Jenna pulled him in a different way, a way that seemed to be even harder to resist.

The room had become quiet except for the carols filtering from the CD player in the other room. To cut the stillness, Dylan turned to Matthew again. "Hey, thanks for looking into job prospects. I'll check with everyone at church tomorrow and then at work on Monday."

"Oh, right. Work. Some of us aren't on Christmas break this week," Logan joked, earning a frown from Haley, who'd been taking some graduate classes.

"So you two, we're all dying to know how your work went today," Dylan said.

"Us?" Haley asked.

"We got along just fine," Logan retorted.

Lizzie climbed up on her knees in her seat. "But, Mommy, you said Uncle Logan was being ridiculous after he picked up so many cans of ravioli. And Uncle Logan said you picked the bad tuna that trapped dolphins."

Haley didn't get the chance to answer before the room filled with laughter, the solemn mood from moments before having disappeared. Dylan took another look at the others seated around his mother's table. He'd shared a lot of history with the Scott family. He'd hiked down mountain trails, bodysurfed in the Atlantic and taken on the challenges of the newest and fastest roller coasters with Jenna, Haley, Caroline and even Mrs. Scott.

He'd let the painful memories of Jenna obscure the happy times he'd spent with her family. But it didn't have to be that way. He was determined to have a great Christmas with these people he'd known all his life, doing some good and even sharing a few of his mother's traditions. If he could keep things in perspective—and keep his heart under control—maybe these holidays wouldn't be so bad, after all.

The tree looked like a little girl playing dress-up with the contents of her grandma's jewelry case. Okay, an especially tall little girl, Dylan decided, one who wore more strands of lights, glass balls and novelty baubles than any child needed. If that wasn't enough, tinsel clung to the branches like some sort of icing explosion. Despite his determination to enjoy tonight's festivities, Dylan winced at the sight.

After cleaning up dinner together, their families had taken on the challenge of decorating the huge Scotch pine in the living room. Now, as Bing Crosby crooned in the background about the white Christmas they seldom experienced this far south in Indiana, the tree's branches drooped with so much finery he was surprised none of them had broken. After he'd spent the morning with a family who'd lost everything, the holiday display felt like a symbol of excess.

"Isn't it beautiful?" Lizzie stared up at the monstrosity with awe on her face.

"It sure is, honey." Amy gave her granddaughter a squeeze.

"It's amazing, that's for sure." Matthew backed down the ladder he'd used to place the angel on top of the tree.

Dylan tilted his head, trying to see the display from a child's perspective. What kid could resist all those pretty ornaments and lights? He hadn't been able to when he was a little boy. Even now he could pick out a few ornaments that he and his brothers had made in Sunday school or bought for their mother by pooling their quarters. Those pieces represented happy memories, even if they were buried beneath tinsel in the chaos of extremes.

"Well, that's done."

His mother's words brought Dylan back to the present. He turned her way as she brushed off her hands.

"Now we can draw names for the gift exchange," Amy added. "I was thinking we could—"

Dylan held up a hand to stop her. "Wait, Mom. I thought we were going to focus on the Dentons' Christmas, instead of ours. You know, sacrifice a little."

"Believe me, we already have." His mother lifted out her chin, looking offended.

"Sorry, Mom. I know how important all this is to you."

"Do you?"

The sharp question and the frown came from his mother's best friend. Usually Dylan appreciated Mrs. Scott's undying support for his mother, but this time he felt his mother needed to get her priorities straight.

Leaning against the fireplace, Mrs. Scott crossed her arms over her chest. "Do you realize she turned in her third-row *Nutcracker* tickets so they could be resold?"

Dylan coughed into his hand. As a matter of fact, he *hadn't* realized.

"She plans to use those proceeds to add to our project fund."

Jenna spoke up before Dylan had the chance to recover. "That was so nice of you, Mrs. Warren. I'm sure the Dentons will appreciate every sacrifice any of us make."

"Sure glad you think so, Jenna," her mother said. "Because Amy and I returned most of the Christmas gifts we bought for you kids. We have some mall vouchers for you and Dylan to spend when you buy holiday gifts for the Dentons."

"That's a great idea." Jenna looked at Dylan. "I bought mine in Detroit, but most of those stores will be in the mall here, too, so I can return mine. What do you think, Dylan?"

She'd surprised him again with her charitable gesture. As much as he wanted to help the Dentons, he wished she'd stop saying and doing thoughtful things. If she kept at it, he'd have to leave town for Christmas or risk doing something unwise…like kiss her.

"Sounds good," he managed to reply, pulling his gaze away from her.

"Now can we get back to the exchange?" Amy asked. "Just because we've decided to spend the money we would have used for holiday gifts on our project doesn't mean we can't still have an exchange." She paused for effect, excitement dancing in her eyes again. "This year will be different, though. We'll keep our recipients' names secret until Christmas, and all the gifts must be handmade. Doesn't that sound like fun?"

Lizzie squealed with delight, but the rest of them stayed quiet.

Amy frowned at their lack of enthusiasm. "Now what kind of attitude is that? You mean none of you can handle the challenge of making one gift?"

Matthew held his hands wide. "It isn't that, but—"

"Then but nothing," she finished for him. "Anyway, do you want to disappoint a child at Christmas?"

Amy tilted her head to indicate Lizzie, who must have gotten the hint because she pushed out her lip and batted her lashes.

An "all right," three "fines" and two "okays" later, Amy was smiling again. No one even looked for Mrs. Scott's response, since it was a given that she would agree to whatever plan her friend had in mind.

Crossing to the mantel, Amy pulled off a clear vase filled with red and green glass ornaments and poured its contents on the table. Last to fall out were several strips of white paper, which she stuffed back inside.

"Names for a gift exchange, I presume?" Dylan asked.

"I try to plan ahead. Here, everyone draw a piece of paper and, remember, that name is a secret." She turned to her granddaughter. "Except for Lizzie. She and I will read her paper together, and I'll help her make the gift."

Each took a slip of paper from the vase, and then at Amy's cue, they all unfolded the slips at the same time. When he read the name, Dylan swallowed, trying to keep his expression impassive despite his racing heart. Jenna, of course. He should have known he would draw her name. What were the odds? One in eight if he didn't include the chance he could have chosen his own name.

What would he get her—no, *make* for her? He didn't even know her anymore. A few years ago, he knew her details down to her current favorite in her fickle fragrance collection, but now he didn't know what she liked. The idea of handmade gifts made it more difficult somehow. More personal. *Too* personal. He doubted that one of those pot holders he and his brothers used to make on a plastic loom would fit the bill either.

Dylan stuffed the bit of paper in his pocket. What had he done to deserve a week like this? Wasn't it bad enough that he would be spending several more days working closely with the one woman from whom he most needed to keep his distance? The amazing woman who, he was starting to worry, was destined to keep torturing him, in one way or another, for the rest of his life?

Forget about the two front teeth the old songwriter requested for a Christmas gift—all he wanted this Christmas was a break.

Chapter Five

The next morning Jenna settled into the pew between her sisters, peeking over her shoulder every few seconds to see if the two tardy Warren brothers had arrived. She'd tried to save a seat for Dylan, but her mother and Mrs. Warren clearly had other plans, so she gave up and sat where she was told.

This was the first time she'd attended services at the Community Church of Markston since Matthew and Haley's wedding last June, and the sanctuary looked nothing like the elegant, white-roses scene she remembered. Two huge Christmas trees flanked the choir loft, dozens of poinsettias were gathered on the steps to the podium and greenery and bows were draped along the walls above the stained-glass windows.

Excitement was in the air, anticipation that seemed to be about more than just the retail frenzy that used to be so important to her. All around her, everything appeared to be prepared and waiting for the arrival of the Christ child.

As the organ prelude continued to play and stragglers hurried to their pews, Jenna glanced to the back of the sanctuary again.

"Sit still, will you?" Caroline said in a low voice. "You're making me nervous."

Jenna was nervous, as well, but she wasn't sure why. She wasn't the only one who waited anxiously for Dylan and Logan to show though. On the other side of Caroline, Mrs. Warren had an eye out for their arrival, too.

Some things never changed. Stories about Logan's and Dylan's late arrivals at church and the corresponding lectures from their mother went back as far as Jenna could remember. They lived so close to church that Mrs. Warren would make them walk if they weren't ready on time. Now they came from their own houses or apartments and still managed to be late.

Matthew had already asked the congregation to stand and turn to the hymn "O Holy Night" by the time the brothers slunk in, still wearing their coats. Their arrival was disruptive enough, but the two mothers made it more so by stepping into the aisle to let the two young men in first.

Jenna recognized the tactic to seat Dylan next to Caroline. Would those two ever give up? *Poor Dylan... er, poor Caroline,* she thought. Her sister wouldn't appreciate her lack of family loyalty. Caroline sighed next to her, a sound Dylan repeated as he opened his hymnal.

Jenna leaned forward to offer a waist-high wave to the latecomers, but only Logan waved back. Dylan sat with his gaze focused on the front of the church, his jaw flexing as if he was frustrated over his mother's matchmaking. Strange, as Jenna studied Dylan's profile, Haley's description of his "Greek statue–type cheekbones" popped into her head. She herself had never thought to describe him that way before, but now she could see why he could have been the subject for a sculpture.

Her cheeks burned at those odd thoughts. Even if she wondered why she'd never noticed before how handsome her friend was, she had no business recognizing it now…in church. She glanced around to see if she'd been caught watching him, but no one appeared to be paying attention. Relieved, she bowed her head for the opening prayer.

When next they were seated, Haley pulled her purse off the floor and started digging in its messy contents, probably for her offering envelope or a tissue for Lizzie. As Haley pulled her hand from the bag a few store receipts spilled onto Jenna's lap and another paper fell to the floor. Jenna handed the receipts back to her sister and then reached for the piece on the floor. She recognized the paper because she had one just like it. Only this one read "Dylan."

An idea popped into Jenna's head so quickly that she didn't have time to filter it before she leaned close to Haley's ear. "Hey, let's trade."

"Why?"

Reaching for her favorite designer bag, Jenna had no trouble locating her own slip of paper in an outside zipper compartment. She laid it on her sister's palm, and Haley unfolded it.

"Oh, I see," Haley said as she glanced down at her mother-in-law's name. "She's a tough one."

Haley had misunderstood her reason for wanting to switch, but Jenna couldn't bring herself to clear up the confusion. What was she supposed to say, that she was so desperate to be Dylan's friend again that she had to be the one to give him a gift? She couldn't explain to anyone else why it was so important when she wasn't sure herself.

She knew she'd felt more complete than she had for a long time just having the opportunity to be around Dylan. Something told her that her feelings hadn't always been so intense when they'd hung out together, but the difference had to be that she now realized how blessed she was to know him. At least that was the only explanation that made sense.

"Okay?" she said to Haley now.

"Fine."

They traded papers and then looked to the front of the church in time to see Matthew frowning at them from his seat on the podium. They were setting a bad example for Lizzie by whispering and passing notes in church. Jenna peeked around Haley to the child, but Lizzie was too focused on coloring in the *O*s on the bulletin to notice their bad behavior.

Jenna sat straighter, anyway, and grabbed her Bible as Reverend Boggs asked members to turn to the first chapter from the book of Matthew. Since her family and the Warrens had found a great service project to focus on over Christmas, she looked forward to an affirmation of that in the minister's Christmas message.

"Now Joseph was a decent man," the reverend began, choosing an unexpected character from the cast in the nativity story. "Even when he found out that the woman he was betrothed to was pregnant by someone else, he chose not to have her publicly shamed. Instead, he planned to divorce her privately and put the whole, unfortunate matter behind him.

"But God had other plans for Joseph, didn't He?" Reverend Boggs smiled down at the congregation. "God had tapped Joseph for the important task of being Baby Jesus's earthly father. In verse 20, an angel of the Lord appeared to Joseph in his dream, saying, 'Joseph, son of David, do not fear to take Mary, your wife, for that which is conceived in her is of the Holy Spirit.'"

Reverend Boggs paused, allowing the congregation to ponder those words.

"Wouldn't it be great if God would send an angel to let *us* know His will for us?" he said, chuckling. "Or maybe He could reveal His presence to us in a burning bush like He did to Moses."

Several affirmative murmurs and a random "amen" rang out from around the room.

"For whatever reason, Our Father is subtler these days when He speaks to us. He does still speak to us, though. Never doubt that. We only have to listen."

Jenna glanced down at the biblical text again. She couldn't imagine how the minister had arrived at this message from the story of the nativity, but its unexpected twist spoke to her when maybe the traditional story wouldn't have. It convicted her, too, in a way she completely deserved.

Just like her split-second decision to force Dylan to work on a team with her had been about her needs, instead of his, her whole plan about reclaiming her friendship with him had been about what she wanted. Not only had she never taken into account whether Dylan would even want to be her friend again, she'd also failed to consider God's will in the matter.

She might have become a new person when she'd turned her life over to God, but she still had the same selfish tendencies she'd always had. She'd wanted to be the one to work with Dylan, the one to make his gift.

Well, it couldn't be about her anymore. She could try to be Dylan's friend again but only because he deserved to have a good friend, not because she wanted it to be her. More than that, she needed to trust God to handle this and all the other situations in her life. She needed to concentrate on what God had to say. And, like Reverend Boggs had said, she only had to listen.

Early that afternoon Jenna watched with fascination as seven-year-old Connor Denton spooned the last bite of his caramel sundae into his mouth. She thought he might set a speed-eating record, but one glance across the ice cream parlor to where Dylan sat with Ryan shot down that idea. Connor's twin scraped the sides of his clear ice cream dish and might have licked it, too, if adults weren't watching.

"Aren't you cold?" She shivered at the thought of eating ice cream in December and curled her fingers around the coffee drink she'd ordered, instead. Even if there wasn't any real snow this week in Markston, it was cold enough for flurries.

"Not too cold for ice cream." The boy's teeth chattered a bit, though, and he pulled his new coat closed around his neck. The navy parka fit better than the one he'd worn the night they'd escaped from the fire, with its tight buttons and sleeves that didn't quite reach his mittens.

"Are you ready to work on your Christmas list?

Your parents will probably be done soon at the coffee shop and will want to get you guys back to the hotel."

"Mommy and Daddy like to drink coffee for a long time, so they can talk about mushy stuff." The look on Connor's face suggested what he thought of such nonsense.

"Oh. I see."

Jenna's cheeks warmed as she peeked Dylan's way. She wondered if Ryan was telling private family matters over there, as well. Still, she was glad for the boys that even during this difficult time they never had to doubt that their parents loved each other.

Brad and Kelly probably wouldn't be in a hurry to force their rambunctious twins back into that hotel room, anyway. They'd already admitted to being stir-crazy after two days and had appeared relieved when Dylan had suggested that they go to the coffee shop next door, instead of joining them and the boys for ice cream.

"So, what would you like to put on your list?" She pulled the legal pad in front of her closer and poised her pen, waiting. "Do you want to write this, or do you want me to do it?"

"You can." He grinned. "My handwriting is messy."

"And we wouldn't want Santa to misunderstand your wish list, would we?"

"No way!"

"Okay." She looked down at the lined paper and wrote "Dear Santa" at the top. "What do you want to say?"

"'Dear Santa,'" he began to dictate. "'I know you'll be busy with having to fly all over the world on Christmas Eve and stuff, but if you can find some time—'"

"Um," she said to interrupt him, "let's just start with the things you want, okay?" The peal of laughter coming from the other table suggested Dylan and Ryan were making no better progress than they were. She glanced down at the words she'd already written. "After 'some time,' why don't you say, 'could you please bring these things?'"

He nodded, tilting his head as if deep in thought. "For Daddy…some screwdrivers. Mommy would like…um…perfume. Stuff that smells like flowers. And Ryan likes building sets and puzzles. Oh, and comic books."

Jenna finished writing an abbreviated version of what Connor had just said and then looked at him, waiting. "And," she prompted when he didn't say more.

"That's all."

"What about for you?"

The boy drew his brows together as if he didn't understand what she was getting at. "I want them to be happy for Christmas. I want Mommy and Daddy not to have to worry anymore."

Jenna could only nod, thanks to the lump that had formed in her throat. Her eyes burned. Connor had lost his things in the fire, and when she'd expected him to ask for the mother lode of new toys, he'd thought only of his family. His selflessness humbled her. At seven years old, he'd already mastered the art of putting others' needs ahead of his own. She was still a novice.

"Can you sign it 'God bless you'?" Connor asked her. "Then I'll write my name, so Santa knows it's from me."

"Of course."

She looked away so the boy wouldn't see her blinking away the dampness in her eyes. At the same time, Dylan glanced up from the letter Ryan had been dictating to him, and their gazes connected. Dylan smiled and she felt her stomach drop out, close to what she felt during a plane landing but not quite the same. She expected him to look away as he had all the other times she'd caught him watching her with those evaluating eyes, but her heart must have beat a dozen times before he lowered his gaze to his notebook again.

If she didn't know better, she might have believed that smile was for her. More than likely, it was his response to some crazy gift Ryan had asked for, but she could dream, couldn't she? He hadn't smiled much since she'd returned to Markston—at least not at her.

She noticed how handsome Dylan was, especially when he smiled. It was as if that curve of his lips softened the hard lines of his jaw and chin, transforming granite to moldable clay. His eyes crinkled, too, perhaps the most appealing part of all. Shifting in her seat, her cheeks warm, Jenna looked back at her notebook.

At least he hadn't caught her studying him. That would have been humiliating. She glanced at Connor to see if he'd been watching, but the child was oblivious, his attention focused on her half-eaten strawberry sundae. As she slid it his way, his eyed brightened.

Probably before they wished to end their brief time alone, Brad and Kelly joined them in the ice-cream shop, and then Dylan and Jenna dropped the family off at their hotel.

"Now that was an odd experience," he said when they were alone.

"What do you mean? Going to the ice-cream place with just the boys?"

"No, that was fine. It was the stuff on Ryan's list." He looked away from her as he pulled his SUV into traffic.

"Does he want a laptop like Lizzie?"

The side of his mouth lifted at that. Matthew had confided to them about his daughter's grandiose Christmas list, but the child had only received a lecture on why greedy children ended up with empty stockings.

"Just the opposite. Ryan didn't ask for a single present for himself. Everything he asked for was for his mom, dad or his brother."

She turned sideways in her seat, the belt digging into her shoulder. "Connor, too. I even asked him if he wanted anything for himself, and he wouldn't budge."

"Neither would Ryan." Dylan cleared his throat.

"Well, they are twins," Jenna said. "If one of them asked for presents for his brother, he might be thinking he would get to play with them, too." Even as she said it, though, the words didn't ring true in her ears. "I don't think they had a scheme. That sounds more like something I would have done when I was a kid."

Dylan chuckled. "No, that isn't true. You would have asked for presents for yourself and then asked for some for Caroline and Haley."

"So I could play with all three sets."

"Never accused you of not being a smart child."

"You know me so well." She wanted to say he *used* to know her so well, but this was the best conversation they'd had since she arrived, and she didn't want to spoil it, even if that meant having to joke about the person she'd once been and hated remembering.

"I guess if we use Ryan's list, we'll know what Connor would like, and Connor's list will tell us about Ryan," Dylan said.

Jenna pulled out her notebook and looked at the letter she'd drafted. "And both boys told us things we could buy for their parents, though I wonder if every little boy thinks his mom needs perfume for Christmas and his dad needs screwdrivers."

"Ryan said perfume for Kelly and tools for Brad."

"Definitely twins." She chuckled and then became serious again. "Connor said he wanted his family to be happy for Christmas, and he didn't want his parents to have to worry anymore."

She waited for Dylan to share, but when he didn't say anything, she prompted, "Did Ryan say anything like that?"

He nodded as he cleared his throat again, focusing on adjusting his side mirror. Though he avoided looking her way, Jenna caught sight of his suspiciously shiny eyes. She had to smile at that. Dylan had always been tenderhearted—the protector of anthills, the secret fan of chick flicks.

He probably figured that sensitivity wasn't an attractive quality in a man, which was why he tried so hard to bury it. Jenna was surprised by how his lack of success pleased her. This was the Dylan she remembered. This was the friend she missed.

Though she'd been astonished when he'd taken charge of their adopt-a-family project, it had never surprised her that Dylan would have shown compassion for the family. Particularly those little boys. Whether he saw something of himself in them she didn't know, but she was grateful to Connor and Ryan, anyway. Not only had the boys shown her a great example of selfless love, they'd just given her a glimpse of her best friend, a man with a warm, compassionate heart. A man who didn't seem to be as lost to her, as she'd feared.

Chapter Six

"Now that wasn't so bad, was it?" Jenna glanced back at Dylan as they stopped near the exit of Sycamore Square Mall, their arms laden with shopping bags.

Dylan looked over his shoulder at the stores behind him with glass doors and metal bars already closed over their fronts. When he turned back to her, he wore a pained expression.

"Not as bad as losing a limb. But close."

"You're not overly dramatic or anything." She tried to shrug into her coat and balance several shopping bags at the same time, but finally she gave up and put her packages on the floor.

"Here." Already bundled, Dylan set his bags at his feet and helped her with her coat.

His fingers only barely grazed her shoulders before his hands fell away, and yet her skin tingled all the way down her arms. Startled, she looked back at the closed stores so he wouldn't notice her discomfort. She blamed the chill on the frosty breeze that sneaked through the door as the other shoppers exited. What else could it be? Giving herself a moment to collect her thoughts, she peeked into a few of her packages.

"You know my favorite part?" Dylan waited until she looked up before he continued. "The Sunday early-closing hours. They're great."

"Glad you liked them." She gave him a stern look, but she couldn't hold it.

Dylan swiped up his bags and as many of her bags as he could balance. "Okay, it wasn't as bad as I thought it would be."

Jenna had to agree with that. She'd been expecting the worst, or at least Dylan's worst griping, but he'd been pleasant. Helpful even.

"I couldn't believe how well you did with those store owners." She collected her few remaining packages. "Why did you think they would all be willing to donate something or throw in an extra discount?"

He pushed through the door and held it open for her. "I figured it wouldn't hurt to ask. The worst they could say was no."

"Well, none of them did." She shivered as she stepped out into the wind, wishing she'd zipped her coat before going outside.

"Did you notice I only approached store owners in the independently owned stores, instead of the chains?"

"I did notice that," she said.

"Managers from chain stores have to seek approval from corporate for donations, but local owners have the authority to make those decisions themselves."

"How do you know all that?"

"Mom has always forced us to work with her on charity projects."

Jenna hesitated, then decided to ask her question.

"If your mom is so involved in charity, why was she reluctant when you suggested that we adopt the Dentons ourselves?"

He stopped next to his SUV and pulled open the hatch so they could put their packages inside. "She was just attached to her Christmas traditions and found it hard to let go of them. You know how that is."

"Sure." If she'd had some traditions, she might have been protective of them, too.

"Mom's just… I don't know."

She glanced at him, his strange words piquing her interest, but he stopped and lowered the hatch. He opened the passenger door for her and crossed to climb in the driver's side.

Jenna waited him for to resume the conversation, but he said nothing at all. She couldn't allow the silence to linger—they were finally talking again, and she didn't want that to stop.

"Well, anyway," she began, "I thought you were great today. I'm a good shopper, but you were an amazing negotiator. Because of the extra discounts you got the stores to give, we were able to buy more."

"You learn which store owners are easy marks… er, I mean the most generous souls. Seriously, though, remember, this is Markston. We take care of our own here."

Our own. How appealing that sounded, to be claimed as part of a community, to have a rightful place. Markston. Sure, she was born here and had lived here longer than anywhere else, but she didn't really belong anywhere. Her father had always called their moves "new adventures," but the shine had worn off early on. Jenna still wasn't convinced that the stress of his corporate climb hadn't led to his death from a heart attack.

"Whoa, what did I say?"

She peeked over to find Dylan watching her. He'd always been able to read her moods as if he'd had a personal invitation into her thoughts, so she shouldn't be surprised that it hadn't changed.

"Oh, I was just thinking."

"Must have been a sad thought. Want to talk about it?"

She wasn't sure she did, but she still found herself turning toward him. "My dad," she said finally.

"I thought it might be about him."

"How did you—" she started to ask, but then she stopped, lifting a shoulder and letting it drop. It probably wasn't that hard for him to guess what might make her sad. "It's still hard sometimes."

He nodded, pressing his lips together. "I should have attended the funeral."

"We understood. You had classes and clinicals. Your mom told us when she came. Your brothers couldn't get away, either."

"It was more than that for me, and you know it."

She shrugged because she did know. She also knew how hurt she'd been to receive just a customary flower arrangement when she'd desperately needed her friend's presence and support. "It doesn't matter," she said, because it was probably what he wanted to hear, but when he shook his head, she stopped.

"It does matter. I should have been there for you no matter what..." He let his words trail away instead of rehashing the whole story. "Anyway, I'm sorry I didn't go."

"Thanks."

She didn't know what else to say, and because he flipped on the radio as they drove up Central Avenue on their way to her mother's house, she guessed he wouldn't be saying more about the past today, either.

"I guess I'll get started on my supersecret, homemade exchange gift tonight," she said when the silence stretched too long. She hoped she didn't sound too obvious. Now that she'd exchanged names to have his gift, she needed to come up with a good one.

"Oh, yeah. I have to do that, too." Dylan grabbed his forehead as though it suddenly ached. Then, glancing over at her, he said, "I'm not much of a craft guy."

She smiled. That was another thing she already knew about Dylan, but it didn't give her a hint about what to make for him.

Neither spoke again until Dylan pulled into her mother's driveway, and his question then showed he had other things on his mind besides gift exchanges.

"Did you notice Ryan and Connor squinting when we were at the ice-cream shop?"

"Well—" she paused, considering "—I guess Connor was a little when he was reading off the menu."

"Ryan, too. Could be a reading problem, but more likely myopia." He smiled at her raised brow. "You know, nearsightedness."

"Why didn't you just say that?"

"I wanted to impress you with my medical lingo. Are you impressed?"

"Very." She was surprised he would want to impress her. Surprised, and pleased.

"I'm having Brad and Kelly bring the boys in for eye exams tomorrow. I've convinced the senior partners to write off the exams, and then I'm going to talk them into giving the Dentons the glasses for free hopefully, as well."

"I'm sure they'll agree to it, too." She spoke without hesitation. She had no doubt that this new Dylan could convince the soldiers at Fort Knox to hand over the gold there for charity without anyone raising a weapon.

Dylan was confident in a way he had never been before. It was different, but Jenna liked it. Not *liked* it, not like that...but no matter how she tried to explain it away, she wasn't sure. She couldn't defend her reaction when he'd helped her put on her coat, either. Her chills might have to do with the company, not the weather. Could it be that this confident, charmingly persuasive Dylan was having an effect on her?

No, it wasn't possible. She couldn't be attracted to Dylan. He was like a brother to her. Right?

Right, she told herself.

He'd never been a clock-watcher. Dylan had always liked that about himself, so he hated admitting that he'd spent more time looking at the office clock that Monday before Christmas than he had performing eye exams. The only time he'd been focused all day was when Ryan and Connor took turns in his examination chair, and he was helping the boys to see clearly for the first time in a long time. But after that, he was back to watching the numbers change on the clock.

He was just itching to start work on the rental house tonight. That had to be it, because he refused to believe he might be looking forward to seeing a certain someone after work today. That would be unacceptable.

As he drove to the Pearl Street house, he remained

Dana Corbit 333

hopeful that Matthew had been exaggerating when he'd described the amount of work necessary to bring the rental up to livable standards. That was his perfectionist brother's opinion, and one man's hovel might be another man's castle.

He knocked on the door, and when no one answered, he pushed it open. His optimism sank the moment he got a good look inside, and he dropped the gym bag containing a change of clothes on a semiclean spot near the entry. Matthew hadn't exaggerated, after all. This place was a mess.

Eggplant-colored paint would have been an unfortunate choice for a living room in the best of circumstances, but here it appeared almost as if someone had thrown the color at the wall and carpet. The baseboards were split and falling off the wall, or missing entirely. But his observations were imprecise at best since the whole room was buried under an inch of grime.

"Oh, Dylan, you made it," Jenna said as he entered a bedroom at the end of the hall. She was crouched and scrubbing carpet no one should touch without a hazardous-materials suit.

She'd pulled her hair back in a ponytail again, and was dressed for hard work in faded jeans, an old sweatshirt and huge rubber gloves. As she scrubbed, her long side bangs fell forward over her eyes.

Dylan surprised himself by reaching his hand up as if to tuck the stray strands behind her ear, despite that fact that they were across the room from each other. Apparently that wasn't far enough.

Shoving his hand in the pocket of his khaki slacks, he gazed from side to side, searching for witnesses. Good thing no one else had been paying attention to him or he would have had to explain his tender impulses concerning his former best friend. He was having a tough enough time making sense of those himself.

But Jenna's sisters and his brothers were too busy to notice his strange reaction. They were peering up at a hole in the ceiling big enough for Lizzie to squeeze through. The rest of the room was covered in chipped, pea-green paint and filth.

Logan stepped over and slapped Dylan on the back. "We've got our work cut out for us, bro. Did you get a gander at the kitchen?"

"Do I want to look at the kitchen?"

"Depends," Logan said with a shrug. "As long as you don't want to cook anything, keep anything cold or wash your hands, it's a great kitchen."

"They took all the appliances and the kitchen sink?"

"They didn't want anyone to accuse them of taking everything but the kitchen sink."

Logan's joke earned moans from the others, but he seemed pleased with his comedy routine, anyway.

"It's going to be hard to wash out paintbrushes without a sink," Dylan said.

Matthew, still in his suit from work, grinned over at him. "Not to worry. Caroline and I are headed to the home-improvement store for a stainless-steel sink and some cleaners after I stop by the house to change."

"I hope you're picking up some paint, too."

"We thought we would start with cleaning tonight and then let you and Jenna pick up the paint tomorrow," Matthew said. "That way we can blame you if the colors look bad."

"Anything would be better than this." Dylan caught his brother examining the trousers and dress shirt he'd worn beneath his lab coat at the office. "I brought some clothes to change into."

"Good thing, because we're all going to get dirty," Matthew said.

"Lizzie's going to love that. Speaking of Lizzie, where is she? And where are Mom and Mrs. Scott?" Not that he was dying to meet up with the meddling moms and have Caroline shoved at him again. Caroline would probably catch a flight back to Chicago the day after Christmas, instead of waiting for New Year's, if they didn't stop soon.

Jenna stood up from her spot that didn't look any cleaner for her effort. "They're bringing back take-out." She paused, looking around. "I don't know where we'll eat it."

"In the cars?" he supplied.

"Either that or we'd better clean one good spot and make it into a dining room."

Dylan grinned and glanced at where she'd been scrubbing. "I don't think that one's going to be it."

Matthew and Caroline headed for the door to complete their errand, and Logan and Haley filed out of the room, searching for more damage like the "skylight." Dylan could only hope they didn't find anything to top that.

"We could rent one of those carpet cleaners from the grocery store," Jenna said, though her frown suggested she wasn't convinced it would help.

Dylan shook his head. "We'll have to replace all the carpeting."

She looked at him over her shoulder. "Can we afford to do that? You might be an optometrist and Matthew might be a lawyer, but I fly in turbulent times in the airline industry. I'm not made of money."

"'Turbulent times'?" He chuckled. "Do you have any idea how much in student loans an optometry student can rack up?" Jenna shook her head. "I didn't, either. And Matthew probably won't pay off his law-school loans until Lizzie goes to college."

"Then how will we pay for carpeting, too?"

"Matthew said the owner was willing to split the costs for improvements, and if that's not enough, we can ask some other church members for donations. We should be fine, though, because I know a guy who owns a carpet store, and he'll—"

"Give you a deal, right?" She looked directly at him, her eyes narrowing. "You don't happen to know a guy who designs *haute couture,* do you?"

He studied her, grinning when he realized she was joking about her reputation as a clotheshorse. "Sorry. Can't help you out there."

She snapped her fingers. "Had to give it a shot," she said, and they both laughed.

Her laughter sounded like the tinkling of ice cubes in a tall glass of sweet tea. Before Jenna had come home, he'd forgotten how much he enjoyed hearing that sound, how easily it could touch a place inside him he'd declared off-limits. Now he was remembering exactly what it did to him and warning bells sounded in his head.

"We should replace the carpeting, then," she said. "We should make this place as special as we can for Connor and Ryan. Their biggest worries should be about which toys to play with, not whether they'll have a place to sleep tomorrow night."

"You really like them, don't you?"

"Can't help it. The boys, and Brad and Kelly. I can't imagine how hard it must be to worry about how you're going to provide for your kids. My heart just aches for them."

Dylan looked away, trying not to allow his surprise to show, but he knew he'd been caught.

"Why does it shock you every time I do or say something remotely decent?"

"I haven't been shocked," he protested, but when she looked back at him, her hands planted on her hips, he stopped. He didn't sound convincing, even to himself.

"People can change, you know. Even selfish, self-centered ones," she said.

"I know that."

"Do you?"

He shifted under her scrutiny. He didn't know why he continued to expect less of Jenna when she was proof that people could change. His mom had told him that Jenna had made a profession of faith a year or so ago, and everything he'd seen so far had confirmed a new, more benevolent spirit in her. She'd shown nothing but kindness to the Dentons, and she'd been nice to him, too, though he'd had a hard time being civil to her.

She had every right to her say now, so he waited, but she turned away, instead.

"Well, where do you want to start?" she asked.

Since he was bracing himself for an onslaught, it took him a few seconds to realize she was talking about the house, rather than the dressing-down he deserved.

"I'm sorry," he began, but she waved away his apology.

"Forget about it."

"Well—" he paused, looking around "—we could make a list of painting supplies and then start cleaning. I have a notebook in my bag." He started down the hall toward the bag by the door. "Later, we'll have Matthew get in touch with his landlord friend about the carpeting, so we can rip it out tonight. It'll be easier to paint without having to work around it."

"Will we have time to get it installed before Christmas?"

"Where there's a will, there's a way."

She nodded. In truth, he wasn't sure they would be able to get everything in place before Christmas no matter how much will they had. Dylan reached into his gym bag and grabbed a notebook and pen.

"We're really going to do this, aren't we?"

He smiled, allowing her contagious enthusiasm to push aside his worries. She'd told him to forget about the way he'd offended her, but amazingly, she appeared to have forgotten about it, as well. She forgave so easily, first about the funeral and now this. She didn't hold a grudge, either. As he changed in the one clean room of the house—the garage—he decided he should be more like her.

Now that was a thought he'd never expected to have about Jenna Scott, just as he never could have predicted that he would consider allowing himself to get close to her again. And yet, he was thinking about it.

Boundaries would be a must, of course, and he would never again be the human backhoe, waiting to scoop up the pieces after one of her failed relationships, but he could be some kind of…friend to her.

His confidence in that decision wavered the minute he stepped back into the house and headed for the rear bedroom. Jenna popped out of the closet where she'd been removing a broken rod and she nearly crashed into him. He reached out to steady her, and the feel of her arms nearly undid him. Suddenly his mouth was so dry that the house's lack of a kitchen sink became a personal affront. He simultaneously wanted to hold her forever and run from the room, never looking back.

Friendship with Jenna was impossible for him. It would never be enough. How many more times was he going to have to learn that lesson?

Chapter Seven

Jenna dipped her roller into a pan of butternut-colored paint and climbed onto the countertop to work. She wasn't skilled enough to use the painting pole without messing up the ceiling, so she had to make do. With Christmas only three days away, they were running out of time. Amateur painter or not, she was determined to do her part to finish the house so that the Dentons could spend Christmas in their new home.

Despite the amount of work they still had to do, Jenna was hopeful they would meet the tight deadline. Last night they'd installed the kitchen sink and then spent so many hours cleaning that she'd awoken this morning with stiff muscles. Dylan and Matthew had taken a few days off from work, and they'd all put in an eight-hour shift of painting with more to come.

Dylan had been able to convince the carpet dealer to not only offer a hefty discount but to schedule installation tomorrow. Now Matthew was waiting for a call from his friend at a freight company so they could have the appliances and furniture delivered by tomorrow afternoon. It could be done.

Careful not to drip paint, Jenna stood in a stooped position so she could roll the color along the strip of wall between the top of the cabinet and the ceiling.

"That works best if you put more paint on the wall, instead of on you."

At the sound of Dylan's voice behind her, she startled, bumping her head on the newly painted white ceiling. She glanced down at her sweatshirt, jeans and hands, all of which had been decorated with butternut smears.

"No comments from below, or you'll be up here."

"With you doing such a fine job? I wouldn't dream of interrupting genius like that." He stood, admiring the work for a few seconds before adding, "Hey, someone did a fine job of taping off the wall up there."

"I wonder who that could have been." She rolled her eyes at him.

Although he'd just turned down the job, Dylan snagged the painting pole Jenna had set aside, attached it to a new roller and started on a fresh section of the wall.

His reasons for working with her probably weren't what she would have hoped for—perhaps to cover up her painting mistakes or even to avoid being thrown together with her sister—but Jenna was pleased, anyway. For the first time since she'd returned to Markston, he was making the effort to spend time with her, instead of the other way around. And she found herself looking forward to every minute he was by her side.

At the sound of pounding feet, Jenna turned to see the Denton boys and Lizzie Warren bounding into the kitchen.

"Hi, Aunt Jenna." Lizzie tilted her head to the side to

look up at her. "Look." She held out one of her braids, now tipped in the royal-blue paint from the boys' bedroom. "I have paint in my hair. Connor and Ryan have some, too."

"Mine has specks of blue, Mr. Dylan," Ryan said, pointing to a series of tiny blue dots.

"I have a blue ear." Connor also had a few blue fingers, which hinted at how his ear might have gotten its color.

"You all have a lot of paint on you, but the idea is to get most of your paint on the wall." She glanced at Dylan and found it hard to keep a straight face. "At least that's what I hear."

Haley hurried in with a damp cloth that she used to wipe some of the paint out of Lizzie's hair. She wiped the paint off the boys' hair and ears before whisking her stepdaughter from the room so Lizzie could "help" her parents in the living room.

"Boys, are you working in there?" Brad called out from the master bedroom where he and Kelly were painting the walls a sage green.

"Sounds like duty calling." Dylan stepped over to the small collection of unopened paint cans and selected a container of white cabinet paint. "If you guys help Mr. Logan clean up in your room, I'll teach you how to paint the baseboards with this stuff."

"Will you really? We get to really paint this time?"

Dylan nodded. "Really."

Ryan's eyes were wide with excitement, which could have been as much about the attention from their painting instructor as the opportunity to play with paint. Funny, Dylan seemed as excited as the boys were, though he'd already spent a whole day with brushes and rollers. His attachment to these boys couldn't have been more endearing. The twins probably weren't even aware how blessed they were to have a friend like Dylan. She'd enjoyed that blessing once herself and was beginning to think she might get to again.

"You two sure have done a nice job in here," Mrs. Warren announced as she and Jenna's mother joined the rest of them in kitchen. They rolled in the snack-filled cooler they'd brought over earlier to make up for the house's lack of a refrigerator.

"Almost done," Dylan said as he ran his roller sideways along the strip of wall.

"Well, then, Dylan." Amy cast a sidelong glance at Jenna's mother. "Don't you think that Caroline could use some help painting the hall bath?"

Jenna didn't have to look at Dylan to know that strong jaw of his had tightened. Her jaw was tight enough, and the moms weren't even meddling in her life. She could almost hear the matchmaking wheels cranking up again, and even the imagined sound of it grated on her nerves. Why couldn't they just leave Dylan alone? And, of course, Caroline. There had to be something she could do to help him avoid all this awkwardness. Uh, them.

"Have you ever known Caroline to need help with anything?" When several surprised glances turned Jenna's way, she rushed on, "I mean, she would never admit needing help, even if she did. You know, that whole she-is-woman-roaring thing, an ode to Helen Reddy."

Her gaze slid toward Dylan, and he coughed away what sounded like a laugh before looking back at his mother. "Anyway, I need to finish up in here."

"And then he's promised to teach the boys to paint moldings."

"He did," Ryan announced, his brother supporting his statement with an excited nod.

"Well, I suppose…" Trina Scott let her words trail off, her disappointment obvious.

The matchmakers excused themselves, probably to check in with Caroline and see if she really would refuse all assistance. They weren't going to win this one; Jenna could tell them that right now.

When the boys rushed off to help Logan so they would be ready to start on the baseboards, Jenna and Dylan were alone, and an unexpected awareness of that fact settled over her like static electricity. She couldn't decide whether she liked the sensation, only recognizing its newness.

"Thanks."

"You're welcome," she said without looking at him.

She didn't know for sure what his gratitude even meant—that he wasn't interested in her lovely sister, that their mothers' matchmaking attempts annoyed him, even maybe something completely different. When she finally worked up the courage to look at him, she found him watching her again, his eyebrows drawn together as if he couldn't quite figure her out.

"You go ahead and catch up with the boys. I can finish the rest of this and wash the brushes." She gestured toward the new stainless-steel sink that had already proved its usefulness as they'd all rinsed dozens of brushes, rollers and paint pans in it.

"You're sure?" He glanced up at the wall, unconvinced.

"I've watched you all day, so I know what I'm doing. I can handle it. Really."

He shrugged, then disconnected his roller from the paint pole, resting the roller on the pan. "Meet us in the garage when you're finished."

And then, before he left the room, he winked at her.

Jenna suddenly felt like a teenager again, just like when the captain of the football team had flirted with her. Dylan couldn't have been more different from that Neanderthal or any of the other boys she'd dated in high school and college, and yet she recognized those sweaty palms and the flutter of her pulse. She was not attracted to Dylan. She was just so happy that they were friendly again. That was all.

Dismissing any lingering doubts, she chose to focus on their earlier conversation, instead. She'd surprised him again by doing something nice, this time defending him. In all the years she'd known him, she'd never helped *him* with a problem. All the help and advice had always come her way. So it felt good to be the one watching *his* back. He needed a friend on his side to help him deal with the matchmakers, or he wouldn't stand a chance against their powers of persuasion.

But had she intervened for his benefit—or hers? She didn't want to ponder that because the answer might be as confusing as the electricity that had buzzed between them in the kitchen air. If this were anyone else, she would have read all that wattage as attraction, but this was Dylan, sweet, bookish Dylan, who'd always been more attached to his chemistry set than to any girl.

The new Dylan was different than the boy she remembered, but she still couldn't picture him with her independent older sister. Funny, she couldn't really picture him with any woman.

Except me.

As those words stole into her thoughts uninvited, her hand jerked, leaving a streak of butternut paint on the crisp white ceiling. Crouching down, she jumped off the counter and wet a paper towel before climbing up again. She didn't know where that thought had come from, but she shoved it to the back of her mind where it belonged.

Four years ago she'd messed up their friendship by not recognizing that his feelings for her had changed, and now that she had the possibility of restoring their friendship, she was trying to mess it up again by changing the rules. No, she would not let that happen. Too much was at stake.

Just as she touched the damp towel to the spot on the ceiling, Dylan pulled open the door between the kitchen and the garage and strode into the room.

"Well, there's an *oops*."

"I guess I didn't know what I was doing, after all." She frowned at the spot and started wiping, almost afraid to make eye contact with Dylan for fear he might smile at her and cause her to spill paint or something.

"Maybe you should blot at that, instead of wiping."

Dylan wet another sheet of paper towel, hopped up on the counter and started blotting. He was so close that their elbows bumped a few times and there didn't seem to be enough oxygen in the room for the both of them, but they quickly cleared away the mess.

He squinted as he studied the damp spot from a few angles. "We might have to touch up the white a bit. Let's see how it dries."

All they needed today was something more to paint. "I just got distracted and…"

Dylan scanned the room, appearing to take in the plain wood cabinets, simple laminated floor and spaces where appliances would go eventually. "There's not a lot in here that could serve as a distraction."

Jenna could only smile at that as she avoided Dylan's gaze, hoping he wouldn't see the heightened color in her cheeks.

Dylan lowered the roller into the pan of white paint with a final-sounding *thunk*. They were finished. At least as finished as possible when the newly repaired ceiling in the second bedroom couldn't be painted for a few days. Still, they'd accomplished a lot today, painting all six rooms of the two-bedroom bungalow, plus a hallway. It was amazing what ten adults and three children could do with a short deadline and a lot of heart.

This was really going to happen. Brad, Kelly and the twins would wake up on Christmas morning in their new home, even if some of the smaller repairs would have to wait until after they'd moved in.

Dylan didn't know when it had become so critical to him that they meet this arbitrary deadline, when a few days either way wouldn't harm anyone, but it mattered. He wanted so much to return some small part of what the fire had taken from the Dentons.

"Are we going to nail the baseboards to the wall now, Mr. Dylan?" Connor asked as he rubbed his paint-covered hands together.

Dylan shook his head. "They need to dry longer." He didn't want to promise the boys they could help again when it was already late. That work probably would be completed after they were in their bed back at the hotel.

As if cued by his thoughts, Brad and Kelly pushed through the door into the garage. Dylan couldn't help but smile at the contrast between Kelly and Jenna after a day of work. While Kelly had only specks of green paint on her hands, Jenna wore an abstract painting of colors on her work clothes.

"Hey, you two, it's time for us to get back so you guys can go to bed." Kelly shook her head at her sons' automatic groans. "Now say good-night. We'll come back tomorrow."

While Brad corralled his boys, heading them inside to wash up at the sink, Kelly turned back to Dylan.

"I don't know how to thank you."

"You've already thanked us." He smiled. "Several times, actually."

She shrugged but grinned back at him. "I can't help it. This place is perfect."

"Perfect?" He lifted an eyebrow. "Did you see that drywall job Logan did on the ceiling in the boys' room? I wouldn't call *that* perfect. And the way the bathtub drips, I wouldn't call *that* perfect."

"You know what I mean. Your two families have been a blessing to us."

"Thanks." Dylan's throat tightened. The Dentons had been a far bigger blessing for him than he ever could have been for them. "So hopefully everything will come together, and you'll be home."

When the garage door opened again, he expected to see Brad and the boys, but Matthew came through first, flipping his cell phone closed as he approached.

The rest of the workers tromped out after him, with Brad and the boys taking up the rear.

"I've just received word that we've hit a snag." Matthew sent an apologetic look toward Brad and Kelly before he continued, "The trucking company that was supposed to deliver the furniture and the new appliances couldn't schedule a delivery until next Tuesday."

"Isn't that December twenty-ninth?" Haley asked.

"Is that after Christmas?" Lizzie wanted to know.

Matthew answered both questions with a nod. "Apparently it's hard to get people to volunteer to work extra shifts right around Christmas."

For several long seconds, no one spoke. It was as if someone had let all the air out of a balloon. After riding four days on the drive of having a deadline, Dylan felt deflated.

"Aw, man," Logan answered for all of them.

Connor exchanged a sad look with his twin. "Does this mean we can't move in to the house?"

"You will, but just not yet," Dylan explained. "I know it's tough living in the hotel, but it will only be a few more days." Maybe he shouldn't make promises at all. He'd already gotten the boys' hopes up once, and look how well that had gone.

Ryan grimaced. "But what about Santa? We already left the letter at the old house, telling him we would be in this house. How will he find us now?"

"Now everyone," Jenna said, "let's calm down. This doesn't have to be a big setback." She turned to the boys. "We can go back to the site of the old house and leave a new note. I'm sure Santa will understand."

The boys nodded, looking relieved.

Jenna turned to Dylan. "You know, this isn't all

bad. Sure, it would have been nice for everyone to be settled by Christmas Eve, but you said yourself that there were plenty of jobs still to do around here. The closets, for instance. Did anyone get around to painting them? And what about second coats? A few of the rooms could use them. And the moldings…" She let her words trail away.

Several murmurs of consensus came behind Jenna.

"She does have a point," Brad said. He paused to glance first at his wife and then at his sons before continuing, "And, you know, this setback doesn't mean we can't sleep here on Christmas Eve, either."

He turned to Dylan. "Now, you said the carpet will definitely be installed tomorrow, right?"

"That's when they've scheduled it."

Brad gave a firm nod. "Then we're all set. We'll just bring sleeping bags…" He stopped, his gaze darting back to Dylan. "Do you have sleeping bags we could borrow?"

Dylan indicated his younger brother with a tilt of his head. "What do you say, Ranger Logan?"

Logan grinned. "Gotcha covered, buddy."

"Okay, then." Brad turned back to his sons. "We'll sleep in sleeping bags on the floor, so we can wake up on Christmas in our new house."

"You mean we get to go camping?" Ryan asked.

The room filled with hope again. Dylan had Jenna to thank for getting the process started. She hadn't let a minor setback discourage her, just as she hadn't let any of his off-putting behavior hinder her from trying to reconnect with him.

She'd become an amazing woman in the past four years—he couldn't deny it. She inspired and impressed him at every turn, and he felt...proud. Proud of who she'd become.

When she caught him staring at her, probably looking like a lovestruck teenager, he gave her a thumbs-up, hoping she couldn't read his mind.

Chapter Eight

Flipping on the overhead light in her mother's partially finished basement, Jenna jumped at the squeal coming from the far corner. Under only the illumination of a small desk lamp, Haley stood in front of an easel, a palette and brush in her hands.

"What are you doing down here?" Jenna asked as she padded from the carpeted area with its comfy couches to the section of bare concrete where Haley had set up.

"Shh. What are you trying to do, give away the location of my secret studio?" Haley waited until her sister stood next to her before she spoke again. "Mom said I could work down here on my secret gift."

"Your house wasn't good enough?" Jenna had claimed this place herself the other evening, and she was hoping to get some work done on Dylan's gift.

"Ever tried to keep a secret around a four-year-old?"

"Guess not," Jenna said.

"Matthew's no better. He keeps sniffing around the house, looking for my gift. He's convinced himself I drew his name, and I figured I would just keep him guessing. That's why I told him I had to come work over here."

"Well, aren't you a sneaky one. Does Caroline know you're down here?"

"Sure, but she's been holed up in the guest room for hours working on her own gift."

Jenna stepped closer to the easel where her sister was putting the finishing touches on a painting of daisies in a vase. "Hey, that's amazing."

"I hope Amy will like it," Haley said. "Have you started on Dylan's present?"

"Kind of."

"Well, are you going to show it to me?"

Jenna lifted a shoulder. "I don't think so. It's not as amazing as yours is. You're the only one of us who's good at making crafts."

"I'm sure Dylan won't mind."

"Are you kidding? He'll probably laugh his head off when he sees it."

Haley was swirling a glob of white paint into a spot of yellow, creating a pale yellow color for some of her flower petals. "Why are you so worried about it, anyway? This is Dylan we're talking about. He'll like anything you make." She turned to study her sister. "Come to think of it, why did you need his name so badly in the exchange?"

Jenna noted that she hadn't fooled her sister with her interest in trading names, after all. "I don't know. It's just a friend thing."

"What's the deal with you two, anyway? You used to be so close, and now there's a strange tension between you. It's almost as if—"

"Just a misunderstanding," Jenna said too quickly.

Haley lowered the cloth over her easel. "Well, Christmas is a good time for healing relationships. But then, at least according to the movies, it's also a good time for family brawls over the Christmas turkey."

Jenna frowned. "Thanks for the good thoughts."

"Don't mention it."

Finished for the evening, Haley set her palette aside and started up the stairs with her brushes in her hands. She stopped about halfway up and turned back to Jenna.

"Relax about the gift. And don't try to make it into a peace offering for your misunderstanding. Sometimes things take time to heal."

Haley pressed the fingertips on her free hand to her lips and blew a kiss. "See you tomorrow."

Once Haley had closed the door behind her, Jenna stepped to the row of metal shelves and pulled a shoe-box out from a waist-high shelf. She carried the box over to the sofa and opened it. The scarf inside had uneven stitches, and some rows of gray and white were wider than others were, but she'd made it herself, and she couldn't help being a little proud of her effort.

Had she been making it as a peace offering as Haley had suggested? Was that the whole reason behind her need to have his name in the drawing? Or was it more than that?

Sitting back in the chair, she curled her feet under her and stretched the material across her lap. Then she pulled the crochet hook from the box, looped the yarn twice around it and slipped the second loop over the first.

She had better do a whole lot more looping, and fast, if she hoped to make Dylan's gift long enough to keep him warm this winter and have it finished in time for Christmas morning.

Glancing at the wall clock, she set to work on the first of several hundred stitches she would complete tonight. That would leave little room for sleep before tomorrow morning's cookie-baking event, but she didn't mind. She had a gift to finish. It would be a gift from her heart. No strings—of yarn or anything else—attached.

"Miss Jenna, look at this one."

Sitting on his knees at Mrs. Scott's kitchen table, Connor held up a spruce-shaped sugar cookie, so pitiful it could have been the inspiration for Charlie Brown's Christmas tree. Jenna applauded.

"My star is better," Ryan announced from his seat across from his brother.

The creation Ryan held in his palm had only four points instead of five, and it was sort of smashed in the center, so if anything, Dylan would have given the two cookies equal grades. Only they weren't grading.

"Do you like mine?" Lizzie held up an angel-shaped cookie that apparently had lost a wing.

"They're all wonderful." Jenna took a few seconds to ooh and ahh over each of the cookies before helping the children transport them from the flour-covered tabletop to the cookie sheet. "I'm sure they'll all taste great, too."

Kelly stood up from her chair to get a better look at the creations on the sheet. "Boy, you're all doing a great job."

"Those are some cookies, all right," Brad said with a chuckle.

Last night Jenna had invited the Dentons to join
them for Christmas-cookie baking this morning, hoping to distract the boys from their disappointment that
the house wouldn't be ready for Christmas. Dylan had
been touched by her caring gesture and had also recognized the benefit of having the children out of the Pearl
Street house while the carpet layers did their jobs, but
he'd dreaded the idea when Jenna had first mentioned
it. Just the thought of Christmas cookies had inspired
memories of stress-filled holiday-baking events with
their perfectionist pressure. At-home baking with a
professional had its disadvantages. He'd been hoping
to escape that family tradition when they'd adopted the
Dentons for Christmas.

But so far, Jenna's cookie party had been more about
the fun of creating than the products, more about time
spent together. She didn't worry about cookies that only
a child would eat, and she didn't even mind the flour
in her hair or the food coloring that had splattered on
her sweatshirt.

He was glad now he'd relented and invited his niece
to join them, as well. This was the kind of memory he
wanted Lizzie to have of Christmas.

At the beep of the oven timer, Jenna removed the
first tray of cookies.

"Just look at these, everybody. Have you ever seen
better cookies?"

"Well, not today…er, I mean, not in a long time."
Dylan bit his lip and looked over at her, but Jenna only
smiled. Come to think of it, he'd never seen Jenna bake
before, and she'd never mentioned liking to spend time
in the kitchen. He would have thought Haley had been
the family's crowned baker, but it just went to show

that he didn't know everything about the Scott sisters, after all.

"You never told me how you convinced our mothers not to attend this little shindig," he shouted over the buzz of the twirling beaters as she made frosting. "I'm surprised my mom didn't jump all over it and try to resurrect her Christmas-baking schedule."

"It wasn't easy. Your dear mother could convince a rottweiler to hand over his bone."

"Don't I know it."

"I had to rely on my own mother. I told her I planned to make a huge mess in her kitchen, and I was going to make her watch." She glanced over at him and shrugged. "She really hates messes."

"I remember."

"After I mentioned the mess, Mom was more than willing to convince your mother to go out with her for coffee, instead of joining us."

"Remind me never to stand in your way when you want something."

He leaned against the counter as the truth of his own words settled in. She'd wanted them to be friends again, and he was having a hard time denying her that. He no longer even wanted to. As he watched her, he expected her to gloat, but she wasn't looking his way. Only the slight upturn of her lips told him she'd even registered what he'd said.

Jenna placed the frosting, several butter knives and a plate of cooled cookies on the table in front of Brad, Kelly and the three children.

"I'll be back in a minute," she said. "I have to go scrape some of this flour out of my hair."

As he watched her go, a familiar longing settled over

him. He wanted to be with her, to be around her. But
he tried to fight it. He'd already learned the hard way
that to long for more than friendship from her was to
swing out on a trapeze of faith with neither a safety
net below nor any promise of someone to catch him
when he fell. Only a fool would take a risk like that
again. And he was no fool. What he'd been feeling for
her these past few days was just…attraction. And he
was strong enough to ignore that.

Shaking away those unproductive thoughts, Dylan
glanced back to the table. Kelly must have taken Lizzie
to the restroom while he and Jenna were talking because Brad was there alone with his sons, a new ball
of dough on the table and a rolling pin in his hands.

The image was more a baking free-for-all than a
sweet domestic scene, but no one seemed to mind. In
fact, anyone who didn't already know about the tragedy this family had faced less than a week ago would
never guess it from their happy faces. The boys hadn't
lost everything; they still had everything that mattered.

It was the kind of simple, everyday, father-son moment that every boy deserved to enjoy, the type Dylan
had no recollection of ever experiencing with his own
father. But he wasn't jealous. He was pleased that the
twins would have this kind of memory of their father,
rather than an empty place at a table or an empty smile
in a fading photograph. Like his.

Swallowing, he shook away unwelcome thoughts
for the second time that morning. All these memories
and feelings needed to stay in the past where they belonged. Was it Jenna's reappearance in his life that had
stirred the sand of passing time once again? Or maybe

it was just the holidays. Christmas could be the loneli-est time of the year.

When he glanced at the kitchen doorway, he found Jenna standing there, her hair pulled back in a pony-tail as usual. Only she wasn't watching the scene at the table. She was watching him.

When they were younger, Dylan had avoided shar-ing many of his feelings with Jenna even after his fa-ther had left and he really needed someone to listen. He'd worried that if his friendship became too cumber-some, she would pull away from the weight. But now as he read the warmth in her eyes, the compassion, he came to a surprising conclusion. She just might be one person—maybe the only one—who really understood. And that conclusion scared him more than even the re-alization that he was still attracted to her. Much more.

Chapter Nine

Amy Warren broke off a piece of blueberry scone, slathered it with butter and popped it in her mouth. She needed a sip of her Christmas-mint latte just to swallow it.

"Blueberry sawdust."

Trina grinned at her from across the tiny table at A Fine Cup coffee shop.

"Critiquing the baked goods again, Amy?"

"Why do you let me order things like this when we go out?" she said with a frown.

"A baker's standards are pretty high. That's why I talked you out of joining in on Jenna's baking party."

"Are you sure you weren't more worried about the mess?"

It was Trina's turn to frown. "I'll probably find flour in the crevices of my hardwood floors for months."

Amy spun her cup around. "But it would have been nice to get to share at least one of our Christmas traditions like we'd planned."

"Now, remember that I'm telling you this as your best friend who loves you. You need to quit pouting about the change in plans. You're being selfish, and I didn't even think you were capable of selfishness." Trina pinned her with her stare. "Our families are doing exactly what they should be this Christmas, trying to be God's hands in the world. That's how I raised my daughters, and that's how you raised your sons."

Amy swallowed as the truth of Trina's words struck her squarely in the heart. When she spoke again, she couldn't look at Trina's face. "I've always wanted the guys to be giving men. And they are. It's just that certain traditions are really hard to let go of."

"Especially the ones that helped us make it through the tough times," Trina added.

Amy nodded, though she wasn't ready to admit aloud that Trina was right. She acknowledged, though, that her friend understood her pain. Both had experienced devastating loss, although Trina's had been over losing her beloved husband to death while Amy's husband had deserted her and the boys.

"It's too bad we couldn't convince Caroline to host this activity with Dylan, instead of Jenna," Trina said.

Amy smiled, knowing her friend had purposely changed the subject.

"The Plan isn't working too well this time, is it?"

Trina shrugged. "It wasn't going swimmingly last spring, either, and we still ended up with our two families joined by marriage."

"It didn't turn out the way we planned, though," Amy pointed out. "If we'd had our way, Matthew would have ended up with Caroline, and then our two middle children would have paired off, followed by the youngest. But we were wrong."

"You yourself said that's because God has a sense

of humor. Matthew and Caroline were too alike. But Caroline and Dylan? They're just different enough to be perfect together."

"Maybe too different," Amy said. "I just mean that Caroline is still sticking to her guns about this permanently single plan. She's got this idea that her lofty career aspirations are incompatible with marriage and family."

"Give her time. If anyone is patient, it's your Dylan. He doesn't kiss a lot of lady frogs while he's waiting for his frog princess."

Amy closed her eyes, shaking her head. "Oh, don't remind me." When her eyes popped open, she lifted an eyebrow. "That's quite a fairytale notion coming from a pragmatist like you."

"I was appealing to *your* romantic side."

"Have you considered that we could be wrong again?" Amy asked. "It is possible, isn't it?"

"Of course it isn't. What were you thinking? Caroline with Logan?"

Trina's incredulous tone told Amy what she thought of that. Amy had to agree. The man-about-town and the feminist? That would never happen.

"Or maybe you're thinking of Dylan with Jenna because they're the middle kids," Trina said.

"No, they were good friends for too long."

"So we have to focus on Dylan and Caroline, right?"

Amy nodded. And who knew? Maybe God really did intend Dylan for Caroline and would let all of them know eventually if they were only patient.

"It would be easier if they had an unlimited amount of time to be together."

"You don't think we should try another one of those

ambush-date things, do you?" Amy winced even as she asked it. After their last dinner party, she was blessed that Matthew had ever spoken to her again. It had seemed like such a good idea to fly Caroline in and trick her and Matthew into having dinner together— that is until Matthew blew up and told both mothers to stay out of his love life. The only good thing that came out of that night was that it forced Matthew to admit he had feelings for Haley, instead.

Trina shook her head. "Caroline told me if I ever did something like that again, she would no longer consider me her mother."

Trina pressed her index finger to her lip, trying to come up with a plan. "Do you think either of them got the other's name in the gift exchange?"

"I don't know who has Dylan's name, but I know for sure that Lizzie pulled Caroline's name, since I'm helping her with the gift."

"We should have taken our names out so we could have known who everyone had."

Amy shook her index finger at her friend to indicate that was a great idea. "We'll do that next Christmas."

"We can't wait until next year. Biological clocks are ticking. We aren't getting younger, either."

"Speak for yourself," Amy said in a joke they'd shared many times as she was ten years older than her friend.

Trina pushed open the door, causing the attached bells to jangle. "I am speaking for me…and you." Trina's lilting laugh mingled with the other Christmas sounds in Markston's downtown. "We have to find a way to get those two together in the next ten days."

* * *

"Ho. Ho. Ho. Merry— Hey, is anyone back there?"

The loud thud that followed surprised Jenna as much as the poor imitation of the jolly old elf coming from the living room. Wasn't Dylan supposed to be out running errands this afternoon?

"In here," she called, though she wasn't sure anyone heard her over the herd of buffalo that stampeded down the hall toward Dylan.

Before she'd made it to the living room, the scent told her what all the fuss was about: a Christmas tree. Dylan and Brad were wresting a huge plastic bag off its branches, but she could already tell it was more than big enough to fill the room's empty corner.

Sporting a Santa hat with his field jacket, jeans and boots, Dylan looked over the tree at her and grinned. He was thrilled with his gift, and she was excited for him. She'd been curious when she'd caught him watching Brad with the boys while they were baking. Did Dylan have any happy memories of his own father at Christmas like the ones she cherished, now that her father had passed on?

She must have stared too long because his eyebrow quirked. Disconcerting warmth spread over her neck and face, but she couldn't look away from him at first.

When she finally did, she reminded herself that this was Dylan, the friend of her heart, and she had no business looking at him like that. Even though she was tempted to look at him all day. *Unless*...

She didn't know how to process what was happening, but now wasn't the time. Soon. Sometime soon she would have to sit down and analyze these new feelings that scared her to death.

"Look, Miss Jenna, isn't it the most beautiful tree you've ever seen?"

From Ryan's wide eyes, she could see that he thought so. Having managed to take the bag off, the two men had set the tree in the corner. It brought some much needed color to the room, with its neutral walls and carpeting.

Jenna looked past Dylan to several items piled just inside the front door. Three new boxes of lights were laid next to another box with a star-shaped tree topper. Beyond those, two huge bags of popped popcorn were leaning against the wall.

Jenna cocked an eyebrow. "Hungry?"

"Popcorn garlands." He bent and picked up a small plastic shopping bag. Inside was a pack of extra-large sewing needles, scissors and two spools of heavy thread.

"You thought of everything."

"Not quite everything," Matthew reported as he entered from the kitchen, carrying a hammer and a short piece of molding for one of the closets. "Haley and Lizzie just went home for the shop vacuum. That popcorn's going to make a mess."

"Somebody always has to be the spoilsport," Dylan replied.

In her side vision, Jenna caught sight of Ryan and Connor trying to open one of the bags of popcorn.

"Wait!" Kelly called out, but she was a fraction of a second too late.

The bag split down the middle, and everyone watched as the boys fell away from each other, plastic and popped kernels trailing after them in opposite directions as they collapsed to the floor. Ryan and Connor scanned the mess and turned their guilty faces to their parents.

"See what I mean? We need a vacuum."

Matthew chuckled, and then the others joined him. The boys didn't seem to know what to make of it.

"Sorry," Connor murmured.

Ryan followed his brother. "Yeah. Sorry."

"Congratulations, boys. You've made it a white Christmas, after all," Jenna said.

"Yeah, look at this. You've made it snow."

Dylan exchanged a glance with her, his amazing eyes full of light and laughter. She quickly turned from him and went to the kitchen to find something they could use to clean up the popcorn. At least that was the reason she told herself as she fled the room.

An hour later they had formed several long popcorn garlands, and the boys were winding them around the tree to go along with the tree topper and strands of lights. When they were finished, they flipped off the ceiling lights and all stood back as Brad plugged in the Christmas-tree lights to a chorus of oohs and ahhs.

"It's so pretty," Kelly exclaimed. "Thank you so much for doing this, Dylan."

Though Dylan nodded and smiled, Jenna could tell that something wasn't right, so while the Dentons were preoccupied with the tree, she sidled over to him.

"What's the matter?"

He leaned close and whispered out of the side of his mouth, "The tree looks bare."

"Come on, Dylan. It looks great. And they love it."

He shook his head. "It's not finished."

Jenna studied the tree. She could see what he meant. Like the rest of the house, it looked incomplete. She scanned the room, looking for something they could use for decorations, but used paint cans didn't seem festive enough.

"I've got it." Dylan crossed the room to Haley, who'd returned with the shop vac just in time for cleanup. "Hey, do you think you guys can finish up here? I've got another errand to run."

"What do you have to do?" Jenna tried to keep the disappointment from her voice but knew she'd failed. She couldn't help it. Whatever this thing was between them, their days together were ticking away, and she wanted to spend as much time with him as she could.

Grabbing his coat from the pile by the door, he started out and then turned back to her. "You're coming, aren't you?"

Jenna grabbed her coat. She didn't bother to ask him where they were going. She didn't care. It didn't matter where they went as long as they could spend time together.

Chapter Ten

Dylan stuck his head inside the door, refusing to acknowledge any of the second-guessing going on in his
thoughts. This was a good idea, and he wouldn't talk
himself out of it.

"Mom? You home?"

"In here," Amy called from family room.

He slipped off his shoes and crossed into the room,
waving for Jenna to follow. His mother was curled up
on the sectional with a romance novel.

"I thought you might still be at the bakery." He
walked to the couch and bent to kiss her cheek.

"Then why'd you come here?"

"I *hoped* you'd be here, silly."

Tucking a bookmark into the page, she lay her book
aside and crossed her arms. "What is it, Dylan?"

He cleared his throat, hating that he was nervous.
"We were just over at the Pearl Street house, which
looks great with the new carpeting and the moldings."
He cleared his throat a second time. "Anyway, there's
a Christmas tree at the house now. It's decorated with

lights and popcorn garlands, but that's all. It looks kind of…"

Dylan let his words fall away as he turned to his mother's tree, its limbs drooping with the weight of their ornaments. He was still trying to come up with the right words when Jenna spoke up.

"It looks kind of plain," she told his mother. "Unfinished."

He turned back. "So I was hoping—*we* were hoping that you might be willing to donate a few decorations from your tree. I know they're special and all, but maybe you could spare some."

"It wouldn't have to be many," Jenna added, supporting his request, a request she'd known nothing about until that moment. "Just the ones without a lot of sentimental value."

He sent a grateful look her way, but when he shifted his gaze back to his mother, her bewildered face tore at his heart. She scanned the pieces of her overwhelming collection as if each held a special memory, and the memories were about to be stolen from her, one by one. Immediately, he was ready to backtrack. No charity project was worth making his mother this sad.

"You know, we don't have to—"

"Dylan." His mother spoke his name so softly that he almost missed it in his placating ramblings.

"Yes, Mom?"

She pressed her lips together for several seconds, and when she finally spoke, she didn't look his way. "Take whatever you need."

With that she walked out of the room, and soon her footfalls could be heard on the stairs.

"Why do I get the feeling there was a lot more to

that conversation than the words you and your mom said out loud?" Jenna asked after a long pause.

"Because there was."

Though her curiosity all but thrummed in the room, she didn't ask. She deserved an explanation, Dylan decided, but that would have to come later, when the memories weren't so close around them.

He told her he needed a box from the garage, and when he returned, he found Jenna standing next to the tree, delicately touching ornament after ornament as if without knowing the whole story she understood the pieces' value.

She looked back at him over her shoulder. "These are all so beautiful. I never noticed before."

"It's hard to see any of them when they're all so crowded in there together."

"But that doesn't mean that they're not important to your mom. Are you sure we should be taking them? They all seem to have a lot of sentimental value to her."

"It's okay. Really." He nodded for emphasis because she looked skeptical. "Mom never would have agreed if she didn't mean it. She just left the room because it hurts too much to watch."

Jenna traced her finger over the miniature drum that was attached to a Little Drummer Boy ornament. "I don't know. Your mom seemed to be having a hard time giving up these things."

He pushed the box closer to the Christmas tree. "Some sacrifices are tougher than others."

He pulled off a little red sleigh and stuck it in the box. He didn't bother removing the green metal hook from it since it would be going back on a tree as soon as they returned to the rental house.

"Remember, we're taking from her abundance." He pulled off an animated pig dressed in Mrs. Claus getup and showed it to her. "I promise, we'll only take the ones with the least amount of sentimental value—none that my brothers or I made for Mom."

Jenna seemed to accept that and started removing a few items, showing them to him for approval before lowering them gently into the box. Soon they had enough ornaments to cover the Dentons' tree.

As he closed the top flaps of the box, Jenna turned back to the tree, folding her arms across her chest as she studied it. She glanced around the room at the other items blanketing the tables and windows. "Anything else you want to take?"

He stared at her incredulously.

"Joking," she said with a grin.

"I think we've traumatized Mom enough for one day. We can come back tomorrow and ask her to donate the giant plastic carolers in the front yard." He glanced toward the doorway and then leaned closer and lowered his voice conspiratorially. "I've always thought those old gals should carol somewhere else."

"Well, Dylan Warren, you're not nice at all."

"You're just figuring that out now?"

"I'm a slow learner."

"Maybe, but when you do learn things, you master them so well that you could teach a class." He hadn't meant for his comment to sound so serious, but as soon as he said it, the truth in his words struck him. She *had* learned a lot of things, and he'd become the one who needed to be taught.

Jenna blinked, but she didn't comment on what he'd said.

They gathered the box and their coats. Dylan paused at the bottom of the stairs to call up to his mother, thanking her and telling her goodbye.

"I'll call her later tonight," he said to Jenna when his mother didn't answer.

The only sounds during the drive from his mother's house to the rental house were the whir of the engine and the carols coming from the all-Christmas-format radio station.

He was trying to come up with a way to broach the subject when she turned just as he put the car in park. On one of the shortest days of the year, darkness had already settled, so they couldn't see each other, but he could still feel her gaze on him.

"Tell me something, Dylan."

"What's that?" He shut off the engine and turned to face her.

"What's the real deal with your family and Christmas?"

Until Dylan started laughing, Jenna was worried that she'd brought up a topic that was even more off-limits than she'd guessed. But he'd invited her into this story when he'd asked her to come along to his mom's house, and she couldn't help being curious.

"You sure know how to phrase a question," he said as his laugh tapered off. "My family and Christmas. Let's just say that Hollywood doesn't make warm Christmas specials about Warren-family Christmases."

He seemed to be waiting for her to contradict him, but she'd seen enough now to know that all had not been perfect over the Warren-family holidays. She settled with her back against the car door and waited for him to fill in the blanks. She might know some of this already if she'd only been listening years ago, but there was nothing she could do about that. She was listening now, and now was what mattered.

"Christmas was always a frantic holiday at our house, long before my...father left."

The catch in his voice made Jenna long to reach out to touch him, but she wasn't sure how that gesture would be received, so she clasped her hands in her lap. "Why do you think that is?" she prompted when his pause lingered.

"Mom was always making up for the fact that Dad—my father was never involved in any of it. He never came to our Christmas pageants at church, never had time to look at our Christmas lists. He would show up to watch us open presents, but he always had the TV on."

She didn't miss that Dylan was uncomfortable referring to Elliot Warren as Dad. He had every right to his anger at the man who'd deserted his family. She was furious on Dylan's behalf.

"Your dad sounds so different from the man I knew when our families went on vacations together," she said. "He seemed pleasant."

Dylan shrugged. "He was different at home. Mom must have believed that if she filled every holiday minute with frantic, festive activities, my brothers and I wouldn't notice he was missing. So each year she added more activities, and the holiday seemed more desolate."

"That must have been strange," she said, "feeling lonely and alone in a frenzy of activity and people."

He nodded. "The Christmas celebration was just a symbol of bigger problems."

"You know how jealous I used to be of all your family Christmas traditions?" she said, shaking her head. "As often as we moved, we barely had any traditions at all. You guys had all these amazing events, and I wanted that."

"That coveting thing is in the Ten Commandments, you know. Thou shalt not covet they neighbor's house. Thou shalt not covet thy neighbor's Christmas celebrations," he said in a solemn voice. He tried to keep a straight face, but then he started chuckling. Jenna couldn't help laughing with him.

"We're even, then, because I used to envy *your* family," Dylan said.

"You're serious? Even with all the moves? How could anyone envy that?"

"You took everything important with you each time you moved."

Jenna considered that for a moment. Dylan was right. Even without a permanent landing site, she and her sisters had always enjoyed support from two parents who loved them. Not everyone had been so blessed.

"I never thought of it that way," she said. "I didn't think about a lot of things back then."

"The narcissism of youth."

"Or just mine."

He didn't disagree with her, but she hadn't expected him to, either.

"Why didn't you tell me the truth about your family back then? We talked all the time, but I don't think you ever told me any of it."

"How could I? You had to think I was strange enough already. Being a chemistry-set nerd was bad enough without the sad home life." He lifted a shoulder and let it fall. "I didn't want your pity."

"I wouldn't have pitied you." But even as she said it, she wasn't so sure. The truth was, she didn't know how she would have reacted. She hoped she would have been supportive. "But I told *you* everything. Probably more than you wanted to know."

"I always wanted to know," he said in a quiet voice. Then he straightened in his seat as if his admission had surprised even him.

Jenna didn't know what to make of that confession, but the rest already had made her feel terrible. He'd always been there for her, but she'd failed him again and again. She had to fight the urge to reach over and pull him into a hug. "I'm sorry, Dylan."

"For what?"

"For not being the kind of friend you needed and deserved. I wish I'd been the type of person who put others ahead of herself, but I wasn't."

He cleared his throat a couple of times as if he had something momentous to say. When he finally spoke, though, it was only to dismiss her apology. "It doesn't matter. It was a long time ago."

She wanted to tell him that it did, but he opened his door and climbed out. He went around the back of the SUV and opened the hatch. "We'd better get this stuff inside. We can finally finish decorating the tree."

She didn't want their conversation to end. He'd opened up to her in a way he never had before, and it seemed like he was about to share more. But she had to be satisfied with what he'd told her. Maybe he'd decided she was worthy of his trust again. The thought of it made her as excited as the boys were about the tree. It was happening. She was winning him back.

"All finished," Dylan called out as he hung the final snowflake ornament on the Dentons' tree. "Doesn't it look great, guys?"

"It's cool!" Ryan exclaimed.

"Yeah, cool!" Connor agreed.

All the adults, minus Dylan's mother and Mrs. Scott, had gathered back at the Pearl Street house again. They stood admiring the tree, its pine aroma competing with the smells of fresh paint and new carpeting.

Dylan turned to Jenna. "You see, *now* it's finished."

Jenna smiled, and his chest filled with warmth. He'd been surprised by how much the activity of hanging the ornaments with Jenna, the twins and Lizzie had affected him. Or maybe he was still reeling from his intense conversation with Jenna.

With his history of sharing little with her about his life, he'd found it surprisingly easy to open up to her now. But what he'd been tempted to say to her affected him more than anything he'd actually said could have. When she'd told him she wished she could have been a more magnanimous person, he'd wanted to assure her that she was that kind of person now.

Sharing that with her wouldn't have been so bad if it hadn't felt so intrinsically tied to another admission he would be forced to make to himself. Despite his best efforts at keeping her at a distance, his old feelings for her were back in full force, and there was nothing he could do about it. What happened to his promise that he would never let her get under his skin again? Didn't he ever learn?

"Hey, I recognize some of these."

Logan's words brought Dylan back from the journey of his thoughts. He was relieved that no one seemed to notice that he'd been daydreaming.

Logan took a cherub-shaped plastic ornament in his palm. "Aren't these things from—"

Dylan cut him off with a quick shake of his head.

Logan's gaze darted between his brothers. "Oh, yeah. This stuff looks great." He turned to Brad and Kelly and their boys. "You have a great tree to go with your great new home."

"It's so beautiful. You're all so wonderful." Kelly's eyes were shining as brightly as the Christmas lights.

Brad walked over to his wife and draped an arm over her shoulders. "She's right. You've outdone yourselves. You didn't have to do any of this, but we're so grateful." His gaze flitted to the tree and back. "Where did you get all this stuff?"

"From my mother's tree," Dylan admitted.

Matthew shook his index finger at the tree. "I thought I'd seen some of it before."

Dylan held his hands wide. "They're gifts from my mother."

Dylan didn't miss the raised eyebrows from both his brothers, but that would be a discussion for another time. In fact, for a long time, he and his brothers had needed to have a little Christmas conversation with their mother. Until now, they'd all been reluctant to broach the topic, but things had changed today. He'd opened a door by asking her to donate part of her ornament collection, and his conversation with Jenna had convinced him it was time to talk to her.

Thinking about that discussion would be better than

dwelling on his feelings for Jenna. He needed to step away from her, to find some perspective, but that was awfully hard when they were working together.

He was on dangerous ground, and he knew it. At first, he'd just been struck by her beauty, but that was nothing new. Now, every time he saw her, he found something else to admire about her, from her kindness to her humor to her warmth. Even knowing it would be foolish to allow himself to fall for her again, he found himself standing on the edge of the cliff, waiting for the courage—or madness—to leap.

But, he quickly realized, he was forgetting something important. He shouldn't assume reality had changed just because Jenna had. There was one truth that could keep his feet rooted in place, no matter what was happening to his heart. For whatever reason, he wasn't the guy she wanted. He never had been, and he probably never would be.

He would do well to remember that.

Chapter Eleven

Something had changed between them. Jenna was convinced of it, even though he had agreed to her suggestion that they stop for coffee when they left the rental house. Dylan was across the table from her, sipping a cup of dark roast, but he seemed thousands of miles away and probably would have been if he didn't have to drive her home. Last week she hadn't minded him spending time with her out of obligation, but now she wished he'd chosen to be near her, instead.

That wasn't likely to happen. He'd been acting oddly around her ever since the conversation in the car earlier. It couldn't have been clearer that he was sorry he'd shared details about his past with her. If only she'd minded her own business, instead of nosing into his life, asking about his family's Christmas celebration.

Why couldn't she just let him keep his secrets and his pride? But she couldn't let it go any more than she'd been able to let him keep his distance. She might have known him all her life, but she realized today that she'd never really known him at all.

He'd been her steady rock in the choppy waters of

adolescence, but he'd never allowed her to see that he, too, had been scared and lonely. She wanted to see now. She wanted to know him, to know what made him tick, what made him happy or even still scared him, though the last he tried to hide.

"Hey, I wanted to thank you for listening earlier," Dylan said.

Jenna looked up from her latte. "Thank me? I thought you would never forgive me."

"That, too." He paused and grinned at her over the top of his cup. "But you got me thinking and talking about something I've needed to discuss with my mom for a long time now."

"Why do I get the feeling I've just messed up the delicate balance of noncommunication that has worked so well in the Warren family? The whole clan will probably collapse in a heap."

He shook his head as he set his cup aside. "We're a family of guys. What can I say? Noncommunication works well for us. Well, most of the time. It's families of women that have to beat every subject to death."

She raised her hand,. "Guilty. But our family won't die of heart attacks over bottling up our feelings, either."

"None of us have." He shrugged. "Yet."

He turned his head to glance at the coffee shop's display of baked goods.

"Hey, those cherry turnovers look good. Want one? My treat?"

Jenna smiled at his obvious attempt to change the subject, but at least he didn't suggest they take their coffee to go.

"Are you sure your mom won't be hurt that we're eating treats from the competition?"

"To spare her feelings, we'll keep it between us, okay?" he said with a wink. "Besides, she wouldn't want us to starve to death, would she?"

"Of course not," she said, continuing with the joke.

But as she waited for Dylan at the table, she suddenly felt even more flustered than when she'd first returned to Markston. Her nervousness was different this time, though, as if they were on a first date or something. It was a silly daydream, of course, but part of her wished that dream were real.

"I should have known that all this would come up when we took on this project," he said as he sat down and handed her a plate with a turnover on it.

"What would come up?" she asked, certain he couldn't be continuing the conversation about his family.

"All this...*stuff*." His said the word as if it was something distasteful.

"You mean about your dad?" After his nod, she took a deep breath and decided to forge ahead. "I can see why the Dentons' situation would have hit a little close to home for you. You connected with Ryan and Connor right away, and it was easy to see why you did."

His expression was guarded, but still he asked, "Why do you say that?"

"A pair of little lost boys? You could relate to them because you used to be one of them even if their loss was different from yours." As soon as she said it, Jenna braced herself, certain she'd gone too far. How could she presume to know anything about sad little boys or their losses?

"When did you get so smart?"

"Are you kidding? I've always been brilliant." Although she played down his praise, her cheeks warmed with pleasure. "You just never noticed."

Dylan stared at her, the look in his chocolate eyes so intense that Jenna forgot to breathe. His gaze—so warm, so true—made it clear that she was wrong. She could say a lot of things about Dylan but never that he'd failed to notice her. *She* was the one who hadn't been paying attention.

Chewing her bottom lip, she lowered her gaze. When she glanced back at him again, he was staring out the window. She had so many questions about Dylan now. His thoughts, his feelings and his dreams—she suddenly needed to know all of those things.

"I saw you this morning when you were watching Brad with the boys," she began, choosing just one of her questions. If he didn't want to talk about it, she was sure he would let her know.

But he only nodded. "Ryan and Connor seemed to love his attention."

"I couldn't help wondering what was going through your mind. Were you thinking of your dad? Do you have memories of good times like that with him?"

He shook his head, giving her the answer she expected.

"But I wasn't thinking about that when I watched them," he said. "I don't dwell on stuff like that." He took a sip of his coffee. "It wouldn't fit with my rugged, manly persona."

She smiled but didn't say more because she suspected he was working up to a real answer. Finally, he spoke again.

"I was happy when I watched them," he said. "Happy for Brad and Kelly, too. The Dentons will weather this difficult time because they have each other. That's the most important thing, and a lot of people don't have that."

A lump formed in Jenna's throat. Dylan had missed out on a lot of things in his childhood, and yet he'd still learned to value what really mattered. "I couldn't help thinking about my own dad when I watched Brad with the boys," she told him. "My sisters and I had plenty of war stories from when Dad tried to get us to work together in the kitchen."

She stopped and smiled, the memory warming her now, instead of creating that familiar ache inside. "That includes the time we invited the fire department over to put the fire out in the oven."

"Sounds like a great time to me."

Jenna was suddenly aware that her hands rested so close to his on the table that if she moved her fingers the tiniest bit, they would be touching. She swallowed as she realized how much she would like that. No, she couldn't keep having thoughts like this. Couldn't let herself be attracted to Dylan. Unfortunately the force that pulled her to him was becoming harder to resist.

Her cheeks burning, Jenna gathered her courage and looked up from the table. As she expected, Dylan was studying her.

"You really miss him, don't you?"

Jenna blinked. She hated that he'd misunderstood the reason she'd become quiet and that she couldn't tell him the real reason, but what he'd said was true, as well.

"Yes, I miss him." Her eyes burned, but somehow,

she managed to keep her voice from shaking. "It's worse on holidays."

He nodded, a sad smile resting on his lips, and she ached inside to think how well he understood.

"I told you I used to be jealous of your family sometimes, but it was mostly about your dad."

Of course, he would have longed for what he'd never known. She, on the other hand, had been blessed to have such an amazing father, but she'd taken that blessing and so many others for granted while she'd mourned the lack of permanency in her life. She'd forgotten what really mattered while she was longing for a permanent home.

"My father was an amazing blessing. When he passed away last year, it was the lowest point of my life." She glanced at Dylan and found him looking at her in a way that made her long again to reach for his hand. "When I flew into Indianapolis, Haley met my flight to tell me Dad had died."

"I can't imagine how hard that was for you."

"Your dad is still living, isn't he?"

"As far as I know," Dylan replied. "No one's called us to claim a body or pay off any debts." He closed his eyes, shaking his head. "Sorry."

"Don't be sorry. You have every right to be angry. Your father's desertion totally changed your life, and Matthew's and Logan's."

His eyes opened, but he braced his hands on the edge of the table and leaned back in his chair, staring at his coffee, instead of looking at her. He seemed to weigh her words, deciding if he could agree with what she'd said.

"So…would I have been a different man if my father hadn't left?"

He seemed to be talking to himself as much as to her, but Jenna heard the pain and the uncertainty in his question. The need to reassure him overwhelmed her. She couldn't let him go on thinking he was somehow less than the amazing person he was.

"You might have been a different man," she acknowledged, though she hated agreeing with even that part of what he'd said. He needed someone to ease his doubts, and she wanted to be the one to do it. "But there's no way you could ever convince me that you would have been a *better* man."

Jenna reached over and clasped her hand over his, unable to hold back any longer. It was an act of comfort, of support, and that was all, she told herself. When the strong, firm hand stiffened under her touch, she realized her mistake. Dylan would never want her to see him as weak, as in need of her nurturing. She'd worked so hard to move closer to him these past few days, and in a few seconds, she'd just negated all of that effort.

When she looked up at him, Dylan was staring at their hands in surprise or confusion or some other emotion. He swallowed visibly and didn't speak for so long that Jenna was convinced that whatever he said next would be something she didn't want to hear.

"Thanks," he said finally.

Her sigh of relief had almost escaped her lungs when Dylan turned his hand under hers and laced their fingers together. She drew in a sharp breath. As much as she tried to tell herself that he'd only accepted her gesture of comfort, the strumming tingle that extended from her palm all the way up her arm made the excuse sound flimsy. And though they were in the middle of a coffee shop, she felt as if they were the only two people in the world at that moment, connected in a way that seemed so right.

Giving her hand a squeeze, Dylan unlaced his fingers from hers. "Shall we go?" he asked, standing up.

Jenna's fingers continued to thrum as she put on her coat. She felt strangely empty without the feel of his hand in hers.

Neither of them spoke during the ride back to Jenna's house. Dylan didn't know how he could with the complex conversation already going on inside his head. But the silence only seemed to add to the electric charge between them.

They'd shared too many thoughts and words and emotions for one day. As for him, those words and feelings dug through so many layers of his history that he ached from the excavation.

He didn't know what to make of his willingness to open up to her, let alone that touch they'd shared, which had about as much to do with simple compassion as his mother's holiday-village collection had to do with Christmas.

Okay, Jenna might have reached out to *him* in solace, but the moment her fingers had rested on his hand, he could think of nothing besides her soft skin and her warm touch. His lacing their fingers together had seemed like the most natural thing in the world.

"Did you hear me, Dylan?"

He startled as her words drew him back to the present. He'd just pulled to the curb in front of Jenna's mom's house, so he waited until he'd turned off the engine before he turned back to her. She was watching him in the illumination that filtered in from the streetlight.

"No. Sorry. I wasn't listening."

"I wanted to ask you a question."

Swallowing, he nodded and waited for the expected question. How could he tell her what he'd meant by the whole hand-holding incident when he wasn't sure himself?

"Why did you really end our friendship?" She must have read his surprise because she rushed to explain, "I mean, it had to be more than just that one misunderstanding over my canceling on you, right?"

He shook his head. She still didn't get it. "It wasn't just a misunderstanding."

"I know it wasn't. I mean, I should have gotten it that you thought our date was…well, a real date. And even if I didn't get that, I knew we had plans, and I shouldn't have canceled just because I had…"

"A better offer," he supplied.

"No, that wasn't it," she began, but she stopped herself.

"It was a long time ago. Let's just forget about it."

"I don't want to forget," she said. "I want to know."

"Fine," he said on a sigh. The truth. He'd spent so many years hiding it and then even more trying to forget about it. But she deserved to know, even if it was years too late.

"I was always crazy about you, even when you were eleven and crying over your new braces."

The look of surprise on her face only made him smile. "It started there, but it only became stronger over time. Through every one of your boyfriends and heartbreaks, I was there waiting for you to recognize that I had feelings for you. But you never did."

"Why didn't you ever tell me?" she said in a quiet voice.

"I guess I was afraid of losing the little part of you I did have. The part that belonged to the best friend alone."

"But you changed your mind." If possible, her voice sounded even smaller this time.

"Even everymen reach their limits eventually. You know, like George Bailey in *It's a Wonderful Life*."

"Only you would bring up that movie," she said, chuckling. "You were never an everyman."

"Anyway, when you canceled our date that you didn't even realize *was* a date, that was the last straw for me. I had to do something for myself, and that meant I had to make a clean break."

"So you couldn't be my friend anymore."

The sadness in her voice touched his heart. "Like I said, it was a long time ago."

"That doesn't make it right. I totally disregarded your feelings and made you feel as if you were unimportant. It was wrong, and I'm so sorry about it."

He nodded. They both stared out the front windshield, lost in their thoughts.

"What does all that mean for us now?" Jenna asked finally.

"That doesn't—"

She rushed on, not allowing him to finish, as if she couldn't bear to hear the answer to her question. "I mean, I came here hoping that I could make things right with you. I'll do whatever it takes, but I want you to know that I don't want to give up on us."

"Are you going to let me speak?" A smile pulled on his lips.

"Oh. Sorry." She took a deep breath.

"You've been trying to apologize to me ever since you got here. A long time before that, even. It was wrong of me not to forgive you. Besides being downright un-Christian. So, I forgive you, and I'm sorry." He shifted in his seat, uncomfortable with apologies. "I was hoping that you would, you know, forgive *me*." He shrugged. "You know that whole 'forgiveness is divine' thing."

"You're asking *me?*"

"I guess I am."

"Then I forgive you."

"You make that sound so easy," he said with a chuckle.

"It is when you're feeling blessed to have the chance to appear so charitable." She paused, clearing her throat, and when she spoke again, her light tone had disappeared. "It's just that, Dylan, I can't picture my life without you in it."

He took a deep breath, trying to slow his racing heart. They'd just moved beyond apologies and forgiveness to something less easily defined. He couldn't afford to let himself read anything into her words, though. Yes, she wanted him in her life, but she'd always wanted that. Nothing had changed. It would be dangerous for him to think so.

Still, she sat beside him, so vulnerable, so unsure. He couldn't leave her dangling that way, wondering what he thought about her admission, wondering if he cared at all. He owed her the truth, no matter what it cost him.

Tightening his hands on the steering wheel, he let the words come. "I can't imagine my life without you, either, Jenna."

Chapter Twelve

Dylan sat at the same desk where he'd beaten his head against his calculus textbook on more occasions than he cared to recall. Now he was banging his head for another reason entirely. So he'd drawn Jenna's name. Big deal. He didn't know why he was making it so complicated. Yet Christmas Eve was tomorrow, and he still wasn't sure what gift he would give Jenna on Christmas Day. Or rather…which.

What happened to his thinking he'd received a raw deal when he'd pulled her name in the first place? When had it become so important to him that his gift to her be the right one?

Probably when they'd held hands. Or admitted they wanted to be in each other's lives.

He glanced down at the papers spread out on the desk in front of him. One of them was covered with so much ink that the words on it were almost indecipherable. Another, the one with the ideas on it, had most of its lines crossed out. Settling his elbows on the wood, scarred with the dents and glass rings from the irresponsible teenager who'd once worked there, he looked at the other option, which he'd set in the corner of the room.

Either the birdhouse he'd made as a kid or the gift on the desk would fit the letter of rule if not the intent, as Matthew would say in his legalese. Both were definitely homemade; only the time frame of the creations could be called into question. The birdhouse was almost finished, but the other gift? He could finish the other one if he put his mind to it…and sacrificed his pride.

Was he ready to do that? Was he ready to put himself out there and take a chance at falling flat again? He shook his head. Where was his sense of self-preservation? His answer to her question about why he'd put her out of his life made him wonder. But what did he have left to protect when he'd already told her the truth about the past? Only that he'd never really gotten over her, but he refused to give away that little detail.

He tucked the sheet of blotched paper in the top desk drawer to let the ideas stew again. From the corner of the room, he collected the birdhouse and opened a small can of paint he would use to finish and update it. The pungent smell made his eyes water, but it at least helped him to think of something besides the piece of paper in the drawer. It was an imperfect structure, all right, with its less-than-square walls and tiny door that had shown his amateur skills with the jigsaw. But it might have to do.

There was still time to choose between the two gifts. As much as thirty-four hours, if he pushed it. But he would have to decide eventually, and then he would have to live with the fallout from the choice he made.

* * *

Jenna pulled her coat higher about her throat as she and Dylan trudged through downtown Markston, searching for last-minute gifts for the Dentons. With the fifteen-degree temperature drop they'd experienced since last night, it felt more like shopping farther north in downtown Detroit, instead of southern Indiana. Maybe there was a chance for Christmas flurries after all.

Instead of festive, the air about them felt frantic as shoppers bustled from store to store, all under the pressure of finding the perfect gift before Christmas Eve early closing hour. Jenna's disquiet had nothing to do with the remaining shopping hours, and Dylan's restlessness mirrored hers. Clearly their conversation from the night before had confused him as much as it had her.

"Well, what's left?" Dylan rubbed his hands together to produce heat.

Jenna gestured with a nod toward his hands. "Forget your gloves?"

"In the car." He stuffed his hands in his pockets.

She pointed down the street. "Just the specialty toy store and the candle shop."

"Good. We need to get this over with."

Jenna gave him a sidelong glance as she trudged down Washington Street. Somehow she didn't think his comment had anything to do with shopping. When they reached The Toy Maker, Dylan opened the door for her and then disappeared into the back of the store to browse.

She supposed she couldn't blame him. If he felt even half as vulnerable as she did, she could understand his need to put some space between them. Not that his reprieve would be long. Even after they finished shopping today, they still had Christmas Eve services ahead tonight and the family gathering tomorrow for Christmas Day.

Jenna wished for a little space herself, yet she realized that would do as much good as wishing she hadn't asked him last night why he'd walked away from her years ago. Last night, she'd needed to hear what he would say, but as soon as she'd asked, she'd known the answer. The truth was that in her heart, she'd always known how Dylan felt about her when they were younger. She'd just chosen *not* to know it. How could she reconcile herself with that? Sometimes the extent of her selfishness back then still shocked her.

She'd known Dylan her whole life, so it was strange to feel as if she was seeing him now for the first time. This strong, honest and amazing man had been there right in front of her, and the only way she could have missed seeing him was to have lived her life with her eyes closed. Maybe she had.

She stood before a floor-to-ceiling display of puzzles, barely seeing any of their colorful boxes as she caught sight of Dylan farther down the aisle. He'd squeezed his lanky frame into a junior-size chair at a display table featuring some sort of industrial-style building set, and he was manning the mechanical controls. He was too focused on the task to even notice her gaze or how she smiled as she watched him.

The inquisitive boy she'd always known was still there, the boy who'd put grapes in the microwave just to see the sparks and who'd performed an experiment with toilet-bowl cleaner that had nearly caused an explosion.

Of course, she'd always cared about Dylan. She'd been drawn to her friend in the same way that an injured individual is connected to the crutch that helps him make his way in the world. But this Dylan—the man—pulled her to him in a way the boy never had.

Now, her gaze followed the contours of his beautiful, strong jaw, and those firm lips pressed into a straight line of concentration. The long fingers of his hands were curved around the controls. She now knew how safe and warm his hand could make a woman feel when he laced his fingers through hers. How safe and warm it had made *her* feel.

Jenna blinked, not sure what to do with all the thoughts and emotions clamoring inside her head, each vying for top position.

He said he'd always been crazy about her. Was that a past-tense *always,* or did he still feel that way? If he did, would she have the courage do anything about it?

What was she thinking? Dylan was an amazing man; there was no denying that. He was as gorgeous on the inside as he was handsome on the outside. No wonder she couldn't help feeling drawn to him as any woman with good sense would be.

But it wasn't good sense for her. She'd waited so long for Dylan to give her a second chance, and he'd amazed her by finally forgiving her. Whether they would ever be the kind of friends they'd been in the past, no one could predict, but one way to guarantee they wouldn't get there would be to allow herself to become attracted to him.

As tempting as it was to follow these new and different feelings, she couldn't afford to take the risk. Relationships failed, even more often than marriages, and she knew the statistics on those. If she and Dylan were to begin a relationship, and that relationship were to fail, she would lose their friendship, too. How could she bear to lose him again?

The truth was she couldn't bear it.

She shot another glance Dylan's way and this time found him grinning at her. He gestured with his hand for her to come over to see something, childlike excitement in his eyes.

No, she couldn't risk their friendship again for anything, even some silly daydream that they could be something more than friends. She shook her head to strengthen her resolve and walked over to Dylan.

When she reached the display table, he pointed down at it. "I think Santa should get the boys one of these."

"One of these?" She leaned over the contraption, trying to cover the flush in her cheeks from her earlier thoughts.

The toy was fancy, all right, with its motorized cranes and pulley systems, as well as its trucks and train cars waiting to be filled from huge piles of coal and logs. It wasn't what she would have pictured, but she admitted she'd struggled when they'd been shopping for Ryan and Connor. Although they'd already found some puzzles and comic books, nothing else at the regular toy store at the mall had seemed like a good fit.

"You're sure about this?"

"Oh, yeah. I would have given my eye teeth for something like this when I was their age."

She narrowed her gaze when she looked his way. "Are we shopping for the twins or you?"

"Them, of course. They love to build things. They like to see how things work together and come apart."

"And you know what a boy like that would like because you used to *be* that boy, right?"

He answered with a grin.

"Well, did you find the box anywhere? It is Christmas Eve, after all." Jenna glanced around, and then she saw it. Only one box remained, just to the right of the display table. She pulled it out so she could look at the price, and when she did, she gasped. "Dylan, did you see this?"

She pointed to the two-hundred-dollar price tag, which was more than a toy had any business costing. "This is too expensive."

"But it's perfect," he said simply.

"We don't have this much left in the budget." In fact, their working budget was stretched about as thin as it could be without popping any holes.

"Can't you find something else that the boys would love just as much?" she asked when he didn't answer. "They won't mind. Remember their Christmas lists?" She hoped that by reminding Dylan about their wish lists, he would rethink the plan, but he wouldn't budge.

"Come on, Dylan. Brad and Kelly would never have been able to buy this for their sons, even before Brad's job loss. Even before the fire." She paused, trying to plan her words just right. "We can't buy happiness and security for them no matter how much we'd like to."

She expected him to bristle under the criticism of his motives, but he wouldn't budge. "That's not what I'm doing. Their family gives them all the happiness and security they need. This is only a gift, the kind that encourages them to stretch their minds to see possibilities rather than roadblocks. It reinforces the stuff their parents are already teaching."

Though she couldn't argue with his reasoning, they still didn't have the money to pay for this gift, and they couldn't approach any of the other church members for funds to purchase an extravagant toy. She would have told him that, too, if he hadn't yanked out his wallet and pulled out a stack of twenties.

When he caught her watching him counting the money, he tapped President Andrew Jackson's face on the top bill. "I've been saving up for a new snowmobile." He paused and then shrugged. "It'll be a while longer."

He would probably be waiting a lot longer, Jenna guessed, since this wasn't the first rogue purchase he'd made this week. When the senior partners at his optometry practice offered him a discount on the boys' eyeglasses, instead of the *free* eyeglasses he'd hoped for, he'd covered the rest of the bill himself. Jenna's mother had bound her to secrecy over that bit of information.

It wasn't until Dylan carried the huge box to the cash register and plunked his money down that Jenna realized what had just taken place.

"You'd already picked this thing out for the boys, hadn't you?" She pointed to the box. "You knew how much it cost, and you already had the cash on you."

"Whatever do you mean?" he asked, his lips twitching.

She looked around the store with suspicion. "How often do you come to this place to play—I mean, demonstrate use of the toys?"

He assumed a thoughtful pose, gripping his chin between his thumb and forefinger. "Hmm. Before this week, maybe once or twice a year. You know, gifts for my niece."

"But as busy as we've been this week, you still found time to get over here by yourself and pick this out?"

"Errands, remember?"

She nodded, smiling. "But you hate shopping."

He shrugged as he smiled back at her. Would Dylan ever stop surprising her?

She hoped he never did.

As he came to his feet, taking his place next to Logan among the basses, Dylan looked to the conductor and winked, though he doubted Matthew could see him clearly in the low lights and candle glow. Dylan had to give Matthew credit for pulling together a melodic-sounding choir from this crew of mediocre voices, Dylan's own superior in its mediocrity.

From his place in the back row of singers, he scanned the middle and front rows, his mother and Mrs. Scott joining Haley in the soprano section, while Jenna and Caroline stood side by side in the alto section. His mother positively sparkled as she took in the herd of Warrens and Scotts, all corralled in the choir loft to sing in the Christmas choir.

As the opening strains of "Silent Night" filled the sanctuary, Dylan grinned out at their guests, the Dentons, who were sitting in the second row. It only seemed right that Brad and Kelly and the boys would join them for Christmas Eve service after the week they'd all spent together. Lizzie, who'd insisted on sitting between Ryan and Connor, waved up at her family.

Dylan was happy for his mother that she'd had the chance to share another of their family's Christmas traditions with the Scotts, but he was even more pleased for all of them that it had been this particular custom. This one had been special to him once upon a time.

For reasons he didn't bother trying to explain away anymore, he shot a glance at the person who had also been special to him back then and who had remained in his heart no matter how hard he'd tried to extricate her from it. While the rest of her family appeared to be caught up in the serene spirit in the sanctuary, Jenna seemed edgy, as if she could feel his gaze on her and would have wished it away if she could have.

That same uneasiness had seemed to cling to her the whole time they'd been shopping together. Several times at the toy store he'd caught her watching him with what he thought was pity. During those moments, part of him wished he'd said nothing about why he'd pulled away from her. But only part.

Sure, he hated feeling this vulnerable now that the words were out there between them, instead of tucked safely in his thoughts, but at the time he hadn't been able to stop the words from coming. Just once, he needed her to know what had been inside his heart, even if he regretted telling her later.

He also could have told her that those feelings hadn't ebbed over time, but he wasn't ready to do that any more than he was ready to ban her from his life again. He didn't know how she felt, anyway. Sometimes he sensed something between them, but that could have been wishful thinking. He'd proved years ago that he wasn't above reading too much into simple friendship.

Because none of the questions inside him could be settled tonight, Dylan pushed the thoughts away and focused on the words Reverend Boggs spoke in the opening prayer. Like the others around him, he settled in his choir-loft seat and pulled his Bible from beneath the pew.

He didn't want to go through the motions as he had so often in the past few years. Tonight he wanted to fully experience the service, to absorb the sight of the manger scene in the corner, the scents of pine and candle wax and the sounds of familiar carols and scriptures. More than any of those things, though, he wanted to feel God's sweet spirit, which Reverend Boggs described in his prayer.

Tonight, Dylan listened with rapt attention to the verses in the second chapter of Luke, some of which he could quote by heart. The story sounded so real to him, such truth in the arrival of light for a dark world.

"'And suddenly there was with the angel a multitude of the heavenly host praising God, and saying, "Glory to God in the highest, and on earth peace, good will towards men."'"

As Reverend Boggs had closed the passage at verse 14 and invited the congregation into a moment of contemplation, Dylan couldn't help looking over at Jenna. From behind her, he could see only her profile as her head was bowed in prayer. He couldn't begin to explain now why he'd allowed the fiasco between them four years ago to cause him to lose his way with God.

He hadn't blamed God for not giving him the woman he'd wanted; it wasn't as simple as that. He'd just lived his faith on autopilot, just as he had some other elements of his life. It was the lowest point in his life, and he'd turned his back on his faith, just when he'd needed God's comfort most.

Again he looked at Jenna as she continued her silent prayer. What a contrast there'd been between the way they'd faced their darkest days. While she'd reached out to God in her time of need, he'd turned away from Him, instead. He didn't have to ask himself which of them had found more peace. That was obvious in the serenity on her face.

A smile pulled at his lips as he lowered his head and began a silent prayer of his own. He'd never expected to learn life lessons, let alone faith lessons, from Jenna Scott.

Father, you know I often take the longest path to reach You. Thanks for waiting around for me until I do.

When he looked up again, Jenna was smiling at him. She mouthed the words that would mean more to him this holiday season than ever before. "Merry Christmas."

Chapter Thirteen

"Merry Christmas, dear one." Mrs. Warren crossed the family room, gathered Jenna's mother into her arms and kissed her cheek.

"And Merry Christmas to you." Trina returned her friend's kiss.

Amy was the last to join the crowd, as she'd been finishing up in the kitchen, so they'd all dispatched with coats and pleasantries before she arrived. That just meant another round of hugs and kisses was in order before they could get to the presents that seemed to be occupying Lizzie's attention.

"When are Ryan and Connor going to get here?" Lizzie asked.

"Soon," Matthew told his daughter. "The boys are opening their gifts from Santa at their new house first and coming here for Christmas dinner."

"We'll *never* get to open presents, then." Her voice became a whine.

"Never open them?" Dylan nabbed his niece and swung her around in a circle. "I heard you already opened a bunch of presents from Santa at your house this morning."

Her sour expression immediately disappeared. "I got a bike and two dolls." She pointed to the two curly-haired baby dolls propped up on the mantel.

"Those are really nice. Since you've already had presents, I guess you won't need the one under the tree," Dylan joked with his niece.

"But these presents are special because we made them," she told him.

Those wrapped gifts beneath the tree were special, all right. Jenna was only uncertain about one of them: the one she'd made for Dylan. She'd been pleased with the scarf when she'd finished it last night, but now it seemed woefully inadequate, especially when compared to Haley's painting.

Mrs. Warren practically floated over to the Christmas tree, her holiday spirit back in place. Jenna was impressed with the tree itself, its branches less weighed down now.

"Since the rest of our guests weren't involved in the gift exchange, I don't see any reason why we can't open the gifts now," Mrs. Warren said.

Or we could wait, Jenna wanted to say, but since Lizzie was already jumping up and down and Dylan's mom might as well have been, she didn't bother. Her gift would have to be enough.

Most of them gathered on the sectional and side chairs, and Logan sprawled on the carpet near the fire so that Lizzie could distribute the gifts, with reading help from Haley. The child lowered a box, about twelve inches square, at Jenna's feet. Jenna was more curious about what Dylan would think of the gift in the small red box in his lap than she was about her own gift.

"Who do you think should go first?" Matthew asked.

His daughter raised her hand. "Me, Daddy. Me. Me."

"I don't know, pipsqueak." Logan shook his head. "What do you guys think?"

"Logan Michael Warren," Mrs. Warren said.

Dylan learned over and thwacked his brother on the back. "Whoa, brother, it's not even noon yet on Christmas morning, and you've already earned the three-name threat. You should pace yourself."

Lizzie did get to open her gift first—a sweet rag doll Trina had made—and then the others took turns clockwise around the room.

Jenna held her breath as Dylan pulled the tag off his gift and read the name on the back.

"It's from Jenna." He smiled her way and then pulled the red wrapping from the box. Lifting off the lid, he brushed his hand on the gray-and-white-striped scarf Jenna had crocheted. "Hey, this is great. Thanks."

He pulled the scarf from the box and wrapped it around his neck, preening for their families. Jenna knew he was just being kind—it was the most average crocheting job anyone had ever done—but he made her feel as if she'd just given him the most amazing gift in the world.

As he started to set the box aside, he noticed the other item she'd put in there. He pulled out the card and read it silently. When he'd finished, he met her gaze and nodded. "Thanks again."

"What does it say?" Haley wanted to know.

Dylan brushed away the question with a wave of his hand. "It's just a Christmas card."

And it was. The card wasn't even homemade. The handwritten message inside it was part of the gift, though, and she was relieved he'd chosen not to share her words: *I wanted to return some of the warmth you have always given to me.*

As Dylan tucked the card back in the box and tossed his wad of wrapping paper in the garbage bag Caroline had brought from the kitchen, Jenna finally was able to relax. He not only had liked her gift, he had appreciated the feelings that were tied in with each stitch.

By the time most of them had opened their gifts, Jenna was really enjoying herself. The gifts were as varied in content as they were in craft quality, but each recipient accepted them with the love with which they were made. Caroline fussed over the pair of colorful pot holders Lizzie had made on a child's loom, and Haley couldn't stop complimenting Logan on the tiny pine Christmas tree he'd whittled for her from the small section of trunk he'd cut from the bottom of his mother's Christmas tree.

"Okay, it's your turn, Jenna," Trina told her daughter.

Jenna lifted her box off the floor and glanced down at the card. She flipped over the tag and read aloud the name that made her pulse quicken. Dylan. "It's from Dylan."

"You're the only two who got each other's names," Logan pointed out.

The look her mother exchanged with Mrs. Warren left little doubt that the two of them would have preferred someone else to share the tradeoff with Dylan.

Jenna decided not to reveal that she had orchestrated hers and hoped that Haley wouldn't give her away.

"Aren't you going to open it, Aunt Jenna?" Lizzie asked.

Jenna took a deep breath, trying to look as casual as she could. She was probably putting too much importance on something as simple as a gift exchange, but she couldn't help wondering if Dylan would make a statement with his gift the way she had.

"Of course, I am Lizzie. I love presents."

"Remember, Jenna, this one won't be a designer fashion," Matthew joked. "It's from Dylan Warren, not Calvin Klein."

Frowning his way, Jenna pulled the gift wrap from the box. "I'm sure I'll love it whatever it is."

Fighting her temptation to rush, she removed all the paper before untaping the end of the box.

Jenna could only hope that no one read her reaction when she saw what was inside, because it shamed her. She wanted to be able to appreciate the gift just because he had chosen it for her, but she was having a hard time understanding the gift. The birdhouse he had built when he was a boy? Still, she tried her best to be gracious.

"Thanks, Dylan."

Reaching into the box, Jenna pulled out a red-and-green-painted structure. From its scent, she could tell he'd given it a fresh coat of paint. He'd also personalized the gift with the words, "Jenna's House," which was the only thing personal about it.

"It's great," she added, and she made herself meet his gaze and smile. She tried not to let herself think that a birdhouse was something to be put up at a home, the thing she still didn't have after all these years.

"Hey, isn't that the thing you made when we were kids?" Logan asked.

"The only rule was that the project had to be handmade." Dylan told him. "Not that it had to be made this week."

Logan grinned. "Way to take the easy way out."

"Now, Logan," Mrs. Warren began, "you know how busy Dylan's been this week. And he's right. We didn't say the gift had to be made recently. Just homemade."

She scooted over to Jenna's side and examined the house further. "It was a nice touch to personalize it."

"Thanks, Mom." Dylan, who had crossed the room to stand behind his mother, leaned down to buss her cheek. "Now go open your present. You're the last one."

As his mother returned to her seat to open her present, Dylan stayed where he was, next to Jenna.

"I hope you're not too disappointed," he said in a low voice.

"Why would I—"

"It's not a handmade scarf." He tugged on the tasseled end of the one still encircling his neck.

"I love it. Really." The more she thought about it, the more she did like it. He'd taken a piece of his past and remade it for her. Maybe there was something personal in that, after all.

Dylan shifted next to Jenna, drawing her attention away from Mrs. Warren and the painting she was gushing over. Jenna lifted an eyebrow and waited for him to explain.

"It's just that I had to choose between two gifts,"

he said with a shrug. "So I chose the one with Christmas colors."

If only he'd turned away then, Jenna would have accepted his explanation without question. He didn't. He continued to look at her, his lips pressed together as if he wanted to say more.

Jenna could barely restrain herself from grabbing him by his navy sweater and insisting that he say whatever he'd held back. She was still considering doing that when the doorbell rang, announcing the Dentons' arrival.

Brad and Kelly and their boys paired through the door, Ryan and Connor lugging the box for their building set with them. When the boys immediately found a corner and pulled Lizzie along so they could set up their toy, Jenna exchanged a secret smile with Dylan. He'd been right about this special Santa gift.

The adults returned to the Christmas tree to let Brad and Kelly open a few gifts. One turned out to be a gift from Mrs. Warren alone: a crèche from her collection. But the hit turned out to be the date-night package, which included a gift certificate for dinner, movie passes and free babysitting from Dylan and Jenna.

Once those gifts were opened, Matthew slipped out of the room, and soon the prelude from "Away in a Manger" filtered in from the piano in the living room.

Taking her rag doll with her, instead of the two fancy dolls she'd brought from home, Lizzie skipped out of the room to join her dad at the piano. One by one, the adults and children set aside their gifts and followed the musical sound. Singing voices soon blended with the piano.

Now Dylan and Jenna were alone in the family room. He gestured for her to precede him, but as she stepped next to him, she glanced at him. The intense look in his eyes stole her breath away. Straightening, she took another step, but he reached out a hand to rest on her sweater-covered upper arm.

"Merry Christmas, Jenna."

With her heart pounding so hard and the skin on her arm tingling beneath his touch, she struggled to find her voice. "Merry… Christmas, Dylan."

He squeezed her arm and then pulled his hand away, leaving a warm and prickly place where his touch had been. "We'd better get in there. We have the whole family holiday celebration ahead of us today."

She nodded, unsure whether she could trust her voice not to give away her disquiet if she spoke. She'd never been so nervous around Dylan before. Or so agitated. Or so thrilled. She couldn't begin to know what to do with any of those jumbled feelings.Motioning for her to follow, Dylan started out the door into the hallway that separated the family room from the living room, but Jenna barely had enough time to catch her breath before he glanced back at her.

"It's going to be a great day," he told her. "But soon…"

That he let his words trail away like that made her crazy. She waited for him to fill in the blank, but when he didn't, she couldn't help prompting. "Soon?"

He gave her another meaningful look that made all her nerve endings spring to life.

"Sometime soon, after all this is over, you and I need to talk."

* * *

The long table in his mother's dining room was more cramped than Dylan could ever remember, and food on the platters was disappearing at a rate alarming enough to rule out the possibility of leftovers. But neither of those things dampened Dylan's spirits as he looked along the table that he shared with his family and friends, and Jenna. She looked more beautiful today than he could ever remember. He was nervous about the conversation, but the time had come. Words needed to be said. At least, *he* had to say them.

His mother held court at the head of the table, smiling at her collection of guests, accepting compliments about her legendary Christmas dinner with grace.

As Dylan smiled back at her, the realization struck him that this was his favorite Christmas ever. It didn't matter that the week had been even more hectic than any of his mother's regular Christmas extravaganzas. It didn't even bother him that he was sore from painting and tired of shopping and even that he and Caroline were seated next to each other again. Out of necessity, they'd become adept at ignoring each other in close proximity.

Spending the holiday giving back to others was part of what had made this Christmas special for him. A large part. But he wouldn't lie to himself by saying that was the only thing that had made this holiday extraordinary. He attributed the rest to Jenna.

Automatically his hand went to his neck. It felt bare without the scarf around it, but he would have had a hard time explaining why he had kept his scarf on when even Lizzie had left her rag doll on the mantel with her two new plastic friends. Still, he couldn't get over the thoughtfulness of Jenna's gift. Her lovely, imperfect scarf only made his substitute gift seem more inadequate.

"This dinner is amazing, Mrs. Warren." Brad indicated the turkey and ham and trimmings of the traditional Christmas dinner, plus the Warren family standards of pierogi, kielbasa and cabbage rolls. "Thank you for including us in your family Christmas."

"We're just pleased you could be with us," she said with a smile.

"I don't know how you managed to get everything done with all the time you all spent helping…" Brad let his words trail away, his voice thick with emotion.

Amy Warren waved away his comment with a brush of her hand. "There were plenty of us, and many—"

"—hands make light work," several other voices finished for her.

"Well, it's true," she'd said with feigned annoyance.

Before anyone had the chance to say more, his mother clapped her hands. "It's time for dessert."

"I wonder what it will be." Logan tapped his lip a few times before guessing. "Cake, maybe?"

"Of course, cake," she said, rolling her eyes at her youngest son. "What you should be asking is what *kind* of cake." Her enthusiasm building, she stood up from her seat and waited.

"Okay, I'll bite," Matthew said. "What kind of cake do you have for us, Mom?"

Seated next to Brad and Kelly, Dylan leaned over to explain. "I don't know whether we mentioned this or not, but our mother owns a cake shop."

"This is the *kind* of cake we have today." Amy slipped through the door and returned with a rolling cart and a cake that would have been perfect for a party of one hundred, rather than just thirteen. The three-tier cake was white like Christmas in Markston hadn't been, and it was covered with green piping that looked like garland and red flowers shaped like poinsettias. Like a wedding cake, this confection had a topper, but it was a miniature manger scene, and next to that was a birthday greeting for the Christ child.

"Wow, Mom, you've really outdone yourself this time. I don't even know how you hid this thing," Dylan said.

"I still keep a few secrets up my sleeve." Amy crossed her arms over her chest, appearing pleased with herself.

Dylan felt the resentment of Christmases past disappearing. All his mother had ever wanted was to make her celebrations a fantasy for the children in her life, and today she had mesmerized the three children with her king-size gesture.

"I think Mrs. Warren deserves a round of applause for this one, don't you?" Dylan clapped, and the others joined him.

As his mom handed out pieces of cake, Logan sampled the vanilla mousse filling, closing his eyes. "This is wonderful, Mom, but what are we going to do with all this leftover cake?"

Amy slanted a glance his way as she took her first bite. "Funny that you should ask. We're expected at the Shared Blessings soup kitchen with cake in about an hour." She turned her head to include the Dentons in the conversation. "Everyone's invited to come help us serve. The staff there can use as many hands as they can get."

Dylan leaned over to Brad and Kelly again. "You never know what's going to happen when you get together with the Warrens and the Scotts."

Kelly gave him a warm smile as she covered her husband's hand with hers on the tabletop. "Yes, we do. Only good things."

Her words struck a place deep inside Dylan, making his throat feel thick. Strange, while they'd all been here celebrating together, he'd forgotten how they'd met Brad, Kelly and their sons in the first place. Somewhere along the way, they had become more than benefactors and beneficiaries. They had become friends.

"We wanted to thank all of you again," Kelly said. "You've done so much for us. You've helped to turn what could have been a very dark Christmas into a season of memories. You've given us hope."

Dylan didn't try to speak after that because there was no way he could do it without embarrassing himself by getting choked up. Jenna must have realized it, too, because she smiled at him from across the table. At one time, it would have bothered him to think she saw any sort of weakness in him, but he found that he didn't mind the transparency now.

"Don't you see?" Jenna glanced at Dylan as if to let him know she was speaking for all of them before she turned back to Kelly and Brad. "You're the ones who've given *us* hope. Meeting your family has been a blessing for us. You're amazing examples of faith. No matter how tough the situation has been, you've never wavered in your beliefs."

Finally finding his voice again, Dylan added. "You've helped to make this an amazing Christmas for us, so we want to thank *you*."

"The best Christmas ever," Logan agreed.

"Speaking of great holidays," Matthew said as he reached for Haley's hand, "my wife and I have some special Christmas news."

Before he had a chance to say more, Amy and Trina reached for each other, linking both their hands.

Haley grinned like someone who'd kept a secret too long. "As best as we can calculate, sometime in the late summer, a new little Warren will be arriving here."

"A baby!" The two mothers cheered together.

"A baby brother?" Lizzie's eyes were wide with excitement, and then she frowned. "Or a sister."

Laughter filled the room as everyone stood up to share congratulatory hugs with the expectant parents.

Dylan turned back to Brad and Kelly. "See what I mean? You never know what to expect."

Jenna, who'd just given her younger sister a squeeze, must have overheard him because she smiled at him from across the room, a look so warm he felt tremors all the way to his heels.

He never knew what to expect with this particular Scott woman, all right, from her transformation over the past few years to his heart's willingness to lay exposed for her benefit. Even if she frustrated him and terrified him and drew him to her despite his best efforts to resist her, he still loved the way she kept him guessing.

He swallowed and pulled his gaze away from her. He was in way over his head, and he knew it. Maybe he wasn't as ready for that promised talk with Jenna as he'd thought. But then the side of his mouth lifted. It didn't matter whether or not he was ready to confess his feelings. He could shout it from the rooftops or bury it deep inside him, but the truth would remain that Jenna Scott had again claimed his heart.

Chapter Fourteen

Jenna's muscles ached that Tuesday afternoon, even muscles she hadn't been aware existed until she'd stretched too high, stooped too low and hauled more boxes than anyone ever should. The delivery truck was gone now, but she needed only to look at the stack of boxes in any of the rooms for proof that their work had just begun.

Not that they hadn't already been working so hard since Christmas that the past few days had gone in a blur. She had the blisters and broken nails to prove it.

At the sound of the front door opening, Jenna stepped to the kitchen doorway, so she could see the entry. She patted her hair, trying to restore some order to her messy ponytail, but she didn't know why she made the effort. Dylan hadn't been working that much with her these past few days, anyway. He'd said he wanted to talk to her after Christmas, so it seemed odd that he hadn't yet. It made her wonder even more what he intended to say.

Dylan stuck his head inside the door. "Second shift reporting for duty."

Kelly hurried down the hall toward him. "Oh, good, because the rest of us have dinner reservations."

"Very funny," Brad said as he followed Dylan inside, but he bent and dropped a kiss on his wife's forehead. Unlike the rest of them, who were spending another day in their work clothes, Brad wore his Sunday best, though he'd already taken off his suit jacket and loosened his tie.

"Well, how did it go?" Jenna couldn't help asking.

"You mean the boys' eyeglass fitting?" Dylan lifted an eyebrow. "It went great."

They all knew that wasn't the question she'd asked, but they went with it as Dylan made a production of announcing the twins' entrance. They stepped inside, wearing their new wire-frame glasses, just different enough to show off their individuality.

"Oh, don't you two look handsome," their mother gushed as she hurried over to hug them. "So grown up."

The twins made those miserable faces that boys make when their mothers get too mushy. But her compliments must have given them courage, because they rushed off to show some of the others their new glasses.

After they left, Kelly turned back to Dylan. "Thanks again. It was so kind of you to persuade your bosses to cover the cost of their glasses."

"It wasn't a big deal. The boys needed them."

His gaze darted toward Jenna, but she looked away before he could see in her eyes that she knew. She found it precious that he hadn't shared that he'd covered the cost of the glasses himself, and she wanted him to be able to keep his secret.

Strange, how she'd found so many things endearing about him lately, just at the time when he'd started finding more excuses to put space between them. Not all the time. In fact, sometimes everything seemed okay between them, but then suddenly he would feel the need to work on plumbing with his brothers when he could have been painting doors in the garage with her.

Whether he was reluctant or not, they needed to talk about his gift and the conversation that had followed it, and even about the changes in their relationship.

Now aware that Dylan and Brad had returned, other helpers spilled from different parts of the house. Logan and Matthew had been installing the new electric range, and Jenna's sisters and the two older women had been unpacking boxes at the back of the house, but they all converged in the living room, hungry for information.

"Well, are you guys going to tell us about the interview or not?" Kelly crossed her arms over her chest.

Dylan tilted his head toward Brad. "What do you think? Should we tell them?"

At first, Brad nodded sadly, but then he grinned. "You're looking at the newest custodian at Sycamore Square Mall. After a probationary period, I can be considered for the custodial-supervisor position that's also open."

"Oh, thank you, Lord," Kelly called out as she threw her arms around her husband. "That's wonderful."

A round of hugs broke out as everyone celebrated Brad's new job. Jenna asked Dylan in a low voice, "Your shopping-center contacts?"

"Brad must have wowed them in the interview," he answered just as quietly.

She closed her arms around Dylan the way she'd hugged Brad a minute before and Dylan himself hundreds of times, but the wallop of sensations that filled her when his arms closed around her was something new. It was as if every nerve ending in her hands and arms, shoulders and back had activated at once, and she was left trying to catch her breath without appearing to suffer from an asthma attack.

The hug didn't seem long enough, but since Dylan had to extricate himself from her arms, it couldn't have been that short, either. He turned away quickly, but not quick enough for her to miss the surprise and confusion on his face.

Jenna could relate to that turmoil. If she were honest with herself, though, she would admit she had an idea about what was happening, and that idea scared her to death. Could she be falling in love with her best friend? She'd promised herself she wouldn't let it happen, and yet she couldn't deny that she was in deep now.

No, this feeling couldn't be love. Her impression that her heart expanded whenever Dylan entered a room and contracted when he left it again had to be an exaggeration. He was her friend, and she loved him. But still.

Clearly they needed to talk. At least then they could work out some of her confusion, delineate the boundaries of this new relationship, because for her at least, the lines had blurred.

Jenna looked at Dylan again, but the festive atmosphere from a few minutes before had disappeared. Brad was holding Kelly in his arms, rubbing her back while she sobbed against his chest.

"We're going to be okay," he crooned to her in a low voice. "Gonna be okay."

Jenna's breath caught. For more than a week while

they'd all been working together, Kelly had been forced to be strong, but now that it appeared her family would be fine, she had released her hold on all those over-whelming emotions.

"Miss Jenna, why is Mommy crying?" Ryan asked her, tugging on her sleeve.

The worried faces of this sweet boy and his brother made her heart ache.

"You know, I think it's because she's happy."

He gave her a skeptical look and then turned to watch his parents again. Kelly must have heard the exchange because she pulled back from her husband's arms and started drying her tears. When she stepped over to her sons, her face was red and her eyes were puffy, but she was smiling.

"Miss Jenna's right, guys." She put her arms over the shoulders of both boys. "I *am* happy. Thanks to God and all these nice people, we have a house and clothes and food. All the things we need. Your dad even has a job so we can pay our own bills."

As she lowered her arms, she turned and crouched in front of her sons. "We're going to be all right. I wasn't so sure about that before."

"Why not, Mommy?" Connor wanted to know. "Didn't you have faith?"

"Sure, I—" She stopped herself and reached out to ruffle his hair. "I guess not."

For several seconds, no one spoke, and then Brad started chuckling. "Out of the mouths of babes, huh?"

As he grabbed both his sons and wrestled them under his arms, he turned to Matthew and Haley. "Everyone should have a few of these, don't you think?"

"Absolutely," Matthew answered.

Haley, who'd been green all day with morning sickness, only smiled.

"Yes, everyone should," Mrs. Warren agreed, though she was looking at Dylan and Caroline when she said it.

Caroline pretended to miss the comment, the way she usually did, and without looking at him to see him do it, Jenna knew Dylan would be rolling his eyes.

Soon the call of all those unpacked boxes sent them back to different parts of the house. Leaving kitchen organization to the older women and Kelly, Jenna worked in the boys' bedroom with Haley. Once Matthew and Dylan had mastered the directions for assembling the bunk-bed set, Jenna climbed to the top bunk and wrestled the linens and comforter into place.

She liked the idea that the Dentons would sleep in their beds tonight, instead of sleeping bags. Though Brad and Kelly had gratefully accepted their help with the move today and even with furniture assembly and unpacking tonight, they'd already politely suggested that they would take over the rest of the work.

Jenna was surprised by her bittersweet feelings over the end of the project, but it was time. Her family and the Warrens had done more than just accomplish their goal of making a nice Christmas for another family; they had helped them rebuild their lives.

Only ten days had passed, yet so much seemed to have changed, and not just for the family they had helped, either. Her mother and Mrs. Warren had brought their families together again this Christmas in hopes of them building stronger bonds. Jenna wondered if they realized how successful their plan had been.

No, the holidays hadn't turned out the way Mrs.

Warren had envisioned them, but the results had to exceed her expectations. Not only had her children and her best friend's children connected in a way they never had before, but in sharing their holiday with a family in need, they had experienced the true spirit of Christmas.

"You go this way. I'll go that way." Dylan waited as Jenna took her position on the opposite side of the kitchen table.

"We'll get him this time," Jenna assured him.

"No you won't," Ryan ducked under the table and scrambled out the other side before either of them could catch him.

Connor ran into the room, already shirtless and barefoot. "He wins! He wins!"

"He's not going to be a winner for long if he doesn't get in the shower like your mom and dad said before they left."

Because there was a note of warning in Dylan's voice, Ryan glanced back to see if Dylan was serious. Dylan gave his best stern look to show that he was, though he hadn't a clue what he would tell the boys if they asked what his threat meant. It had sounded good at the time.

"What he means is, anyone who isn't clean, combed and in PJs in twenty minutes will have to skip popcorn and a movie before bedtime," Jenna said.

The boys looked at each other for no more than a second and then both shot down the hall.

"I call the shower first!"

"I already have my clothes off!"

"Hey, boys, there are two showers," Dylan said. He looked back at Jenna. "Here, let me handle this."

"I'll just finish these." She indicated the few dishes in the sink from the macaroni-and-cheese and chicken-fingers dinner they'd just shared.

Resisting the urge to see anything warm and domestic in the scene, Dylan started down the hall after the racing ruffians. The boys weren't accustomed to living in a house with more than one bathroom, so they were used to the evening race. He had to smile at that thought. He and his brothers used to have a nightly bath race, too.

With a little negotiating, he had them both settled in separate bathrooms with pajamas, soap and shampoo. He was still smiling when he started down the hall to join Jenna again in the kitchen.

He didn't know why he'd let himself get all worked up about spending an evening alone with Jenna in the first place. They weren't even alone, unless they didn't count the 110 pounds of seven-year-olds who had kept them hopping from the time the boys' parents had backed out of the driveway. And if he was being technical, he would admit that he and Jenna had already been alone together in this house a few times in the past week.

But he had been nervous, so nervous that he'd had sweaty hands when he'd picked up Jenna at her mother's house. He hated feeling like a teenager on a first date when this didn't even qualify by the broadest sense of the word as a date.

His anxiety wasn't only about being with Jenna, or even being *alone* with Jenna. He was more worried about the conversation that would take place tonight, words that were long overdue. He'd been a coward this week, dodging Jenna to delay the talk. But he supposed his faintheartedness should only be expected since he'd made the suggestion in a rare moment of daring. He still wasn't sure he was ready to explain about his second gift or tell her how he felt, but he owed her something.

When he stepped into the kitchen, Jenna was still standing at the sink. She looked back at him. "You got both of them in the shower and you're still dry? I'm amazed."

"Well, you should be. What happened to those sweet little boys their parents left two hours ago?"

She lifted a handful of suds from the dishwater and blew them into the sink where she'd been rinsing. "Poof. They disappeared just like all well-behaved children do the moment the babysitter comes. I take it you didn't babysit much—oh, I guess I already knew that about you."

She smiled that smile that would still get to him even if he was catatonic. She did know him better than anyone else; that was something that had never changed.

"Here, let me help." He moved to the sink and grabbed a dish towel. "There's a dishwasher down there, you know." He pointed below the counter.

"But it's brand-new, and I don't want to be the first one to use it."

"Or to break it."

"That, too."

He was just drying the last dish when the twins rushed into the room, sporting pajamas and wet hair.

"Popcorn!" Ryan cheered.

"And movie!" Connor chimed in.

"And then bedtime," Dylan and Jenna said at the same time and laughed. That the kids didn't think it was funny only made them laugh harder.

By the time the last of the popcorn was gone and the movie credits had rolled, Dylan didn't know who was sleepier, the adults or the children, but the boys would never admit it. After piggyback rides to their room, some lengthy bedtime prayers and finally lights out, which involved leaving one closet light on, Dylan pulled their bedroom door closed, and he and Jenna trudged back to the kitchen.

"How do parents do it?" Jenna dropped into a kitchen chair and rested her head on her arms.

"I think they drag around just like this." He lowered himself into the chair opposite her.

"Well, I, for one, am amazed by them. Brad and Kelly in particular." She held her hands wide to indicate the room. "Can you believe they already have curtains up and pictures on the wall?"

"They do only have possessions collected in a week rather than over years, but it still was a lot of work putting them away."

"An incredible amount of work." She looked around again, and when she turned back to him, she was smiling. "They sure looked excited about going out tonight."

"It was a great Christmas present, wasn't it?"

"They could have warned us that the boys are like gremlins someone fed after midnight when they have a babysitter, but it still was good gift." She stifled a yawn. "I don't know about you, but I could veg out in front of the TV for the rest of the night."

Dylan glanced at her. Instead of looking back at

him, she was studying her hands, folded together on the tabletop. She was giving him an out, and he knew it. He was tempted to take her up on it, too, to let the talking box keep them from really talking.

It was too easy, though, and he was sick of taking the easy way out.

"How about I make some tea, instead?" He took a deep breath and added, "Then we can talk."

Chapter Fifteen

Jenna wrapped her hands around the mug of hot tea that Dylan had placed in front of her and waited as he set out another for himself. Making tea had required some creativity, since the Dentons didn't have a kettle or a microwave yet—Dylan had boiled water in a saucepan and found two mismatched mugs on the cabinet's top shelf. He set a bowl of sugar and two spoons in the center of the table.

"Now that wasn't as easy as it sounded. I probably should have checked to see if there was any tea before I offered to make some."

Instead of taking the seat across the table so he would face her, he settled in the chair next to hers.

"I was worried that you'd have to go out and grow the tea leaves before you could brew a cup."

"Yeah, me, too."

Were they really sitting there talking about tea? What would be their next topic? Shelf liners? Jenna knew she should keep quiet and give him the chance to say whatever he'd planned to, but she couldn't help herself. She hated seeing him so uncomfortable as he appeared to search for the right words, especially when she had something she needed to say, as well.

She waited as long as she could, but she couldn't hold back anymore. "I'm sorry I stood you up on our first date."

Dylan blinked a few times, and then his tongue slipped out to moisten his lips. "Our first date?"

"I knew when you asked me that you were talking about a real date, not just hanging out." The sweet memory that popped into her head then made her smile. "You were so nervous…" She stopped, her gaze darting his way before she continued, "Anyway, I could tell that you'd worked up the courage to ask."

Jenna hated seeing the embarrassment on his face. She'd only just acknowledged the truth to herself, so it was harder to share it with him. "I wanted to go at first. It felt right. But then the misgivings started setting in, and I didn't know what to do."

"But why?"

She stirred her spoon around in her tea, though she hadn't put any sugar in it. "I chickened out. I knew that if we went out together and started a relationship, and then things didn't work out between us, I would lose my best friend. So when that other guy asked me out, the one who was the same kind of awful guy I always dated, it was an easy decision to cancel on you and go with him, instead."

He raised an eyebrow. "Easy?"

"The coward's way out."

Jenna braced herself, waiting for him to respond. She deserved whatever he had to say and more for having treated his feelings so cavalierly to protect her own. She could have shielded herself by not telling him now, but he deserved to know the truth, no matter what it cost her.

Still, when he pushed back from the table, a fresh ache settled in her heart. She could only watch as he went into the laundry room and grabbed his coat off one of the wall hooks. Only he didn't put it on. He dug through the pockets, instead, his hand coming out with a white, letter-size envelope.

Hanging up his coat again, he returned to the table, set the envelope on top and slid it her way.

"What's this?" she asked as she rested her hand on it.

"Your other present. You know. The one I told you about." He swallowed. "You see why I picked the one with Christmas colors?"

She didn't see anything except the white envelope that he'd obviously been too nervous to give her. The birdhouse had been a substitute for whatever was inside that envelope.

"Aren't you going to open it?"

Jenna took a deep breath, not at all sure she was ready to see what was in there, but she pushed her thumb under the lip of the envelope and dragged it across.

She pulled out what appeared to be a letter written on lined paper, but when she unfolded it, she discovered it wasn't a letter at all. It was a poem, entitled simply "For Jenna." Yet it wasn't even recopied. The paper had yellowed, and all the words in the draft had just been marked out as he'd revised.

For Jenna
Roses are red, but not as red as her lips,
Violets are blue, never as blue as my heart.

When she calls me, my pulse trips,
To tell her, I don't know where to start.
I don't want to be just her friend.

Daisies are white like the white lies I've told,
Daffodils are yellow like the coward that's me.
She is the one I long to hold.
Will she never hear my heart's plea?
I don't want to be just her friend.

Her heart squeezed after she read those first two stanzas. Those were the musings of a lovesick adolescent, feeling hopeless and invisible. Jenna hated that she'd ever made him feel that way. She didn't want to read more, didn't want to know more of his pain and to realize she'd been the one responsible for it, but the words called out to her.

The room is aglow when she steps inside.
Her laughter heals old wounds like a salve.
From these feelings I can no longer hide.
An answer from her heart I must have.
I don't want to be just her friend.

Change has painted her lovelier throughout.
Her compassion seeks out those who are broken.
My heart waits for hers; I have no doubt.
These words I can no longer leave unspoken.
I don't want to be just her friend.
I want to be her man.

As soon as she read the last words, Jenna understood why he'd left the work as it was, instead of recopying it. This poem had been written at different times by two different people: the boy Dylan used to be and the man he'd become.

And suddenly she knew. She loved Dylan. She'd loved that sweet boy, and she loved the man even more. How could she not have known it before? How could she not have seen that what she'd always wanted had been right there in front of her eyes?

Dylan just might love her, too. At least that was what the poem seemed to say in black and white. He'd cared about her when they were teenagers, and he still did, no matter how much pain she'd caused him, no matter how unwise he believed his feelings to be.

For several long seconds Jenna could do nothing but stare at the weathered page, though her eyes began to fill. She brushed her hand over the smooth surface of the page, her fingertips following the dented places where he'd marked out the wrong words.

Dylan's gaze seemed to follow the slow slide of her hand. "I guess I'm not a great poet. Then or now."

"I think it's beautiful."

It took her a few seconds to gather the courage, but finally she looked up at him. His eyes were cautious, searching, as if he didn't know what he would find, but he had to know nonetheless.

"Thank you. I love it." Jenna didn't even stop to think. She leaned forward and pressed her lips to his.

It was the briefest of kisses, just a tentative touch, and yet it changed everything. Jenna pulled back and stared at him, her pulse ticking in her temple. Dylan looked as surprised as she felt, his eyes wide with unspoken questions. She could see the exact moment the surprise in his eyes turned to joy.

"I've waited my whole life for this," he whispered and then reached for her, his hands tracing from her forearms to her upper arms and then over her shoulders to settle at the back of her neck.

Dylan leaned in close and hovered, so close that she could feel his breath as a warm caress on her lips. This wasn't to be a kiss of gratitude, one to be explained away as a whim. In his hesitation, he was waiting for her consent, asking if this was something she really wanted. With a small smile, she granted her permission.

She didn't have to say it twice. He lowered his head and pressed his lips to hers in the sweetest, most loving kiss Jenna had ever experienced. A lifetime of adoration settled into that one moment, filled with hope and promise and love.

Dylan's heart raced as he held her, but he forced his kiss to remain unhurried. This was Jenna, the person who'd filled his thoughts and dreams for as long as he could remember. There was no rush. Kissing her felt like the answer to a lifetime of prayers, the one clear view in an otherwise foggy sky.

She tasted sweet, but then he'd always known she would, and he'd had a lot of years to predict. Not only smooth, her lips were also pillow soft, and he couldn't help but sink into their softness. He didn't even know when he deepened the kiss, only that he was expressing the feelings he'd held so long in his heart.

When he would have preferred to go on touching and tasting, Dylan's good sense prevailed, and he pulled back, just far enough to press his forehead to hers.

"Do you have any idea how many times I've thought

about this moment? How much I dreamed about holding you in my arms?" he breathed.

"Is the reality as nice as your dream?"

He couldn't help smiling, his mouth still just a breath away from hers. Even if he'd had a lot of basis for comparison, he knew that anything from his past would have paled when measured against this moment.

"Reality is perfect."

Her sweet smile then only made him long to kiss her again, so he took her hands in his and eased his forehead back from hers, putting a cushion of distance between them. The last thing he wanted to do was to lose firm control over his better judgment and cause her to believe he thought of her as anything less than precious.

"I tried to avoid you when you came back for the holidays, and I was so frustrated when you made it impossible." He sighed, shaking his head. "Even after I decided to forgive you, I still tried to keep you at arm's length. But no matter how many times I warned myself to be cautious, to separate friendship from any closer relationship, I ignored the warnings.

"As absurd as it sounds, something inside me kept asking, if you and I were both different now, then why *not* now?"

For several seconds Jenna said nothing, looking at him with a wide-eyed expression. He'd gone too far, and he knew it. Why couldn't he just have seen the gift in her kiss and accepted that it would be a journey of baby steps toward a dating relationship between them? Now he'd pushed her, and she would probably go running in the opposite direction.

"Not absurd."

"What did you say? I didn't understand you." He thought he'd heard her, but she'd said it so quietly that he couldn't have heard her right.

"I said it's not absurd."

He would have demanded that she explain what she meant by that, but he couldn't trust himself to speak. Like the words of a jury foreman, the next thing that Jenna said would either be a gift for the future or a sentence to a life without her.

The look on her face as she met his gaze made him brace himself for news that would hurt. Her eyes shone too brightly, as if she was only a comment away from tears. But then she smiled, and the clouds in his heart separated, allowing the sun to shine through.

"You're right. Why *not* now?"

"I can't believe we were almost busted." Jenna shook her head and smiled as Dylan pulled the car to the curb in front of her mother's house.

She still felt a little jittery after tonight's events, but she pushed aside her uncertainties. He was still Dylan, and she was still Jenna. Only their relationship was in flux.

"Just like a couple of teenage babysitters." He shut off the ignition and turned in the driver's seat to face her. "Not that Brad and Kelly would have found anything all that shocking if they had busted us. Just a kiss."

"They wouldn't have been that surprised, either."

"What do you mean?"

"Kelly's always wondered about us. Ever since that first day at breakfast."

Dylan drummed his fingers against the steering

wheel. "After that scene tonight, she's probably more curious."

"Why would you say that?"

"We had to look suspicious when we both jumped up from the table after Brad and Kelly came through the door."

Jenna frowned. "What do you mean? We were just picking up because they were home and we needed to get going."

"You told them the boys were sleeping like 'little baby lambs.'"

"Do you think it was overkill?" She thought about it for a second. "Don't worry. They probably thought I was kidding, anyway."

"Either way. But this does bring up another subject. What are we going to tell everyone else?"

"You mean about—" she paused, gesturing back and forth between them "—us?"

"Yeah."

She shot a look at her mother's front door, illuminated by a pair of porch lights and the glow of the living-room lamp her mother would have left on for her. The house appeared quiet, so she turned to Dylan again. "We haven't even defined what 'us' is yet. Or even if there is an 'us.'" She shook her head. "And I have to fly back to Detroit in a few days."

"Maybe it would be best if we wait a while to share, at least until we figure out what to say." Though Dylan suggested it, he didn't sound as if the idea would have been his first choice.

"That's probably a good idea. Just a few days...to see." To see what exactly, she wasn't sure. If they could survive as a couple that long? A few days were hardly the test of a relationship's endurance.

"Our moms will probably be disappointed, anyway." He lifted a shoulder and let it fall. "You aren't Caroline, and she was part of their plan."

In a huff, she turned in her seat to face him, crossing her arms over her chest. "And why Caroline in the first place? I'm not saying she's not amazing. She is. But how could our mothers ever have thought she was right for you?"

"You know how they are," he said with a shrug. "If they had the ability to look at the big picture, they wouldn't be trying to set up their kids at all."

"I just hate that they've made you the consolation prize for Caroline because Matthew and Haley ended up together. I mean, not that Caroline ever wanted a consolation prize. She doesn't want any guy." After the first vehement comment and all of that backtracking, Jenna glanced at him sheepishly, glad he couldn't see her blush in the darkness of the car.

It was to his credit that he didn't laugh. When he finally spoke, he didn't make a single wisecrack.

"You've defended me ever since you arrived here, and our mothers' new game began. I really appreciate that. You really have been a good friend to me. Thank you for that."

Jenna blinked. There were so many things he could have said to her, but this one touched her more than anything else could have. She'd returned to see him here, hoping to restore the friendship of their past, and she'd surpassed that goal, becoming the kind of friend he deserved.

He must have understood how his words moved her because he continued without waiting for a response. "You know, it was unfair of our mothers to change their game plan just because my big brother ended up married to your baby sister. Remember in their master plan, they talked about the two oldest, two youngest and two—"

"Middle," they said at the same time and laughed.

As their laughter died, Jenna sensed that the atmosphere in the car had changed, had become more intimate. For what felt like a long time, neither spoke, but she could sense his gaze on her, and she couldn't help peeking back at him.

Finally Dylan shifted in his seat. "We'd better get you inside." Instead of waiting for her answer, he opened his car door and then hurried around to the passenger side to open the door for her.

Jenna swallowed, feeling more nervous than she had even for her senior prom. But when Dylan held out his hand to her, she didn't hesitate to take it. Laced through hers, his fingers felt warm, even through her thin gloves. The temperature outside had dropped another ten degrees with promise of a white New Year's, but Jenna didn't even feel the cold. This was Dylan, the friend of her childhood and the surprise of her adult life. She felt warm just being next to him.

On the porch Dylan turned her to face him. She was tempted to glance at the front window to catch her mother watching as she always had whenever Jenna had gone on a date. But this wasn't a date, only a babysitting job. Her mother wouldn't have any reason to snoop. She wouldn't even be worried about Jenna when stable Dylan was there to make sure she made it home safely.

"Are you okay? Warm enough?"

Dylan stroked her cheek with the back of his fingers as he asked, and Jenna could have assured him that she wasn't the slightest bit cold. She looked up into those warm, chocolate eyes, and she nodded. This was the man she'd always known. The one she'd always loved, but she'd been too afraid to admit it.

Stepping closer to her and shielding her from the wind with his body, he settled his hands on her coat at her waist and bent until their faces were only inches apart.

"I really want to kiss you again, Jenna. Would you like me to do that?"

Jenna had been staring into his amazing eyes, but at his words, she blinked. He hadn't asked for permission. Instead, he wanted to know what she wanted. It was so like him to worry about her feelings, even when it would have been so easy for him to overcome any reluctance and muddle her brain with his kiss. He wanted her to come to him of her own free will.

His kindness in itself would have been enough to win her over, even if she wasn't already willingly tumbling headfirst into his eyes. "I'd like that." She expected her voice to come out shaky, but it sounded strong.

By small increments, Dylan moved closer until a tilted chin would be enough to bring their lips together. Jenna closed that distance herself. As their lips touched, Dylan's arms closed around her in an embrace that shut out the world. Rather than just a touch of lips, Dylan's gentle kiss felt like the promise of a lifetime together. She wanted nothing more than to be able to accept his offer.

Too soon he lifted his head away and took a step back from her, his hands still resting on her waist.

"Well, good night." He glanced at something over her shoulder. "Did you see that?"

"See what?"

"The curtain moved."

Jenna swallowed. "Oh." She looked from the window to the door and back to the window. What was she supposed to do now? The idea of being with Dylan was new. She wasn't ready to share it with the others, but now she wouldn't have a choice.

"Let's go." Dylan held out a hand to her. He pulled open the door so quickly that he caught Jenna's mother and Mrs. Warren before they could jump back from the window.

Amy jerked her hand to her chest. "Dylan, you just startled the life out of me."

"Me, too," Trina agreed.

"Could be that you were too close to the window," Dylan answered in a flat tone.

"Perhaps." Amy smiled at her best friend. "But it was worth the shock."

Instead of saying more, their matchmaking moms just stared at their offsprings's joined hands with self-satisfied grins, as if they'd arranged the whole budding romance between them.

"You knew all along?" Jenna couldn't help asking.

Trina grinned at her daughter. "Well, not all along, but—"

"But nothing," Dylan said with a chuckle. "You didn't have any idea."

His mother smiled at her son first and then at Jenna before lowering her gaze again to their joined hands. "But we did plant the garden. Only God gets to decide which things grow."

Chapter Sixteen

For the tenth time in the past fifteen minutes, Dylan took his gaze off the checkers game he was supposed to be playing with Logan and looked out the living-room window, searching for car lights. The snow had start fluttering down early in the afternoon, and now, just in time for New Year's Eve traffic, it was coming down in earnest. Jenna, Caroline and their mother should have already arrived, and the wait was killing him.

With another look up the street, he turned back to his brother and the game. Logan grinned at him as he executed a triple jump that landed his game piece on the opposite side of the board.

"King me." Sitting on the floor next to the coffee table where they'd arranged the game, Logan leaned back on his elbows as Dylan turned away again. "Either pay attention or this is going to be a really short game."

"What?" Dylan looked back from the window. "Oh. Sorry."

"Relax, man. She'll be here." He coughed into his hand. "I mean they'll all be here. It's the Warren family New Year's Eve movie marathon. Who would miss that?"

"Yeah, who would?"

Dylan didn't even bother wondering how his younger brother knew about the *she* who would be there. No one in either of their families could keep a secret. This time he didn't even want it to be a secret. After all these years of first hiding how he felt and then pretending he didn't feel it, he couldn't wait for tonight, when they would attend the party as a couple. He didn't have to hide anything anymore.

But more than having the chance to announce that he'd begun a relationship with the woman of his dreams, he couldn't wait to see her. He looked forward to the stroke of midnight, too, when he could gather her in his arms again.

"Dylan, I'm killing you here." Logan pointed to the game, where another of his pieces was prepared to be kinged. "Jenna's really muddled your brain again, hasn't she?"

"Just like in high school," Matthew added.

Dylan was just registering that Matthew had returned from the kitchen, where he'd been helping their mother and Haley with the appetizers, when he realized what his brothers had said. Both of them. He stood up from the sofa, which he'd been using as his perch to watch for arriving guests.

"Aw, come on, buddy," Logan said. "We're your brothers. Did you really think we didn't notice how you used to moon over Jenna? Or how you'd hide in your room for days every time she smashed your heart like a bug by telling you about another new boyfriend?"

Matthew shook his head, chuckling. "Nobody could

be as good a friend as you were to her through all those breakups if he didn't secretly hope she'd wake up and smell the coffee and finally see him there waiting for her."

Dylan looked back and forth between his brothers, humiliation welling in his veins. He'd thought he'd done such a good job of hiding how he felt, and now he learned he'd been a miserable failure.

Logan must have recognized they'd stepped on sensitive ground with their comments because he held his hands wide. "But hey, look who won out in the end. Mom said you two looked pretty close on the porch last night."

Dylan could feel the heat creeping up his neck. "If you two knew all that stuff before, why didn't you ever say anything about it to me?"

"A guy has the right to a little privacy with his misery," Logan told him.

"What can we say? We're guys." Matthew strode over to Dylan and gave his back two firm pats. "And we were already in the habit of hiding our feelings about Dad. We were good at avoiding communication by that time."

"Too bad you couldn't stick with that now," Dylan joked, and they all laughed.

But he wasn't really kidding. His brothers' comments had struck too deep. He needed no reminders that he'd always cared for Jenna more than she had for him, that he'd always been the one more invested in their relationship.

He hated that one conversation could cause his misgivings to reappear, but that was all it took. Would he always be the one with more to lose if he allowed his relationship with Jenna to move forward? He didn't want to answer yes to that question, but he couldn't say a positive no, either.

A relationship should be based on trust, and yet he wasn't certain he could ever trust her completely. Would he allow his heart to be that bug Logan so eloquently described, the one just waiting to be smashed again?

"They're here," Lizzie called out as she came running into the room.

Sure enough, like the proverbial watched pot that never boils, Mrs. Scott's car had pulled into the driveway at the very moment he wasn't staring out the window and waiting. Unfortunately that also meant that the woman he loved had also just arrived, right when he wasn't ready to see her.

Beside him, his niece was chattering on about how Grammy had told her she could pick out the first movie, but Dylan was focused on that car and the woman climbing out of it.

Even with just her eyes, nose and cheeks peeking out from the fluffy faux fur of her hood, Jenna still looked so pretty that Dylan couldn't take his eyes off her as she hurried up the walk. Her mother and sister trailed behind her, taking more care to walk without slipping on the ice.

He had already started toward the front door when Lizzie pulled at his hand. "Uncle Dylan, is Aunt Jenna your girlfriend?"

Matthew nabbed his daughter under his arm so that her arms and legs were dangling. "Hey, let's check out what kind of cakes Grammy has for the party." He headed toward the kitchen without giving his child a chance to get an answer.

Dylan reached the door before Jenna could ring the bell. He pushed open the storm door and stepped back for her to come inside.

"Hey there."

"Hi." She paused awkwardly as if she thought he might greet her with a hug or a kiss, but then she stepped past him, slipped off her shoes and removed her coat.

Caroline and Mrs. Scott followed her inside, and though both looked back and forth between Dylan and her with curious expressions, neither commented on what they saw. Caroline smiled his way, probably a sign of gratitude for finally letting her off the hook in their mother's matchmaking game. Then the two of them continued into the kitchen.

He glanced around, surprised to see that the others had made themselves scarce, as well, probably hiding in the dining room or kitchen. Touching the back of Jenna's arm because he couldn't bear not to touch her for long, he guided her into the formal living room.

She turned a full circle. "Do you get the feeling no one wants to be around us?"

"They must be trying to give us some space."

Her beautiful mouth curved. "That's kind of them."

"Yeah, it is." But he couldn't look at her when he said it.

"Is something wrong?"

"Everything's fine," he said automatically.

When he glanced back at her, she was staring at her stockinged feet. He never remembered her being shy or bashful, but she seemed that way now. Vulnerable.

Despite his uncertainties, he hated that he would ever make her doubt how he felt. He would have had to be pinned to the wall to keep from drawing her into his arms and pressing a kiss to her hair.

Jenna released the breath she'd been holding as his arms closed around her. For a moment she'd been worried that something might have changed since she'd talked to Dylan on the phone earlier in the day, but with his arms around her now, her world righted itself. She'd thought he was looking forward to their chance to spend New Year's Eve together as much as she'd been, but the truth was, she didn't know what he was feeling.

Maybe he was just uncomfortable sharing these early moments of their new relationship with all their relatives. She couldn't blame him for that. She had to expect some awkwardness in their transition, but strangely, she didn't feel embarrassed at having the others see them together. With Dylan she had finally seen the truth that had always been in her heart, and she no longer had any desire or will to hide from it.

A few days ago she wouldn't have allowed herself to think about a possible future with Dylan, and now she couldn't think about anything else. Just as her life didn't make sense without him in it, a romantic future for the two of them together made more sense than anything ever had.

Jenna would like to have discussed that future with him, but the others returned then, putting an end to their private moment. It was just as well. She would probably have rushed Dylan just when he needed them both to relax and take a breath.

"Aunt Jenna, Uncle Dylan didn't tell me. Is he your boyfriend?" Lizzie asked as soon as she reached them.

Jenna glanced sidelong at Dylan and then down at the preschooler. "We're really good friends. I know that."

Matthew scooted over and wrapped his arm around his daughter's shoulders. "Now, kiddo, what did I say earlier about asking people such personal questions?"

Instead of making everyone more uncomfortable, the child's question seemed to put them all at ease. Jenna knew she'd answered right, because no matter what else they were or what they might become together, she and Dylan were friends, and over the past two weeks, they'd become better ones.

They gathered in the family room for movie night, complete with snacks and, of course, one of Mrs. Warren's cakes, this time devil's food. Because Jenna dreaded the moment their mothers would begin the third degree about her budding relationship with Dylan, Jenna appreciated that the movie format for the New Year's Eve party didn't offer many opportunities for chatter.

They all took their seats on the sectional, and as she'd hoped, Jenna ended up seated next to Dylan. Through the first movie, a short, animated flick Lizzie picked to watch before bedtime, Jenna was too distracted to even watch the colorful characters.

She couldn't focus when Dylan was so close she could smell his woodsy cologne and brush his shoulder if he shifted in his seat. His hand was mere inches from hers, but he never reached out to take hers the way she hoped he would. She tried to tell herself he was simply trying not to be too public with displays of affection, but the thought didn't ring true, since he'd held her hand in front of their mothers last night.

When she caught sight of exhausted mom-to-be Haley resting her head on Matthew's chest, Jenna reminded herself she would only have to wait for the strike of midnight for Dylan and her to have a special moment of their own.

"Okay, everyone, it's almost time," Mrs. Warren announced as she distributed New Year's party hats and noisemakers.

"Ten…nine…eight…seven…six…"

Jenna counted down with the others, but her gaze was on Dylan. He caught her watching him, and his lips curved, but his smile didn't reach his eyes.

"Five…four…three…two…one. Happy New Year!" they all shouted.

Everyone jumped up and started exchanging hugs. When Dylan stepped her way, Jenna turned to face him, waiting for the kiss they would share in front of the others, the one that would make a statement about a possible future between them.

"Happy New Year, Jenna."

"Happy New Year." Her eyes fluttered closed in anticipation, but all he gave her was a brief kiss on the cheek. She glanced away so he wouldn't see the disappointment in her eyes, only to catch newlyweds Matthew and Haley sharing a sweet kiss.

Releasing her shoulders, he stepped away from her and gave Caroline the same kiss on the cheek he'd given Jenna. He did the same thing three more times with Haley and then his mother and hers.

Jenna tried not to let his actions bother her as she shared hugs with the others. He hadn't ignored her, just treated her exactly like everyone else when she'd wanted to be special. She was probably overreacting, anyway, just being paranoid because she'd taken a risk by getting involved with him.

His mixed messages confused her, though. Last night he'd given her every reason to believe he loved her. The poem was proof enough. But tonight he seemed to be pushing her away with both hands. What had happened between then and now?

With the midnight celebration complete, Amy prepared to start the next movie. There would be at least one more feature before their party broke up so they could all crawl into their beds. But before Dylan could sit again, Jenna touched his arm. "Could we talk for a minute?" She indicated the doorway to the hall with a nod of her head.

Dylan glanced around the room, but finally he nodded.

Jenna led him into the living room and turned to face him. "I don't understand. Something's wrong, isn't it? Tell me what it is."

He shook his head and started to deny it, but then he stopped. "Do you want to go for a drive with me?"

She shot a look at the front window where the snow continued to fall and was beginning to blow. "In that?"

"I have an SUV, remember?"

Within a few minutes, they had informed the others, endured all the speculative glances, grabbed their coats and headed out into the snow. She waited, but he didn't take her hand this time, either, even when no one else could see.

It didn't do any good for her to tell herself she was overreacting this time. She couldn't convince herself that she was imagining things or that everything was okay between them. As the snow crunched beneath the car tires, her heart filled with dread.

Dylan stopped the SUV in the parking lot of the supermarket three blocks from his mother's house. Though inside the store was dark, parking-lot lamps still poured their full light over the nearly empty lot, illuminating the interior of the SUV.

The location mirrored the conversation that was about to take place, Dylan decided, because in both he felt completely exposed.

"I thought this place never closed," Jenna said as she looked to the store window.

"It doesn't except on Easter, Christmas and New Year's Eve." He didn't know why they were having this inane conversation when there were more important things they needed to say.

She stared out the windshield into the emptiness of the parking lot. Her arms were wrapped tightly about herself as if to provide protection from an onslaught. He wanted to take her in his arms and protect her from anyone who would hurt her, and it shocked him to realize he would be battling himself. But her hurt would only be temporary, he reminded himself, just a scratch compared to the pain he could foresee in his own heart.

Finally Jenna unfastened her seat belt and turned in her seat to face him. "Okay. Are you going to tell me now?"

"I don't know what it is," he began, but he realized that wasn't quite true. He did know. He just wasn't sure how to share it.

"Well, it's something." She still had her arms crossed but more in frustration now than for protection. "Last night you told me…well, you know what you told me. And the gift you gave me…" She turned away and cleared her throat before she tried again. "And then tonight after you knew full well that everyone there knew about us, you didn't want to be anywhere near me. It doesn't make sense. What changed?"

"Why was I never enough for you before?"

Dylan wasn't even sure he'd spoken the words aloud until he saw the confusion on her face. Confusion, then shock, then guilt. He'd never expected to pose that critical question to her aloud, and he felt trapped by it. He didn't want to know her answer, but then he couldn't bear not knowing, either.

Maybe his earlier conversation with his brothers had triggered some of his misgivings today, but if he was honest with himself, he would admit he'd always had questions. The one he'd asked Jenna tonight had never been far from his mind. Now that their relationship had changed, he needed that answer more than ever.

Jenna swallowed, her eyes and nose burning. She tried to meet his gaze, but he only stared out the driver's-side window. Guilt flooding her veins, she stared at her gripped hands.

"Why would you ever think you weren't enough?"

Before he could answer, though, she shook her head to tell him she wouldn't need an answer. She'd probably given him dozens of reasons over the years, the primary being the date that never happened.

Only now did she begin to realize how much she'd hurt Dylan again and again. How could she have been so blind? She'd been so careless with his heart that he'd begun to question his own worth. This amazing, brilliant man had started second-guessing himself because of her. Worse than just knowing she'd hurt him was the reality that she couldn't take any of it back.

"I'm so sorry, Dylan."

"I thought it wouldn't matter," he seemed to say as much to himself as to her. "But when Matthew and Logan started kidding me about my pining after you when we were kids, I started remembering that. And then I remembered other things I would have preferred to forget."

Now she understood what had changed in a day's time. Maybe he'd believed, as she had, that their history wouldn't touch them now, but they'd both been wrong. She didn't want him to relive the pain she'd caused him then, but Dylan deserved an answer to his question, so she braced her hand on the armrest and began.

"It amazes me sometimes how selfish I was back then." He didn't look at her, but from the way his hands flexed and unflexed on the steering wheel, she could tell he was listening.

"Part of me always knew how you felt about me. I hate admitting that, but it's true. I didn't acknowledge your feelings because I was afraid if I did, I would lose you."

"Why were you afraid of that?" He still didn't look at her as he asked it.

She took a deep breath and pressed on to the hardest part of what she had to say. "As long as I didn't recognize your feelings, I wouldn't have to admit that I didn't feel the same way about you. I could still have you and all the boys I dated. I didn't want to give up…either."

By the last word, her voice faltered. How could she have been such a terrible person? She didn't know why he'd ever decided to be her friend again, let alone consider building a more tender relationship with her.

Dylan cleared his throat, his fingers never releasing the steering wheel. "I appreciate your telling me." His voice sounded flat, resigned, as though if he hadn't made any permanent decision before, he'd made one now.

"But, Dylan, I'm not that person anymore. You know that. We're both different now. We'll be different together."

"But is *now* really that different?"

She'd been staring at her hands, but his strange question brought her head up again. "What do you mean?"

"You knew what you didn't want then. How would I ever know whether I was what you really wanted? I might have once been willing to settle for the crumbs in your life, but I'm not that guy anymore. I won't be the man you settle for."

"You've got to know that I'm not settling. I want you. I *choose* you."

"How could I ever know that for sure?"

Jenna opened her mouth to tell him he had to trust her, but the sad reality caused her to close it again as anguish twisted in her heart. Of course he couldn't count on her feelings for him. There was no way he would know for sure that she had chosen him, instead of ended up with him by default. How could they build any sort of a relationship when he would always wonder if her feelings were real or fleeting?

"I don't want to be anybody's safety net," Dylan continued when she didn't answer his question. "Do you understand that? Not even yours."

"But you're not a safety net. I—I really care about

you. You have to know that." She'd almost told him she loved him, but she'd never said that aloud and she wasn't ready. Would he even believe her if she told him that now?

"You've always cared about me the way that best friends care about each other. But you also wanted to be around me because I was safe. You might even think there's more to us now because you lost that friendship for a while and found it again." He shook his head slowly.

"Don't you see? I can't do it. I don't want to be anyone's consolation prize. I want to be someone's everything."

Settling her elbows on her knees, Jenna held her head in her hands. "No, Dylan. It's not like that." But even she couldn't say that for sure. Her feelings for him—or at least her recognition of those feelings—were still too new for her to have analyzed them.

But she did want to be with him, so much it hurt.

Jenna didn't know when she started crying, but suddenly her cheeks were wet. As she lowered hands and leaned back against the headrest, Dylan reached over and wiped away a few of those tears.

"I'm sorry, Jenna. I don't mean to hurt you, but I can't do this relationship thing. And for a while at least, I can't be your friend, either."

Jenna sniffled and then nodded. *I don't want to be just her friend.* The line from his poem filtered into her thoughts again, but those words did no more to change their situation than anything else she'd said tonight had. As Dylan drove her back to her mother's house, offering her the chance to skip the end of the holiday party, she reflected on how close she'd come to having everything she'd ever wanted.

It wouldn't be a happy new year, after all.

Chapter Seventeen

Jenna woke with a start in the late morning of New Year's Day, surprised she'd slept at all. Her eyes gritty from crying, she stared at the floral wallpaper in the guest room of her mother's house, which would never be home to her.

It had only been a few hours since Dylan had backed out of her mother's driveway, but already she missed him so much that all her muscles ached with loss. He was the one man who'd ever really mattered in her life.

If only she'd have realized her true feelings for Dylan sooner. Maybe then she wouldn't have caused so much damage, so much hurt, that she couldn't take it back no matter how much she'd changed.

Vaguely she took note of the light spilling in from the open drapes, not from sunlight but from the glare off the snow. Movement next to the window caught her attention. Blinking, she sat up in bed. Still dressed in her flannel pajamas and a robe, Caroline sat in the oak rocker.

"What are you doing in here?"

"Mom wanted me to check on you," Caroline said

with a knowing smile. It wasn't uncommon for their mother to send one of the sisters in as a surrogate when situations promised to be too emotional for her comfort zone. "She thought this situation might be messy, but I assured her that you'll survive."

Jenna pushed a hand back through her hair, which felt like it was going every which way. "I'm fine."

"You don't look fine."

"Thanks. I feel better already."

"Glad to be of service. So what happened? I thought Mom's current matchmaking target for me was suddenly off the market, much to my chagrin, of course, and then he showed up back at his mother's house alone and refusing to talk to anyone."

"Sorry I messed up your reprieve." Jenna tried to smile but didn't quite manage it. "I assure you Dylan's still available."

"Are you kidding? Even if I was interested, which I'm not, that poor man is definitely *not* available." Caroline frowned as she tucked her feet under her in the chair. "Dylan's never been available. Why I never noticed it before, I'm not sure. I'm usually more observant than that."

"It doesn't matter, anyway, now. The relationship that took fifteen years to kindle took about fifteen hours for me to destroy."

"You?" Her sister popped out of the chair and climbed onto the bed to sit facing Jenna and holding her hands. "Dylan was the one giving you the cold shoulder last night when you were shining like a new penny."

Jenna shook her head, refusing to accept her sister's loyal defense. "No, it was my fault. I'd done so much damage years ago that I didn't need to do anything new to cause everything to collapse." She tried to pull her hands away, but her sister wouldn't let go.

"Do things you did a long time ago really matter that much now?"

"Dylan said I always wanted to be around him because he was safe, and I think he was right. Not only was he the polar opposite of any of the guys I ever dated, but he had these bookish, nerdy qualities that made him a little embarrassing." She closed her eyes, smiling at the memory of that awkward boy.

"I remember. He and Matthew were both kind of nerdy."

When Jenna opened her eyes, her sister was smiling back at her.

"All those things made him off-limits for me as a boyfriend. Safe, like he said," Jenna continued. "I could always love him without worrying he would leave me. But then he did leave after he finally asked me out and I stood him up."

"You mean about four years ago?" Caroline had an incredulous expression on her face. "Well, then. Better call the rest of us chronically unobservant."

"What are you talking about?"

"How could we have missed that Dylan was in love with you? How could Mom and Mrs. Warren, who've been doing all this crazy matchmaking, have missed that they had a match in the bag?"

Jenna pulled her hands away. "Only it won't work. Last night Dylan asked me why he was never enough before. He's decided he can't be with me because he doesn't want to be the guy I settled for. He's wrong— I know what I want now, but I'm too late. He'll never be able to know for certain that he's the one I really want." She hated that the tears started again, but she couldn't stop them.

Caroline reached out and brushed away a few of them. "Trust. That's a tough one."

"Without it, any relationship is impossible," Jenna said as she wiped at the tears that kept coming.

"Impossible, huh?" When Jenna lifted an eyebrow, Caroline continued, "I know you say you've found faith, but is it really true?"

"Of course it is."

"Then you might want to think about what Jesus said in Mark 10:27. 'With men it is impossible, but not with God; for all things are possible with God.'"

Jenna opened her mouth to retort, but then her lips curved into a smile. "Thanks. I'll keep that in mind."

"It probably seems unwise to be taking relationship advice from someone who isn't in a relationship and has no intention of being in one, but I do know a little about getting what you want out of life."

"And I appreciate your advice. Really." Jenna leaned forward and hugged her sister.

"You said you know what you want. Now you have to decide what you're going to do about it," Carline said.

She was right, Jenna decided as her sister left the room, probably to report to their mother that all was well. Jenna didn't want to give up now that she realized she and Dylan belonged together. She had to believe that it might be possible someday for her to earn his trust. But even if she didn't, he would always hold the key to her heart.

Dylan felt so alone as he sat at the kitchen table in his apartment, eating soup and staring out at the dark sky. His life had never felt more bleak or lonely. The first day of the new year had passed in a long series of gray minutes.

Part of him felt his decision to cut his losses with Jenna before there were any more of them was justified, unavoidable even, but the other part worried he'd made a huge mistake.

Jenna, the one woman he'd ever loved, was finally ready to be with him, and all he could do was turn her away with excuses about safety nets and consolation prizes. Why had he let his misgivings get to him in the first place? His brothers might have been encouraging him to proceed with caution, but he was certain they hadn't been going for this outcome.

He knew he shouldn't feel guilty for walking away from a woman who hadn't even been able to say that she loved him, but that offered him no comfort. Jenna had only recently recognized her feelings. He'd known how he felt for years, and he'd never said the words aloud, either.

The hopelessness he'd seen on her face when he'd told her they couldn't be together had almost been his undoing. He'd longed to hold her and tell her he was wrong, but the idea that she would change her mind someday over another rugby player or, more likely now, a pilot on one of her flights, had helped him keep his hands on the steering wheel.

He knew he'd hurt her. Were they even now? Was that what he needed, for them to be even? Would he feel comforted in his justice next Easter, next Fourth of July and next Christmas when he was still missing her?

His challenge, though, remained just where it had been before. How could he be sure that she wouldn't change her mind? Faith. The word came to him in a small voice from inside. Jenna had found faith, and then she'd helped him to open his heart to his own again. Maybe God could help him to have a little faith in her.

Lord, please give me the strength to follow my heart, if it's where You're leading. And teach me to have faith in the people I love, too. In Your Son's name I pray. Amen.

He had another long night of sleeplessness ahead of him, but he needed the time for prayer and for introspection. He needed time to find the courage to do what he knew was right.

Jenna sat in the terminal at Indianapolis International, early for her late-night flight. She was almost relieved to be surrounded by throngs of post-holiday travelers, all equally exhausted and crabby. At least when she was being elbowed and stepped on and tripped while walking barefoot through airline security, she wouldn't think of Dylan and the fact that he hadn't called all day.

Not that she knew what she would say if he did call. That he'd made a mistake was too much to ask. But she hadn't heard a word from him or from any of the other Warrens, including her own sister, Haley. At least Haley had an excuse—Jenna had heard she was suffering from worse morning sickness and had spent the day in bed.

Though Jenna wasn't looking forward to returning to her lonely apartment, she would appreciate the chance to be out of her mother's and Caroline's curious study. They were only concerned, but she felt like a bug under glass, waiting for the oxygen to run out.

At least now she could stop coming up with new versions of her harebrained plan to go to his house and convince him they could find a way to be together. She'd picked up her keys and dialed half of Dylan's number so many times today that her fingers ached almost as much as her heart. Her plans were courageous, but her execution was not.

The advantage of being at the airport early also turned out to be a disadvantage in that she had even more time to think, more time to ruminate on the reality that he hadn't called. If there was any hope for them, he would have by now.

Sitting in the uncomfortable chair, she held her head in her hands as her hope dwindled in small increments. What would she do now? She'd come to Markston hoping to reconnect with her friend, and she was leaving more alone than ever. She reminded herself that she'd lost more love in a matter of days than some people do in a lifetime, but somehow it didn't make her feel any better.

As she reached her lowest point, she pulled the smaller of her two Christmas gifts from Dylan out of her purse. She'd tried to fit the birdhouse in, too, but eventually gave up and gave her mother money to ship it. Just holding the folded-up paper made her feel better somehow. Even if Dylan no longer felt these tender feelings for her, there was a time he had.

She opened the poem and began to read what she'd read so many times in the last twelve hours.

Roses are red, but not as red as her lips,
Violets are blue, never as blue as my heart...

Sure, some of those thoughts had been written by a lovesick teen, but the others, the ones that mattered more, Dylan had written only recently.

I don't want to be just her friend.
I want to be her man.

By the time she reached the final line, her hope had returned. His words reminded her that he'd loved her. If he still did, there had to be a chance for them. Jumping up from her seat, she rushed over to the flight desk to request that her bag be removed from the luggage bin.

Blood pumped at her temples. She couldn't walk fast enough out of the secured part of the terminal to the car-rental department.

For once, though, her plan was more about Dylan's needs than hers. No matter what Dylan felt about her now, whether he was willing to accept her or not, there were things she had to tell him in the morning. Things that meant the world to her and, if God willed it, could mean a future for the two of them.

As Dylan merged onto Interstate 465 the next morning, anticipation and anxiety melded inside him, making it difficult to watch for the signs to Indianapolis International. There was more traffic than usual on the last Saturday before the end of the traditional Christmas vacation, but he was still sure he would make his flight on time. He'd been blessed to get a last-minute ticket, but since he was heading north, instead of the warmer south, he'd found a seat.

The plan was crazy, but taking the risk felt exhilarating. He wasn't even sure where she lived, but he would figure all that out when he landed in Detroit.

He could almost picture the surprise on her face when he showed up at her apartment. He had so much to tell her, things he'd never said, things he should have said if he hadn't been such a coward.

In all the years he'd loved Jenna, he'd never once made it clear what he wanted. Today he would make it clear. He'd never told her he loved her for fear she would reject him. Today he would tell her. He would no longer allow fear and pride to keep him from taking a chance with the love of his life.

If he fell on his face after this, then at least he would no longer have to live with regrets.

As he parked at the airport, his cell phone rang. Jenna's number came up on the caller ID. He considered waiting to call her back until he landed in Detroit, but he was dying to hear her voice.

He flipped open the phone. "Jenna?"

"Hi, Dylan," she said.

He swallowed. Should he tell her he was coming or just wait and surprise her after he landed?

"Are you already home?" he asked casually. He tried to come up with an apology for not calling before.

"As a matter of act, I'm not."

"Was your flight delayed?" The thought of that made him frown. If hers was delayed because of weather, then his flight might be, as well, and he would hate having to wait any longer to see her.

"Actually, right now I'm at the optometrist's office."

"What do you mean?" His eyebrows drew together in confusion. She wasn't making any sense.

"To be specific, I'm at *your* office."

"What…?" he began again, but that lilt in her voice, the one that appeared whenever she thought she'd done something clever, cut through his confusion. "You didn't fly back to Detroit? Why?"

"I had to talk to you, so I showed up as a new patient. And if what your mom told me about your being at the airport is correct, then I'm guessing you wanted to talk to me."

Dylan smiled into the receiver. "That was supposed to be a surprise."

"And it would have been if you'd landed in Detroit and I was here in Indiana."

His thoughts raced as fast as his pulse pounded. He needed to see her now, to hear what she had to say and tell her what was in his heart, but fifty miles was too far and an hour was too long to wait. Suddenly an idea popped into his mind.

"Do you know the southbound rest stop on I-65? You know, the one about halfway between here and Markston?"

"Sure… I guess."

"Can you meet me there in half an hour?"

"I'll be there," she promised.

"And, Jenna." He paused until he was sure she would hear him. "I can't wait to see you."

Chapter Eighteen

When Jenna pulled into a spot near the rest stop's main entrance, Dylan's car was already there. Her heart was beating out a percussion solo, but she didn't want to waste time catching her breath. Since she was in a new rental car he might not recognize, she climbed out and hurried toward his SUV.

Before she reached it, his door flew open and he hopped down. He reached her in five long strides. Dylan closed his arms around her, parka and all, crushing her to his chest. She didn't even care if the hug was too tight to be comfortable. Then he pulled her hood back, and his mouth found hers in a kiss filled with adrenaline and joy.

"I can't believe you're here," she said when he pressed her to his shoulder again. Her arms clung tightly to his waist in an embrace she hoped would go on until they froze in front of the all tourists and truckers.

He did pull back far enough to look down at her face, but he didn't release her completely. "I can't believe I almost flew to Detroit."

"I can't believe we almost missed each other."

"So what's this about an optometry appointment?"

"It was kind of a grand gesture, but it was foiled. I wanted to be your patient because you helped me to see." She glanced at the snow-covered asphalt beneath her feet and then back up at him. "I guess it was kind of corny."

"Corny's good." He withdrew his preprinted boarding pass from the front pocket of his coat. "One grand gesture deserves another. Kind of a 'Gift of the Magi' thing."

"It was almost a Gift of the Mixups, but our moms saved us from that. I called my mom when you weren't at the office, and she called your mom and here we are."

"Meddling moms are a blessing," he agreed.

Jenna glanced around. They were still standing in the parking lot in each other's arms, and though they'd shared a kiss, neither had said anything that would change the situation they'd faced on New Year's Eve. She pointed to the opposite side of the lot. "I saw a nature trail over that way for walking dogs. Would you like to walk with me?"

Immediately, Dylan took her gloved hand and laced their fingers as he had the other night. That was a message in itself, but Jenna needed to say more and hoped to hear more, as well.

"I love you, Dylan," she said in a quiet voice as they walked along the path, the snow crunching beneath their feet.

He stopped walking, his breath appearing to hitch, and suddenly he was crushing her to his chest, holding her so tightly that she felt out of breath. He must have recognized her distress because he loosened his arms and took a small step back so he could look down at her. His eyes were suspiciously shiny.

"Do you know how long I've waited to hear that? I hoped for it and prayed for it, but I didn't really believe—" He stopped himself and grinned. "I really should have said it first, you know. I've had more years to feel it."

She couldn't help smiling at that, her heart already filling. "Oh. Okay. You go first."

Instead of speaking as they walked, he stopped and turned to face her. "Jenna, I love you. I can't remember a time when I didn't. I'm still afraid sometimes that I might lose you, but I can't allow that fear to keep us from having the future God has planned for us."

She stared into his eyes. "I love you, Dylan. You are my everything. You always were, even before I realized it. You never have to worry with me. My heart is yours…for keeps."

He pressed his lips to hers again in a warm, unhurried kiss. When he finally stepped back, Jenna didn't really need her parka anymore. He started chuckling, and when her eyes fluttered open, Jenna caught a few different dog walkers watching them curiously.

"There's a picnic area over here." He took her hand again and led her to a grouping of wooden picnic tables. He picked one and used his other gloved hand to wipe the snow off the top. Like a footman, he helped her up to sit on the table with her feet resting on the picnic bench.

When she was seated, he sank onto one knee in the snow. "Jenna Claire Scott, may I ask you a question?"

Was he really going to do what she thought he was

going to do? Her pulse pounding her ears, she couldn't speak, so she simply nodded.

"Would you like to go out to dinner and to a movie with me the next time you come to Markston?"

Instead of answering, she laughed out loud and shoved her hand through her hair. "Oh, dear," she said when the ripples of laughter finally calmed. "I thought you were going to propose to me before we even had our first date."

"So, what do you say?" He met her gaze. "To my question."

"Yes, Dylan, I would love to go on a date with you the next time I'm in town."

"Thank you." He popped up to kiss her lips once before he knelt again. "You know the knee of my pants is getting pretty wet here."

"Well, get up, then," she said, pulling up on his hand.

"Wait. I have some other questions for you."

"So ask." She was still giggling when she noticed that his expression had become serious.

"Jenna, you're my best friend. Will you also be my wife?"

Jenna coughed into her hand, her thoughts racing faster than the cars on the Indianapolis 500. "Are you sure there aren't other questions you want to ask me before that? Did I mention that we haven't been on a single date yet?"

"I could, but every other question I have is dependent on your answer to that question."

She thought about it for a second, and her pulse relaxed again. "I guess there probably isn't anything I could learn about you while bowling or eating pizza or playing miniature golf that I don't already know."

"So?" He quirked an eyebrow. "What do you say?" He glanced at the ground. "The knee's starting to go numb."

"Yes. Absolutely. I'll marry you. I never knew a real home until I found it in your arms."

Immediately he was up from the ground and kissing her as if he hadn't seen her in months. His kiss spoke of permanence and hope and the kind of friendship that is transformed by years into the love of a lifetime. When his mouth left hers, he kissed her forehead, nose and cheeks, all of which were starting to feel wind-burned.

When he stopped he climbed up and sat next to her on the tabletop. He put his arm around her, and she snuggled against his shoulder.

"Now what other questions did you have for me?"

"Will you live with me, be the mother of my children and grow old with me?"

"Yes times three. You were right. All of your other questions were dependent on the first one." She chuckled again. "Any more questions?"

"Will you fly in next weekend to go out with me?"

"Yes." She nodded for emphasis. "Anything else."

"Will you come the next weekend? And the next weekend? And the next? And the next?"

They were both laughing until he stopped and stared into her eyes. With a gentle touch, he lifted her chin and touched his lips to hers once more.

"My Jenna," he breathed, his words sounding like a prayer of thanksgiving.

"We'll have to do the distance thing for a while, until I can get a transfer to Indianapolis International," she said, her mind suddenly in planning mode. "And then we'll have to plan the wedding."

Making affirmative sounds, Dylan kissed her between each comment.

"I'd like a simple one."

"Uh-huh."

"Just family and friends."

Dylan stopped and looked her in the eye. "Didn't you mention before that we haven't even gone on our first date?" He waited for her nod before he continued, "Then there's no rush. We'll do it in our time. So shh." He held his fingers to her lips. "Just kiss the guy, why don't you?"

She was happy to oblige there in the unromantic rest stop that had just become the most romantic place in the world. Her kiss offered him the promise of a future. A future with his best friend—and true love.

* * * * *

"Are you okay?" Stone asked, tightening his hold around her waist and gripping one of her hands.

"I— Yes." She didn't have time to explain to Stone why this had nothing to do with her sore ankle, nor why avalanches were her worst nightmare and that was the real reason why she'd suddenly swayed in his arms.

Not when there was work to be done. There were people in Holden Springs who needed help, and she knew she should be there.

Tugger whined and pressed against her leg as he'd been taught to do as a therapy dog. He could tell her heart rate had increased and her pulse was pounding in her ears, even if she didn't show it in her expression, although there was probably that, too. The dog was responding to cues most humans couldn't see, and Felicity reached out and absently ran a hand between Tugger's ears to steady her insides.

"Have they set up a temporary disaster shelter yet?" she asked.

"Yes. At Holden High School," her sister said. "They're using the cafeteria and the gym, I think. I'd go myself except I have clients in the middle of service dog training back at the center. Do you mind taking Tugger and heading out there?"

Felicity did mind. More than anyone would ever know, because she never talked about it, not even to her siblings. But now was not the time to give in to those feelings. She could cry into her pillow later when she was alone and the people of Holden Springs were safe.

"I'll take Tugger." She nodded. "And Dandy, too," she said, referring to a young black Labrador retriever who was part of the therapy dog program.

"I can tag along, if there's anything I can do to assist," Stone said. "That way you'll have an extra person for the dogs."

Felicity was going to decline, but Ruby spoke up first. "Thank you, Stone. They need all the help they can get. From what I hear, there are a lot of families who were suddenly evacuated from their homes."

"It's settled, then," Stone said. "I'm going with you."

Felicity didn't feel settled. The last thing she needed was Stone alongside her. It would distract her from her real work.

She sighed deeply.

A bruised ankle.

Stone's unnerving presence.

And now an avalanche.

Could things get any worse?

Don't miss
Their Unbreakable Bond *by Deb Kastner,*
available January 2022 wherever
Love Inspired books and ebooks are sold.

LoveInspired.com

LIEXP1221

LOVE INSPIRED

Stories to uplift and inspire

Fall in love with Love Inspired—
inspirational and uplifting stories of faith
and hope. Find strength and comfort in
the bonds of friendship and community.
Revel in the warmth of possibility and the
promise of new beginnings.

Sign up for the Love Inspired newsletter
at **LoveInspired.com** to be the first
to find out about upcoming titles,
special promotions and exclusive content.

CONNECT WITH US AT:

Facebook.com/LoveInspiredBooks

Twitter.com/LoveInspiredBks

Get 4 FREE REWARDS!

We'll send you 2 FREE Books plus 2 FREE Mystery Gifts.

Love Inspired books feature uplifting stories where faith helps guide you through life's challenges and discover the promise of a new beginning.

FREE Value Over $20

YES! Please send me 2 FREE Love Inspired Romance novels and my 2 FREE mystery gifts (gifts are worth about $10 retail). After receiving them, if I don't wish to receive any more books, I can return the shipping statement marked "cancel." If I don't cancel, I will receive 6 brand-new novels every month and be billed just $5.24 each for the regular-print edition or $5.99 each for the larger-print edition in the U.S., or $5.74 each for the regular-print edition or $6.24 each for the larger-print edition in Canada. That's a savings of at least 13% off the cover price. It's quite a bargain! Shipping and handling is just 50¢ per book in the U.S. and $1.25 per book in Canada.* I understand that accepting the 2 free books and gifts places me under no obligation to buy anything. I can always return a shipment and cancel at any time. The free books and gifts are mine to keep no matter what I decide.

Choose one: ☐ **Love Inspired Romance**
Regular-Print
(105/305 IDN GNWC)

☐ **Love Inspired Romance**
Larger-Print
(122/322 IDN GNWC)

Name (please print)

Address   Apt. #

City   State/Province   Zip/Postal Code

Email: Please check this box ☐ if you would like to receive newsletters and promotional emails from Harlequin Enterprises ULC and its affiliates. You can unsubscribe anytime.

> ### Mail to the **Harlequin Reader Service:**
> **IN U.S.A.:** P.O. Box 1341, Buffalo, NY 14240-8531
> **IN CANADA:** P.O. Box 603, Fort Erie, Ontario L2A 5X3

Want to try 2 free books from another series! Call 1-800-873-8635 or visit www.ReaderService.com.
